HOUSE
OF SAND
AND FOG

ALSO BY ANDRE DUBUS III

The Cagekeeper and Other Stories

Bluesman

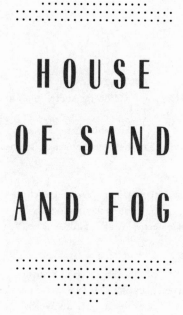

HOUSE
OF SAND
AND FOG

ANDRE DUBUS III

W. W. Norton & Company | New York London

For information about permission to reproduce selections from this book,
write to Permissions,
W. W. Norton & Company, Inc., 500 Fifth Avenue, New York, NY 10110.

The text of this book is composed in Goudy
with the display set in Radiant
Composition and manufacturing by the Haddon Craftsmen, Inc.
Book design by Chris Welch

Library of Congress Cataloging-in-Publication Data

Dubus, Andre, 1959–
House of sand and fog / Andre Dubus III.
p.   cm.
ISBN 0-393-04697-4
I. Title.
PS3554.U265H68   1999
813'.54—dc21   98-35255
                                                          CIP

W. W. Norton & Company, Inc., 500 Fifth Avenue, New York, N.Y. 10110
http://www.wwnorton.com

W. W. Norton & Company Ltd., 10 Coptic Street, London WC1A 1PU

4   5   6   7   8   9   0

For my brother, Jeb, and for my four sisters,
Suzanne, Nicole, Cadence, and Madeleine

Beyond myself
      somewhere
   I wait for my arrival
—*From "The Balcony" by Octavio Paz*

I am grateful to Capt. John Wells of the San Mateo County Sheriff's Department for all of his generous technical advice. I am indebted to my old friend Kourosh Zomorodian, who for two years was my Farsi teacher over Friday night pitchers of Lone Star Beer in Austin, Texas. With gratitude, as well, to Ali Farahsat for relieving me of some of my ignorance of Persian culture. Thanks also to my agent, Philip Spitzer, for his faith and determination.

Finally, I am deeply grateful to my diligent and gifted editor, Alane Salierno Mason.

HOUSE
OF SAND
AND FOG

PART I

THE FAT ONE, THE RADISH TOREZ, HE CALLS ME CAMEL BECAUSE I AM Persian and because I can bear this August sun longer than the Chinese and the Panamanians and even the little Vietnamese Tran. He works very quickly without rest, but when Torez stops the orange highway truck in front of the crew, Tran hurries for his paper cup of water with the rest of them. This heat is no good for work. All morning we have walked this highway between Sausalito and the Golden Gate Park. We carry our small trash harpoons and we drag our burlap bags and we are dressed in vests the same color as the highway truck. Some of the Panamanians remove their shirts and leave them hanging from their back pockets like oil rags, but Torez says something to them in their mother language and he makes them wear the vests over their bare backs. We are upon a small hill. Between the trees I can see out over Sausalito to the bay where there are clouds so thick I cannot see the other side where I live with my family in Berkeley, my wife and son. But here there is no fog, only sun on your head and back, and the smell of everything under the nose: the dry grass and dirt; the cigarette smoke of the Chinese; the hot metal and exhaust of the passing automobiles. I am sweating under my shirt and vest. I have fifty-six years and no hair. I must buy a hat.

When I reach the truck, the crew has finished their water and the two Chinese light new cigarettes as they go back to the grass. The Panamanians have dropped their cups upon the ground around their feet and Tran is shaking his head, and saying something in his language as he stoops to pick them up with his hands. Mendez laughs. He is almost as big as the radish and there is a long burn scar the

15

color of sand upon one of his fat arms. He sees me looking at it as I drink my ice water and he stops his laughing, no longer does he even smile, and he to me says: "What you looking at, *viejo?*"

I drink from my cup and let him look at my eyes. His brothers have started to go back to work but now they stop to watch.

"Old *maricón*," says Mendez. He takes up his trash spear from the orange tailgate, but my eyes look at the burn again long enough for him to see. His face becomes more ugly than it already is and he yells something at me in his language and his teeth are very bad, like an old dog's. I don't give him rest from my eyes and so now he steps to me, yelling more, and I smell him, last night's wine and today's sweating of it, and now Torez is yelling louder than Mendez. Again it is in their mother tongue and it is over quickly because Mendez knows this crew can manage very fine without him, and he needs money for his sharob, his wine. He is *goh*, the shit of life. They are all *goh*.

"*Vamonos*, Camello." Torez moves by me and closes the tailgate. Tran is already working ahead of the truck while the smoking Chinese and the lazy Panamanians walk to the shade of the trees, pretending there is trash there.

I pull my sack over my shoulder and to Mr. Torez I say: "In my country I could have ordered him beaten."

"*Sí*, Camello? In Mendez's country he would have beaten you himself."

"I was colonel, Mr. Torez. I was colonel in the Imperial Air Force. Do you know this, Mr. Torez? I was a *colonel.*"

He hands to me my garbage spear and looks me in my eyes. His are gavehee, brown as coffee, like all his people, like my people also. But I see he has made up his mind about me.

He says to me, to Genob Sarhang Massoud Amir Behrani: "Okay, Colonel, but today I'm Señor General. *Comprende?*"

At the lunch hour, Torez drives the highway truck down to the trees and we all remove our paper sacks from where we left them in the tool chest this morning. We eat in the shade. Many times Tran eats with me and I do not mind this because the little Vietnamese speaks no English and I am able to do my work in the classified pages of the newspaper. In my country, I was not only a desk officer; I bought F-16 jets from Israel and the United States, and when I was a captain in Tehran, a genob sarvan, I worked on the engines with my own hands. Of course, all the best aerocompanies are here in California but in four years I have spent hundreds of dollars copying my credentials; I have worn my French suits and my Italian shoes to hand-deliver my qualifications; I have waited and then called back after the correct waiting time; but there is nothing. I have had only one interview and that was with a young girl in college who I believe the company was simply giving personnel experience. That was over two years past.

But today and all week, I do not even attempt to look for a position. My daughter Soraya was married on Saturday and I feel already there is a hole in my chest with her gone. There is also a hole in our home, but now we are free to leave that place that has cost me three thousand dollars per month for four years. And I turn straight to this area called Legal Notices/Auctions. This is a part of the paper I have never before investigated. I have been speaking and reading English for over twenty-five years but the language of law in both our countries seems designed to confuse. Of course I know what is an auction, and this morning, when the air was still cool and we garbage soldiers sat upon the metal floor of the highway truck as it drove under the tall span of the golden bridge, the smell of the ocean behind us, I held the newspaper tight in my lap so no wind would touch it and that is when I saw the short notice of Seized Property for Sale, a three-bedroom home. Though of course this has not been my plan. My plan has been highly simple: stop spending money from home so we may use it to start some sort of business. I have been looking into many possibilities; a small restaurant, or a laundry, a video store perhaps. Though I know these American papers, I know what they say of this economy, still I see small shops going out of business on both sides of the bay. And of course we have no money for to buy a house as well, but there are many auctions in my country. There it is known as the legal way to rob.

Tran is eating rice and vegetables with a large plastic spoon from waxy paper in his lap. He is very small and yellow-brown. There are deep lines around his mouth and between his eyes upon his fore-head. He smiles and nods at my own food. I eat rice also. Soraya used to save the tadiq for me, the hard cake of rice at the bottom of the pot Americans throw away, but for us, for Persians, it is the jewel. We cook it with very much butter so when the pot is turned upside down all the rice comes out onto the plate, even the brown and burned part we call tadiq. Now, each night, my wife, Nadereh, saves half for my lunch. She also packs for me radishes, bread, one apple, and a small thermos of hot tea. The Panamanians watch me pour the steaming tea into my cup and they shake their heads as if I am a stupid child. They do not know what I know of the heat, that there must be a fire inside you to match the one outdoors. At Mehrabad, my base near Tehran, sometimes the tarmac would become so bright off the sands even we officers, with our European sunglasses, would close our eyes. Of course we spent most of the days inside our air-conditioned offices. Many times there, between appointments or briefings, I would have my attendant phone Nadi at our home in the capital city. She and I would speak of the small events of the day, then she would let the children to the telephone. One morning, when my son Esmail was one and a half years, he said his first word to me, then, over the wire: "Bawbaw-joon," father most dear.

With my fingers I tear out the small notice of the home to be auctioned and place the paper in my front shirt pocket beneath my vest. Today is Wednesday, the only day I do not work my night po-sition at a small convenience store in El Cerrito, a neighborhood where I am not likely to see any Persian people, not the rich ones, the pooldar, those who live alongside us in that high-rise of overpriced apartments on its hill overlooking the bay and San Francisco and the Golden Gate Bridge. In four years, this two-bedroom flat has cost me over one hundred forty thousand dollars in rent. But I will not let myself think of that now. I cannot.

Tran finishes his lunch. With his fingers he brushes off the wax paper and folds it neatly before putting it back into the bag with the plastic spoon. He pulls out a chocolate bar and offers to me a portion, but I shake my head as I sip my tea. I know that he will use that tired paper for his lunch tomorrow, and the spoon will probably last him

half the year. I know, like me, he is a father, perhaps even a grandfather. And perhaps I will be a grandfather soon as well.

Of course I argued many times for a more reasonable place to live,
but Nadi fought me; we must keep up our appearance. We must act
as if we can live as we are accustomed. All because it was the time of
hastegar for our Soraya, when young men from good families send
roses to her and our family, when their fathers call me to talk, and
their mothers call Nadi to introduce. If there is no family match,
there can be no match. And naturally, because our daughter is very
beautiful, with long straight black hair, a small face, and the eyes of
a queen, she had many offers and of course could not make up her
mind. Meanwhile, Nadi had to make certain our daughter did not attract any common Persians; she ordered all the best furniture and
lamps and carpets. On the walls she has hung French paintings, and
the mosaic-frame portrait of the battle of martyrdom in the Karbala.
On the silver coffee table are crystal bowls filled with pistachios,
dates, and fine chocolates. And near the sliding glass doors to the terrace are fresh green plants as large as small trees.

There are many other Persians living in the building, all rich, all
pooldar. Many of them are lawyers and surgeons. One was a judge in
Qom, our holy city before it became the headquarters for the mad
imam, but the mullah is dead now and we still are on the list of those
who will be hanged or shot if we are to return home. He left behind
many such lists as that.

I think of these things as I look over at Mendez, sleeping in the
shade, his brown stomach visible beneath his peerhan. When we
flew from France—Nadi, Esmail, and I—I carried bank checks worth
two hundred eighty thousand dollars. A man like Mendez would
drink that money, of this I am quite certain. But many nights my
sleep does not come when I think of how unwisely I let that sum be
burned up, burned because my dear Nadereh could not and cannot
bear to let other families know we have next to nothing left from the
manner in which we used to live. If I had been stronger with her, if
I had not been so sure I would have work soon with Boeing or Lockheed, making a respectable salary, then I most for certain would have
invested in real estate. I would have told Soraya her hastegar must

wait for a year or two, I would have rented us a modest apartment under one thousand dollars per month, and I would have purchased a partnership in an office building or perhaps even a residential property in a growing neighborhood of new homes. I would have watched the market like a wolf, then, in short order, I would have sold for an honest profit only to do it again.

We have forty-eight thousand dollars remaining, this is all, an amount my fourteen-year-old son will need for the first two years of university alone. It has been my hope to begin a business with this, but I fear now to lose it all, to become bankrupt like so many Americans. Of course, I have always seen the samovar as half full, and Nadi may have been right; Soraya has married a quiet young engineer from Tabriz. He holds two Ph.D.s in engineering and we can rest to know she will be taken care of and I thank our God for that. The young man's father is dead and that is a pity because he is supposed to have been a fine businessman, a possible partner for myself. Perhaps it is the seized property I must begin to view, the used, the broken, the stolen. Perhaps there is where we can get our start.

BECAUSE OUR WORK is finished at half past three, the sun is still high as Torez drives us through San Francisco down Van Ness Street. I sit with Tran and the Chinese opposite the Panamanians, and I look over the pig's head of Mendez—he stares at me with the tanbal eyes, the lazy eyes of a man who wants sleep then more wine—and I regard all the mansions of Pacific Heights, the high walls covered with white and yellow flowers, the iron gates that allow in only fine European automobiles: Porsches, Jaguars, even Lamborghinis, the cars of the old Tehran. My driver in the capital city, Bahman, he drove for me a gray Mercedes-Benz limousine. Inside was a television, a telephone, and a bar. Under Shah Pahlavi, we all had them. All the high officers of the Imperial Air Force had them.

The skin of my head is burning. Each morning, Nadi gives to me a sun-blocking lotion I rub there, but now, even with the warm wind in the open truck, my scalp burns and I promise to myself again I will purchase a hat. We continue south through the city past Japantown

and its five-acre Japan Center, where one can buy electronics, porcelain, and pearls. Many Persian wives from our building shop there,
and so I must sit low in the bed of the truck and stay in this manner
until Torez turns onto Market Street, then down to Mission Street,
where is the Highway Department's depot. He drives us under a freeway, past a movie theater which shows films only in the Spanish language. On both sidewalks are no pooldar people, only workers,
cargars, brown-skinned men and women carrying bags for their shopping. And there are many small food stores, restaurants, laundries,
and clothing shops, and they are owned by the Nicaraguan people,
the Italians, and Arabs, and Chinese. Last spring, after our thirty-day
fast of Ramadan, I from an Arab purchased a shirt in his shop near
the overpass bridge. He was an Iraqi, an enemy of my people, and the
Americans had recently killed thousands of them in the desert. He
was a short man, but he had large arms and legs beneath his clothes.
Of course he began speaking to me right away in his mother tongue,
in Arabic, and when I to him apologized and said I did not speak his
language, he knew I was Persian, and he offered to me tea from his
samovar, and we sat on two low wooden stools near his display window and talked of America and how long it had been since we'd last
been home. He poured for me more tea, and we played backgammon
and did not speak at all.

Torez drives into the dark building that smells of motor oil and
dust. It is so large it reminds me of an airplane hangar, which I appreciate. He parks the truck beside the gas pumps opposite the office
and we crew of garbage soldiers walk to punch our time cards. But
Mendez and one of his friends stay behind. Each day it is different
who Torez will choose for tool and truck cleaning duty, and I am certain the pig Mendez holds me responsible for today. I walk through
the bright truck yard surrounded by a tall chain fence and I carry
nothing but my newspaper and bag and thermos. Every day at this
time it is the same; my back and legs are stiff, my head and face are
burned by the sun, and I must walk four city blocks to Market Street
to the Concourse Hotel where I pay to keep my white Buick Regal
in their underground parking facility. Of course it is an added ex-
pense, but there is no secure location for my auto so close to the

Highway Department. Also, it gives to me opportunity to clean myself and change clothes before returning home.

In the beginning I would enter the hotel through the carpeted
lobby. At this time of day there is only one employee at the desk, a
man of forty years with very short black hair and a large black mustache. He is dressed in a fine suit, but pinned in one of his ears is a
tiny bright diamond. Each day he would regard me in my work
clothes dirty from road dust, wet with my sweat, and each time he
would ask, "May I help you, sir?" Soon enough I stopped explaining
and simply pointed to the elevator I would take to the garage. But
one afternoon, when there was a well-dressed lady and gentleman
settling their account at the desk, the diamond man, the kunee, the
one who gives ass, who in my country would be hanged, he looked
over their shoulders and asked very loud of me: "May I help you, sir?"
The lady and gentleman turned around, and I could see they were
tourists, perhaps Germans, but they viewed me no longer than a man
would take for a dead insect upon his windshield while driving. And
for the thousandth time in this terrible country I wished to be wearing my uniform, the perfectly tailored uniform of an honorable
colonel, a genob sarhang in the King's Air Force, the King of Kings,
Shahanshah Reza Pahlavi, who three times in my career his hand I
kissed, twice at formal gatherings at Sadabaad Palace, once at the
grand home of my dear friend General Pourat. But of course my uniform then, in the lobby of the Concourse Hotel, was damp work
clothes with blades of grass on my lower pants, dust on my back. So
I did nothing but move quickly away, once again the hot blood of a
killer dropping from my heart to my hands.

Now I simply eliminate the lobby and every day walk down the
concrete auto ramp into the shadowed belly of the building, where I
unlock my automobile and retrieve the clothes I wore early this
morning. I am never certain if there will be Persians in the elevator
of our apartment building or not. In the cooler months I wear a suit,
but now, in summer, I wear a short-sleeve dress shirt and tie, dress
pants, and polished shoes with socks and belt. I leave these in a
zipped garment bag laid out quite neatly in the trunk. The hotel elevator is carpeted and air-conditioned. I breathe the cool air into my

lungs and soon I am in the second-floor lavatory opposite the ice machine, where I remove the auction notice from my front pocket, pull
off my shirt, and wash my hands and bare arms and face. I shave for
the second time today. I dry myself with the hotel's clean paper towels, and I use cologne on my cheeks and deodorant under my arms.
Today I change into brown slacks, a white pressed shirt, and a tan silk
tie. I fold the auction notice into my wallet, wrap my work clothes
and shoes in paper, then put them in the garment bag. When I step
into the hallway and walk to the elevator, my covered clothes over
my arm, my tie knotted correctly and straight, and my face shaved
clean, I pass a Filipino maid pushing her cart and I take notice that
she smiles. And even bows her head.

THE GENTLEMAN FROM the San Mateo County Tax Office gave to me
a map for finding this home to be auctioned. He informed me to arrive by nine o'clock in the morning and be prepared to offer a ten-
thousand-dollar deposit should I have a wish to purchase the
property. He also to me said it was located upon a hill in Corona and
if there were a widow's walk on the roof, you would see over the
neighbors' homes to the Pacific Ocean below. I had not heard before
this term "widow's walk," and so after traveling to the bank for a
certified check of ten thousand dollars, I drove home to the high-rise
and eventually last evening, after a dinner with Esmail and Nadereh
where I revealed nothing, a dinner of obgoosht and rice and yogurt
with cucumber followed by tea, I dismissed my son from the sofreh
upon the floor where we eat barefoot and I searched for "widow's
walk" in our Persian-English dictionary. I found only "widow," a word
in Farsi I know quite well enough, and I felt a sadness come to me because this did not seem a good sign for the purchase of a home.

But this morning, that feeling had every bit disappeared from my
body. Many summer evenings, instead of sleeping upon the sofa in
my office, I rest on the carpet near the sliding door of the terrace with
my head on a pillow beneath the leaves of the tree plants my Nadi
cares for like her own children. Last evening the sky was clear, and
sleep came for me as I watched the stars through the screen.

I rise with the first light from the east, and, after a shower and shave and a breakfast of toast and tea, I wake Esmail for his newspaper route. Then I dial the Highway depot and inform them of the summer flu I am suffering. I prepare tea for Nadi and bring it to the bedroom on a tray. The room is of course dark, with the shades drawn and the drapes closed, and I know she is awake because a cassette tape of Daryoosh's sentimental music is playing softly beside her bed. I rest the tray on the bureau and open the drapes and both shades.

"Eh, *Behrani. Nakon.* Chee kar mekonee?"

My wife's voice is still hoarse from sleep, and I know she again has not slept well. She says to me, "Don't." And, "What are you doing?" But this morning, for the first time since perhaps France, I know what I am doing; Colonel Massoud Amir Behrani knows what he is doing.

She sits up and I put carefully the tray upon her legs. I bend to kiss her cheek, but she turns her face from me and I sit down in the chair near her bed. My wife's hair is thick and short, an area of gray near her face that she dyes black. Sometimes she applies too much and that part of her hair appears the color of a plum. Nadi has always worried about all that is not as it should be, and the overthrow of our society has aged her more than myself. But even still, her face is small and beautiful and many times when I am allowed to stand or sit in this shadowed room where she spends so much of her days, I hear the domback drum behind Daryoosh's singing, and I see her and she has no longer fifty years, but twenty-five, and again, I desire to be with her in the fashion a man is supposed to be with his wife.

"What do you think you are looking at, Behrani?" she says in our mother language as she reaches for another sugar cube. She does not take her eyes from me. Her hair is tousled in the rear. I think of our children, and I smile at her and the cassette tape ends and the machine clicks off at once.

"Nadi-joon, today there may be a big opportunity for us." I of course say this in English, but it is never any use for if she answers at all it is only in Farsi.

She says nothing. She turns over the Daryoosh cassette and she does not wait for me to proceed about this opportunity. She reaches to turn up the volume, and I rise and leave the room and dress into a summer's weight gray suit.

It is not one of my finer sets of clothes, for I do not wish to appear pooldar, nor however do I wish to seem like a beggar in the market-place. Before leaving, I kiss my son on the top of his head as he eats his cold cereal at the small breakfast table in the kitchen. His hair smells of sleep and needs washing. He is dressed in a loose T-shirt and shorts, and beside him on the floor is his skateboard and bag of news-papers. He has only fourteen years, but he is already my height—175 centimeters—and he has his mother's face. Both my children have Nadi's small, beautiful face.

THE HOUSE IS one-story but in a good state of repair. It is painted white and appears quite bright in this early sun that is already hot on my head that still carries no hat. There are hedge bushes beneath the windows and a small lawn of grasses in front that is in need of trim-ming. The street is called Bisgrove, and it is on a hill with houses built closely together on one side, a woodland on the other. But the county tax gentleman was correct; the street is not so steep one can see the water, only the pale morning sky so high and wide over the rooftops. Opposite the road are evergreen woods and brush and far-ther up are even more homes, all small, many with bushes and fences separating the lawns. I look once more at the woodland, at the fash-ion in which the sunlight drops through the branches, and I am thinking of our summer home in the mountains near the Caspian Sea, of how the light was the same in those trees along the winding earth road to our bungalow, and for a moment, I feel a sense of sarne-hvesht, of destiny, and as soon as I do, I stand erect and look back at the property with as cool an eye as I am able, for I do not wish my judgment to be weakened at the point of sale.

Within thirty minutes we are all assembled, the county tax gen-tleman, the auctioneer, and only two prospective buyers: a young couple, a boy and his wife, who has not as many years as my daughter Soraya and is dressed in blue jean pants and white basketball shoes; and a gentleman close to my years, though very fat, as large as Torez, and he is dressed in a fine pair of suit pants but no jacket, simply a loose tie and white dress shirt that is stretched over his belly, and he is sweating on the forehead and above the lip. It is him I view as my main opponent, and all of his sweating makes me straighten my shoulders and I feel quite calm.

First, the county tax gentleman takes us for a walking tour through the bungalow. There is no air-conditioning, but the rooms are cool and I note every floor except for kitchen and bathroom is carpeted. The living room is large enough, and the dining area is a counter with stools where the kitchen begins. In the rear are three rooms, and as we step out in the backyard, I pat my breast pocket and touch the certified check from the Bank of America.

The young wife is very fond of the rear lawn, which is small and surrounded by evergreen hedges taller than a man. They shade us from the morning sun, and she begins to tell to her husband of the privacy they might have here, but it is the sweating gentleman, the radish, I am regarding. He stays close to the county tax officer and the auctioneer, who has as many years as me, carries a notepad and pen, and wears a department-store necktie and shirt. He has upon his face a confused expression, and he pulls the county tax gentleman aside for a quiet word.

Then we continue around the side yard to the front, and the sale begins with the auctioneer's suggested starting price of thirty thousand dollars. I am at once so astonished at this low figure that I do not respond and the young wife raises her hand and the auctioneer acknowledges her and the radish nods his head and the price is thirty-five thousand. The wife lifts her hand again, but the young husband forces it down and begins whispering loudly to her that they do not have that much saved, reminding her they are expected to pay all at once. My hand raises slightly from my side and the auctioneer points to me and the price is now forty thousand. The radish regards me with his wide wet face and his eyes become small, as if he is at once assessing me and my intentions as well as the numerous numbers in his head, and now it is clear to me he is a professional, a speculator, and he most possibly buys and sells dozens of these bungalows. I turn my face towards his and smile a most relaxed smile, one that is meant to invite him to bid all afternoon for I am prepared to do the same, sir, though of course I am not; I can barely go further than this, and I am not so certain any of this is wise.

"Forty-two fifty," says the radish, his eyes still upon me.

"Forty-five," my voice answers.

"Will there be a fifty-thousand-dollar bid for the property? Do I hear fifty, ladies and gentleman? Fifty thousand?" The auctioneer regards all our faces, our hands and fingers. The county tax officer consults his watch, and I feel the fat man's eyes upon me, and I make my own look to the house as if I am prepared to bid and bid. The sun is hot upon my head.

"Forty-five thousand, going once, going twice—"

The radish turns and walks to his car, and now the auctioneer cries, "*Sold,*" and the county tax gentleman steps forward to shake my hand and receive the deposit which I hand to him from my jacket pocket. I sign his papers, and I hear the young couple drive back down the road, but already I am calculating what this house on this street might bring me in the open market, and I am certain I will surely be able to double my money. Yes, yes, I will put it up for sale as soon as we move in.

NADI NOTICES THE new hat upon my head before she says anything of the flowers I have brought her, tiger lilies, the flower gentleman in Ghirardelli Square named them. My wife still wears her sleeping gown, and she is polishing the silver tea table. On the carpet around her she has rested the crystal bowls of nuts, dates, and chocolates, each covered with plastic wrapping to protect them from the fumes of the silver polish. In Farsi she says: "You should have a brown colah on your head, Behrani, not blue."

I know of course she is correct. The new hat I wear is of an artificial material, with a short visor like taxi drivers wear, and it is the color of a swimming pool. But I purchased it because in the shop's mirror it gave ˄ the appearance of a man with a sense of humor about living, a n˄˄n who is capable to live life for the living of it. And when I bought the flowers, I naturally hoped my Nadi might also for a moment see things in this way. But as I put the tigers in a water vase and set them upon the floor, I find myself preparing a proposition of numbers in my head. This must be handled quite delicately.

"Nadi-joon?"

"Why are you not working today, Behrani?" She does not look up from her work. I want tea, but I feel the moment is now to be taken. I sit upon the sofa, close to the silver table and my wife.

"Nadereh, do you remember our bungalow near Damavand? Do you remember I ordered the trees cut down on the north side so we may view the Caspian?"

"Saket-bosh, Behrani. Please, be quiet." My wife's voice is weary and there is fear in it as well, but I must continue.

"Do you remember when Pourat brought his family there for our New Year's and we celebrated spring on our terrace? And his khonoum, your dear friend, said what a gift from God to have the sea spread before us?"

"Hafesho, Behrani! What is the matter for you? *Please*." She stops polishing and closes her eyes, and when she does this I see water gather beneath one eye, and I feel the moment has come.

"Nadi, I today bought for us another bungalow."

She opens her eyes slowly, as if perhaps what I said is something she did not hear. "Do not joke. Why are you not working?" Her eyes are wet and dark and I think how in our country she would never let me see her like this: no cosmetics upon her face, her hair untended, still wearing what she slept in beneath a robe, doing what before only soldiers or women from the capital city did for us. But we have not looked at one another this directly in many months, and I want to hold her tired old face and kiss her eyes.

"I am not joking, Nadi." I begin to tell her of the auction and the price no one would believe I paid for the home, and how of course the open market will pay us three times that, which is the point,

Nadereh; this is the way for us to make significant money now, not Boeing or Lockheed, but real estate; we will live in the home for a short time and perhaps we will build a widow's walk to increase further the value of the property and we will take our tea there where we can view the ocean and you will be very comfortable there, Nadi; you will enjoy to invite Soraya and our new son-in-law there until we sell it and find an even better home and perhaps—

It is now that she stands and throws down the polish rag and yells at me in Farsi she did not come to America to live like a dirty Arab! So kaseef! Some family roaming the streets like gypsies! All their possessions being damaged and ruined along the way! She stops and closes her eyes, raises her hand to the side of her head, her fingers trembling at the knowledge she has invited one of her migraine headaches. I watch her walk back to her room and close the door behind her. Soon I hear Daryoosh's music on the cassette player in her room, the domback drum sounding as steady behind him as a march to bury the dead.

I lie back upon the sofa, no longer wanting tea, only rest. My wife has always been afraid. Both our fathers were lawyers in Isfahan, colleagues, good friends, and our marriage was their design since we were children. But I believe when I came of age I would have sent Nadi the flowers of hastegar anyway. She was always such a quiet girl, forever standing or sitting out away from the center of things, and her large brown eyes, so gavehee, looked often to me shiny with feeling.

Her confidence grew as an officer's wife, and she began to speak back to me, but she always was so fair and kind with our children, and with the soldiers who served in our home. The night we fled, she trembled like a wet bird, and she let me direct everything while she held the children and repeated to them whatever it was I had already said when, at three o'clock in the morning, one week to the day after Shahanshah flew to Cairo and the imams and ayatollahs were making massive crowds in the streets, I and two captains stole a large transport plane and flew our families across the Persian Gulf to Bahrain. Nadereh and our driver, Bahman, and I loaded five suitcases of all we could carry into the trunk of the limousine. Nadi was afraid to drive through the streets in it; she was afraid a mob would attack us for being pooldar, and only six blocks west one of our finest hotels was burning. University students with beards were breaking open cases of Dom Pérignon champagne and pouring the contents of each bottle into the street drains. I assured my wife a dark car was best in the night, one with bulletproof windows.

On the flight over the black water, our wives and children sat in the middle of the wide cargo floor wrapped in blankets and the women sang songs to the youngest children who were so afraid because they had heard what had happened to our dear friends, the Pourats. They had heard how my rafeegh, General Pourat, and his family were stopped at the airport the previous day, accused of taking what was not theirs; the children had heard how the entire family was put on trial there in an empty baggage room, how they were made to stand in front of a wall with a large cloth banner which read in our language: MUSLIMS DO NOT STEAL FROM THEIR MUSLIM BROTHERS. MUSLIMS DO NOT TORTURE AND KILL THEIR MUSLIM BROTHERS. It was under this banner my friend's wife and three young sons were one at a time shot to death. They were first forced to read aloud from the Koran. Then they were killed. My friend, an officer admired by even the lowest of soldiers for his generosity and strength, was saved for last. They shot him numerous times in the head and chest. They then dressed his body in full uniform, and from the observation tower, hung him by the feet.

I close my eyes. I have grown accustomed to these images in my head, and it is not long before sleep begins to take me and I dream once again of a large cave full of naked children. They are dirty, their thin arms and legs streaked with dust. Hundreds of them. Thousands of them. And yet they are quiet, their faces raised to the darkness as if they are awaiting bread and water. Then Shah Reza Pahlavi and Empress Farah float through the crowd in a convertible limousine. They are dressed in long red robes covered with diamonds, rubies, emeralds, and pearls. Some of the children move from the path of the auto, but others are too small or weak and they are crushed beneath the wheels. Shahanshah and his queen wave to them, their wrists stiff and their smiles fixed. I sit in a pilot's chair behind a large rock. My hands are on the controls, but I can do nothing but watch. I watch them all.

WEDNESDAY EVENINGS ARE not so busy at this convenience store/ gasoline station near San Pablo Avenue in El Cerrito; it is on Thursdays and Fridays when I am forced to hurry behind the counter like the young man with whom I work on those nights, and of course my legs are already very heavy from the long day working for Mr. Torez on the highway crew. This evening that is not the case, however, and for this I am grateful.

After my sleep this afternoon I made for myself tea, and I ignored the sound of more melancholy Persian music coming from Nadereh's room. I gathered the telephone book and telephone upon the floor, and I dialed six Realtors in the Corona–San Bruno–Daly City area. I described to each the home I owned, and I inquired as to a fair selling price. Each of them reminded me of the recession in which we live, Mr. Behrani; this is a buyer's market, and still, unfortunately, hardly anyone is buying. Yes, I said, but are there many good three-bedroom homes selling for under one hundred thousand dollars? Each Realtor—four women and two gentlemen—said no, not usually, and they of course then asked me if I had anyone representing my interests in this matter. I had just terminated my final conversation when my son Esmail returned home from practicing skateboarding with his friends. Both his knees were skinned to the start of blood, and I told to him he must wash them before he thought of having a snack.

"Mohamneest, Bawbaw-jahn." No problem, Daddy, he said, and I followed him into the bathroom and I sat upon the toilet seat while he removed his Nike basketball shoes and stepped into the tub to run water over his knees. I remained silent as he washed himself, and I noticed once again the black hair he is growing on his legs like a man. In front of his ears is the shadow of hair that in only a year or so will become reesh, a beard. And for the very first time, I felt the difficult position I was in with him as well.

"Esmail-joon?"

"Yeah?" My son turned off the water and looked at me quickly in the face. I handed to him a towel and he began drying himself.

In English I said: "I did not work today. Do you know why?"

He shook his head, then stepped out of the bathtub and folded the towel.

"I bought for us a house, Esmail. There is a beautiful hill for your skateboarding, and your friends can take the BART train to see you."

"Cojah?"

"In Corona. You remember that beach village we have before driven through on Sundays?"

My son of fourteen years looked at me then with Nadi's beautiful face that becomes so ugly so easily with bad feeling, and he walked past me and said in our language: "I don't *want* to move."

It is my practice halfway through this nightwork to purchase a Coca-Cola and drink it while I eat a package of peanut butter crackers. By nine-thirty or ten o'clock, the majority of my customers come only for gasoline or cigarettes, though many times a young husband or wife will arrive to buy milk and bread, ice cream perhaps. I sit upon the stool behind the counter and have my snack, and I am thankful of the long cigarettes display rack over me for keeping the bright fluorescent light from my eyes. Today has been a day of many decisions. After my son left the bathroom I stood quickly and felt the hot blood fill my hands and fingers, and I kicked my bare foot through Nadi's clothes hamper basket, then rushed into Esmail's room where he had turned on his television and I switched it off and stood over the bed where my son lay. I pointed at him, yelling in full voice, and I do not remember all I said except I know Esmail became hurt, perhaps frightened; I saw it in his eyes—though he lay there very relaxed-looking, his hands loose at his sides, and he would not show any of this to his father. I told to him he would do as I said without question, and then I heard the music stop in Nadereh's room, the bedsprings squeak as though she were sitting up to listen, and I pushed her door open and I went directly for the cassette player and pulled it free of the wall and threw it to the other side of the room where it knocked over the bureau lamp and the lightbulb shattered and Nadi began screaming, but I shouted back and soon she became quiet, but I did not lower my voice; I yelled in our language that, yes, perhaps she did not come to America to live like a gypsy, but I did not come here to work like an Arab! To be treated like an Arab! And then I did lower my voice because even my son does not know the manner of jobs I have been working here. He has seen me leave dressed in a suit and he knows I work at two jobs, but that is all he knows, and many nights at this convenience store, even though it is situated two towns to the north of us, I have worried about his older schoolmates with driver's licenses making this discovery. So I lowered my voice to almost a whisper, and I told to my wife that beginning tomorrow she will begin packing and there is no more to discuss, Mrs. Behrani. *Do not open your lips.*

Once, before dinner at our home in the capital city, while Nadereh and Pourat's wife were in another room and after I had just raised my voice at our daughter of seven years for something I do not now recall, Pourat said to me softly: "Behrani, every night you must leave your work behind you."

Pourat and I were of the same rank then, both captains, genob sarvans, and I did not at first understand him until he nodded at Soraya, at her brown eyes wet from my yelling, from my orders. My face became warm with embarrassment, and after that moment I have worked hard to discipline myself from viewing my wife only as a junior officer, my children as soldiers.

But I am prepared now to give all the orders necessary until we are out of that pooldar apartment. The rent is paid through the month, two more weeks, but the Behrani family will be discharged this weekend, I promise that. I have a security deposit of three thousand dollars to claim. This leaves a total of six thousand dollars for us after I pay the remaining thirty-five on our new property. Tomorrow, Friday, I will receive my checks from this store and from the Highway Department, and I will leave these jobs with no notice. Torez and Mendez, and even Tran, can watch my backside as I go, as Genob Sarhang Behrani prepares for a new life, a life in the buying and selling of American real estate.

. . . .
. . . .
. . . . . .
. .

Mᴀ HUSBAND GOT TO MISS ALL THIS, THAT'S WHAT I KEPT THINKING, that he didn't have to be around for any of this, and I was stuck at the El Rancho Motel in San Bruno. It was a shitty little one-story L of rooms wedged between an electrical parts warehouse and a truck-stop bar near the 101 freeway ramp. The TV in my room got sound but nothing on the screen, and it was only a Wednesday night but there was a live country band playing at the truck stop and the management must have had all the windows open, so I turned the TV up and listened to an old movie with Humphrey Bogart and in the end he gets shot and his girlfriend weeps and says he's free now, he's free.

But I was still so mad it had backed up on me and now I felt weak and a little sick. I was dying for a cigarette, which made me even madder because I hadn't smoked one since a month after Nick left, and I hadn't really craved one in five. So I chewed gum.

I was getting out of my morning shower when they knocked on the front door of my house: a man in a suit, two cops, and a locksmith with a huge gut that hung over the tool belt at his waist. I answered in my robe, my hair wet and scraggly around my face. Parked out front was a van, a big LTD, and two police cruisers. The man in the suit did the talking. He handed me some kind of document and said he was from the civil division of the San Mateo County Sheriff's Department. He had a crewcut and a double chin, the rest of him slim. The policemen had star badges on their light blue shirts, sheriff's deputies. One was tall and skinny with black hair and a mustache he'd trimmed too much on one end, and he kept staring at me. I read over the court order, then handed it back to the man in the suit, my fingers shaking, and I told him the truth, that my husband and I had never operated any damn business out of our home and did not owe a business tax. I went to the county tax office myself and told them so, even signed a statement and had it notarized, and I thought that was the end of it. The man in the suit asked to be let in and when I stepped back, all four of them walked into my small living room while I stood there in my robe, still naked and damp underneath. The fat locksmith squatted at my door and started unscrewing the knob and lock.

"What is he doing?"

The man in the suit handed me back the court order. "The county has petitioned the court in its behalf, Mrs. Lazaro. This should come as no surprise to you. I'm sure you had ample warning; your house is up for auction starting tomorrow morning."

"*Auction?*"

The pager on his belt went off. He asked if he could use my phone on the kitchen counter, then went to it without waiting for an answer. I stared at the court order, but didn't see any of the words; I was picturing all the county tax mail I'd been throwing away unopened since last winter, sure I'd done my part and they were now after the wrong person.

"Is your husband home?" It was the tall deputy with the crooked mustache.

"That's none of your business."

The deputy looked like he was about to say more, but then just looked at me.

"*What?* Why do you need to know that?"

"We need to notify all residents of the house, Mrs. Lazaro."

"Well, he doesn't live here anymore."

The tall deputy nodded at me, then folded his hands in front of him and looked down at my bare feet. I walked away from him, but I didn't know where to go.

The other deputy was short, chewing gum, watching the locksmith like he wanted to remember how to do that himself. The man in the suit finished his call and waved the tall deputy over, whispered something to him, then came back into the living room and said he had to leave but Deputy Sheriff Burdon will assist you in vacating the property. That was his exact word, *vacating,* and he said it in a low tone, like it was a skill not many people had. Then he was gone, and the tall deputy with the crooked mustache asked where I kept my coffee. He suggested I get dressed and he'd make up a pot. I hesitated a second, but I felt like all three of them could see through my robe. I went and changed into jeans and a sweatshirt and when I came back out, the short deputy was using my phone, the locksmith was already going at the back-door knob, and Deputy Burdon was setting four of my cups on the counter. He glanced at me and said I might want to put on something cooler, there's no fog today and it's going to get hotter.

"That's all right 'cause I'm not leaving." My throat felt dry and stiff.

The locksmith looked up from his work on my back door.

Deputy Burdon rested one hand on the countertop, and he had an understanding expression on his face, but I hated him anyway. "I'm afraid you have no choice, Mrs. Lazaro. All your things will be auctioned off with the property. Do you want that?"

"Look, I *inherited* this house from my father, it's *paid* for. You can't evict me!" My eyes filled up and the men began to blur. "I never *owed* a fucking business tax. You have no right to *do* this."

The tall deputy handed me a napkin from the counter. "Do you have a lawyer?"

I shook my head and wiped under my eyes. "I can't afford a lawyer, I'm a house cleaner."

He took a notepad and pen from his front shirt pocket, wrote down the name of a Legal Aid office in San Francisco, then ripped out the page and handed it to me. "Nothing's written in blood. You just have to clear out today. Who knows? You might be moving right back in next week. Do you want to phone some friends to come help you pack up?"

"No." I kept my eyes on my full coffee cup.

"I'm afraid everything has to go today."

The locksmith was using a battery-powered drill on my back door. I could smell the sawdust spilling onto the linoleum. "There's no one to call."

He looked at me, his brown eyes narrowed like he thought he

knew me from a long time ago. I felt my cheeks get hot. He reached out his hand. "My name's Lester."

I hesitated before I took it. He stood then used my phone to call the Golden State Movers, signed a slip of paper for the locksmith, took from him the new keys I wasn't supposed to have, and stepped out onto the front stoop with the other deputy. They were standing close to the screen door and I heard Deputy Lester Burdon tell his partner to go back out on patrol, he was going to call in some personal time and help this lady clear out.

The storage sheds across from the El Rancho Motel were his idea. It took only four hours to move my life from the only house I've ever owned to one of those steel shacks with the padlock I now have to pay for and can't afford. The movers didn't have any boxes to sell me, so the tall deputy went out for some while the moving men—three college kids—started hauling out my Colonial living-room set with the plaid upholstery, a wedding present from Nick's mother and father. I was feeling kind of numb, stuffing the small things into plastic trash bags, each one thrown into a moving truck like this was all natural, part of some bigger plan that shouldn't have surprised and upset me so much.

AFTER A WHILE, the band quit for the night and I turned off the lamp and sat there against the headboard. I heard an eighteen-wheeler pull into the lot, and the last call noise inside the barroom. I was fighting the urge for a cigarette. I stretched out on the motel bed, rested my hands over my breasts, and closed my eyes, but I couldn't sleep. I was wondering again where Nicky was, Los Angeles maybe, or Mexico, though nobody back East knew he'd even left me. So I lay there in the dark, remembering what Irish Jimmy Doran said to me. He was from Dublin, small and wiry with bad teeth, and he tended bar where I used to waitress at the Tip Top on old Route 1. I saw him in the grocery store parking lot right after Nick got his job offer in Frisco. It was a gray day in April, but Jimmy was squinting his eyes like the sun was on him, and when he saw me he came over and gave me a big hug, smelling like Chesterfields and Schnapps. I told him we were off to California, the land of milk and honey.

"Dat's what they say of this cauntry back home, Kath: 'America, the Land of Milk and Honey.' Bot they never tell you the milk's gone sour and the honey's stolen."

AT THE FIRST sign of daylight spreading over the cars in the El Rancho parking lot, I gave up trying to sleep and drove the Bonneville down the coast on Highway 1. The sun was still coming up from the east. The ocean to my right was maroon, the sky above it silver. There were sand trails through the thick purple ice plant that grew along the roadside. The few cars I passed had their headlights on, and I kept hearing Deputy Burdon's voice in my head warning me to stay away from Bisgrove Street until I'd talked to a lawyer and straightened things out or else I'd be trespassing and up for arrest. This got my heart beating fast, and I kept the radio off and drove for twenty minutes, past the state beaches through the tourist-shop town of Montara to Moss Beach, where I stopped at a gas station/beach supply store and drank coffee at a table by the window. The morning was still quiet. The beach across the road was empty, and I watched a seagull dive into the water for a fish. At the front of the store was an old woman behind the register. I went to the cigarette machine, stuck in my coins, and pulled the knob hard: *Who did they think they were evicting? And for **what**? A tax they billed to the wrong fucking house? My dead **father's** house?*

I backed out the Bonneville and drove south along the water. I lit another cigarette and I kept seeing Nick's face the morning he left, the way he looked in the shadowed room after he woke me with a nudge, sitting on the side of the bed. At first I thought I'd slept late and he was on his way out the door to work, but then I saw how early it was, and I could smell all the cigarettes on his breath, and I knew he'd been up a long time. I moved to switch on the bedside lamp but he touched my hand to stop me. Then he held it. In that dim light, I couldn't make out his eyes.

"What, honey? What?" I said. I was thinking of his father or his mother, a late-night phone call I'd missed. But as soon as he opened his mouth and said, "Kath," I knew it was about us again, and I started to sit up, but he put his other hand on my chest and I stayed still and waited for him to say what he was going to say. But he never said another word; he sat there and stared in the direction of my face, and even when I asked him what, what's the matter, Nicky, my heart jerking all confused under his hand, he only stared, and then, after another half minute of nothing, he squeezed my fingers and left the room, and I jumped out of bed in just a T-shirt and followed him through the house to the front door, saying, "Wait, wait." I stopped and watched him get into the used Honda we'd just bought as a second car. Daylight was breaking out over the yard and the woods across the road. Then I saw the two suitcases and his bass guitar in the backseat, and I ran out into the driveway, the January air hitting me like a bat. He was already backing up and I rapped on the driver's window and screamed his name and kept doing it until he shifted gears in the street and drove down the hill, not once looking back at me, even in the rearview mirror.

I started to cry as I drove. The sun was lighting up the ocean, and the sand was getting bright.

IT WAS CLOSE to ten when I drove into the parking lot of the motel. Most of the trailer trucks next door were gone, and the sun was starting to shine bright off the cars in the lot. As soon as I got into my room, I lit another cigarette and called the lawyer's number Deputy Burdon had written on the back of his card. A man with a soft voice answered and I started to tell him how I'd been evicted from my own home yesterday. I almost cried again and I hated myself for it. The man said he was sorry to hear of my dilemma but you've reached the Walk-In Legal Aid Society and all you have to do is come in and explain all that to one of our attorneys. He gave me the address in the city and wished me luck. Before we hung up I asked him what it would cost and he told me all services were delivered on a sliding scale.

I undressed and put on my robe and sat on the edge of the bed. I had about eight hundred in checking, fifty in savings, and this month the house insurance was due. Now I had the storage shed to pay for, and this new lawyer, and there was no way I could pull my shit together for my two cleaning customers today. One was a house over on the San Andreas Reservoir, the other a doctor's office in town. I called and postponed both, leaving me three jobs to do tomorrow, then took a long shower. I dried myself with the motel's thin green towel, thinking how even this place could sink me, though I knew there was nowhere else to go.

I started to blow-dry my hair, which had grown out past my shoulders the way it hadn't been since I was nineteen and married to Donnie, my first cokestorm, my period late, and we both told ourselves we weren't ready and he drove me to the clinic in Brookline and the whole family found out. Dad had never really looked right at me anyway, but then he stopped doing it at all, would only give me his quiet profile, usually in his recliner in front of the TV. And Ma started giving me that look, her eyes locking in on me dark and flat, like I was something from her bad dreams that kept showing up in her day life, in her home, and just who did I think I was?

I went through my suitcase for the least wrinkled clothes there, which was a new pair of jeans and a white blouse with horizontal pleats in the front. Just before I left I thumbed some blush onto my cheeks that were pale from no sleep. My eyes looked sunken and I brought them out with black eyeliner.

The Legal Aid office was in the Mission District in San Francisco. I had to drive around the block a few times before I saw the window sign on the second floor of a building on 16th and Valencia. It was above one of those New Age coffee shops this city is full of, the Café Amaro. It was a half hour before lunch and all the small tables were full of west coast men and women eating food like tabouleh salads and miso spread on sesame crackers, the men skinny and clean-shaven, a lot of them with ponytails, but I was really seeing only the women as I went by, their unmade-up look, their long thick hair tied up in back with more hair, their colorful T-shirts, their breasts small,

or else hanging long and heavy underneath the cotton they probably only bought from catalogs. They had handmade jewelry hanging
off their ears, around their necks and on their wrists. They wore
shorts or homemade skirts or loose jeans and there wasn't a painted
finger or eyelash or lip on any of them. Some of the women glanced
up at me, then looked back down again, not really interested after all,
and I was back in high school walking down a hallway crowded with
the girls in clubs and organized activities I wasn't interested in but
felt left out anyway, my face a doughy mask.

The receptionist upstairs had the same soft voice as the man I
talked to on the phone. He wore jeans and a bright aqua silk shirt.
He was my age, thirty-five or -six, and when he stood to greet me he
smiled and said his name was Gary, then handed me a clipboard with
a form to fill out. There was no one else in the waiting room. On the
walls were posters of women's movement marches, announcements
for lesbian poetry readings, boycotts of fruit and vegetable farms in
the state.

After I filled out the personal information sheet, including my in-
come and how I made it, the receptionist led me to a corner conference room that was small but full of daylight from all the tall
windows that faced the street below. He offered me bottled water,
herbal tea, or coffee. I told him I'd take as much coffee as he had, and
I laughed, but I wasn't feeling funny; really, I felt like an old magazine somebody finds wedged under a chair cushion, and I knew that's
where I wanted to be, under a huge cushion somewhere, curled up
cool and private, to sleep a long time.

AFTER LEGAL AID, I made the mistake of taking a nap at the motel.
When I woke up the room was dark and there was talking and laughing coming from nearby. The air smelled like cigarette smoke, and I
didn't know where I was. Then an eighteen-wheeler started up outside, its driver revving it until something metal began to rattle. I
switched on the bedside lamp and read my watch: almost nine. I lay
back down and took a deep breath that made me shudder, but I re-

fused to cry. I concentrated on a brown water stain on the ceiling, and listened to the early drinking crowd at the truck-stop bar next door, and remembered the spring before last, when both our families gave us a going-away party at my brother's house in East Boston. Frank had taken the afternoon off from his car dealership in Revere, and he was still dressed in a gray double-breasted suit with a loud silk tie. He was big and handsome, his black hair moussed back. There were forty or fifty people there, just relatives and in-laws, and they filled all three floors of my brother's house. It was a party with no cocktails or beer—my mother-in-law, mother, and aunts made sure of that—not even red wine to go with the veal and sausages and spaghetti. Most of the older women stayed in the kitchen, where they warmed the food and kept telling each other the right way to cook. All the little kids were on the first floor, where the Ping-Pong table and dartboard were, and because it was a Saturday in March, most of the uncles and guy cousins sat in the family room watching basketball on Frank's wide-screen TV. One or two were out on the second-floor deck with Nick, wanting to hear about the new job. I was standing in the doorway of the kitchen with Jeannie, sipping a coffee before dinner, my eyes on Nick out on the deck. I could see the huge Mystic Bridge behind him, the gray clouds, the skyscrapers of Boston. We were a few days from spring and it was warm enough that I didn't wear a coat. My new husband was standing there in a bright yellow cashmere sweater and black jeans, smoking a cigarette and flicking the ash into his Coke can. He was nodding his head at something one of his cousins was saying, and I felt so much love for him right then my eyes filled up and Jeannie put her hand on my arm and asked what's wrong, K? What's the matter?

Later, Frank led everyone out of the house to the driveway and the shiny red Bonneville. There was a wide white ribbon running from the front bumper over the roof and into the trunk. And somebody had taped to the driver's window a huge card both families had signed, though I knew the car was from Frank, a low-mileage sales bonus he usually took for himself but this year gave to us. One of the uncles videotaped us climbing inside, then backing out for a test drive. We didn't want a big American car, though; we were planning to buy something small. But on the drive west we kept it on cruise control the whole way and steered with two fingers. When we weren't talking, we stretched out and played cassettes till one of us needed to crawl into the backseat and lie on the maroon upholstery with a pillow and blanket and go to sleep.

I got up off the motel bed and washed my face with cold water and soap in the bathroom. I had cried more in the last eight months than in the rest of my life and I had to stop it because it seemed like the more I cried the less I did to change things, or to even avoid the shit coming at me. My new lawyer couldn't quite understand that, why I threw away all that mail from the county tax office without opening it. I liked her right away, I think because she wasn't wearing any shoes, just round glasses, a white blouse, and gray slacks over bare feet. She poured herself a cup of coffee, then sat down a chair away from me with her legal pad and pencil. She asked me to tell her everything, which I did, including that I already went to the county tax office in Redwood City and signed a statement saying we'd never run a business from our house, so why the five-hundred-thirty-dollar business tax?

"Five hundred dollars? They evicted you from your house for *that?*"

"You got it." I lit a cigarette, enjoying my lawyer's shock at this. She asked where my husband and I were staying, and I looked down at the table, at a worm of a cigarette burn. "He's not in the picture anymore." I reached for a seashell ashtray. "I'm booked in a motel in San Bruno."

She paused a second and made a straight line with her lips like she was sorry to hear that. Then she asked me a bunch of questions about my inherited ownership. Was there a devise in my father's will? Was it completely paid for? Who was the bank? Do you have a copy of your signed statement to the county tax office? That's what she wanted more than anything, and I said I could get one to her, though I had no idea where it was. After all her questions she stood and took off her glasses and smiled. "First thing we have to do is keep them from selling your home. Then we get it back. And they can pay your motel bill, too." She checked the form I'd filled out to make sure she had my room number, then she shook my hand and said not to worry, call her tomorrow late afternoon.

I turned on the TV and sat at the foot of the bed, but still there was only sound, a commercial for a diet drink. I heard a woman laugh out in the parking lot, and I wondered if this truck stop was like some back East: cold beer and live music in the bar, hot steak and eggs in the diner, hookers for the rooms upstairs. I sat there and listened to the beginning of some TV show about cops and DAs and the streets of New York City. Outside my window was the twangy beat of another country band playing next door, and for the fortieth time since last January I looked at the telephone and tried not to call someone back home.

For a long time my mother would call every Sunday afternoon to catch us up on things, but really to see how *we* were. The first few Sundays after Nick left, when I answered the phone and heard her voice, I had to hold my hand to my mouth sometimes to keep from crying. But then I'd start lying about how well he was doing at his new job. I told her how his office was on the seventeenth floor of an earthquake-proof building overlooking San Francisco, and that he was making good money and would probably get promoted in no time. This used to be true.

Sometimes she would want to talk to him and I'd say he was taking a nap and I didn't want to wake him up, or else he was working (she never liked hearing that, not on a Sunday), or he was playing basketball with some guys from his office. She seemed to like hearing that the most, that Nick was out making friends and doing something healthy.

"What about you, K? Have you made new friends, too?"

"Yeah," I'd say. "I get together with some of the wives and we shop and, you know, do things like that." There'd be silence on her end. "And there's one girl, Ma. She's my age and kind of overweight. She lives nearby and we go jogging together four nights a week."

That helped, a lie about making friends and taking care of myself. As soon as she seemed satisfied with my news, she'd go on about Frank and my nephews, their house, her thinning hair, the gambling trip to Atlantic City her two sisters were planning. But behind all this talk was the question she'd never ask: have you been going to those recovery groups out there, K? And that was one lie I couldn't pull off, anyway. So instead she would finish her calls by asking me the other true question stuck inside her like something she could only ease out by hearing me finally give the right answer:

"When do you think you two will have children, K?"

And for once in our calls I could tell the truth: "As soon as I can talk Nick into it, Mom." Which was true when Nicky still lived with me. Saying this long after he'd been gone though, my voice sounded hollow.

ONLY THREE YEARS ago we were both into our second week at the program, and we had the same double dose—coke and alcohol—but the day before in Group, Nick had owned up to a third, porno. A lot of us couldn't accept this as a real addiction, but Larry told us to pipe down and "hear" Nick. That wasn't hard for me to do because even then, Nick's body still coming off the ten-day binge of lines and beer and Southern Comfort that got him into an emergency room then the program, his fingers always trembling while he smoked, I couldn't not look at him, at those hard blue eyes, at his thick black hair and pale face with pimple scars on the cheeks. His arms and legs were skinny, and he had a belly that showed more when he sat down, but all I ever wanted to do from the start was to feel my whole wasted body up against Nicky Lazaro's.

Whenever he talked he threw me because his voice was so deep and didn't go with his boy-look, and also, he spoke well, like he was educated or else read a lot of books. He said it was always worse when he was trying to stay straight, that instead of drinking or doing lines he'd be doing dirty movies. Sometimes he even called in sick at work and he'd rent a half-dozen hard-core tapes and spend hours and hours with them.

"*Hours?*" I said, and I started to laugh, though I felt pretty disgusted. Larry cut me off and said how "inappropriate" remarks like that were in Group. I looked at Nick. He was studying the burning cigarette in his hand like he wasn't part of this conversation at all. Then he glanced at me, his eyes dark and a little shiny, and my cheeks got hot and I had to look away.

On visitors' day, while I was waiting for my brother and his wife, I kept watching Nick on the other side of the room sitting straight across from his parents, who reminded me of my own, though Dad was dead and Ma couldn't face seeing me anymore. Sometimes he'd glance in my direction and I'd look away. All around us were visiting families in plastic chairs around fold-out tables, some of them hardly looking into each other's eyes, others loud, telling stories and jokes like they were relieved everything had only come to this, a Get Well helium balloon floating in the haze of cigarette smoke above them.

But I felt grateful just to be sitting there. In the two weeks I'd been at the program, the lining inside my nostrils had already stopped bleeding, I hadn't drunk anything stronger than coffee, and the only stranger I would wake up to was me. But more than that, I had already stopped wanting what I'd been craving off and on since I was fifteen, for Death to come take me the way the wind does a dried leaf out on its limb.

QUITE EARLY FRIDAY MORNING, AS I LIE SLEEPING UPON THE CARPET near the open sliding screen, my son touches my shoulder and wakes me to a glass of hot tea and four cubes of sugar. Outdoors, in the trees below us, a bird calls, but the sky is gray and the air through the screen is cool.

"Bawbaw-jahn. Man goh khordam. I am sorry."

My son is already dressed in shorts and T-shirt, his hair dry, but combed. I sit up and take the tea and drink it without sugar. I look through the screen at the small concrete terrace outside, and I hear my Esmail sit upon the carpet beside me.

"I know you work very hard, Bawbaw. All the days and almost all the nights of the week."

I look at my son, at his brown eyes that on a woman would be beautiful, and in Farsi I thank him for his apology and for the tea, and I tell to him he must begin preparing his room for moving.

Today, on the freeway crew of garbage soldiers, we work the south-bound lanes of Route 101 where it runs along the tall evergreen trees of the Golden Gate Recreational Area. I wear my new blue hat all the day long but of course the morning fog never lifts and I wish for a light sweater. At the lunch break I eat quickly beside Tran, then rise to speak with Torez as he sits behind the wheel of his truck, the door open very wide, as he studies one of those odd crossword grids in the newspaper. I stand there a moment until it becomes clear to me I am standing at attention. I discipline myself to relax my shoulders and speak.

"After today I will no longer be working here, Mr. Torez."

He completes writing a word with his pencil, then he looks up and says: "You tell the office, Coronel?"

"No."

"So why tell me, man?" He regards his newspaper. "You know an-other word for hurricane?"

I return to Tran and my tea and I have a wish to tell the Viet-namese goodbye, but when I point to my chest then to the road, he smiles and nods his head as if I were telling to him a very old and hu-morous story.

And now it is evening at the convenience store and my legs are heavy, my eyes are beginning to water from fatigue, but I am filled with cheer as I work my very last shift. Rico, the young man work-ing beside me, has always possessed the habit of chewing gum which on other evenings bothered me a great deal—that nasty sound it makes in the mouth—but tonight this is not the case; none of the usual irritants have their power over me, not the bright fluorescent lighting over all the shelves of overpriced boxed and canned food; not the university students who enter with their stupid smiles after drinking too much beer to purchase chocolate bars and cigarettes; not even when people hand to me a gasoline credit card and I have to use the cumbersome machine beneath the magazine display rack; and even those kaseef and dirty magazines of naked women on their covers, which I have always despised having to touch or sell, even they cannot upset me as they have so many times before. Because this I know of life's difficult times: there is always a time for them to begin and a time for them to end, and the man who knows this knows he must thank God for each day he has suffered because that is always one day closer to the sun, the real sun.

But many nights after many long days in America, I have forgotten God and thought only of my troubles, of the manner of jobs I was forced to work here, jobs I would not have assigned a soldier under me back in my old life. Here I have worked in a tomato cannery, an auto wash, a furniture warehouse, a parking lot, two gasoline stations, and finally the highway department and this convenience store. Yes, I have earned enough to slow our spending, but each check cashed felt to me like one less bone and muscle in my back, those a man needs in order to stand straight.

My young colleague and I close the store promptly at one in the morning. We lock the evening's receipts into the small safe in the rear office, and we post our inventory sheet for the day gentleman before removing our paychecks from the coin drawer of the register. We lock the doors and walk beneath the light over the gasoline pumps to our vehicles, and to the young man I only say, "Good night, Rico," nothing more, and as I drive my Buick Regal down San Pablo Avenue beneath the streetlights so early in the morning, my body feels sewn into the car seat with tiredness, but I nod five times to the east and thank God, my mouth beginning to tremble, for the freedom He has granted me once again, for the return of the dignity I was beginning to believe I would never recover.

FRIDAY WAS THE BEST AND WORST DAY SO FAR. IT WAS BEST BECAUSE I worked it straight through, cleaning my normal residential plus the reservoir house job and the pediatric office I'd skipped the day before. There was a fog bank pushing in from the beaches and on another day it could've sent me over the edge, the way it covers the town in gray, but Friday I just tuned it out and cleaned with more energy than I'd had in a long time.

My customers leave me a key in their mailbox or under a rock on their lawn, which means no one is ever there except for a dog or cat, and I can work alone and fast, chewing gum and listening to the Walkman I keep clipped to my shorts; Nick's old tapes mostly, loud fast rock that keeps me moving at a good pace and keeps me from thinking too much. When I woke up early Friday morning at the El Rancho, I made up my mind I was going to stop wallowing in my problem and start concentrating on the solution instead. I had to turn it over to Connie Walsh. She *was* my lawyer. By the time I was dressed, I'd convinced myself I'd hear something positive by the end of the day about getting my house back. So instead of booking my room through the weekend, I went down to the office and paid another thirty-one dollars for Friday night only.

I got back to the motel just before the end-of-the-work-week traffic heated up on the freeways. My arms, legs, and lower back were tired out, and my sweat had dried three times on my skin, but before I took a shower I called Legal Aid and Gary had me wait on the line almost five minutes before Connie Walsh picked it up: "I'm sorry, Kathy, but evidently the county has already sold your house."

I stood still and took short, dry breaths. *"What? How?"*

"The auction date's been set for months, Kathy; that was in the mail you've been throwing away." I pictured my mother's round face, her eyes dark and flat-looking. I heard my brother Frank, who told me and Nick the house was ours as far as he was concerned; he might want his half in twenty years, but hey K, One Day at a Time, right? Then I felt the tears come, my stomach twisting up. "Those moth-erfuckers."

"Can you get that to me Monday morning, Kathy?"

"What?"

"Your copy of the tax statement. Hopefully I'll have their paper-work by then, and we can go from there, all right?"

Connie Walsh was quiet on the other end. I wiped my nose and asked her what she was planning to do.

"Just what I said, Kathy. We'll demand they rescind the sale or we file a lawsuit against the county." She said not to worry too much, then reminded me to get that paperwork to her Monday morning.

I spent the first part of the night in the steel storage shed across the street looking for the signed tax statement from the county. But it was already too dark to see much, and I didn't have a flashlight, so I drove to a convenience store on the other side of the freeway to get one. The streets were fogged in and the air was wet and too cool for shorts. Back in the shed I found one of Nick's old sweatshirts and pulled it on. It was black-and-white with the logo of a band he used to play bass for years ago. It was clean so didn't smell like him, but I could still picture him in it, lying on the couch while he read a pa-perback with the TV or radio on, sometimes both. That was always how he read.

After over an hour going through my boxes and bags, my neck stiff from holding the butt of the flashlight between my chin and chest so I could use both hands, I almost gave up when I remembered my trunk. I pulled two full trash bags off it, then lifted the heavy wooden lid. Inside were things I hadn't even looked at since moving west: old clothes and shoes, towels and blankets, a dozen rock albums from high school—mainly the Rolling Stones and the Allman Brothers, but no paperwork.

"Hello?"

I screamed and swung around and dropped the flashlight. A man picked it up and shined it in his face. It was shadowed and I stepped back, but then recognized the crooked mustache. Deputy Sheriff Burdon smiled, then handed me the flashlight, and I took a breath and let it out. "Shit, don't *do* that."

"I'm sorry, I didn't mean to scare you."

"Well you *did*." I put the pictures back in the trunk, then stepped out of the shed and padlocked it, squeezing the flashlight between my ribs and elbow. My heart was still beating fast, and it was completely dark now. Fog hovered in the lot and street. In the light from the security lamps over the sheds I could see Lester Burdon was wearing jeans and sneakers and a windbreaker.

"Did you get hold of Legal Aid?"

"Yeah, thanks." I turned off the flashlight and began to walk across the lot. My bare legs felt cold, my nipples were hard against my shirt, I didn't know how I felt about him being here. "You working undercover or something?"

"Excuse me?" He looked down at his sneakers. "Oh, no, I'm off. I just—I drive by this way. I thought I'd check in on you, see how you're holding up."

He sounded like he meant it, and he seemed even softer than the day before when he'd led those men in kicking me out of my house. When we got to his car, a Toyota station wagon parked at the edge of the lot near the chain-link fence, I kind of hoped he'd keep talking; Connie Walsh was the first person I'd had a real conversation with in over eight months, and that was more of an interrogation than a talk. I wanted one, even with a sheriff's deputy in the fog. He was looking across the street past the motel to all the tractor trailers parked behind the truck stop. I could hear the bass drum of the country band through the walls, cars moving over the freeway bridge down the block. He looked back at me, his face all somber. "Can I buy you a cup of coffee, or something?"

"That'd be all right." I told him I had to put on something warmer first. He waited in his car in the motel lot and I changed into the same clothes I'd worn to Legal Aid. I rubbed deodorant under my arms and ran some eyeliner under my bottom lashes.

We both agreed the truck stop would be too loud, so we ended up at a Carl Jr.'s a mile past the freeway on the outskirts of San Bruno.

The place was brightly lit and smelled like fried chicken and pota-
toes. I hadn't eaten and my stomach felt hollow, but I didn't want to
order food and change the offer of drinking coffee together into
something else. We sat at a table by the window. Deputy Burdon
had taken off his jacket and was wearing a striped golf shirt. His
arms were tan, and the gold of his wedding band stood out bright
against his skin. His mustache was as crooked as it had been the day
before, his dark eyes a little moist. I had to be looking at the most serious man I'd ever met.

Our coffee came. I added Sweet'n Low to mine but he sipped his
black, his eyes on me. On the ride over he'd asked me if Legal Aid
had a lawyer for me yet and I told him yeah, then Connie Walsh's
news about the county already auctioning off the house. Now he
looked down at the tabletop and shook his head. "Boy, they don't
fool around, do they?"

"It's not hard to rescind these things, though, is it? That's my
lawyer's plan." I felt shaky at his reaction. I lifted my coffee cup, but
then put it back down; I felt a little sick to my stomach. I lit a cigarette and blew the smoke out the side of my mouth.

"I really don't know much about that, Mrs. Lazaro."

"Kathy. Nicolo's my maiden name."

"It suits you." His eyes stayed on mine a second, then he glanced
out the window. I wanted to ask if he had any kids; I wanted to know
that, but I didn't ask and took a drag of my cigarette.

"Anyway, we never should have been charged a tax at all, and I
only own half the house in the first place. My lawyer's confident,
though, so I'm trying not to harp on the negative."

"Your husband hold the rest?"

"My brother. He doesn't know about any of this yet. No one
does."

The waitress came by and topped off our coffee. Lester Burdon
smiled at her, but sadly, I thought, like he knew something about her
that wasn't good. His face changed when he saw me studying him
and he sipped his coffee.

"Do you have any kids, Mr. Burdon?"

"Two." He put his cup down and folded his elbows on the table. His eyes were on mine again, but this time he didn't look away and neither did I. I wasn't used to being looked at so closely, to being seen.

"My husband left me eight months ago. No one back home knows that either."

"You always keep so many secrets?"

"Just when I have to."

He kept his brown eyes on me, and I looked away to stub out my cigarette.

"I understand."

"Do you?"

"I think so." He nodded once, the way cops do.

IT WAS A short and strange ride back to the motel. Neither of us talked and the fog still moved slowly through the streets. The lights over the diesel pumps at the truck stop looked misted at the edges, so did the blue and red neon beer signs in the bar window, and across the lot the tall yellow letters of the El Rancho Motel over the office, all dulled and spread out a little.

He pulled into the lot and I put my hand on the door handle. "I want to go back to my house, but I'd have to break a window just to get in there."

He touched four fingers to my knee, lifting them just as quick, but they left a warmth in my leg that loosened something in me all the way to my diaphragm.

"Do you mind if I give you some professional advice?"

"I guess not."

"Keep your head and do it all through your lawyer, Kathy. If I were you, I wouldn't even drive up there until the keys were back in my hand."

He looked dark-eyed and somber again and I didn't want to get out of his car, but I didn't want to stay either. "Thanks for stopping by."

He looked at me with his handsome face and crooked mustache and I got out and closed the door, watching his little station wagon turn up the foggy street, its taillights vanishing in no time.

SATURDAY AND SUNDAY all the coast towns were fogged in. I spent the weekend in my room smoking and reading magazines, watching my own color TV I'd pulled from the storage shed. When I got hungry I went out for fast food. Late Sunday night I drove under the freeway to go buy cigarettes and a Snickers Bar and when I got back, I couldn't be sure, but I thought I saw Lester Burdon's car pull away from the curb across the street, its small foreign engine straining to shift gears.

I LOOK AT MY NADI OVER THE PIZZA WE ARE EATING UPON THE FLOOR of our new home. She is dressed in a fashionable sweat suit the color of roses. She wears no cosmetics upon her face, and there are shadows beneath her eyes. Esmail has worked very hard all weekend, and he reaches for a fifth slice even before he has finished chewing his last. But Nadereh will not return my look. She has spoken to me very little, in Farsi or English, since I yelled and broke her cassette player by throwing it in the bedroom of our pooldar apartment. We complete our eating and I give my son permission to leave the sofreh for his room. Nadi rises to prepare the samovar.

The movers finished with their business by nightfall yesterday, my wife working until midnight bringing order to her new room, the largest, with two good windows overlooking the rear lawn. My room and Esmail's are smaller and face the front grass and the street and woodland beyond, and we will share the bathroom as a family. Even though she would not speak to me, I enjoyed listening to Nadi talk

ANDRE DUBUS III
55

with the large moving men in *English,* informing them please to be calculated, and please to work slowful and avoid to shatter very supreme furniture, thank you, sirs.

I lie back upon one elbow on the carpet, but I can no longer see my wife in the kitchen area due to the bar counter and its stools. This is something quite western, the design of a drinking saloon in one's own home, and if I were not planning to sell the property to Americans, I would have it removed. The sound of televised laughter comes from Esmail's new bedroom. Yesterday he was excited to discover this hill brought as many programs to his screen as the pooldar apartments, and for two hours today, after he had organized his room, my son rode his skateboard down the long hill of Bisgrove Street again and again, those minature wheels sounding on the road like a quite distant F-16 in the clouds.

Nadi rests the tea and sugar at my bare feet, then quickly removes the empty pizza container and returns to the kitchen, which she has been putting into order all the afternoon. Upon the sofa are unpacked boxes, lamps, folded drapes and blankets. She is reserving this room for last, which is good, for I know she has enough work to keep her busy for at least the first week. Fardoh, tomorrow, I will for her purchase a new cassette player and even a new tape or two, Googoosh perhaps, that zeebah Persian woman who is a less sentimental singer than Daryoosh.

I rise and carry my tea out the front door and walk barefoot upon the grass. The blades are long, at least two centimeters, and as I walk around to the side of the house I make a note to purchase a grass cutter as well, something used, nothing extravagant. The sky has lost most of its light and my new neighbors have turned on the lamps in their homes. I was disappointed there was no sun all the weekend long, only that strange cool fog, but I am grateful for the tall hedge bushes around our little bungalow, and I like the heavy smell of pine they release into the air. Through the kitchen window I can barely see my Nadi working for she has turned on no light. Tomorrow begins my new work, that of buyer and seller. I will give it the best hours of the day, like any office position, and that is what I must do with my room, arrange it with a proper desk and chair and a telephone and perhaps a typewriter as well. But first I must become a seller; I must double my investment with a buyer very soon. And of course this must be handled more delicately than anything else. I cannot push Nadi too far too quickly, asking her to pack and move again so immediately. Perhaps I should wait a month or two for her to settle herself here, away from all the lying and play-acting of our life at the high-rise of our ruling pooldar. But will it not be more difficult, after I sell the home on the open market for a fair price, to ask her to move once again? But then I will of course be able to show her eighty or ninety thousand dollars in our hands, the opportunity to purchase another auction property to sell for profit or even begin a business of some kind right away.

I regard the slope of the roof above me, the sky growing quite dark, and I decide to telephone a najar as well, a carpenter, to give a price for the building of a widow's walk. I can then refer to this bungalow as Waterview Property, and in the meanwhile, my wife and I may sit together in the early evenings so high on the house and hill, to look out at the sea, and the sky.

THE NAJAR IS a polite young man, not quite thirty years, and he has given to me a price of eleven hundred dollars for the construction of a widow's walk. We will not be able to enter this from inside the home but must walk outdoors to new stairs in front of the kitchen window in order to reach the roof. There is no other affordable way to construct it, the najar assures me, so I accept this compromise, but I will not inform Nadereh of her window.

This morning, Monday, while my son rides his skateboard down the hill of Bisgrove Street to explore the town of Corona in the sunshine, I spend time here in my new room organizing it as an office, and I have no time to waste. As soon as I rid my desk of all unnecessary papers and boxes I begin immediately to write an advertisement for the sale of this house. I study the language used in other realty advertisements of the town's newspaper, and I use the same for my own, yet I do not feel I am qualified to name a price. So many of the homes advertised sound no larger or more well-maintained than this bungalow, and they are in "quiet residential areas" as well, but the prices for these homes are well over one hundred seventy thousand dollars. My fingers begin to shake; I am once again in amazement at the low price I paid for the home and I imagine if I could sell for even one-fifty I would more than triple my investment. Outside my door and down the hallway, Nadi works in the living-room area. From time to time I am able to hear her voice as she speaks to herself. It is a habit she has always possessed and I am pleased to hear it for it only comes when she is deeply involved with a project or task of some kind.

Early this morning she rose from her bed with the rest of us, her son and I. She for us prepared toast and tea, and when she poured for me I thanked her and she said: "Haheshmeekonam, Behrani," which is the proper response, though I have never cared for her using my family name when addressing me. When we were younger she called me Massoud-joon or, often, Mass. But for many years now—since the revolution I am quite certain—my Nadi has called me Behrani. One evening in our large apartment in Paris, on the Right Bank of that dirty but beautiful river the Seine, Nadi had a long telephone conversation with one of her sisters in Tehran. After hanging up she began immediately crying. I gave her a few moments of solitude, then I went to comfort my wife but she pushed me away and yelled very loud in Farsi she should have never married me, a kaseef soldier! None of her family were forced to leave the country; *their* names were not upon a *death list*, just *her* because she married *me* and the filthy kaseef air force and it is all your fault, Behrani! Our country is ruined because of *you*, you and your SAVAK friends!

It was then I hit my wife very hard across the face with my open hand and she fell to the floor and lay there crying, "Man meekham bemiram." I want to die, she wept. I want to die.

Of course I would not have let her stay upon the carpet in that fashion if our son was in the home, but Esmail was playing in the streets with his young French friends, so I allowed Nadereh to lie upon her face and weep. Because she was quite wrong of my involvement with the secret police, SAVAK. I had very little to do with any of their affairs. And of course she before never complained of all our privileges; she never complained of the maids and soldiers she used for the upkeep of our home; she never complained of the skiing trips in the mountains to the north, or of our bungalow there overlooking the Caspian in Chahloose; she never complained of the fine gowns she was able to wear at the parties of generals and judges and lawyers and famous actors and singers; she never complained when on a Sunday afternoon I would order Bahman to drive our family to the finest movie house in Tehran and of course there would be a long queue of people waiting, but I was dressed in my uniform so we never waited, we never even paid; we were ushered up to the balcony reserved for the Very Important People, away from the crowd. And yes, I often saw fear behind the smiles of these theater managers as they bowed and led us personally to our seats, and yes, no one waiting upon the sidewalk outdoors dared make a complaint I may hear; but there was no blood on my fingers. I purchased fighter jets. I was not with SAVAK.

But there were moments in my career I had spent time with these men. In the final years, every Thursday evening, five or six of we senior officers would meet at General Pourat's home for vodka and mastvakhiar. And how I have wished for that sort of company today. At the high-rise of pooldar Persians in Berkeley I attempted to organize some of the men together for an occasional evening, but these young doctors and engineers have spent so many of their years being educated in the west they do not even know the proper way to drink with each other like men; they do not know that the oldest and most experienced in the room is the saghi, that he, and only he, holds the vodka bottle and he will fill, or not fill, those cups around him. Each Thursday evening at Pourat's, he, of course, was the saghi. In his large home a soldier would escort us to the den where we gentlemen would remove our shoes at the doorway, and we would sit in a circle on the dark red carpet from Tabriz. In winter, there was a fire burning in the tall stone fireplace behind us. Two or three musicians and a singer would stand in the far corner softly playing songs more than a thousand years old and still only a third as old as our country. Hanging on the east wall was a long woven tapestry of Hazrat Abbas and his holy companions charging down the sand hill of Karbala, racing to the thousands of enemy soldiers who would yield them to martyrdom.

And in front of each of us was placed a small earthen cup, relics from Pourat's family in Isfahan. A box of long Havana cigars lay closed, for we never smoked until our host did first, nor did we dip our two fingers into the chaser, as Americans might call it, the bowl of mastvakhiar—that wonderful sour yogurt mixed with bits of cucumber—that moment would not come until after our first drink of cold Russian vodka, which Pourat would pour as soon as he entered in a smoking jacket, silk pants, and fine Parisian socks. He was a handsome man, khosh teep, and bald with wide shoulders and a flat belly. Of course we would stand, but Pourat would wave us back to the floor and he would make a joke about one of us, something he may have heard that week at Mehrabad, and we always laughed at Pourat's jokes, not out of respect, but because he was truly an amusing man. Sometimes he would tease one of the younger or more ambitious men by passing his cup over while pouring the very first drink, something a saghi rarely did, for the main purpose of a saghi is to keep a man from drinking more than he is able. The young senior officer with the empty cup might lower his head out of shame, his face a reddened study in concentration as he attempted to remember how he may have insulted the general. But then Pourat would laugh quite loudly, as would the rest of us, and he would pour the vodka for the relieved and smiling young man, then fill all our cups.

When we toasted our health, each man, including Pourat, attempted to tap his cup beneath those of the others, which is a true sign of respect in Persia. "Man nokaretam," we say, meaning: I am your servant. And of course each man wants to honor another more than himself, if it is truly deserved, so he will not allow his cup to stay higher when they touch; he will instantly lower his cup to the bottom of the other man's as if to say, "No, I am *your* servant." But the other will sometimes insist by lowering his again and more than once

I have seen grown men lower their cups in this fashion, each after the other all the way to the floor, then stand to fistfight over who respects whom the most. But at Pourat's this would never occur. We prided ourselves on being not simply high officers, but Persian gentlemen as well.

One winter evening, General Pourat invited a seventh man to his home, his nephew. He was dark-skinned and younger than us all, with not more than thirty-three or thirty-four years. He possessed good looks, the wide jaw, small nose, and deep eyes I would see in film actors, and his physique was quite fit and powerful-looking beneath his finely tailored dark suit. Each time he raised his vodka cup to drink, his upper arm muscle would bunch into a round stone, and when one of the men commented on the young man's power, Pourat said, "Yes, Bijan outlasts them all at the zur khaneh."

One of the older gentlemen seated beside me began to speak of his boyhood in Rasht, how he would go with his father to the zur khaneh and witness all the large men there, half naked and sweating, lifting the milos over their heads while the chanter sang and played the domback drum in front of a fire and the hot stones a boy would pour water over to bring on more steam. And I did not care for the fashion in which Pourat's nephew listened to this story; he drank his vodka and dipped three fingers, not two, into the mastvakhiar, and as he licked his fingers clean he would not even look at the older man speaking of his boyhood in Rasht. The young man kept his eyes on his stocking feet in front of him as if he were hearing something for the five hundredth time, something he of course knew completely before he'd heard it the first. When the gentleman beside me finished telling the story of his father and the zur khaneh, Pourat poured each of us more vodka and when we raised our cups in a toast to our past and to our traditions, I watched to make sure the younger man, this Bijan, held his cup low out of respect, which he did, though his face appeared impassive, and it was plain for me to see that here was a boy who was not only accustomed to being admired and looked at and listened to, he expected it as well.

"What is your nephew's position, Genob General Pourat?" This was asked amiably by Mehran Hafsanjani, a small man who held a high rank and was a specialist in radar communications. The young man looked directly at Hafsanjani and he insulted Pourat, his uncle and host, by answering ahead of him: "I am with SAVAK, sir."

Pourat immediately made a joke to us all to watch our manners, you never know what secrets these policemen have, but his nephew did not smile; he sat with his back erect, his thick arms resting at the wrist upon both knees, and he absently tapped two fingers on the carpet.

"My Bijan was trained in America, in New York."

The handsome Savaki shook his head in a pretended show of modesty. I leaned forward. "And what did they teach you there, young Mr. Pourat?" I did not try to disguise the contempt in my voice, and my use of the word young, javoon, came out sounding like an insult, but I did not care; General Pourat was my oldest friend, the vodka was warm in my belly, I was a colonel. The handsome nephew looked directly at my eyes. "They taught us techniques, Genob Sarhang."

"What sort of techniques?"

The young man surprised me; he glanced at his uncle to see if he should answer. Pourat nodded slightly, the light of the fire behind him in his eyes.

"Torture, Genob Sarhang."

"They teach you this in America?" said another gentleman, a big radish of a bureaucrat named Ali.

"Among other things." The trace of a smile passed over the young man's face.

"I have heard some stories," said Ali. "We all have." He regarded General Pourat and cleared his throat. "I heard of a man in the Tudeh Party who was forced to watch his wife raped at the city prison."

Young Pourat waved his hand as if at a fly upon his nose. "That is only effective for so long. If you want real information, you must take their children. Make a subversive watch his little one lose a hand or arm and they will tell you everything." He smiled, his eyes on his vodka cup upon the floor. "But the difficult part of the work is knowing whom to arrest."

Two men laughed.

I had heard these stories as well. We all had. But I felt the vodka inside me turn cool. "Do you enjoy your work, Mr. Pourat?"

The Savaki narrowed his eyes immediately. "Enjoyment has nothing to do with it. I serve Shahanshah, sir. I can only assume you do as well."

The musicians had just completed a song and the room was quiet. A dry log crackled in the fire, then shifted in the coals. I felt the heat of my heart drop to my hands and for a brief moment I imagined my thumbs buried in the young policeman's eyes.

General Pourat clapped his hands twice. "All right, all right, enough of this talk. You two surprise me. You are colleagues, you should act as such." He turned to the musicians. "Play something festive!"

The general poured us all more vodka, and the moment passed. Soon I was mast, half drunk, with the others and we lay back upon our elbows on the carpet to smoke cigars and listen to the music. Occasionally I would look over at the young torturer and see him gazing into the fire, his eyes empty, and I wished he would leave our group early and not come back, for I did not like to be reminded of the secret police and all the people they made disappear in our land, these students and professionals, wives, mothers, husbands, fathers, children, illiterate cargars living in small homes of mud and wood scraps less than a kilometer from the grand palace with all of its fine ornaments imported from around the world; I did not like to think once again that America, with whom I did close business in the purchase of fighter jets, had such a hand in all this; I did not like to think this was the manner in which our king retained his throne and our way of life; but, most of all, I did not want to accept that General Pourat was correct when he said the young policemen and I were colleagues, so, once more, I drank more vodka than I should have, and the rest of the evening I did not dip my two fingers into the same bowl of mastvakhiar as the young torturer Bijan.

"Behrani?"

My wife stands in the doorway. Since moving, she has dressed each morning in lady's cotton trousers and a loose pullover shirt in which she can work. Over the last few months she has lost too much weight. She wears a gold costume jewelry belt to hold her pants up and her hips look as slim as a boy's. But she has applied cosmetics to her lips and eyes, and her thick hair is pulled up and back with a scarf.

"Yes, Nadi-jahn?"

"When must we move again?"

I take a breath. "Not too soon. Perhaps once we get a buyer we will tell them to wait until fall. Would you prefer that?"

She looks by me to the window, at the sun on our long grass, the road, the woodland beyond, her eyes becoming moist. "I will do as you wish, Massoud."

I stand and hold my wife, and for a brief moment she allows this. I feel the softness of her chest against me. I smell her clean hair, the familiar scent of lavender and tea. But she steps away and walks quickly down the corridor to her work.

Nadi has always had more pride than a queen, and I am certain what just happened between us was an apology. But as I sit at my desk, I feel that caged heaviness in my belly that comes with a failure of courage, for it is I who should apologize; it is I who have helped to fly us so far off course.

．．．．．．．．．．．．．．．
　．．．．．．．．．．．．．
　　　．．．．．．
　　　　．．

I WAS ON CORONA BEACH, STILL WEARING THE SHORTS I'D WORKED IN, leaning back on an El Rancho Motel towel. The sky was clear and blue, no sign of the fog that can float in whenever it feels like it. The tide was low, and green waves curled in long and lazy, spreading out on the wet sand where four kids squatted building a hill for a red plastic truck.

My Monday job was a two-story duplex on the Colma River. The owner was a quiet CPA who had custody of his twelve-year-old daughter on the weekends. He had a beard and thick glasses and once he left me a typed note asking me out and I wrote in pencil on the bottom that I couldn't, I was married, which was true, though Nick had already been gone for months. The CPA wrote an apology in a second note, and I'd felt like a liar and a chickenshit, and he never wrote any more notes, just left the check under a rainbow magnet on the fridge. After cleaning his small house, I drove straight to the motel and called Connie Walsh. It took her almost ten minutes to get to the phone and when she did she told me she was running late for court, she still hadn't heard from the county, then she asked me to drop off my copy of the notarized tax statement. I told her I couldn't find it. She said that wasn't good news but keep your chin up; it'll probably be in the records they're sending. "And Kathy, I recommend you try and stay with friends. County bureaucrats are notorious for dragging their briefcases. This could take a few weeks to iron out."

"A few *weeks?*"

"Yes, that's right."

I was about to tell my lawyer that's too long, I can't afford it, but she hung up, and soon after the front desk lady buzzed my room and asked if I was checking out or staying another day. I didn't know where else to go, but told her I was checking out. I packed my suitcase, then carried my TV across the street and locked it back in the storage shed. A trucker was backing his rig into the yard to turn around and as I crossed the street again he honked once, then stuck his head out the window, smiled hard, and said something to me I couldn't hear over his engine. I should've given him the finger, but instead I went back into my room and packed two of the motel's towels to take with me, revenge, I guess, for the broken TV, though I never told them it was broken.

Behind me an engine with no muffler started up and I turned to see an old Malibu pull out of the beach lot, a First Things First bumper sticker above its rusted tailpipe. Nick hated those twelve-step, Higher Power slogans, especially when they were on cars he'd see on his way to work or just running errands. "Big Brother ruling you from somebody's fucking tailpipe," he'd say.

"They're not rules, they're reminders."

"They're fucking reminders to obey the rules, Kath."

But I didn't feel that way. Every time I saw one—usually on a back bumper—I felt like when you're in a crowded city street and you see a face you knew once and even if you don't talk to that person you feel suddenly more tied to your past and present. When I was using I never liked seeing them. But after the program, whenever I saw one I felt a kind of sad attraction for whatever it had to say: Live and Let Live, Let Go and Let God, One Day at a Time, Take It Easy, Keep it Simple. Nick's the one who got me to stop going to meetings. In the program they let you try both ways: AA, that says we're powerless over our addiction and have to give it up to something higher, and RR, which is based on *The Small Book*, which has only been around a few years and says we're *not* powerless, and thinking this just makes it easier to fail; all you have to do is recognize the Beast in you, the addict, the Enemy Voice that wants to use, accuse it of malice against you, remind yourself what a worthwhile person you are and that you treasure your sobriety, and then it's not so hard to use all this against the Beast and not let it get what it wants. And they spelled B.E.A.S.T. in capital letters:

> B=Boozing opportunity
> E=Enemy Voice recognition
> A=Accuse the voice of malice
> S=Self-control reminders
> T=Treasure your sobriety

This all left me cold, like a foreign language I'd never be able to learn. It's where Nick went though, so I went too. But I missed the few AA meetings I'd been to, everyone sitting in a cloud of their own smoke, telling their stories and backing each other up, nobody any wiser or more together than anyone else.

Nick loved the part about Enemy Voice recognition. On that five-day drive west in our new car, hauling a tiny U-haul trailer, he drank thermos after thermos of coffee and he'd go on and on about how there's a part of all of us that wants to kill ourselves, K, even when things are going well, especially when things are going well. And the only way to beat it is with reason and ratonality. Like a mother or father with a young kid. And he'd smile and slap the steering wheel with both hands, looking over at me, his cheeks and chin bluish with whiskers. He was so sure about it I wanted to believe it, too. But there was always that nagging pull inside me. I'd look back out at the rushing white lines of the highway, or else put the passenger seat back and close my eyes; it wasn't a problem for me to hear an enemy voice in my head and accuse it of malice; it was the next part, drawing on all this self-love everybody's supposed to have deep down, then telling yourself that life without getting high is better. That's what I could never do. And after the program, as I sat next to Nick at our weekly Rational Recovery groups in Cambridge, no one talked about being powerless and living life one day at a time, which was really more how I felt. Instead, we were powerful and rational— powerful *because* we were rational—and we talked about living life one *life* at a time. A lot of RR people had even given up smoking that way, so there was hardly an ashtray in the room, though there was coffee and we all seemed to drink a lot of it.

I always left these meetings feeling like a fake. Nick didn't though; we'd walk down the sidewalk across from the high brick walls of Harvard and he'd grab my hand and then kiss my neck, pulling me along, telling me there was a little voice in his pants he could only accuse of love. Sometimes we'd walk down to Harvard Square to eat or see a movie. I always wanted to do both, eat something heavy and delicious like lasagna or prime rib, then go to the small theater past the newsstand and all the teenagers in loose pants to snuggle down into the red seats in the dark with a large Coke and about ten chocolate peanut butter cups, just let the flickering light of the story shut up my rational, reasonable voice for a couple of hours. But then the lights would always come up and I'd blink to see Nick sitting beside me in a funk. Very few of the movie characters had control of any of their impulses and problems, and Nick said it was too depressing and exhausting for him to watch. So we stopped going to movies on RR nights. Soon we left the East Coast.

So many nights after Nick left I'd just get into the Bonneville and drive. I'd drive up the coast and down the coast and I was always looking for that gray Honda. Most of the time I knew he was far away, though sometimes I pictured him living in a neighborhood less than ten miles from Bisgrove Street, playing bass in a band maybe, living alone or with a twenty-year-old girl who had no intention of saddling him with kids, saddling him with anything. I'd still feel a little sick whenever I thought of him with somebody else, but I was sure if he was with anybody, she had to be young enough he could mold her into what he wanted. He was such a chickenshit. And I didn't even know this until he'd been gone almost two months. I got the insight while I watched a rented movie. That's what I did almost every night, right up until Deputy Lester Burdon showed up to evict me. I'd rent two or three movies and watch them back to back. Sometimes I'd even start in the late afternoon. Including weekends I averaged close to twenty a week. I knew how addictive this might look to anyone back in the program, or in RR, but I wasn't putting anything into my body, not even cigarettes then, so I rationalized there was no real Enemy Voice to accuse of malice, was there?

It was a porno I grabbed from the adult section and slipped in with two PG-13s. I read once that over ninety-five percent of men masturbate while only forty-six percent of women do, and I'd always thought I was somewhere on the borderline; I did it once every few months, not enough to ever miss. But when I put in the videocassette and heard the electric moan of the recorder pulling the tape along I was already wet and there was still daylight outside, so I went around and pulled all the shades, turned off the light in the kitchen, then sat on the floor as the credits came up yellow with names like Fiona Lace and John Rod and before they were over a young blond girl was on her knees sucking off a tanned Italian in a shirt, tie, and suspenders. I had seen skin flicks before, but not many, usually at parties where I was too loaded to see, so I was a little surprised when they started to fuck and I didn't feel like unzipping my jeans. Instead I sat back against the couch with my ankles and arms crossed and watched as the man directed the blonde to do this and to do that, to bend over his desk so he could spread her cheeks and enter her from behind.

Then I pictured my husband jerking off to this and I felt my stomach and insides get pulled down a second, and I jabbed the eject button and flung the tape behind me without looking.

I went outside to my backyard. It was March then, and chilly. The ground was hard and I stared at it. Nicky was a good lover. He didn't fuck like those men. He didn't direct me like a rag doll to probe. It had always seemed mutual to me. But what was so clear to me for the first time was this: when all was said and done, Nick Lazaro had to have total control.

It was close to noon and the sun was getting too hot on my legs and face. I stood and brushed the sand off, and after a fast-food lunch of a fish sandwich and Diet Coke, I drove back to the storage lot to look for that signed tax statement again. But there were no air vents in the shed, and even with the doors swung wide open, it was so hot in there my tank top and shorts were stuck to my skin in just a few minutes and my throat needed another cold drink. I padlocked the door, put the air conditioner on in the car, and just started driving. I was kicking myself for not taking a shower before checking out of the El Rancho. I turned into a gas station, filled the tank on my gas card, and gave myself a cat bath from the sink in the ladies' room. Then I changed into a clean cotton pullover, bought more cigarettes, and drove twelve miles south on 101 to the mall Cineplex. There were ten movie theaters there and I was planning to sit the afternoon away in at least three of them.

I DO NOT KNOW IF IT WAS THE GLASS OF CHAMPAGNE MY NADI DRANK, or if it was because Esmail had fallen asleep early before his television in his room, or if it was simply the joyful news of the real estate appraiser who I hired to come here yesterday, the news I thank God for and cannot yet believe, that this bungalow is worth four times what

I paid for it and the appraiser sees no difficulty in our finding a buyer for it, especially with the new widow's walk that will overlook the sea. Perhaps it was that, or the new cassette player I purchased for her at Japantown in San Francisco late yesterday afternoon, I do not know. Man nehmee doonam. All I can be certain of is yesterday God kissed our eyes, and last evening my wife invited me to her room for only the third time in the years we have lived in America.

We lay together in the darkness listening to a new cassette of a singer reciting the rubaiyats of Fayez Dashtestani. Behind this a man softly played the ney, a shepherd's flute, and soon she pulled me to her and it was almost too much; I felt I was a young man again, lying with my new bride. Nadi held my back so tightly and I saw again my father on our wedding day carrying the fat sheep to the doorway of our new home. It was summer and very hot and because of the west wind there was dust upon our fine clothes. My father wore a suit of black, and his forehead and cheeks were shining with sweat as he carried the sheep under his left arm, the long knife in his right hand, and he knelt and held the sheep at the open doorway, the sheep beginning to bleat, struggling and kicking beneath my father's weight, Nadi squeezing my hand in both of hers as my father pushed the blade deep into the sheep's throat, pulling it free, letting the blood fall onto the threshold of our new home, Nadi's father squatting and rubbing the blood into the wood with his fingers, behind us the women and men clapping and a hot wind blowing over us all, Nadi's breath upon my neck, the crowd pushing us into the dark house past the dying sheep, its rear legs twitching and jerking in the dust.

The shepherd's flute continued. My wife moved to rest my face upon her shoulder and she rubbed her fingers gently on the skin of my head as if I were her own child.

Soon the music ended and she was asleep, but I could not sleep. I went to Esmail's room and turned off the television, then I covered him with his sheet. Even curled there, his body took up nearly all the bed. He is growing so quickly, faster than did his sister Soraya, that standing before him in my robe, I felt proud and frightened all at the same moment.

And now I wake upon the living-room sofa just before the sun and

I feel a sadness that I did not stay in bed with Nadereh, for I do not know if last evening will come again anytime soon. And I remember Soraya when she was a girl. Her legs were long and thin and brown, and her mother forever had her wearing a pretty dress of some kind. One evening upon my return home, when she had no more than seven or eight years, I remember my daughter stepping out onto the rear veranda to greet me. I heard her laughing and I looked up from the auto and saw her standing at attention in her yellow dress, her tiny knees barely touching one another, wearing the visored hat from my old sarvan's uniform. The captain's hat was of course so large it fell forward and covered her eyes and I remember that lovely gap between her two front teeth as she laughed and saluted, even though she could not see me or anything else.

She is now a man's wife. At this thought I rise from the couch, dress, and take my tea outside to the rear lawn. The tall grass is slightly wet and it begins to itch my bare feet as I walk around the bungalow with my hot cup. It is still quite early. Stars are visible in the sky. Today the young najar begins construction of the widow's walk, and I do not know if it was perhaps a mistake to begin advertising the sale of the home before the job is complete. I lower my eyes to the dark woodland across the road and I stop still, for parked there beside the trees is the appraiser's red automobile. I feel a sudden lightness in my chest and a heaviness in my legs; I am certain he has driven here to inform me it is all a mistake, this bungalow is not worth anything. But as I step over the hard cool road I am embarrassed at my fear, at my doubt; the car is quite new-looking and not the appraiser's at all, and of course he would not drive out for business at so very early in the morning. Pourat many times told to me I was not a man of faith and of course I was forced to agree with him. It is why I am forever expecting disaster around the corner from God's smile.

There is a slight movement within the automobile. I approach and peer through the window glass to see a young woman sleeping upon her back in the front seat. She is dressed in short pants and a shirt without sleeves. Her arm rests over her eyes. I look in the rear window, but she is alone. Once again I shake my head at how these American women live. I look once more at her naked legs and feet, then I return to my yard with my tea.

. . . .
. . . .
. .

THE SKY IS DARK AND NICKY IS ON A BROWN HORSE STANDING IN A stream. I'm there too, knee-deep in water. He sits in the saddle, looking down at me the way he did the morning he left, like it's too late to do anything and he's made up his mind to leave right away before he gets too sad about it all and won't be able to move. Except his horse won't move. It keeps looking at me with its big eyes. Every time Nick jerks on the reins the horse opens its mouth and lets out a high-pitched whir. And when Nick kicks its ribs with his heels it sounds like a rock hitting a hollow tree. I put my hand on the horse's damp neck and look up at Nick, then everything changes and he and I are sitting on a couch somewhere, both smoking, me pleading about wanting a baby, Nick sitting so still and quiet, looking straight ahead like I've just asked him to drink cyanide. I can hear the horse outside, the whirring and knocking. But who's the rider?

Who is the rider?

I opened my eyes and sat up in the front seat of the Bonneville. I could taste last night's cigarettes and I turned the ignition key halfway to light up the digital clock. It wasn't quite eight in the morning but already the sun was coming warm through the windshield and on the maroon upholstery and me. The woods were thick and shaded as always, and deep inside were spots of sunlight. Then I heard the sound that had been in my sleep, and I turned and looked across the street at the house. Two carpenters were up on the roof above my kitchen.

They were both shirtless and one of them was ripping away shingles with the claw of his hammer while the other was using his power saw to cut through my roof, my *father's* roof, *Frankie's* roof. Their pickup truck was parked in front of the house close to the driveway where last night I saw a new white Buick in the shine of my head-lights as I drove up the hill, but now it was gone, and I should've lis-tened to Lester Burdon and stayed away from here. But it was the only place I could think to go so late at night after driving around for over an hour, talking myself out of checking into another motel somewhere. Now the two carpenters stood together and used crow-bars to pry a huge square of my roof off. They let it fall to the ground, then they stood on the floor of my attic between the rafters. The one with the saw started cutting right into one of them and I scooted be-hind the wheel and jerked open the door and ran across the street barefoot. I yelled up at them, but they couldn't hear me over the saw, so I stepped around my roof and climbed up the ladder. They were both tan and one of them had a tattoo of a diner on his shoulder. The other one stopped cutting and looked from me to the one with the tattoo, then back at me again.

"What are you *doing?*"

The one with the tattoo dropped his hammer into his tool belt. "Excuse me?"

"Who said you could *do* this? This is *my* fucking house!"

He peered over the roof down at his truck and my car. "And you are?"

"I *own* this house. *Me*. Get off my *roof*."

"Are you Mrs. Behrani?"

"No."

The other carpenter reached into his apron, shook a cigarette from its pack, and lit it. I could feel him looking at my bare arms and legs, and at my hair all ratty from sleep. It was cold last night and now my head felt stopped up and I felt so out of place and wrong.

"Mr. Behrani hired me. You'll have to talk to him."

I looked from the tattooed carpenter to the one smoking his cig-arette. He glanced away from me and took in the view and I turned and saw the rooftops of Corona below, then the green-gray ocean stretching out from the beach to the horizon. Somehow this made me madder and I climbed back down the ladder and began stepping over the shingles and one of the carpenters yelled to watch out for nails just as I stepped on the upside-down plywood where dozens of nail points were sticking out and now four or five of them were sinking into the heel and ball of my foot. I screamed, jerking my knee up, the blood dripping. "*Shit.*" I hopped and sat down, then twisted my foot up, but there was so much blood I couldn't see where the holes were. "*Fuck.*"

"Here." The tattooed carpenter squatted in front of me and tied a bandanna tight around my ankle. He helped me stand and guided me to the front steps, *my* front steps, and he knocked on the screen door. I had my hand on his bare shoulder, my elbow against his back. His skin was warm and damp and I could feel the muscle under it. I was thinking how I hadn't brushed my teeth or washed my face, that I'd slept in my car last night and now was bleeding on my own doorstep waiting for a stranger to answer.

A black-haired boy came to the door. He was maybe fifteen and he wore bright orange surfer shorts and a loose T-shirt. He glanced down at my foot I wasn't letting touch the ground. A woman came up behind him. She had short thick hair and dark eyes with hardly any makeup. She was wearing a designer sweat suit, and there was a big ring on her left hand. I wanted to say that she was in my goddamn house, that she had no fucking right to remodel it, but the carpenter spoke up first and asked her if we could use the bathroom to wash my foot, and if she had something we could use to keep the blood from getting on her rug. And it was *her* rug. I could see it on the wall-to-wall carpeting behind her, a huge deep red and brown Persian rug. The woman told the boy something in what sounded Arabic or Israeli, and the boy went to the kitchen and came back with a plastic trash bag he handed to the carpenter, who bent down and pulled it loosely over my foot. I felt like throwing up, my stomach contracting. The woman was looking at my hair and face, my wrinkled shirt, and her eyes seemed so full of caring I took a weak breath and didn't say anything as she stepped back and let the carpenter and me inside.

I had one arm on the carpenter's shoulder, the other holding the plastic trash bag onto my foot. We passed a silver coffee table with bowls of nuts and wrapped chocolates set on top of it. There was a plush sofa and expensive-looking lamps. The carpenter stopped at the kitchen and asked the woman where the bathroom was, but before she could talk I told him to go all the way down the hall. I leaned on his shoulder and hopped through a house that didn't seem like mine anymore; the door to my bedroom was open and I caught a glimpse of a queen-size bed with brass posts. On the floor near the windows were huge potted green plants, and on the carpet around the bed were small rugs, deep purple, green, and black.

In the bathroom I sat on the edge of the tub and let cold water run over the sole of my foot as I watched the blood swirl down the drain. The carpenter stood beside me with his hands on his hips. He still had his tool belt on and his hammer handle was swaying against his leg.

"When's the last time you had a tetanus shot?"

"Ees she yet bleeding?"

The woman reached by me, her arm brushing my face, and I smelled lavender and cotton. She knelt on the floor, adjusted the water temperature, then took a bar of soap and washed my foot under hot water. She called to her son in their language, then she sat on the edge of the tub, gently took my foot and swung it to rest in a towel in her lap. It was a white towel, thick and soft, like only five-star hotels use, and I started to pull my bleeding foot from it.

"Ees it to hurting so much?" She looked into my eyes with hers that were so dark, the lines in her face delicate-looking, like she hadn't had them long.

"I don't want to ruin your towel."

She smiled but I don't think she understood what I said. Her son came to the room with a box of cotton balls and a roll of Ace bandage. He said something to her—Arabic, I decided—then he said to me with no accent at all, "I use it for skateboarding. Don't worry, I washed it."

"Sorry, but I have to know what the story is before I continue the job." The carpenter stood in the doorway and watched while the woman swabbed the bottom of my foot with a clear liquid that smelled like ginger. My face got hot, and I held my finger up to him to wait a second, though I didn't know what I was going to say next. The woman pressed a cotton ball to each puncture in my foot and she started to wrap it tight with the Ace bandage. Every turn or so she would glance up at my face to see how I was. Her son left the bathroom and I heard a TV go on in what used to be the room Nicky practiced his bass in. I looked up at the carpenter and said quietly: "I'll talk to her husband."

"Fine. Sorry about your foot."

I watched him walk down my hallway with his tool belt and shorts and no shirt. I felt abandoned.

The woman pulled the last bit of tape up around my ankle, kept it there with her thumb, then held it down with a safety pin. She smiled at me and we both looked at each other a second, which made me pull my leg from her lap and stand up, but I couldn't put weight on my foot without a burning ache shooting up my shin. She helped me out of the bathroom and I half-leaned on her all the way to the living room, where she guided me to the sofa behind the silver coffee table. I was about to say no but she moved a pillow, slid the bowl of sweets off to the side of the table, then rested the folded towel there for my foot; all I could do was sink into the softness of the couch.

"I carry you tea and sugar. You must for rest."

I watched her walk into my kitchen and reach into a cabinet for a clear glass cup. On the wall across from me were paintings of mountains on a waterfront, of bearded men in robes on horses. On the lamp table beside me was a family portrait of the woman smiling next to a bald man in a military uniform. Sitting in front of them was the same boy who'd answered the door, only he was younger, his face more smooth and round, and beside him was a beautiful young woman with long black hair that went past her shoulders and hung over her white blouse. She had her mother's eyes and the gentle smile too.

"That is of course our family pictures." The woman rested a black breakfast tray on my lap. The tea steamed up into my face as I sipped it, and she went into the kitchen and came back with a small bowl of red grapes.

"Thank you," I said. She smiled at the other end of the couch and put a cube of sugar in her mouth before she sipped her tea, placing the cup in a saucer on her lap. She was looking at my bare legs, the high hem of my cotton shorts, her face taking them in like my mother would. My cheeks flushed. I could hear the muffled noise of the carpenters cutting through wood above us, then hammering something, then cutting some more. The woman was sucking softly on the sugar in her mouth. The grapes were cold and sweet, but I wished I'd never driven up here last night and I put the tray on the table, sat up, and stood on my good foot.

"No, you must for rest your foots. Your friend must to the hospital bring you."

I made my way around the table and hopped to the door. Draped over the edge of the silver table was the folded white towel, my blood drying all over it. "Thanks for your help, but he's not my friend. I don't even know his name."

CONNIE WALSH WAS in a meeting when I limped up the stairs above the Café Amaro and told Gary I wanted to see her and I'm not leaving till I do. He looked down at my bandaged foot and asked what happened, but I sat without answering because I felt like killing somebody right then, *anybody*, but not him, especially when he dragged a chair over for me to rest my foot up on while I waited.

Connie Walsh's morning clients were two women a little older than me and better dressed. They walked out of the conference room laughing, but when they saw me sitting there with my foot up on a chair that almost blocked their way, their laughter dropped down to smiles as they squeezed by and disappeared down the stairs.

My lawyer stood in the doorway. "What happened to *you?*"

"They're tearing my fucking house apart."

"*What?*"

I hopped by her into the meeting room that smelled like clove cigarettes. All the tall windows were open and the room was full of sunlight. I leaned against the table and crossed my arms over my chest to keep my hands from shaking. "They're *remodeling* it. What are you going to *do* about that?"

"Have a seat, Kathy."

"I don't want to sit down. I want to fucking kill somebody. How come they don't even know they're squatting in somebody else's home? I'm tired of this shit." I lit a cigarette.

Connie sat down and called out to Gary to please bring us two cups of coffee. She looked up at me with a patient look on her face. "The courier just brought over the paperwork from the county this morning. I was planning to review it and call you this afternoon."

"I don't want you to call *me*, I want you to call those *Arabs* who are cutting up *my house*." My voice broke, but I wasn't going to let whatever was under it break through. Gary came in and left the coffee. My foot felt swollen so I pulled out a chair, sat down, and rested my leg on another.

"What *happened?*"

"My yard is a construction site."

"You were there, Kathy?"

"That's right." I emptied a whole packet of Sweet'n Low into my coffee, stirring it while Connie launched into a soft-voiced lecture on why it's a good idea to stay off the property so she can do her work unencumbered.

"It's very important we're both clear on this," she said. "Agreed?"

I looked at her, at the premature gray in her hair, at the serious look in her face, and I was still so mad at how far all this was actually going my throat felt closed up, but I said yes, then drank from my coffee. Connie excused herself to go get the paperwork. Outside, on the flat roof of the Roxie Theater across the street, two pigeons were perched on a brick chimney stack in the sunlight. They stood together looking out over the street below, their beaks jerking front and back, right and left, as they took in the scene.

My foot hurt. I smoked another cigarette and thought how at least today was my off day with the cleaning and if I was lucky I might be able to put enough weight down tomorrow to work. But on the drive over my right sole ached so much I had to sit almost kitty-cornered and use my left foot on the gas and brake pedals, making me sit as low in the seat as an old lady. I started to stand to go find my lawyer, but then she walked back into the room smiling, carrying a manila folder in front of her.

"I was right. They sent your signed statement with everything else. Here."

I took it from her. It was the original statement both Nicky and I signed in front of the notary. I looked at his signature, each letter of his name written so neatly while mine was a hurried scribble. I used to think he did that so people wouldn't have to decipher it, so he wouldn't make things hard for anyone, so he wouldn't leave behind a mess. I used to think that.

Connie Walsh said a few things and I looked up and nodded at her like I'd heard.

"And it's obvious they decided to put it to rest with that statement, so I'll fax them a letter today and we'll follow it up with a phone call before offices close. If they don't offer to rescind the sale immediately, we'll sue the county for a bundle. Are you still at the motel?"

I shook my head no. "I want you to call those people in my house, too. They're already more at home there than I ever was. That's not right."

My lawyer tapped her pencil in the palm of her hand. "Did you get their names?"

"I don't know, Bahroony or Behmini, something like that. They're Middle Eastern. Please call them up and tell them to put the roof back together and get out."

She left the room and I heard her tell Gary to draft a letter for the courier service. The pigeons flew off, and I told myself I should feel good the county had sent the sworn statement that would get me back into my and Frankie's house, but there were four holes of heat in my foot, a stiffness in my neck from sleeping in the car, a tightness in my throat, and for a second I saw myself emptying most of the storage shed into the Bonneville and driving straight back East, just pull into my mother's driveway and tell her everything, that I had no friends, I was smoking again, I just scrape by cleaning up after other people, all I do is watch movies I don't remember, my husband left me, and I lost the house, Ma; it's gone.

"Where are you staying, Kathy?" Connie walked in reading some paperwork. She had on her round glasses.

"Nowhere."

"You're not with friends?" She was giving me eyes that were sincere but holding back too, and I pegged her right away for the kind of person who couldn't live with herself for not doing the right thing, but also the kind who could never say no, so they really wanted you to lie to them so they wouldn't have to *do* the right thing like invite me to stay a week with her.

"Yeah, I'm with a friend."

"You are?"

They always did that too, pushed your lie till it almost broke. "I want to be back in my house by this weekend, Connie, all right?"

"I can't promise you anything, but we'll do our best." She smiled and stood and showed me to the door. As I hopped to the stairs, she said not to worry and she hoped my ankle would feel better soon.

It's almost easier being down and alone than when you're up and no one's there to share the view with you. Not that I was feeling that great as I drove south on Skyline Boulevard through Daly City in the sunshine. Addicts are supposed to be famous for expecting disaster around every corner from good luck, but now I did have my hopes up a little Connie Walsh might have this mess straightened out by the weekend. I needed some distraction.

I rested my right foot on the hump in the middle of the floor beneath the console. The ache wasn't as sharp, but now there was a warm throbbing that came with my heartbeats which were faster than normal because I was smoking practically one cigarette after another. I was also thinking of Lester Burdon again, his sad eyes and crooked mustache, his little station wagon driving off into the fog. I knew I'd been thinking of him off and on since then; I kept seeing that dark need in his face as he sat across from me at Carl Jr.'s. Men who have that look usually want to bite into you like you're a fresh cool plum; and after they've bitten, sucked, and chewed they expect your juices to come back and stay sweet. But Lester's need seemed different than that. There was a gentleness there too, a patience. So maybe it wasn't really a need at all, but a wanting. Maybe he wanted.

In Daly City, I pulled into a gas station and hopped to the rest room with my makeup bag and toothbrush, a clean T-shirt and pair of underwear. I cleaned myself up, climbed back into my Bonneville with my wrapped foot, then dug through my pocketbook for Lester Burdon's card. It had slipped into my checkbook between two blank checks: Lester was something called a field training officer and his office was at the San Mateo County Sheriff's Department in Redwood City. I put the car in gear, used my left foot for the gas, and drove onto the Bayshore Freeway, heading south.

THE SUN IS WARM UPON MY ARMS AS I PUSH THE BRIGHT RED LAWN cutter that started with one pull of its rope and I smell benzine and that American scent of green grass that is cut in the heat. The engine is loud but still I hear the work of the najars upon the bungalow. The afternoon remains in their first workday, but already they have completed building the frame of the widow's walk into the roof and I push the cutter from one end of the property to the next and I see them lay new boards of lumber across the structure and drive nails with their steel hammers in the sun.

The tall grass falls away beneath my machine like dead soldiers, and I am grateful for the silly blue hat upon my head, for it keeps the skin there in the shade, and even my forehead and eyes are protected. But I am grateful for so much more than this; after a lunch of chicken, tadiq, and radishes, I gave to Esmail permission to ride his skateboard down to the BART train to go visit his friends until early evening. The young najars had left in their truck to purchase building materials, and I sat at the kitchen counter reviewing the real estate pages of the newspaper when my Nadi paused in her cleaning and kissed me on my cheek. She stood close to me, holding the folded sofreh to her breasts. "Why did you not stay with me last night, Massoud?"

My wife has fifty years, but she spoke as would a young girl, a new bride. I thought perhaps she was disappointed in me, but then I regarded her smile, the fashion in which she held her chin low, looking up at me with those gavehee eyes, and as she took my hand and led me back down the corridor to her room, my heart was a flat stone moving over water and my breath was held like the boy counting the skips of his good fortune.

Afterward, as the najars resumed their work above us, Nadi put the blue colah upon my head and laughed as I stepped out into the midday sun. I laughed as well, for except for an occasional television show she barely understands, Nadi has not laughed. Not in the pooldar apartments, she has not. But here is different; here she seems to be living as if she is no longer waiting for life. Here she is free of our own masquerade, our own lies.

I continue to cut down the tall grass with ease, making straight and orderly lines of the dead green, and I make the decision, yes, we must stay here for the summer season; it will be good for us, a good rest. I will continue to work daily for securing a buyer, but I will enter into the contract that the property will not be available until autumn. This will also give me the necessary time for finding new properties to purchase, for it is clear I must buy only bungalows such as this, homes that are auctioned by county or bank. Perhaps I will discover a pleasant home or apartment we can rent while I continue to buy and sell for a profit.

These have been my thoughts, and they have been most pleasing thoughts for I feel once again like a man with his hands on the reins of his own beast. The najar tells me the platform overlooking Corona and the sea will be ready in two more days' time. Soraya and her new husband end their honeymoon trip on Friday and so we must invite them and the groom's family to our home for a small celebration. I will instruct Nadi to prepare her best chelo kebab, both barg and the tender meat of the kubehdeh. I will purchase champagne and arrange chairs on the widow's walk, and we will all toast the health of the bride and groom, to our own health, salomahti.

At the street, I extinguish the engine, leaving the rows of cut grass for Esmail to rake into a bag upon his return. I wipe the sweat from my face. I am unable to cut the grass at the side of the house due to the najar's ladders, tools, and the new lumber they have stacked neatly upon the ground beside the small section of old roof. As I push the cutter past all of this, a najar calls down to me.

I raise my face to the two young men, but the sky is bright and even with the new colah upon my head I must further shade my eyes with my hand.

"Yes sirs, you are doing a superior job."

"Thank you," replies the one with the tattoo of a restaurant upon his shoulder. "Did you get everything settled with that woman?"

"Excuse me. To what woman are you referring?"

"The lady who cut her foot. She didn't talk to you?"

"If you please, come down here so my neck does not freeze this way."

The najar descends the ladder with his leather apron of tools hanging over his short pants. He is not wearing a shirt and I see his back is almost the color of a Bombay Indian. When he reaches the ground he turns to me and wipes the sweat from his forehead.

"I just wanted to make sure she talked to you. She said she would."

"Oh yes, my wife told to me your girlfriend cut her foot. I am sorry to hear this."

"Girlfriend? I never saw her before. She came up to the roof this morning all upset because we were doing this job. She said *she's* the owner."

My hands become heavy and my voice trembles. "What are you talking, young man? *I* am the owner of this home. I have for it paid cash. Who is this woman?"

"She looked nutty to me," the other najar says from the roof, smoking a cigarette. "She's swimming with one fin. She's probably down the street telling somebody she owns their house, too."

The najar beside me laughs and I smile, but I do not quite believe in this smile and stop. "In my country crazy people are put in hospitals, but here you let them wander as free as sheep."

"This is true," the young najar says, picking up from the ground a paper bag of nails, then climbing back up the ladder to his work. The other one extinguishes his cigarette beneath his foot upon the new boards.

"Please tell to me if the woman returns, thank you very much." I continue pushing my grass cutter to the rear lawn that is completely in the shadow of the house. There is only a thin line of sun upon the ground at the base of the tall hedge trees and it is there I stop to pull the cutter's rope two times before the engine starts. I give it as much benzine as it can drink, and I feel thankful for all the noise it makes.

FOR ALMOST THIRTY MINUTES I SAT IN THE CAR PARKED ACROSS THE street from the Hall of Justice building in Redwood City. It was eight or nine stories high, and the concrete sidewalk was so white under the sun I had to lower the visor and put on Nick's old Ray-Bans that were too big for my face. Across the street from the Hall of Justice was an old courthouse building with a huge dome of stained glass, and there were no trees on either side of the main street, just parking meters and shining cars. Every few minutes I got the urge to open the door to go find Lester for a possible lunch date, but then I'd think of that ring on his finger, that sadness in his eyes, and I'd smoke a cigarette, tap my own wedding ring on the wheel, and wonder just what it was I thought I was doing.

I watched a couple of uniformed deputies walk into the Hall of Justice. One was big like my brother Frank. I thought again how much I'd like to see him, just him and me sitting at a restaurant table in the North End of Boston for lunch somewhere like we used to.

He'd be dressed in one of his polo shirts, turquoise or mango orange, and whether I was talking to him about money I owed or somebody I was seeing, he always gave me the same advice which pissed me off, but sometimes made me feel better too.

"It's easy, K. On one side of the page you got your Costs and on the other side your Benefits. All you do is mark which one is which, then you weigh one side against the other and you get your decision just like that. That's all you ever have to do. I live by this."

Sometimes it was comforting to be around someone who looked at life like this. And I would've told my brother months ago about Nick if I'd known he wouldn't tell his wife who I knew would tell my mother. "But what if you don't know the difference between a benefit and a cost?" I would always ask him. "What if you've never been very good at telling a plus from a minus?"

It was lunchtime and small groups of men and women were leaving the building for food. I kept smoking and watched three women in business skirts and blouses sit at a concrete bench not far from my car. They were eating from small plastic yogurt containers. One of them laughed, finished her yogurt, and bit into a cookie. I knew I didn't want the office life they were living—I knew that—but from where I sat watching them eat and chat in the sunshine, I felt like I'd been apart from groups of normal people and their nice conversations my whole life. On another day I might've let myself feel homeless and husbandless and with no friends, but now I felt almost better than them, tougher, like I knew more about life from having really lived it out here on the rim.

I inhaled the last of my cigarette to the filter and stubbed it out in the ashtray. I was getting ready to leave, forcing myself to think about finding a safe place to park my car for tonight's sleep, when someone tapped on the window glass at my head and I jerked back. Lester Burdon was standing there in the sunshine in his uniform, holding a sheaf of papers. I lowered the window all the way and the heat from outside hit my face. My mouth was dry and I wished I had something for the cigarette breath.

"This is a surprise." Lester said, glancing at the empty passenger seat like he was trying to see who brought me here.

"A good surprise? Or a bad one?"

He smiled, his crooked mustache straightening a little. "Good. It's good."

"My lawyer thinks she can get me back into my house. I thought you'd like to know."

"I'm glad to hear this."

"You had lunch yet?"

"I'm due in court." He pointed his thumb over his shoulder at the domed courthouse building behind him. "I'm usually out on patrol right now. I'm surprised you found me."

"Hey, you found *me*." I smiled and started the car but I felt like a woman caught peeing behind a shrub, her butt sticking out. "Well, gotta go."

"Wait, I'll be up near you this afternoon." He rolled up the papers in his hands, wringing them a little. "Coffee?"

"Depends on what time," I hoped I didn't sound as see-through as I felt.

"Four o'clock? I'll swing by your motel?" There was a line of sweat right above his eyebrows.

I thought of last Sunday night, seeing his car pull away from the El Rancho when I got back from the store. "I'm not there anymore. I'm staying at the Bonneville."

"I don't know it."

"You're looking at it, Lester." I put the car in gear and rolled the window up halfway. "I'll meet you at the Carl Jr.'s in San Bruno. Have fun in court." And I pulled into the street without hardly looking, but no one honked at me and there was plenty of road ahead and behind, and I felt my luck might really be changing after all.

I MADE SURE I wasn't at the restaurant first, but when I drove into the parking lot in San Bruno at five past four the sun was in my eyes and I didn't see his Toyota station wagon or even a cruiser. I waited in my car till a quarter past, then hop-walked into the restaurant, keeping the weight off my wrapped foot, and I scanned the people at the counter, in the booths and sitting at the tables, but he wasn't there and I didn't want to be standing near the door when he came, so I made it back to my car and sat behind the wheel another twenty minutes, eyeing everything that drove into the lot. But no Lester. At quarter to five I drove away, though I had no idea where I was going or what I would do once I got there.

I felt more than disappointed. I drove around San Bruno, past short stucco houses and small dried-up yards, vaguely hoping I'd see Lester's car and follow him back to our late coffee date. My throat felt thick, my eyes burning a little. I hadn't felt this lonely in weeks, and I knew it was because I'd gotten my hopes up and I guess I just hadn't pictured kind Deputy Sheriff Lester Burdon standing me up. At a traffic light, a bald man in an open jeep winked at me and my eyes filled and I pulled away without waiting for the light to change.

I was so sick of being in my car, sick of even the idea of driving around to find a place to stow it and me for the night. But at least it was familiar, though the rest of me was in a storage shed across from the El Rancho Motel. After almost an hour of wasting gas I drove back there, parked the car beside my shed, and sat looking out the windshield at cars going by, thinking how I should really break down and rent another room at the El Rancho across the street, one with a TV that worked, just lie on the bed in front of it and watch hour after hour of whatever trash came on. When I got hungry I'd pick up the phone and have something delivered. I'd write checks I couldn't afford to write; I wouldn't go to work; I wouldn't leave that bed and that room until Connie Walsh called me to move back into my house.

That's how I felt. But back into *what* really? Cleaning people's houses and offices? Chain-watching movies on the VCR? Waiting for my husband to come back? Lying to my family?

I lit a cigarette and blew the smoke out the window. In the program, they'd tell you at these times in life to HALT. If you're Hungry, Angry, Lonely, or Tired—any of these—you should slow down and watch your step. I happened to be all four, I knew it, and the last thing I felt like doing was facing the B.E.A.S.T. in the air and recognizing the enemy voice in my head so I could start accusing it of fucking malice.

My foot throbbed. I leaned back against the door and propped it on the passenger's seat. The Arabic woman had done a good job wrapping it up, I had to admit that, but how come I didn't explain the situation to her when I was back in the house? This is what I was wondering just as a San Mateo County Sheriff's Department car pulled off the street into the lot, its long radio antenna swaying, Lester Burdon lifting his hand off the steering wheel to wave hello.

He left his engine running and walked over to my window and I swung my leg off the seat and sat up. There were sweat stains under his arms, and his gold star hung away from his shirt. "I'm sorry about the coffee, Kathy, I got a call on a domestic. Did you wait long?"

"Just an hour or two."

"I am sorry, I—"

"I'm kidding. Forget it, I drove around." I hoped I didn't sound as happy as I felt seeing him now. "Still want coffee?"

"Yes." He had both hands on the door, looking right at me with that dark look again, a wanting, I thought, definitely a wanting. I glanced down at my hands on the steering wheel.

"You mind riding in a patrol car?"

"Only if you're not busting me."

He smiled and I parked the Bonneville behind the truck stop between two eighteen-wheelers. I hop-walked to Lester's cruiser and when I slid in and pulled the door shut he asked about my foot, his face hard and soft at the same time. I told him about waking up this morning on Bisgrove Street, about the carpenters and the piece of roof in my yard. Lester started to shake his head and get that long-eyed look for me I didn't want, so I told him again how Connie Walsh promised to have me back home by the weekend and now I had someone I could celebrate with. I felt a little too naked putting it that way, and Lester didn't say anything back, just put his cruiser into gear and pulled out of the truck lot heading west.

I looked at the black radio set into the console, the green and orange scanner lights. There was a shotgun clipped under the dashboard, and I glanced over at Lester behind the wheel. He was shaking his head.

"Does your lawyer know you're sleeping in your car?"

"She thinks I'm with friends. That's what she wants to think any-way."

"What do you mean?"

"I mean there's a limit to how much she wants to help, that's all; she has her limits."

He drove onto the Cabrillo Highway and went quiet a minute. "There's no one you can stay with, Kathy?"

I shrugged, my face heating up. "You don't meet a lot of people cleaning houses, I guess."

I felt his eyes on me. I squinted out at the bright ocean. My foot ached and I wanted my sunglasses. We passed a few cars and I watched the drivers hold their heads still, glancing down at their speedometers and keeping their eyes on the road, only looking up once we'd pulled away.

"You ever get used to that?" I said.

"What?"

I nodded out the window at the slowing traffic. "People you don't know being scared of you."

"You really think they're scared?"

"Scared enough to mind their P's and Q's."

Lester turned off Cabrillo into the lot of a hot dog and ice cream shack on the beach. There were picnic tables on both sides of it and in back, and five or six teenage boys and girls sat at one near the order window. Their arms, legs, and faces were tanned or sunburned. When they saw Lester get out of the car they looked away like he was the fourteenth cop they'd seen in the past ten minutes, and I liked being on the other end of that look. I could smell cooked hot dogs, the cig-arette smoke of the teenagers, somebody's tanning lotion. The girl working behind the window told Lester they didn't have coffee so he said two Cokes would be fine, but then he looked over at me to check and I smiled at him.

In the shadow behind the shack Les carried our drinks while I hopped through the cigarette butts in the sand. We sat at a weath-ered picnic table, and way ahead of us the Pacific Ocean seemed to be pulling out into low tide, its waves coming in long and small before they finally broke. Out on the water was a blue-gray cloud bank, the kind that usually came in as a fog, and the sky around it was a haze. Lester sat next to me on the bench facing the beach and for a while we just looked out at the water. I drank from my Coke and turned to him enough to take in his profile, his deep-set brown eyes, the small nose and badly trimmed mustache. Again, there was this gentleness to him, this quiet.

"How did you ever end up in that uniform, Lester?"

"Les." He glanced at me and smiled.

"Les." I was smiling too, but like a flirt, I thought. Like I wasn't really interested in the answer to my question.

"I was planning on being a teacher, actually."

"*That's* what you look like. I mean, that's what you *seem* like to me." I wanted to light a cigarette, but didn't want the taste in my mouth, not right now. "So then how come you're a boy in blue?"

He shook his head and looked down at the old tabletop, at a plank where someone had carved two breasts with X-shaped nipples. "My wife was pregnant. The academy was cheaper than graduate school, the guaranteed job afterwards. That kind of thing."

"You like it?"

"Mostly."

"Mostly?"

He smiled at me, but his eyes had gone soft and he suddenly seemed too tender so I looked straight ahead again, at the cloud bank that had moved closer in just the past few minutes, the haze around it too. The beach sand wasn't as bright as before, and I caught the smell of seaweed. "Fog's coming in," I said. I could feel him still looking at me. I drank from my Coke until the ice slid to my teeth.

"Kathy?"

"Yeah?"

"I'd like to ask you something personal, if I could."

"All right, get it over with." I was kidding him again but I couldn't look at him so kept my eyes on the green water, on the haze it seemed to make.

"Why is your husband not with you any longer?"

I watched a low wave ride all the way into the beach, and just before it broke, I felt I was rooting for it, hoping it wouldn't. "I wanted kids and he didn't. I don't know, I think if he really wanted me, he would have wanted them too, you know?"

Lester put his hand over mine on the table. It was warm and heavy. "He's a fool."

I looked down at his hand. "Have you been watching me, Officer Burdon?"

"Yes."

"Good."

"It is?"

"That you didn't lie."

He took a breath. "I haven't stopped thinking of you since the eviction, Kathy." I looked at him now. His voice was quiet, but there was something like boldness in his eyes. My right foot ached but our knees were touching. He lowered his eyes, but then, as if he'd made himself do it, he looked back at me, his brown eyes not bold anymore. He reminded me of me. He squeezed my hand and I suddenly felt so close to him that kissing him didn't even feel like a forward movement. His mustache was prickly and soft against my upper lip and I let my mouth open and I tasted his sweet Coke. I held his back and he held mine and the kiss went on for a long time, it seemed, until we finally took a breath and pulled apart and the fog was floating in close to the beach and it was getting hard to see the water. I looked at him, at his small straight nose, his lower lip beneath his mustache, his shaved chin. When I got to his eyes that were taking me in so completely, my mouth felt funny so I focused on his gold star badge, his name etched on the tag beneath it, and I wanted to run my fingertips over the letters. The temperature had dropped and I had goose pimples on my arms and legs.

"Let's find you a place to stay." Les stood up and grabbed our empty cups, and as he helped me over the sand to his car, I didn't say anything. We rode quietly through Corona into San Bruno, where he turned north just before the El Camino Real Highway. Under the gray sky we passed one-story houses with small grass lawns. Behind them was the highway, and I could see the cars and long trucks going south for towns like Hillsborough, I guessed, San Carlos, Menlo Park, Los Altos, and Sunnyvale, towns I'd driven through alone for months now, telling myself I wasn't looking for Nicky's gray Honda. Les was quiet behind the wheel and even though we were in his police cruiser, it was so familiar to be sitting on the passenger's side of a car with a man driving again that I felt sort of up and down all at once. Then we were away from houses and in a neighborhood of gas stations, fast-food restaurants, and a shopping center right next to the highway. "So where're we going, Les?"

He looked at me, then rested his hand on my knee and turned left, driving past the shopping center to a stretch of motel and travel inns on a grassy hill along the El Camino Real Highway.

"You want a pool?"

Without waiting for me to answer he turned into the small parking lot of the Eureka Motor Lodge, a two-story white brick building with a fake-looking terra-cotta roof. Outside the office door were two Coke machines and an ice machine. A carved wooden sign hung over its window: *Eureka: I have found it!*

"This neighborhood's better than the other one, Kathy. I can't let you sleep in your car."

"I'll have to pay you back."

"Shh." He put his finger close to my lips. I pretended to bite it and he smiled, then went into the office, all uniform, gun, and wedding ring. For a second I asked myself just what I was doing anyway, but then I concentrated on how good a bath would feel, a firm bed with clean sheets.

The room was in the back, away from the highway, facing the pool. Les helped me in, then excused himself to go to the bathroom. I sat at the foot of a queen-size bed covered with a periwinkle spread. The floor was carpeted and clean. Against the curtained window were two cushioned chairs on each side of a small glass-topped table. In front of me was a color TV on a stand next to a walnut dresser and mirror. I couldn't see my reflection from where I sat, so I started to stand on my good foot when the toilet flushed, the water ran, and Les walked back into the room drying his hands on a towel he dropped on the dresser.

"Looks like you've done this before," I said.

"Why do you say that?" He stood where he was, a hurt look on his face, his hands resting on his gun belt.

"Sorry, it was just a joke."

He opened his mouth like he was going to say more, then he squatted at a mini-fridge on the other side of the dresser and pulled out two cans of Michelob, handing me one. It was cold in my hands and I looked down at it in my lap, like I was seeing an old Polaroid of somebody I used to know and for a second didn't know why I didn't anymore. Les opened his and drank from it right there, standing over me. But I couldn't even look up at him. I let the can drop to the floor and I flopped back on the bed and covered my face. What was I *doing?* My foot hurt, hanging off the bed like that, and I actually wondered if my thighs looked fat from where he stood. I heard him rest his beer can on the dresser, then squat to pick up the other, the leather of his gun belt creaking. The mattress sank with his weight and I lowered my hands and he was looking into my face, leaning on one arm so his shoulder moved up to his ear. He looked almost feminine that way, and for some reason it made me want to kiss him again. He was moving his middle finger over my wrist and forearm, and his eyes didn't have that boldness in them anymore, but they didn't look sad either.

"You have no idea who I am, Lester."

"I think you're the most beautiful woman I've ever seen."

I put my hand on his warm hairy arm and he leaned down and kissed me. His tongue was cool from the beer and I could taste it and that did something to me. I scooted away from him and sat back against the headboard.

"What, Kathy?"

I wanted a cigarette, but didn't know where I'd left them. I crossed my arms in front of me. Les sat at the foot of the bed looking at me like I was about to say something deep. "I haven't had a drink in almost three years, Lester."

"I'm sorry, I didn't know."

"I know you didn't, but you don't know much about me, do you?"

His lips were parted beneath his mustache and he looked away, stood, then walked over and took his can of beer into the bathroom and I could hear him pouring it down the sink. I wanted to tell him he didn't have to do that, but I didn't trust my voice not to sound bitchy. The air conditioner in the wall came on, though the room was already too cool, but my foot felt squeezed and hot and I leaned forward and undid the safety pin the Arab woman had put in the Ace bandage. It felt good to unwrap it, and as I pulled it off Les came out of the bathroom and I was afraid my foot would smell a little. It did. Lester squatted and looked at the sole.

"You should soak it." There was a new look to his face now; distracted, like he was late for being somewhere else but wasn't quite sure where that place was, or if it even existed.

"You didn't have to dump that beer, Les. It's not like that."

His eyes caught mine. "What's it like then, Kathy? I'd like to know."

"You would?"

"Yes. I would."

I believed him, and I didn't like him standing over my smelly foot like that. I put my hand on the spread. "Come here." He hesitated a half-second, as if he didn't know what I had in mind, and truthfully, I don't think I had anything in mind. I just wanted him to get away from my foot. But when he sat on the bed beside me, then leaned over and kissed my forehead, my cheek, my lips, his hand pressed to my rib cage, the other stroking my hair back, it was like I was an empty well and didn't know it until just now when he uncovered me and it started to rain and I pulled him on me and opened my mouth and I held the sides of his head and kissed him so hard our teeth knocked together; I kissed his cheeks, his eyes, his nose; I licked his mustache and kissed him open-mouthed again. I began to unbutton his shirt and he pulled my T-shirt over my head, then everything slowed down as he touched my breasts. A change came over him, and me too. He looked into my eyes, checking on something one last time, then he sat up and very slowly untied his shoes. He put them aside, unsnapped his pistol from its holster, and laid it on the bedside table. When he pulled his shirttails from his pants, I swung my legs to the other side of the bed, unsnapped my shorts, and pulled them and my underpants off. My fingers were shaking, and I was thirsty, but now the throbbing heat of my punctured foot had moved up between my legs and I lay back on the bed just as Les stepped out of his boxer shorts, his rear small and dark. He turned to face me and I made myself look up at his crooked mustache, at his messed-up hair, his narrow shoulders. I was sixteen all over again, Ma gone shopping, Dad at work, plenty of time before we get caught. I gripped his shoulders, drew my heels up along the backs of his legs, and pulled him forward.

EARLIER THERE WAS FOG, BUT NOW THE SKY IS THE COLOR OF PEACHES and the sun is low over the ocean I cannot yet see from our home. The najars have for two hours been gone. Before leaving, they cleaned up the area well, covering the new lumber with a large green canvas they weighted with old wood from the roof. I sit upon the front step and view my son using the rake to gather the cut grass in the yard. He wears what is called a tank shirt, and short pants which are quite loose, and I see the long muscles beginning to show in his arms and legs, his shoulders as well. Set over his head are the yellow earphones of his Walkman radio Nadi purchased for him in Japantown. I am certain he is listening to California rock and roll music that to me sounds as pleasant as five F-16s flying over one's head. In this final light of day his skin is a lovely golden brown and for a moment I find myself thinking of our dead Shah Pahlavi.

It is not often I take alcohol, but last evening Nadi and I drank only one glass of champagne each and the bottle cost over thirty-five dollars. Now it is somewhat flat, but I do not care, frekresh neestam, and I drink from one of the crystal flutes we acquired on the Rue de Touraine in Paris. I tell to myself I am not allowing waste by drinking this champagne, but I know I am simply attempting to prolong the feeling of celebration I had when I purchased it; for inside my head I continue to hear what the najar told me of the young lady, saying she was the owner of this bungalow, and I try to replace his words with those of his colleague who insisted she seemed crazy, deevoonay, and she is likely claiming ownership all over the town.

After cutting the grasses, I thought of phoning the gentleman at the county tax office who supervised the auction, perhaps make an inquiry of this woman, but I was not able to pick up the telephone; if there is no snake at your feet, do not lift rocks at the side of the road.

Through the screened door at my back I smell the meat broth and stewing tomatoes of obgoosht, the steaming rice and tadiq. As she works in the kitchen, Nadereh is singing softly to herself one of Goo-goosh's songs of love. Of course I have said nothing to her of what the najars informed me. Instead I asked her to prepare a menu and shopping list for the dinner party we will host for our daughter, new son-in-law, and his family. My wife's face became so lighted with happiness at this, at the modest fashion in which our lives appear to be returning to the old ways, that she pinched my cheek and said, "Oh, Jujeh-man," my little chicken, something she has not said to me in many years.

My son bags the cut grass and moves his head up and down to the music only he hears, my wife hums contentedly in the kitchen, and I feel foolish for worrying more than God ever wants us to. I call out to Esmail that he dances like a rooster, but he does not hear me and I begin to think of Soraya, of how tightly I will hold her upon her return. And I am thinking so deeply of this moment, of the love I hold for that dear girl, that when the small white automobile drives up the hill and stops in front of the woodland across the street I stand, thinking it is them returning early, surprising us at our new home. But written on the driver's door is Bay Area Couriers, and soon I am holding in my hand a sealed envelope from a Society of Legal Aid, Lambert & Walsh, Attorneys at Law. My name is misspelled upon the front. I tear open the paper, but I must go indoors for my glasses, and I close the office door and sit at my desk.

Dear Sir,

I am writing to inform you this firm has determined the property
at 34 Bisgrove Street, Corona, California, to have been auctioned
to you under improper and erroneous circumstances by the tax officers of San Mateo County. We have today notified the county
regarding this matter, and we request the sale of the aforemen-
tioned property be promptly rescinded so the rightful owner may
be restored proprietorship of her home.

Please be advised you will be expected to vacate the premises
as soon as possible. We regret any inconvenience this may cause
you.

> Sincerely Yours,
> C.S. Walsh, Attorney at Law

Three times I read the letter, and I begin a fourth time to read it
when my hands tear the paper to pieces and I throw them at the trash
basket where they scatter and fall to the floor. My heart beats as if I
have just climbed a mountain. I pick up a pen and break it, the blue
ink spraying once into the air. Oh, this *country*, this *terrible* place;
what manner of society is it when one cannot expect a business
transaction to be completed once the papers have been signed and
the money deposited? What do they *think*? No, it is clear they do *not*
think; they are idiots; and they are weak; and they are stupid. And
what of the widow's walk? What of *that*? Will they return my eleven
hundred dollars? Will they return to me my forty-five thousand
dollars? But I must not even *think* of such an event, for I will not accept the return of *anything*! I will proceed as planned; I will sell this
bungalow for the profit to which I am entitled, and may God damn
them all to hell: *a sale is a sale*. They cannot stop it now. It is too late.
How can this be a legal practice? I must phone them immediately.

I lower myself to my knees and search through the bits of paper
for the letterhead of this lawyer. Nadi steps into the room, polishing
a silver serving bowl she holds with two hands.

"Chee kar meekonee, Massoud?"

"Heechee, nothing, I am doing nothing." But she must see something in my face for her eyes darken and she stops passing the rag over the bowl. I begin to gather the letter pieces from the floor.

In Farsi she asks: "What is wrong, Massoud? What is this mess?"

"I missed the container, that is all. Is it time for eating? I feel a bit weak."

This answer seems for her enough, and she tells to me she said not to stay in the sun so long. "And the champagne, Massoud. Come, you must eat. Come."

I stand and she takes my hand and leads me down the hallway but I pull free and say I must wash my hands, then I am coming.

"You must hurry. Esmail is hungry."

In the office I fold the lawyer's envelope into my pants pocket. It is too late to call these leeches, these modargendehs, these mother whores, but tomorrow I will drive there myself. I do not want them telephoning here; Naderch must know nothing of this. Nothing. In the bathroom I wash my hands and arms with hot water and some of Nadi's lavender soap. The water is very hot and I let it grow hotter still and I fill my hands with it. I want to open them but I lower my head and splash my face, scalding my nose and cheeks, the lids of my closed eyes. I shut the water and leave the bathroom, sitting upon the floor at the dinner sofreh with my wife and son. In Farsi, Nadi to me says: "Eh Massoud, your face is wet. Why did you not dry yourself?" She rises and brings to me a towel. "What is wrong with you, Behrani? Sometimes you act like a child."

. . . .
. . . .
. . . . . .
. .

WE MADE LOVE TILL WE WERE BOTH SO HUNGry WE HAD TO STOP AND Les left to go buy us something to eat. While he was gone I stayed under the sheet and blanket, lying on my stomach and breasts, one knee drawn up beside me, damp and sore between my legs. When Les opened the door to leave, I could see that the fog had lifted outside and the sun was almost down, but now the dusky light coming through the curtained window made the room dim.

For a while I stared at the pistol he'd left on the bedside table. It had a black checkered grip and square-looking barrel. It was so strange he was in that job; he made love so tenderly, moving as if each push and pull depended on if I liked it or not. And it made me think of Nick, the difference in their two bodies; Nick's back was smooth and cool, a little fat, while Lester's was hard, his skin heated; Nick would bury his face at my neck and sometimes suck on my skin, while Lester kept kissing me on the mouth and face and shoulders like he'd been on a long trip and was finally home. He came twice, both times inside me, but I didn't say anything, just held him. For a black second I thought of the virus, of being unprotected from it, but then reminded myself I was with a married man, which made me feel better in one way, but worse in another.

Nick wasn't coming back. Waiting for Lester in the Eureka Motor Lodge, I think I knew this for the first time, that my husband was really gone, that one day I'd hear from his lawyer, get a phone call or a letter or both, but not from Nicky himself. And for some reason, because I'd just slept with a man, I knew that day was closer in coming than before, than even this morning when I woke up in our car across from our house like some refugee.

I took a long shower like there was nothing more to feel about this afternoon than the hot water on my face and breasts, my upper back and rear, the steam clearing my nose and lungs, the slip of the bar soap in my hands, the slightly bruised feeling between my legs, and the ache in my shin and foot. I felt as connected to the ground as an old newspaper blowing down the street. I started to feel a little scared, and as I turned off the shower I could hear Lester out in the room, taking something from paper bags. The mirror was too fogged to see my face, but I didn't want to anyway. I wrapped myself in two towels, then limped out to the room and sat at the glass-topped table near the window across from Les, who'd just finished laying out paper plates and plastic forks and take-out boxes of Szechuan food that smelled like soy and cooked meat. He was smiling at me, taking me in. He leaned down and took my face in his hands, kissing my cheeks and lips. I held his wrists and kissed him back, surprised at how grateful I felt when he did that.

We ate beef teriyaki on pointed sticks, fried rice, spring rolls, and hot mushi pork we wrapped in thin pancakes. Sometimes I would look over at him and he'd smile and I'd smile back. I was still eating when he stood up, took something from the bag, then squatted in front of me and started rubbing ointment on the bottom of my foot. It tickled more than it hurt and I laughed. "Okay, that's *enough*."

"It's antibiotic. I bought you some gauze too."

My legs were parted and he was rubbing my foot with both hands, smiling up into my face, his mustache a straight line, his deep brown eyes as warm as any I'd ever seen. I was suddenly wet and I stood, twisted from his hands, and lay back on the bed, opening my towel for him, and almost immediately he was inside me again, his pants around his ankles, his star and name tag pushing against my skin.

After, he took a shower. I knew he was washing the smell of us off him, and I wondered how he would explain getting home so late to his wife, the wet hair. The word "wife" sort of sunk into my stomach like hot metal, but then I thought how I was a wife too, and that my husband was probably with somebody else right this second. But this was such a lame excuse for what I was doing, and I could hear the water shut off in the bathroom, the curtain jerking open.

My WEDNESDAY HOUSE was the CPA's on the Colma River. There was a small deck overlooking the trees down to the water and I stood out there now, leaning on the railing to give my right foot a break. I'd been hopping around on the toes of it all morning while I vacuummed, dusted, and straightened up, and every few minutes my calf muscle started to bunch up in a cramp and I had to stop and knead it until it relaxed again.

The deck was cool and shaded, but the sunlight was all over the river, bringing out the green in it, a layer of pollen floating along the surface. The air smelled like sewage and bark, and I could hear the crows up in the trees. It felt good to be working, even though I prob-

ably should have listened to Les and rested another day. Last night
he drove me back to my car in San Bruno. We kissed goodbye in the
light of the storage shed lot, then I came back here, lugged in my suitcase, and bagged the leftover Szechuan food and stuffed it into the
mini-fridge bar on the floor. Inside were small green bottles of In-
glenook white wine, nips of Smirnoff vodka and Bailey's Irish Cream,
two Heinekens and the can of Michelob. I flicked on the TV, lay on
the bed, and watched most of a movie about a man who kills his wife
and three kids and gets away with it for almost twenty years before
they catch him living a new life with a new family only a state and
a half away. When the phone rang I didn't know I was almost asleep.
It was Lester, saying he was at a phone booth down the street from
his house, he already missed me. Then he paused, I think to give me
a chance to say I missed him too, but I couldn't say that; I was used
to being alone and right then I needed something I was used to. He
asked if he could take me to breakfast. I told him yeah, though when
I hung up it was as if I wasn't anchored all the way to the ground, like
when you've had too much to drink but you don't know it until you
lie down and it's that instant right before the room begins to turn
when you feel the chains break away. I was glad he'd called, but I also
felt like a kept woman and I guess I told him that this morning over
coffee at Carl Jr.'s.

It was only six-thirty, but almost all the counter stools were taken
up with men in trucker caps, some in suits and ties, drinking their
coffees and reading newspapers between bites of eggs, toast, and
home fries. Half the tables were full too. Lester was in his uniform,
already thirty minutes into his six-to-six shift, he told me. His shirt
had neat creases in the sleeves and I pictured his wife ironing it for
him the night before. It was hard to look right into his face. I was glad
when the waitress came to take our order and left us with two cups
of coffee.

"This is on me, Lester."

"I said I'd take *you* to breakfast."

"You did. You drove me here, now I'm buying."

"Keep your money, Kathy, you'll need it." He sipped his coffee, his
eyes still on me.

"You're paying for my room, what do I fucking need money for?"
I was a little surprised at how mad I was.

Lester put down his cup. He started to reach over for my hand but
then stopped himself. He leaned forward and said quiet and low:
"I'm not sure what's happening here either, Kathy, but I do know I'm
not trying to make you some toy of mine. I just had to see you before
it was another day."

"And what?"

"That's all."

"No, what?" I touched his hand. I didn't feel mad anymore. "Before it was another day and what?

"You'd forget." He looked into my face and scrunched his lips up
sideways, his cheeks and throat darkening. He had to be the
sweetest-looking man I'd ever seen.

"*Ha,* you're lucky I even remembered how." I leaned forward.
"You'll have to wear something next time though, cowboy."

"I'm embarrassed."

"Yeah, well—" I lightly slapped his hand. "Don't do it again."

Our waitress showed up with the food right then, and we both
started to laugh.

When he dropped me off at the motor lodge, we kissed a long time
in the front seat of his cruiser. He asked if he could stop by after his
shift and I said yeah, he could. But as I left I felt that off-the-ground
sensation again, things turning too fast, and I knew I had to get back
into my normal routine, hurt foot or not.

I watched a leafy branch float down the river in the sunshine,
then I limped back inside to finish up, but first I had to check on
Connie Walsh's progress because I knew nothing was going to make
me feel more rooted than getting back into my house. I sat on the
arm of the black Naugahyde couch so many middle-aged men
seemed to buy, and I punched in the number that by now I knew as
well as my own mother's.

. . . .
. . . .
. . . . . .
. .

THE MOTHER WHORES ARE LOCATED ABOVE A COFFEEHOUSE NOT FAR
from the Highway Department Depot and the Concourse Hotel. I
walk from the cool darkness of the underground garage that smells of
car exhaust and dried oil upon concrete, carrying my leather valise
under my arm, and for this meeting I have dressed in my finest suit,
a summer-weight cashmere-and-mohair black double-breasted I purchased from a Pakistani in North Tehran. The shirt is white, the tie
is blue and brown, the color of steel. As I left the bungalow, Nadi
asked me why I was dressed so, and I told to her the truth: I am taking care of important business today, Nadi. Investment business. She
asked no more questions. This morning Nadereh wore a cotton
pantsuit the color of red sharob. She had brushed her hair until it was
full and well-shaped upon her head, and she had applied cosmetics
to her eyes, cheeks, and lips. She smiled and handed to me the shopping list for this Saturday's party for our daughter, and Nadi looked
so zeebah then, so beautiful in her new expectations, that I drove
from the bungalow and down the hill with a furnace in my stomach
for what I must accomplish.

And of course I feel it even more so as I walk from the Concourse
Hotel for I am thinking of long days under the sun with Tran, Torez,
and the Panamanian pig Mendez. I am recalling the highway dust
upon my clothes that stick to my skin with sweat, the burn on my
bare head, the kunee behind the desk in the hotel's lobby who would
see all these things and give me not enough respect for even the
common cargar I had become. But as I walk beneath a sky that is full
of sun I advise myself to practice discipline and forget these things for
they leave me also with a feeling of having been beaten before I
have even fought. I am a genob sarhang, a retired colonel of the Imperial Air Force. I have honored all the legalities in the buying of this

bungalow, and I am certain there is nothing they can do to change this fact.

The waiting area at the top of the stairs is small and shabby and this gives to me more hope. I tell the smiling kunee at the desk my business, and he offers me to sit but I stand and wait. On the walls are advertisements for parades of women who love women and kunees who love kunees. This sort of freedom I will never understand. What manner of society is it when one can do whatever one feels like doing? I have been told other cities in America are not as free as this one. A young pooldar doctor in the high-rise apartments of Berkeley told me this, that the heart of this country, a place called the Middle West, is more proper than the cities of both coasts: Ohio, he said. Iowa. Perhaps, after selling the bungalow, I will move my wife and son there. But Nadereh would not wish to live so far from Soraya, not now with the possibility of grandchildren. And I would miss the sea, for even though it is the Pacific and not the Caspian, its vast presence is a reminder to me.

"Mr. Barmeeny?"

The lawyer's secretary is dressed nicely in a gray skirt and blouse, but she wears no shoes upon her feet.

"*Behrani*. My name is Colonel Massoud Amir Behrani. I wish to speak with Mr. Walsh, please."

She smiles. "I'm Connie Walsh. This is my office, Colonel. Please come with me."

The woman lawyer gives me no time to apologize for my mistake, and I follow her into a room with a large table and many chairs and tall windows open to the bright air. She offers me coffee or tea. I would like tea, but I tell to her no thank you, and when I sit, I do not allow myself to become too comfortable. I take a short breath to begin my talk, but it is as if she knows what I have come to say and raises her hand. "I'm sure our letter came as a shock to you, Colonel. The situation is this: San Mateo County has made a number of mistakes. First, they levied a tax on my client—the previous owner of the property—she did not owe. Second, they evicted her for nonpayment. And third, they auctioned the property. Unfortunately, sir, this is where you come in, and I'm afraid we have no choice but to demand the county reverse this whole process by rescinding the sale so my client can reclaim her home."

I feel a heaviness in my fingers, a heat in my chest and face. "But *I* now own the home."

"Is the sale final?"

"Of course. I paid for it cash, I have a bill of sale." I open my valise and withdraw all the paperwork from the sale of the home. The woman lawyer examines them a moment. She sits back in her chair and looks into my eyes as directly as would a man, a man of influence and status. "Are you willing to sell the county back the house? I'd see to it they made it as comfortable a transaction as possible."

"Please to me listen very carefully, Miss Walsh. The only comfortable transaction possible is if the county tax office pays to me one hundred and seventy thousand dollars for the property. If they pay me this, I will move, but only in the autumn season. My wife is sick and she needs a summer's rest. I also will require time to find a new home."

"Mr. Behrani, you paid a *quarter* of that."

I stand and step away from the chair. "The market will already pay me this. I believe this is something you should discuss with the gentlemen at the county tax office. Good morning, Miss Walsh." I offer my hand to this woman lawyer. She takes it very briefly and she stands as well.

"The rightful owner of that house is living in a motel, Mr. Behrani. All her belongings are locked in storage. Why should she have to wait any longer than necessary to get back into the home that was wrongfully taken from her?"

Again, I feel the blood in my chest, my face, behind my eyes. Who are these people? To whom do they think they are speaking? "Of course you do not understand what I have said: *I* am the rightful owner of this property. *I* am being wronged. You have heard my offer. You are fortunate I have decided to sell the property at all."

I leave quickly and without another word. The downstairs café is full of people seated at small tables drinking coffee, eating pastries. There is music playing, one of the European composers, and men and women who have dressed in only T-shirts and blue jeans look up at me as I pass them by. They view my face, my suit, the valise under my arm, and as I return their eyes back to them, they look away as if I have come to collect something they cannot pay.

:::::::::::::::
::::::
::

I SPENT THE LAST OF THE AFTERNOON IN A LAWN CHAIR AT THE DEEP end of the motel's pool. No one else was around and I closed my eyes to the sun, smoked, sipped a Diet Coke, and kept tapping my good foot on the warm concrete; I couldn't relax: I still didn't like the way Connie had sounded on the phone earlier; she'd said she'd seen the "new owner" this morning and the good news was he was willing to sell the house back to the county, but the county still had to admit their mistake, want to rescind the sale, then actually buy it back. She sounded tired and put out, like she had nine other things on her mind. She told me to call back at the end of the day, then she made herself sound cheerful and told me to stay optimistic, we're just warming up. I didn't like how she put that; if I was going to move back into my house this weekend, shouldn't we be heated up pretty hot already? Still, I was glad to hear the Arab family was willing to sell and move, and I was trying to concentrate on that piece of news.

A shadow moved over me and I looked up into Lester's smiling face. I hadn't heard his car pull up. The top two buttons of his uniform shirt were undone and he stood with his fingers resting on his hips.

"Hey," I said.

"Hey, yourself." He squatted, his leather holster creaking slightly. He took my hand and kissed it. "Let me take you on a proper date tonight, Kathy."

His eyes looked hopeful and I couldn't help myself. "We gonna fight over the check again?"

"No, because you're going to let me pay."

"Only if we go someplace nice."

He smiled under his mustache. "That was my plan."

"My lawyer says the Arabs will sell my house back."

"Really?"

I nodded. "A bunch of other bullshit has to happen before I can move back in though."

"With the county?"

"Yep."

"Still, it's progress."

"That's what I keep telling myself."

"Then we should celebrate." He leaned forward and kissed me. His mustache tickled and he tasted like one of those eucalyptus lozenges, though I didn't think he had a sore throat or cold. I hoped I didn't taste like somebody's ashcan. He stood and asked if seven-thirty was okay and I said I'd be ready, should I dress up?

He nodded and smiled and I watched him walk out to the motor lodge parking lot, get into his Toyota station wagon, and drive off. I wondered what he'd tell his wife about tonight, about where he was going and who with, and I wondered again what I thought I was doing, having been with a married man only once before, back in Saugus, Mass., for one night when I was still using. He was a bar customer, a salesman who dressed in custom-tailored suits, silk ties, and even gold cufflinks. We all thought he overdid the wardrobe, but one night Jimmy Doran let him stay after hours while we cleaned up and soon four or five of us were doing lines and drinking and moving to the sound system. After a while the salesman was making moves on me and the Enemy Voice in my head was a cooing dove.

ALREADY NADEREH IS DRESSED AND IN THE KITCHEN AREA SLICING
eggplant for one of the many dishes she will prepare for tomorrow
evening's dinner party. But it is only Friday morning, no later than
eight o'clock, and I sit at the counter with hot tea and toast.

"Nadi-joon, do you not think you will be able to cook one meal
in one day?"

"Khawk bah sar, Massoud." Dust on your head, she to me says.
And she smiles as she turns to rinse her hands in the sink's water. Before her, the kitchen window is only partially blocked by the staircase
to the new widow's walk, something I was grateful to see, for Nadi has
said nothing of it. The najars completed their work yesterday not
long after the lunch hour. I was so pleased with the final appearance
of it, the long straight rails of the staircase, the strong wide boards of
the walk, the railing there too, that when I wrote the young najar his
final check I included a fifty-dollar bonus for such a professional job
well done. I was of course still feeling the beneficial effects of the visit
I had made to a lawyer in downtown Corona that afternoon, a very
short gentleman wearing a silk bow tie who, for one hundred fifty
dollars, heard the details of my situation, examined the paperwork of
the sale from the county, and then advised me there was nothing
anyone could do against me. The property belonged to me now and
I could do with it what I wish.

Last evening Nadi, Esmail, and I stood on the new structure and
watched the sun disappear. It was a ball of bright saffron sinking into
the sea, turning the water purple, the sky orange and green. Nadi put
her arm around our son's waist and she began to tell him of the
beauty of the Caspian, did he remember any of it? But, for the first
time, there was very little evidence of pain in her voice when she

spoke of our old life, and I put my hand upon her shoulder and listened to her speak to our son and as the sky and ocean colors slowly darkened I felt a certain regret that I must sell this property that has brought my Nadi back to herself. But I felt also all the more determined to make it worth my troubles, to earn back at least three times my original investment. For two days I have heard nothing from the woman lawyer in San Francisco. Nor have I heard from the county tax office. And this is as it should be; I will not contact them. They have heard my offer. And if they refuse it, I can turn to the open market. Yesterday I received two telephone inquiries regarding the home and I have made appointments for showings on Monday.

I rise from my breakfast and go to the door for my shoes. I see that Nadi has hung something new on the wall above the sofa. In a gold frame it is the prized photograph of myself and General Pourat addressing Shahanshah at a Persian New Year's celebration at the Imperial Palace. The king is dressed in the finest of European suits while Pourat and I are in full uniform, our hats in our hands, smiling at something complimentary the king has said of our air force. Also in the photo are three men, a foreign minister from Africa and two large Savakis, their hands folded before them, their faces and eyes empty of all humor. I know Nadi has hung this picture not only for Soraya's benefit, but for her own as well, for of course Soraya's new relatives have already seen the photograph at our expensive apartment in Berkeley. They have investigated us and they know the caliber of people we are, but I suppose Nadi must remind them, so they do not regard this small bungalow and perhaps forget.

My wife rinses radishes and cucumbers in the sink for a meal we will not eat until tomorrow evening. I wish to tell her to slow herself, to rest; our daughter is already married and we must no longer break our backs. But I know my Nadi. My lack of concern will worry her further and then she will insist we paint the walls and hang new drapes before tomorrow. No, for this moment I leave her to herself. I will drive down the hill into Corona and purchase tasteful outdoor furniture for our widow's walk, and perhaps I can find what is called a love seat for the young husband and wife, my lovely daughter who

I last saw two weeks past, stepping into the rear of a limousine dressed in ivory satin, her long black hair tucked up upon her head beneath a spray of baby breath flowers which she wore like a crown.

IN ONLY TWO NIGHTS AND TWO MORNINGS LESTER BURDON WENT from being a distraction for me to the main movie, and I wasn't even sure how that happened, though I know it started when he picked me up right at seven-thirty Wednesday night wearing polished black cowboy boots, black pants, a gray tweed jacket, and a white shirt buttoned at the throat. His hair was combed straight back and his mustache looked less crooked. He was so handsome I immediately doubted how I looked; I'd changed only twice, finally ending up in black rayon slacks, a white dress blouse, and a short rust jacket I always liked because when I buttoned the bottom it pulled into my waist and made me look like I had more of a bust. I wore my black dress pumps and the pressure of the right one felt almost good, like a fresh bandage. I had put my hair up too and now I wondered if I looked womanly enough, but Les took me in like he'd never seen anything so perfect before and on the drive up the highway for San Francisco under the setting sun I wondered if he left his house dressed like that, what did he tell his wife?

The Orion Room was at the top of the Hyatt Regency close to the long wharfs of Embarcadero Street. The restaurant took up the whole top floor and was surrounded by carpet-to-ceiling windows that leaned out at a slight angle. A large square bar was in the middle of the room and three bartenders were working back there now, their shirts and ties and faces bottom-lit with green light. The bar was full of well-dressed men and women laughing and talking over the music of the piano player, who sat on a raised platform, a dim light on him as he played and sang an old song I couldn't name. The maître d' led us past crowded candlelit tables and I tried not to limp as much as my foot still needed, which was hard to do in heels and I was sure everybody must be looking. Our table was small, covered in white linen, and it was right up against one of the glass walls. I could see the tops of skyscrapers looking gold and pink in the dusk light, the blue stretch of the bay, but the whole picture was moving and I had to sit down in the chair the host pulled out for me.

"It's a revolving room," Lester said. "Would you rather go someplace else?"

I looked at him, then back out the window. He was right. Already I was seeing less of the tall office buildings and more of San Francisco Bay, a half-dozen tiny white sails, the yellow hills of Berkeley on the other side. I laughed. "This is weird."

"Do you like it?" Lester was smiling, though his eyes were in a squint like there was only one answer he could really handle.

"Yeah, I like it." And I did once I got used to it. Our waiter showed up fast, his blond hair so short he could've been in the military. He asked what we'd like to drink and when I ordered a mineral water Les did the same. After the waiter left I lit up a cigarette. "You don't have to go without because of me, Lester."

"Oh, I don't miss it. I'm not a big drinker anyway."

"Me neither. I mean, I *wasn't*."

"You weren't?"

"Only when I did lines. That's what almost killed me."

Lester's brown eyes looked more deep-set than ever.

"You've done them too, haven't you, Officer Burdon?"

Les shook his head. " 'Fraid not."

The young waiter came with our mineral waters. He handed us tall menus, then recited the night's specials. I watched him walk back to the main dining area, then I looked over all the full candlelit tables to the piano player, who wasn't singing now, just playing something slow and sad, and I turned and looked back out the window. This time I could see the Bay Bridge to Oakland, the long gray cables in the twilight. "Have you *ever* done anything against the law, Lester?"

"That's a strange question."

I blew smoke at the glass. "A conversation starter. We've already slept together and I don't even know your middle name."

"Victor."

"Lester Victor?"

"Not very musical, is it?"

"No, it isn't." I sipped my mineral water. "Well?"

"Recently? Or a long time ago?"

"How recently?"

He glanced down at the tablecloth. The restaurant was turning to the east now, our windows facing out over south San Francisco, so Lester's face was shadowed. "It's pretty big."

"How big?"

"Big enough not another soul knows about it. Can you handle that?"

"You mean can you trust me?"

"I already trust you, Kathy. Do you want it in your lap?"

"Do I have to keep it there?"

Lester smiled. "I guess not." He looked once around the restaurant then leaned forward and said in a low voice: "I planted evidence."

"You *did?*"

He nodded, slowly, like he was trying to see how I felt about this.

"Not our schoolteacher boy in blue." I felt an almost electrical current in my arms and face.

Lester smiled again, a little sadly, though.

"Well?"

"There was this guy out near the reservoir, this little runt who used to beat up his wife like it was a pastime. He was an engineer or something, a teetotaler, but he'd go off the deep end and take a belt or a piece of garden hose to her. We never found out what exactly. The neighbors would call us, and my partner and I would show up on a hot night, talk ourselves in, and there'd be these bloody welts on her arms and legs, but they'd both stand there together, sometimes arm in arm like it was nobody's business. I'd take her off to the side and ask if she was staying quiet out of fear of him, but she just looked at me with these big wet eyes like she didn't know what I was talking about. This was before the domestic violence law, Kathy, when we couldn't bring the batterer in unless the victim filed a complaint."

"You think she liked it?"

"My partner thought so; I didn't. Anyway, at least once a week we'd get called out there and after a while I couldn't stand the sight of them, especially him. Bastard had the longest, skinniest neck you ever saw."

I let out a laugh, and Lester did too.

"We had something on him, though—he had a prior conviction for possession of your old habit, and I didn't agree with my partner, I thought she was scared to death. So on one of those hot tedious nights, I excused myself to go to the john, where I stuffed two eight balls in their closet behind a stack of towels."

"No way." I felt a tickle rise in my throat.

He raised a finger to his lips. "My ex-partner doesn't even know about this."

"Where'd you *get* it?"

"A recovered Lincoln the day before."

"So what *happened?*"

"We didn't have a warrant, so when I got home that night I put in an anonymous call to the department, then slept like a baby. They both got picked up, but because of his prior he got some time. A few months later I drove by the house to check on her, but the new residents said she'd moved." He shook his head. "She was scared to death of him."

"Shit, Lester, you just do what you want to do, don't you?" I slipped my shoes off under the table. My right sole pulsed but didn't hurt much.

He smiled carefully and sipped his mineral water.

"But what if you were wrong? What if she did like it?"

He sat back a little, cocking his head at me. "You really believe that?"

"Maybe."

"Would *you* like that?" His voice was sincere, naked, and it was hard not to play with him a bit.

"No, but I've known some real sickos."

"But how much better are they going to get if we allow them to live like that?" There was that tightness in his face again and I didn't know if it was covering something hard or soft. The piano player was singing an upbeat Sinatra tune, and a busboy brought us warm rolls in a linen-covered basket. I broke one in two.

"So how come you need to wear this cape and mask, Les?"

"That's a good question." Lester sliced into a roll and buttered it. Our waiter showed up just then and asked if we'd picked out an appetizer. I thought he was doing a nice job trying to get the final bill as high as possible for himself, but we decided to skip the appetizer and ended up ordering two of the night's specials instead, the chicken Provençale for me, swordfish with lemon caper sauce for Lester. He started to hand the wine menu back unopened, but before the young waiter disappeared I told him to bring us a decent Napa Valley chardonnay.

"What're you up to?"

I couldn't help smiling. "I ordered it for you. I know you want some. So, what's the illegal thing you did a long time ago?"

He looked at me a second. "I'm still stuck on your other question."

"Okay, answer that one."

Lester smiled at me, all the tightness in his face gone, nothing but the gentleness now. The piano player was singing an old jazz tune. Les touched the tines of his salad fork and started to talk about his boyhood in a town called Chula Vista on the Mexican border, and I should've been taking in every word but I was thinking of the chardonnay I'd ordered; I was thinking how it really was true I'd never had any problems with alcohol until I'd started doing lines, snorting those long white snakes straight to my head. Then the waiter was at our table with an ice bucket. Lester paused and tasted the sample splash in his glass. He said it was fine, but when the waiter started to pour, Lester touched his arm and told him thanks, but we'd prefer to serve ourselves. The waiter left and Lester filled his own glass, glancing at me before he wedged the bottle back into the ice bucket.

"What was I rattling on about?"

"Chula Vista."

"My brother Martin and I. We were the only anglos in the whole school and just about every day we'd get taunted into a fight with somebody about something."

"That's why you plant evidence?"

"*Planted.* I only did it once." He tried to smile, but it wouldn't finish itself on his face. "What's wrong? Do you think I did a horrible thing?"

"No, I think you did a good thing actually. I'm sorry, Les. Tell you the truth, the wine's distracting me."

"I'll send it back."

"No." I rested my fingers over his. "See, whenever I think of my sobriety I don't think of wine, I think of cocaine. That's what I'm proud of staying away from. My husband—my ex-husband, whatever you want to call him—*he* was a bad drinker, and I haven't ever said this before but I think I just let him sweep me up into *his* recovery program, you know? Whenever I needed to go to RR it wasn't because I wanted a glass of wine, it was because I had to do a mile of coke."

Lester was giving me that long-eyed look again, squeezing my hand back as I spoke. "Don't you mean AA?"

"No, RR. Rational Recovery. Your Higher Power is your ability to reason. It's all a crock of shit really, but—I don't know." I let go of him and looked out the window. We were facing west now and I was looking out across the northern edge of the city, over all the buildings and piers to the orange sweep of the Golden Gate Bridge and the ocean on the other side of it, the sky a band of red and purple. The restaurant had gotten more crowded and I could hear behind me the low din of people talking and laughing through their meals, the tink of silverware on porcelain, the piano player finishing the jazz number and going right into something else. But I kept my eyes on the ocean while the restaurant continued its slow turn away from it, then I heard Lester pouring something into my wineglass and I turned to see him holding the bottle of chardonnay.

"You're a grown woman, Kathy. Maybe you threw the baby out with the bathwater."

"But what if the baby was a demon?"

"Then you toss it out for good and don't look back."

"Do you ever look back, Les?"

"All the time." He smiled. "That's my problem, Kathy—I'm sentimental about my fuckups."

"Me too." I smiled and picked up my glass, felt the cool weight of it in my hand. He touched it with his and I kept my eyes on him as I raised the wine to my lips and tasted what I hadn't even let myself smell in three years. For a second, I had the thought there was still time to spit it out, but if there was an enemy voice in my head it was the one that would keep this from me, the swallowing, the dry heat spreading out in my chest; it was such a familiar taste and feeling inside me, almost like it'd never left, that I suddenly felt more like my true self than I had in I didn't know how long.

"So far so good?" Les said.

"Yes." I sipped once more, then put my glass back down, holding the stem lightly with my fingers. "Tell me more about you, Les."

Our food came then. Lester topped off our glasses and I knew, according to the rationally recovered, I should be looking at this whole dinner as the B.E.A.S.T., nothing more than a Boozing opportunity with an Enemy voice in my head that I had to now Accuse of malice while my reasoning powers started giving me reminders of my Self-worth leading me to Treasure my sobriety and then successfully abstain. But there was no Enemy Voice in my head, I told myself. If there was, it would already be ordering a second bottle, which I didn't feel the need for at all. So there was nothing to accuse of malice. And I didn't feel like accusing anyone of anything anyway, not tonight. I was even feeling all right about the Arab family living in my house, the kind-faced woman who'd wrapped my foot, the people who had agreed to sell back to the county. Between bites and sips, Lester told me about his mother and father divorcing when he was twelve and his brother was nine, how his father, who was a customs officer, used to visit once a week until he got another job in Texas and the two boys only saw him twice a year when they had to go on a fifteen-hour bus trip to do it. He said his mother was a looker with long brown hair and high cheekbones and this quiet way about her that drew men right in. She was a typist at a lumber company and once word got out she was divorced, Lester and his brother were watching men come to the door for her almost every night. I sipped my wine. My face felt warm. I loved watching him as he talked, the way the candlelight showed the dips in his cheeks, made his crooked mustache look as thick as straw, his eyes deep and dark.

"That's why," I said.

"What?"

"You had to protect your mother, so now you protect the peace."

"You think it's that simple?"

"Nope." I smiled. "But I wish it was. I wish everything were that simple." I looked out the window to see where we were and my own candlelit reflection looked back. On the other side was night and all the lights of San Francisco spread out below. I drank the rest of the wine from my glass and I couldn't remember the last time I felt so free of all the shit that pulled at me like the gravity of two planets. I was feeling some of the wine, but not much. I'd eaten half of my baked potato and chicken. I looked back at Les and I could see he'd been staring at me.

"Let's go dancing, Lester."

"What about your foot?"

"Shit, I forgot about that." I laughed.

WE RODE QUIETLY together. The Bayshore Freeway was lit up with orange streetlights, and Lester drove with his warm hand on mine and I was thinking about Nick, him and me driving west in the new Bonneville, driving all day and night. I took in Lester's dimly lit profile. "Sometimes I think husbands and wives, maybe they're just meant to get each other farther down the road, you know? Almost like it doesn't really matter whether or not they stick around for the final act. Is that a sad way to look at it?"

"Depends on your situation, I suppose."

"What's your situation, Les? You haven't breathed a word about · it."

Lester flicked on his indicator, glanced in the rearview mirror, then steered into the exit lane. I could feel myself sort of go still while I waited for him to speak. He took the off-ramp, pulled his hand from mine to downshift, and kept it there.

"My situation is my wife thinks I'm working overnight patrol till tomorrow morning. I guess that's pretty presumptuous of me, isn't it?"

"Is that really your situation?"

Les didn't answer. We rode by the shopping center, the display windows partially lit, the dark parking lot empty. Les pulled up to my door at the Eureka Motor Lodge, and he turned off the headlights but kept the engine running.

"I married my best friend, Kathy, that's my situation. We have a son and a daughter, but for seven of the last nine years I haven't wanted to give her more than a hug or a peck on the cheek."

The light from the walkway was catching the side of Lester's face, lighting up only one half of it and making his cheekbone stand out more, his mustache, and I thought I knew what he might look like as an old man; handsome, sad, and quiet.

"Do you still love her?"

"Like a sister. I don't have one, but I feel like I do."

"What about her?"

"It's not the same for her." He was looking out the windshield at the door to my room. "I understand if you don't want me to spend the night—and I'm not telling you this to make you feel obligated—but I'm not going home anyway. I do need to think."

I thought of Nick, the way his face looked the morning he left, like he was sure he was killing me by leaving. Lester almost had that same look now and I started to feel mad about it, but then he turned to me as if I'd just told him what I was thinking and he said if it were only him and Carol, he'd be gone, but it wasn't; it was his kids, his daughter Bethany, his son Nate. "I'm sorry, Kathy. I don't mean to dump any of this at your feet." He got out of the car, opened my door, and helped me out. The engine was still running. I wrapped my arms around his neck and kissed him. "Turn the damn thing off and come inside."

That night we held each other under the covers, and he asked me question after question about myself, how I'd ended up in that small hillside house in Corona, what my life had been like until then, and

I told him about growing up in Saugus with its shitty strip of neon car dealerships, Italian and Chinese restaurants and tanning parlors, shopping malls, my father's small linen delivery business, how, when I was little, I would ride with him on his Saturday-morning runs delivering aprons and tablecloths to restaurants, drinking too many Shirley Temples along the way until I was giddy and my father smoked Garcia y Vegas while he drove and listened to ball games on the radio and sometimes I'd feel sick but I wouldn't tell him because he hardly ever spoke to me, and I didn't want to spoil my chances.

I snuggled in close and pulled my leg up over his. His skin smelled good, like the ground somehow. I didn't talk about my first husband or Nick, and I didn't mention rehab again, or that it was my brother Frank who'd found me in my apartment, the white snake wriggled so deep inside me I was classified a suicide risk as soon as Frank and Jeannie admitted me. I didn't mention any of this, and Les seemed content for now to hear of me only as a young girl, though he got quiet after that, and I wasn't sure if it was because of the girl I'd told him about, or maybe his own daughter at home. I fell asleep with my cheek on his chest, and sometime during the night we woke up making love.

THE NEXT DAY, Thursday, he went home to his family and I spent the morning doing my laundry at the shopping-center Laundromat. I was still hopping on my good foot, but the other was feeling better, and after a lunch of cold Szechuan food in my room I soaked both feet in the bath. By the middle of the afternoon, I worked up the courage to call Connie Walsh's office. Gary said again she was out but that they were making progress on the house. His voice sounded different to me, not as businesslike.

"What kind of progress, Gary?"

"My boss will kill me, but oh what the hell, the county has admitted their mistake, Mrs. Lazaro! Evidently, they should have billed a 34 Biscove Street all along, not Bisgrove. And apparently they're willing to rescind the sale."

"By Saturday?" I stood up and danced across the carpet, com-

pletely forgetting my foot. Gary said he'd already told me more than
Connie would appreciate and I should really talk to her about all this;
she still had to work things out with the new owner. Then he told me
to call back sometime tomorrow; he knew for a fact she'd be in the
office.

"I could kiss you, Gary."

"Goodness, no." He laughed and hung up.

In the late afternoon I cleaned my Thursday house, then drove to
the pediatric office near San Bruno and went to work on that. I was
working up a good sweat, and even limping along with the vacuum
I was staying at a fast pace. Lester and I planned for him to meet me
at the motor lodge at seven-thirty, and I was stepping out of the
shower when he came, telling him the good news as I dried off and
dressed in the bathroom with the door a little open. He walked in
and hugged me and said we should go out and celebrate, but I was
tired from trying to stay off my sore foot all day, and when I told him
this he looked disappointed only a second or two before he left, then
came back a half hour later with an avocado-and-black-olive pizza,
a pint of chocolate ice cream, and two bottles of Great Western
champagne.

We sat cross-legged on the bed and ate half the pizza, drinking the
first bottle out of Eureka Motor Lodge plastic cups. We started to kiss
and Lester opened a package of condoms, but the bed was such a
mess we made love on the floor near the bathroom and I was halfway
to being loaded, or maybe I already was; behind my eyes were a hundred bees and I remember hearing something big go by out on the
highway as Lester's body froze up and he pushed into me one more
time, let out a moan, and said into my ear, "I love you, Kathy." I
wasn't ready to say that back; I laughed and pushed on his shoulders
until he had no choice but to finish me off with his tongue. He did,
and it didn't take me long at all.

We drank the second bottle in the bath. Les sat back against the
faucet, his black hair so wet his ears stuck out and his mustache
dripped water. I laughed and couldn't stop until he snapped me out
of it by singing a Mexican song he'd learned as a boy. He sang it in
Spanish, looking right at me, like he were trying to caress me with

each beautiful foreign word. Then he paused to sip from the bottle of Great Western and recited the last verse to me in English, his small brown eyes a little bloodshot.

> *"Your love was lightning on the mountain—*
> *Your love was a river in the trees—*
> *Your love was sun upon the desert—*
> *Oh, but where is your smoke,*
> *Your stream, your salt?*
> *Why are the coyotes silent?*
> *When will they call your name?"*

Friday morning we woke up hungover. The curtains were closed and the room was dark. Les sat naked at the edge of the bed, called the front desk for coffee, then took his watch from the bedstand and held it up in the pale light. My mouth was dry, my head ached above the ears.

"I should've been home two hours ago." He fell back on the mattress and I scooted over and let his neck rest between my hip and ribs. He looked up at me. "I'm sure she called the department and I'm sure they asked her if I was feeling any better." He laughed, but it sounded like air forced out of a box.

"Do you really feel like laughing?" I let my fingers rest in his hair.

"No, but things are finally in motion. Maybe I'm relieved in a way."

There was a knock at the door. Lester answered it with a towel wrapped around his waist and took our coffee from a blond teenage girl in baggy shorts. He handed her a five and told her to keep it. I put on my robe and used the bathroom before opening the drapes to a much too bright day, the sunshine reflecting off the cars in the parking lot, the white concrete beside the pool, and I sat at the table with the pint of chocolate ice cream from the mini-fridge that overnight had melted. Lester and I took turns eating it with the tiny plastic spoons that had come with our coffee. But he didn't seem to be in the same room with me; he was looking at a spot on the table and he would take a bite and shake his head, then sip his coffee and

shake his head again. My eyes hurt and I had to squint against all the
light coming through the window. I got up and limped to the dresser
and put on Nick's Ray-Bans. Lester was looking outside now, the
hair at the back of his head sticking out like dog's ears. I was getting
that off-the-ground feeling again, a little shaky about things between
him and his wife coming to some sort of a head. I hadn't planned on
that; I hadn't planned on anything. I suddenly wanted to be alone,
alone in my father's house on the hill of Bisgrove Street. But then
Lester turned and said I looked like a movie star standing there in
that robe with those sunglasses, my hair all loose around the shoulders. He came over and kissed me. He tasted cool and sweet from the
chocolate, and I hugged his bare back, wanting to say something but
I didn't know what. Lester said: "Tell you the truth, I feel more scared
than relieved."

"Me too."

"You?" He stepped back to get a look at me, his hands on my
shoulders. "Why?"

I shrugged and took a breath. "I don't know, I feel lost; I just—feel
lost." I started to cry. He pulled me to him, turning slowly from side
to side, kissing the top of my head.

"You'll feel better once you get back into your house. Why don't
you call your lawyer and ask her to tell you when you can rent the U-
Haul?"

I went to the bathroom and blew my nose. My mouth was dry and
I ran cold water in the sink and drank out of my hand again and
again. Lester was dressed when I came out. He sat at the foot of the
bed pulling on his boots. Behind him, the sunlight through the window made him look like nothing but a shadow. Then the shadow sat
up straight and looked at me. "I'm going to go get it over with,
Kathy."

"It?"

"Telling her the truth. Stopping this masquerade ball I've been at
for years." He stood. "It's strange, isn't it? You feel lost, but I feel
found. I do; I'm scared, but I feel *found.*" On his way out the door he
turned back to me: "And you will too, Kathy, I promise. I'll move you
back in myself."

THERE'S A HARDNESS that happens, this dulling of everything that leaves you feeling minus instead of plus, hollow instead of solid, cool instead of warm; men always hear everything so wrong. I told Lester I felt lost and he instantly thought it's because I'm living out of a suit-case. I didn't know this until he said that, but I guess I was expect-ing more from him, from his sad eyes and crooked mustache, his narrow shoulders and dark skin, the Mexican songs of his youth; maybe I expected some kind of wisdom. But what I got was a dis-tracted cop on his way home to maybe leave his wife, which left me feeling like some witch waiting for her brew to take effect miles away and I wanted to get up and run as far as I could, but the inside of my head was too dry for my brain and every time I moved it hurt. I lay down on the mattress and placed a pillow over my eyes, but then the coffee and ice cream seemed to spread out level behind my ribs and I felt queasy and sat up. Why did we drink *both* bottles? But the ques-tion left me in a black cave. I picked up the phone and called Con-nie Walsh. I was going to ask her when I could start hauling my boxes and bags, and I guess a part of me wasn't surprised when she got on the phone and gave me the news in her flat lawyer's voice; I guess I was really expecting something like this, that the new owner was asking an impossible price and not only would I not be moving back into my house this weekend, but she wasn't even sure it would hap-pen anytime soon.

"When then, Connie?" I was looking at the two empty cham-pagne bottles, one upside down in the waste basket, the other on its side on the floor, the label hidden. Connie was saying something.

"I'm sorry, what?"

"I said I think you should come down to my office, Kathy. Drive over today."

. . . .
. . . .
. . . . . .
. .

SATURDAY AFTERNOON I DRIVE MY NADEREH TO SAN FRANCISCO TO have her hair done by an Italian kunee who charges more than we should pay. His business is located in Ghirardelli Square amongst all the specialty shops, restaurants, cafés, and galleries whose doors are open to touring people from all over the world. In the morning I trimmed the rear hedge bushes and I am still dressed in the cargar clothes I before would wear only for the Highway Department, so I do not enter the Italian's shop, knowing, as I do, the many Persian wives who make appointments with him.

I sit upon a bench in one of the lower courtyards and watch the people pass by. Over our bungalow in Corona the sun was shining, but here in the city, in that area of large piers and wharfs they call North Beach, there is cool summer fog, a fine mist in the air, and many of the tourists look out of place in their short pants, sandals, and shirts with no sleeves that show the undisciplined flesh of their bodies. Many of them pause in their shopping, asking one another to take their photograph as they stand beneath a shop sign or in the center of the courtyard, dozens of strangers walking by them. I hear the speech of Orientals, Greeks, Germans, and French. But the majority are the more large, more fed, pink-in-the-face Americans, who carry their shopping bags, eating ice cream cones or drinking sweet sodas from cups as they walk past, their small loud children leading them.

I sit and I regard these cows, these radishes, and I again think to myself: *These people do not deserve what they have*. When I first came to these United States, I expected to see more of the caliber of men I met in my business dealings in Tehran, the disciplined gentlemen of the American military, the usually fit and well-dressed executives of the defense industry, their wives who were perfect hostesses in our most lavish homes. And of course the films and television programs imported from here showed to us only successful people: they were all attractive to the eye, they dressed in the latest fashion, they drove new automobiles and were forever behaving like ladies and gentlemen, even when sinning against their God.

But I was quite mistaken and this became to me clear in only one week of driving my family up and down this West Coast. Yes, there is more wealth here than anywhere in the world. Every market has all items well stocked at all times. And there is Beverly Hills and more places like it. But so many of the people live in homes not much more colorful than air base housing. Furthermore, those late nights I have driven back to the pooldar apartment in Berkeley after working, I have seen in the windows the pale blue glow of at least one television in every home. And I am told that many family meals are eaten in front of that screen as well. And perhaps this explains the face of Americans, the eyes that never appear satisfied, at peace with their work, or the day God has given them; these people have the eyes of very small children who are forever looking for their next source of distraction, entertainment, or a sweet taste in the mouth. And it is no longer to me a surprise that it is the recent immigrants who excel in this land, the Orientals, the Greeks, and yes, the Persians. We know rich opportunity when we see it.

Nadi looks lovely as she exits the kunee's salon, her hair styled thick and black around her face. She pauses to put the checkbook into the green alligator-skin bag she purchased in Bahrain not long after our flight from home. She wears a handsome green suit, the jacket buttoned at her waist that has grown too small these days, her hips and legs as well—too thin. Even from where I sit I am able to see the lines around her mouth and between her eyes above her nose. My Nadereh is so easily made nervous. Even this intimate dinner party for our daughter has tested her. And I have worried she may bring on one of her headaches that send her to bed for hours, or days. But she is a beautiful woman, and I rise to meet her in the crowded courtyard.

On the drive south to Corona we stop at a florist's shop in Daly City and purchase flowers Nadi chooses herself, so many they fill the large trunk space of the Buick Regal. I am of course concerned about the money we are spending for this affair; Nadereh also insisted on some of the finest champagne, three bottles of Dom Pérignon at well over one hundred dollars each. She even made telephone calls in her questionable English to the city for finding Persian musicians to play the kamancheh and domback for us, and I was relieved she found no one at such short notice. But my Nadi appears quite contented. She sits beside me as I drive down the coast highway into Corona, and she hums an old American pop song I recognize about tying a yellow ribbon around a tree of oak. The sun has remained in Corona, and now, two hours before the arrival of Soraya, it shines on the green ocean, making it nearly too bright to view more than a second or two.

"We will have a beautiful sunset for our guests, Nadi-jahn."

Nadereh nods her head only very briefly before telling to me again the final list of tasks to be completed in only the next hour: all the flowers must be arranged around the home and above on the roof porch—this is what she calls it—amongst the new outdoor furniture; our Waterford flutes must be dusted and properly chilled in the freezer; you must set up the new tape player for music in the living room; and make certain Esmail has put his room in order, bathed, and dressed in his French-made suit. I nod my head and reply, "Baleh, baleh." Yes, yes. But there is no need for me to listen any longer for I know the list very well. As I accelerate the Regal up Bisgrove hill, I am thinking of my daughter Soraya, of her small lovely face I will hold in my hands, and that is when I see Esmail speaking with a young woman on our grass under the sun. Her hair is straight and dark. She wears blue jeans and a white blouse, and there is the red Bonneville I have seen before parked against the woodland. I steer into the driveway and she regards me directly: it is the woman who last week was sleeping in her automobile so early in the morning. Nadi touches my shoulder and says to me in Farsi: "That is the woman who hurt her foot, Massoud."

I extinguish the engine and tell to my wife yes, she has come for a tool her najar boyfriend may have left behind; I've been expecting her. I step out of the car and walk over the cut grass smiling and extending my hand to the woman, who hesitates a moment before taking it.

"I am happy you came." I take her by the elbow lightly. "Please, this way, I will show you." I turn to my son and say low in Farsi, "Help your mother and tell her nothing. Later I will explain."

Around the bungalow's corner, at the stairs to the widow's walk, the woman to me says: "I'm sorry, but I think you have me confused with someone else."

"No, I am quite certain who you are."

"I'm Kathy Nicolo." She to me offers her hand and I take it and release it quickly. The sun is upon us and in this light her cosmetics stand out too much. She regards the ground: "I know my lawyer talked to you, but I thought we could just meet face to face, Mr. Bahrooni."

"My name is Behrani. Colonel Behrani."

The woman inhales deeply and looks upon the new widow's walk. "My father left us this house. He left it to me and my brother."

Esmail appears carrying a large pot of chrysanthemums in his arms for the roof. I tell to him to please rest them on the ground and go. He leaves and I say to this woman: "I am sorry, miss. But you should be telling these things to the bureaucrats at the county tax office. They have made the mistake, not I."

"Yes, but they've already admitted it. They said they'd give you your money back. Look, I know you put a new deck on; I'm sure they'll pay for that." The woman pulls from her front pocket a package of cigarettes, lighting one with a cheap plastic lighter. She inhales deeply upon it and I feel a hot impatience begin to move inside me. I hear the water running in the kitchen sink. I look at the window screen beneath the widow stairs, but it is shadowed and I cannot see my wife inside. I step forward, hoping the woman will follow, but she does not move. "I am sorry, miss, but as far as I am concerned I have nothing more to say to anyone. Why should I be penalized for their incompetence? Tell me that. You should sue them for enough money to buy *ten* homes. I will even sell you *this* house for the right price. This is all I require." The rear door to the bungalow opens and shuts and I take the woman's arm and begin walking her back over the grass. *"I am sorry, I do not know where he left his hammers."* The woman begins to pull away, but I squeeze her arm more tightly, stopping in the center of the lawn under the sun. "My family knows nothing of this, miss. There is nothing more to say of it."

"Let *go* of me." She pulls her arm free, her cigarette falling to the grass. She steps backward, an incredulous expression upon her face. "You can't just move in here and try and make *money* on this. That's not *right!* I look once back at the bungalow, then cross my arms over my chest, feeling the push of my heart against them. The woman shouts at the unfairness of me, and she begins to use profanity, but I only shake my head at her patiently; if Nadereh is watching from the window, she will quickly believe what I tell her, that the najar's girl-friend is crazy, deevoonay, thinking I am someone I am not.

The woman abruptly stops, as if she has suddenly realized the futility of all she is saying. She pulls her hair free of her face and she regards me for a long moment, then she turns and hobbles back across the street to her expensive sedan. I watch her turn the large car around, and as she drives down the hill, I step on her smoking cigarette, crushing it beneath my shoe.

I DROVE SOUTH ON THE CABRILLO HIGHWAY PAST THE STATE BEACHES, smoking one cigarette after another. I'd forgotten my sunglasses back at the motel and the sun off the water made me squint, but I kept seeing my brother Frank stomp that Middle Eastern prick into the ground. I wanted to drive fast, but the road was crowded with late-afternoon beach traffic, so at Montara I turned into the parking lot of a bike and surf shop and I got out of the car and just leaned against it for a while, the last of the sun on me, my arms folded.

Ten feet away there was an empty phone booth. I wanted to call
Frankie so much it made my stomach hurt, but I didn't move. For all
I knew Nick was back on the East Coast by now anyway, showing up
at all the old places, and the word had gotten back to my family and
that was that; they'd be able to see with their own eyes who left
who. *But not this*; not to have Dad's house taken from us while *I lived
in it.* Yesterday, Connie Walsh told me in her office that the county
had done their part and now it was up to the new owner to go along
with the deal, but he wouldn't and she said the only thing we could
do was sue San Mateo County for the value of the house. My champagne hangover had gotten worse as the day went on. My head felt
heavy and dry, and the panic I was starting to feel about all of this
seemed bigger than me. "You mean sue for damages and just go buy
another one?"

"Yes."

"You mean I can't legally get my house back?"

"Not unless the owner gives it back to the county and they give
it back to you. And I'm sorry, Kathy, but that no longer seems very
likely."

After the call, I canceled my afternoon job, closed the drapes in
my motel room, and lay on my bed for a long time. The phone rang
and it was Lester. He didn't sound like himself, his voice up but sad
too, like he couldn't quite believe his own words. He said he and his
wife had a long talk, and they'd decided he should move out.

"You mention me?"

"Yes. But Kathy, I told her you're not the reason. And you aren't."

Then he said he would call me today. Who knows? Maybe we'd
rent the same U-Haul. I wanted to tell him then, tell him about my
house, but there was a weight in his voice, a weight on a thread.

I spent the night in front of the TV smoking, and this morning I
sat in my motel room waiting for the phone to ring, waiting for Les
to say he was coming to take me to breakfast, for Connie Walsh to
say she'd been wrong, everything's set, go get your stuff out of storage. I just sat there, my lungs sore, thinking of the Arab woman
wrapping my foot, the way she smiled at me like I was something to

be pitied. I thought of the oriental carpets and the brass bed in my room, of the nomads and horses on the living-room wall, the construction shit in the yard, and I dressed and applied some color to my face; I would just go there and explain things myself.

And now my arm felt bruised from where that Arabic son of a bitch had squeezed it. A warm wind blew from the beach, smelling like seaweed and hot blacktop, and the sun was getting close to the horizon and I had to put my hand over my eyes. The traffic had slowed even more, and I watched a jeep full of teenagers go by. They were tanned. The boys' heads were practically shaved and their girl-friends' hair was all loose and rat-nested around their shoulders, though they were moving slow now, the road so wide open in front of them, a hundred free choices to be someplace different.

Les was already back at the motor lodge when I got there. His small station wagon was parked next to a Winnebago with Pennsylvania plates and in the rear of his car were shirts on hangers draped over a suitcase. His uniform hung in dry cleaner's plastic on a window hook. My hopes went up, but I felt like I was dreading something too, and I got out of the Bonneville and was stepping up under the awning to my door when he called my name behind me. He stood by a chair at the side of the pool wearing jeans and sneakers and that same striped shirt from that first time at Carl Jr.'s. At his feet was a tall Budweiser can. When I got close he smiled.

"Your limp's getting better."

I stepped onto the white concrete around the pool. I'd thought I'd go over and hug him, but something was holding me back. We stood there and looked at each other. He seemed taller and thinner to me. Even without the cowboy boots, he seemed taller. "You still feel found?"

Les looked at the pool water, his hands on his hips. "I feel so much I hardly feel anything at all." He looked back at me, his dark eyes half squinting.

"What did you tell your kids?"

"A lie. I told them a lie, Kathy." His lips came together in a flat line and I went over to him and hugged him. He smelled like cotton and sweat. He hugged me back and I felt something sort of jolt inside him, but when he spoke his voice was okay: "I don't want to scare you off, Kathy. I really don't."

My cheek was to his chest and I could see the cars go by out on the Camino Real. He stepped back and looked at me.

"I'm not, am I?"

I could smell the beer on his breath and I wanted one. "Oh be quiet, I'm glad you're here." It was true; I was. I took his hand and led him across the parking lot and into my room. I squatted at the mini-fridge and grabbed two cold Michelob cans, opening both, handing him one. I held mine up in a quick toast, then drank. It was cold and delicious and I felt reckless and I didn't care. I told him Connie Walsh's news, about my trip back to Bisgrove Street, of trying to have a human moment with the fucking Arab who hadn't even told his family the situation, who squeezed my arm so I'd stay quiet about it.

"He put his *hand* on you?"

"You could say that, I guess." I drank and looked at Lester, at the way he was shadowed with the sunlight behind him, only his mustache and eyes darker than the rest. "You remind me of a cowboy."

"How was it left?" Lester's voice was high and tight.

I shrugged and drank some more. I never drank beer much, except on days like this, hot days when you're tired and a little hungry and there's an edge to everything. Les sat forward in his chair.

"You mean if this guy doesn't want to sell your house back he doesn't have to?"

I nodded and let out a short laugh. "Look at us, Les. We're both homeless." Then I laughed harder, like maybe I didn't care about anything at all, and I couldn't stop.

"That's not right."

"What *is?*" I was smiling now.

"You're a complicated woman, aren't you?"

"Nope, I think I'm a simple woman, actually. I'm just good at complicating things." I finished off my beer, but lowered it back to my lap like it wasn't quite empty yet.

"Do I complicate things?" Les said.

I looked at him. "No. I mean, yeah, you do a little, but I'm glad you're here. I really am, Les."

He stood and pulled me to my feet. He put his arms around me, locking his fingers together at my lower back. "Spend the night with me."

"I don't want you paying for this room anymore, Les. You've got to think of yourself now, you know."

He kissed me so I'd shut up, it seemed. "I've got a fishing camp south of us. Another deputy's lending it to me till I know what I'm doing, or, you know, where I'm going." He kissed me again. "Come help me sweep it out. Then we'll sit down and figure out how to get your house back. I know so many damn lawyers it isn't funny."

I was starting to get that off-the-ground feeling again, like it didn't matter what I did because I wasn't connected to anything real in the first place. But I wanted to drive back to Bisgrove hill with this man, to walk right into my house with tall Lester Burdon in front of me, his uniform on, his gun at his belt, some sort of paper in his hand kicking the Arab family right back to the sands of wherever the hell they came from.

"Are they good lawyers?"

"Better than what you have now, I'm sure."

I don't know why I thought his lawyers might know more than mine. I did, though. I kissed him and he kissed me back, pushing me onto the bed, but I told him no, let's wait, let's wait and make it special.

My hopes were up again, and on the way out of town, sitting in the passenger seat of his car with five cool Budweisers in my lap, I asked him to drive up Bisgrove Street. As we got near the top of the hill, Les drove slowly. In my driveway behind the white Buick was a green Mercedes-Benz, and in front of the lawn was a shining new Saab or something like it. We had our windows rolled down and there was laughing and some kind of tinny music, like Greek or Lebanese. Lester pulled his car over beside the woods. "Jesus," he said. "Look at them."

In the last of the sunlight up on my roof on the new deck were seven or eight strangers, the men in suits, the women dressed in reds, peach, and pink. One of them was big and had short hair and a gold necklace so wide I could see it clearly. They were sitting in white chaise lounges, holding champagne flutes, and there was a table up there under a huge white umbrella. Bahrooni was the only one standing, and he wore a black suit, one hand in his pocket. He held up his glass to a sitting couple I couldn't see too well because of the flower pots on the railing, and he was saying something, his back to the street.

"He's some kind of colonel, you know. He wanted me to call him Colonel."

"The hell with these people." Les turned the car around, meshing the gears once before he gave it gas. Bahrooni and a few others looked out at the street, but I only looked at him, his smile fading right away. Les sped up and we drove down through the one-story shops and stores of Corona, then onto the Cabrillo Highway, the sky plum and green, the sun out of sight, already on its way to shine on Asia, and the Middle East.

NADEREH HAS LIGHTED TEN CANDLES THROUGHOUT THE ROOM AND our family and guests have sat for many hours upon the floor at the sofreh, eating and drinking, talking and laughing. Now we lean back on large crimson cushions from Tabriz, sipping hot tea and sampling pistachios and mints as Googoosh's music plays from the tape machine. Soraya is telling stories of our old life in Tehran when she was a young girl, of our driver Bahman and how he would allow her and her playmates to sit in the rear of the limousine as he drove throughout the neighborhood and they pretended to drink tea and speak of palace affairs. Nadi has brought into the room our leather-bound photo albums and I watch my daughter's new family as Soraya shows to them picture after picture. My son-in-law is a quiet, respectful young man. Dressed in a gray pinstripe suit, all the evening long he has stayed at Soraya's side but he has not once touched her, which is proper. With his eyeglasses and very short hair, he appears older than his thirty years. Both his mother and sister are large women, though they have dressed very tastefully in the latest colorful fashions, and they are quite warm, laughing with ease at the smallest opportunity. The girl's husband I find more difficult to bear; he is young, with barely twenty-five or -six years, and he owns a jewelry shop in San Francisco. His suit is elegant, but on two fingers of both hands he wears gold, diamond, and ruby rings. And throughout our dinner of chelo kebab, khoresh badamjan, and obgoosht, whenever he reached for his Coca-Cola glass his shirt cuff pulled back to reveal gold chain bracelets on both thin wrists. And when he addressed me it was as Genob Sarhang, Honorable Colonel, but with a tone of such exaggerated respect I did not believe his sincerity. So now it is a relief he has gone into Esmail's bedroom with my son to play computer video games.

But still, I cannot become fully relaxed. I watch Soraya's face in the candlelight. She has become such a lovely young woman, now wife. She wears a conservative white blouse with jacket and a skirt that matches, her legs folded like a lady's beneath her. Her black hair is held up on her head. Around her neck she wears the pearl necklace her mother and I gave her as a wedding gift, and her eyes are alive with flame, her teeth white, but her talk and laughter leave me unable to relax; as soon as she stepped out of her husband's automobile, she regarded the bungalow and her eyes lost something before she rushed to meet us on the grass. The Dom Pérignon upon the widow's walk, the fresh flowers and new furniture, the view of the sea, seemed to help relieve her of appearing from a lower station in life. But all the evening long she has been talking of our summer home in Chālūs, our home in the most fashionable section of the capital city, the parties at all the homes of all the high officials of Shahanshah Pahlavi. Our guests have listened politely, and Nadi—who has been a wonderful hostess all evening—has interrupted Soraya to ask her new mother-in-law questions of their family, their health. And now, of course, the photos have Soraya reminiscing all over again. Earlier, as Nadi was serving the tadiq and mastvakhiar, my son-in-law asked me how I was enjoying retirement. Did I have any hobbies? I had anticipated this question even before our guests had arrived and I had prepared myself to speak of my activity in the real estate markets, but at the time of the question Soraya was telling her new mother and sister-in-law of the night our home received a telephone call from the Shah himself, and I felt such an embarrassment I was not able to tell of my buying and selling bungalows without appearing to apologize for the manner in which we find ourselves living at the moment. I told my daughter in a warm voice to please change the subject, beekhoreem, let us eat.

And now, as I sip Persian tea through the sugar cube between my teeth, I am anxious for them all to leave, Soraya as well, but not before I take her aside and scold her for all her grandstanding, not before I hold her to me and tell her not to worry, this little bungalow is only temporary, your mother and I are expecting quite a profit, please do not worry about us.

And I am worried about my son. Nadi's list of chores was long and the time was short, so I was not able to speak with him about this American woman Kathy Nicolo before the evening began. Esmail is an honest boy, and he sometimes speaks before thinking. I imagine him sitting at his video game he is able to win with closed eyes, perhaps talking out of boredom to the young jeweler, telling to him of the crazy woman who visited today. Nadi and my daughter's mother-in-law talk now of our home country, how they miss the flowers of Isfahan, the mosques of Qom, how the price of saffron here is not to be believed. Soraya is leaning close to her husband as she smiles and shows him a girlhood photograph of herself, the candlelight reflecting in his eyeglasses. I excuse myself and go to Esmail's room. The only light comes from the computer screen and they are both sitting at the monitor, their eyes and faces hard with concentration. My son is taller than the jeweler, I notice. I stand in the doorway and listen to the beep beeps of the electronic game. I listen to the voices of the women in the other room, Googoosh singing one of our three-thousand-year-old love songs on the Japanese tape machine, and I suddenly feel I am a mardeh peer, a very old man. Soon it will be Esmail's new wife we will invite to dinner. But where will Nadi and I

be living then? Will we still be in this country? Tonight, I am long-
ing to be back in Chālūs, the Caspian Sea stretched out before us,
Pourat and his family alive again and visiting us in our home. Earlier
this evening, when the sun was setting into the Pacific and we drank
French champagne amongst flowers and family, toasting our health,
I began to feel the old ways once again in my blood. But then there
was the loud sound of an automobile engine and I turned to see this
woman Kathy Nicolo staring at me from the passenger's seat, a man
at the steering wheel, although I could not see him clearly before
they drove away and I was left feeling accused of a crime I did not
commit.

I feel quite tired and hope our guests will leave very soon. For days
I have been looking forward to this dinner, to seeing my only daughter again, but like so many things in this life it is never as you dream
it. And it is clear to me my daughter does not respect me as she once
did; throughout the evening, in between all of her talking, I would
sometimes catch her viewing me with a distant sadness, the fashion
in which people regard the blind or very ill. And it is perhaps this
more than anything else that leaves my arms and legs so heavy with
fatigue. Because Soraya is right: how far it is we have fallen if everything we have is invested in a small bungalow on a hill in California.

Nadereh laughs quite loudly at the sofreh, but it is not a genuine
laugh, and I want to sleep now. I want to sleep, and dream of kings.

LAST NIGHT WE STOPPED AT A GROCERY STORE IN HALF MOON BAY,
Lester and I walking down the food aisles under all that fluorescent
light, stopping to pick out Wheat Thins, steaks, and coffee as quiet
and relaxed as if we'd been living together for years. But I wasn't relaxed and I don't think he was either. The trip to my house had
pissed him off, and he talked about it as we left Corona and drove

south through all the beach towns on Highway 1, the sky a bloody mess out over the water. He kept asking me who the hell those people thought they were. What were they celebrating with their pricey cars and clothes? Taking a woman's house? I kept quiet and we shared a beer while he drove. I teased him about a cop drinking and driving and Lester seemed to calm down and told me how up until a few years ago it was legal in Texas to drink while you drove as long as you weren't drunk. At the store he acted cheerful again, asking me if I liked this or would I prefer that before he dropped it in our cart. But I still heard a drag in his voice, like he was holding something heavy in his arms. I was hungry and the beer had gone to my head and I didn't like it. I was tired of feeling like my feet weren't all the way on the ground, like the real me was waiting for me somewhere outside my body, and I made a vow I wouldn't drink anymore for the rest of the night.

Five or so miles south of Half Moon Bay Lester turned off the coast highway and we drove along what he said was the Purisima River, a dry bed of stones with a thin ribbon of water moving through the middle, making whitecaps over small boulders as it flowed west for the Pacific. There was a pale green light left in the sky, and I looked out my window at low fields of artichoke plant, then woods and an occasional house or trailer. There were lights on inside, so I guess I expected electricity when we got to where we were going. I had turned on the radio on the highway but now, maybe because of all the trees and the mountain I knew was somewhere ahead of us, not much was coming in, so Les turned it off. He was being very quiet and I wanted him to talk more.

We left the main road for a much more narrow one, the pavement worn to dirt in places. Then Les turned the car onto a trail of flat rocks and pine needles, the woods dense on both sides of us, and he drove slowly and we rocked in and out of shallow ruts in the ground. A couple of times the bottom of the car grated against rock and Les said shit under his breath. When the trail got even more narrow and low pine branches started scraping the top of the roof, Lester stopped the car and we locked it and I followed him along a path as he carried two bags of groceries and I carried one. It was almost too dark to see without a flashlight and the air had gotten cooler and smelled like pine and dried eucalyptus. I could hear the Purisima River through the woods on my left, then Lester walked up three wooden steps and onto a porch with me right behind him. Mosquitoes started to light on my face and hands, and one got his stinger in my back through my blouse. Les put his groceries down, unlocked the door, then felt his way along a wall and struck a match to one of those camping lanterns that hiss and give off the light of a bare bulb. He took the lamp and hung it by its handle from a ceiling hook in the middle of the room, the walls and floors made of pine planks that were weathered or stained a dark brown. I smelled something a little rotten.

Lester took my grocery bag and put it on a three-foot-thick chopping block beneath the hanging lamp. On his way to get the groceries from the porch he stopped and kissed me, hugged me to him. "You hungry?"

"I could eat," I said into his chest. I could smell his aftershave, and I hugged him tight before he went outside.

Under a wooden staircase against the wall was a black iron woodstove. Les got a fire going in it in no time, and even though it made the room a little too warm, it was nice seeing the flames and smelling the smoke. Next to an army cot in the corner was a plastic ice chest, and Les opened it and found an old chicken carcass floating in the water. "Shit."

"Nope, I think it's a chicken, Lester."

He let out a laugh, carried the cooler down to the river, taking the gas lantern with him. In the firelight I unloaded the groceries onto the chopping block, then looked around for something to cook with. On a crate underneath the stairwell was a short stack of pots and pans, and I dusted off a black iron skillet, put it on the stove above the flames, then unwrapped the steaks and laid them in.

When Les came back he opened a bottle of red wine he'd bought and I poured some over the cooking meat. He handed me a paper cup of it and stood with me in front of the stove, drinking. I drank too, swallowing my vow not to, feeding the enemy voice in my head. I thought he might put his arm around me or something, but he didn't. He just stood there beside me looking down at the wood fire in the stove, the steaks cooking. So I put my arm around him.

After a very quiet supper we ate off paper plates on our laps in front of the flames, we went upstairs to the loft, undressed in the light from the gas lantern, and got into bed, a queen-size mattress on the floor. The sheets felt cool and a little gritty against my skin and I wondered when they were last washed, who slept here before. I wanted to wash my face and brush my teeth but there wasn't a bathroom, even a sink. I curled up to Les and rested my hand and cheek on his bare chest. I could hear the gas hiss from the lantern. It made a kind of shadowed light, and I saw how low the ceiling was, the bare rafters running at a steep angle to short walls, just two half-windows on each side, mosquitoes and moths flying at the screens, Lester's heart beating against my hand. Without lifting my head, I asked him if he was all right.

"Yes. I'm all right." His voice was tired, and sounded weak.

"All right but *sad*, huh?"

He took a long breath and let it out his nose. I could feel it move my hair. "I just keep seeing my father drive off in his packed station wagon. I swore I'd never do that to my own, Kathy."

Something fluttered inside me. "Do you want to go home?"

"That's not home."

I thought I knew what he meant, but I didn't want to press him. I moved my hand down just to let let my fingers nestle in the coarse hair there, but he grew hard right away and our conversation seemed to continue though neither of us spoke again.

THE NEXT DAY, Sunday, was just that, full of sun. I had to pee first thing, so Lester handed me a roll of toilet paper, kissed me, and told me to find a spot in the woods. After, he told me to bring my toothbrush and he showed me a trail behind the camp that led through the pine trees to a clearing at the river. In the soft ground was an upside-down aluminum rowboat resting on a tree stump. The river was calm and wide here and seemed to end in the trees. It looked more like a pond, surrounded on three sides with woods, which was strange because I could still hear its water running back down through the stone bed.

"Won't it drain itself?"

Lester put his arm around my shoulders. "It's fed by an underground river. How often do you get to see that in life? The *source* of something?" Three dragonflies ticked along the surface to tall grass at the edge of the water. Les squatted and began to brush his teeth. I did too, spitting on the ground behind me, rinsing my mouth with cool water from my cupped hand. Lester filled a tin pot, and back at the cabin we drank scalding coffee on the small front porch and ate bread we'd toasted on the stove. Lester's hair stuck out a little in places and he hadn't shaved. He was leaning back in his chair, his sneakered feet up on the railing, drinking his coffee, and he looked good, like the pain he'd felt last night was only from his dreams. I lit a cigarette. "We gonna clean this place up or what?"

"How's your foot?"

"I can put all my weight on it."

"We should get damages for that too, the bastards."

"Who you going to call about that?"

"A bunch of people. Tomorrow's lawyer day." He looked at me and smiled, then stood and tossed the last of his coffee over the railing. "Let's do it."

We spent the morning and early afternoon cleaning the whole cabin. And it was filthy. Under the dust on the floor around the chopping block were fish scales stuck to the planks. I got down on my hands and knees and scraped them off with a spoon. In the corners were dust webs four and five feet long, and all around the card table by the window were cigarette and cigar butts. While I was sweeping Les heated two small pots of river water on the woodstove, then he mopped the floor after me. He didn't have any detergent to use so I poured in some glass cleaner I'd found under the pots-and-pans crate. There was a ripped T-shirt there too, and I went to work cleaning the windows and screens. At first, I'd wanted my Walkman, some fast beat in my head to keep me going, but after a while I didn't miss the music. It was nice just hearing the squeak of the rag on cleaner against glass, the gurgling of the Purisima River through the trees, Lester working with me.

In the corner of the porch next to a rusted-out barbecue grill was a dirty blanket and under it was a long ax, a yellow chain saw, and a plastic gallon jug half full of what looked like oil and gas. Les found a pair of pliers and a screwdriver and he tightened the chain blade, then got the thing started. It spewed out blue smoke and was as loud as a dirt bike and he carried it off into the trees and I heard him cutting for a long time. I was glad when he stopped. I walked out there, still limping a bit, and helped him carry logs back to the camp. He had cut up some kind of smooth-barked tree, maple, he thought, a hardwood that would burn well in the stove. We made three trips each. He'd load my arms up, then grab two armfuls and follow me to the house. On the way back for more logs we held hands and Lester pointed out different kinds of wildflowers in the trees, or else we'd just walk through the heat of the woods together, sweating and breathing a little hard from the work, the sun on us in places, nothing but the sound of the river and a few birds.

Once we got all the logs in a pile in front of the porch, Lester took off his shirt and started splitting them with the ax. I went down to the Purisima with a plastic cup and filled and drank three times, then brought Lester some. The sweat was dripping off his nose and mustache and he smiled and thanked me, drank the water, then leaned over and gave me a short wet kiss. I smoked a cigarette on the porch step and watched him split wood awhile. His shoulders and back were gleaming with sweat, and veins were starting to come out in his long arms. Sometimes he would let out a little grunt as he swung the ax down onto the end of a log, then he'd kick the split wood aside, bend over to prop up another full log, and swing again. A fly landed on his face and walked across his cheek to his ear, but Lester didn't even seem to notice it. I thought at first it was because he was concentrating so hard on what he was doing, but then I began to wonder if it wasn't something else, if Lester was maybe thinking about his family, his wife and kids. And I hoped he wasn't.

I left the porch and went inside to make tuna fish sandwiches. After a few more logs, Lester stopped and walked back through the trees towards his car. Then I saw him walking back to the camp, carrying his suitcase, his dry-cleaned uniform and clothes on hangers draped over his shoulder. He was still bare-chested, the sunlight on him as he stepped into the clearing whistling some tune through his teeth. I was relieved to hear it; I really liked being with Lester Burdon. I thought how this morning I'd felt more like myself than I had in a long time, maybe since the first days with Nick. And I wanted it to be good for Les too, and when I heard him whistling, I hurried to the door to take his clothes on hangers from him, and he kissed me deep, pulling me to his slick chest.

Up in the hot loft we took off our clothes and lay down together on the mattress. The room smelled almost like an attic, like dry wood and old furniture stuffing. But I could smell the woods outside the open screen windows too, the pine and eucalyptus, the hardwood tree Lester had cut up. And I could smell my own wetness as I lay on my back and Les licked me and I reached down and held his head in both my hands, my eyes on the rafters above me. I thought of Nicky the morning he left, the way he sat on the edge of the bed and just looked at me. Just that. Looked at me. Then I thought of my house, mine and Frank's, of that Arab family living there, having parties there. What Les was doing felt good, warm and slightly electric, but I was thinking too much to let go into the orgasm I knew he was trying to give me. I pulled away and took him in my mouth, until he came against the back of my throat and I swallowed. I moved up and kissed him while he tried to push himself back inside me but he'd gone soft and so we lay there awhile, holding each other, our skin sticking.

I wanted a cigarette, but I didn't want to move.

"My wife never did that to me."

"Did you like it?"

"Did you?"

"Yeah."

"Good."

"What if I didn't like it, though?"

"You didn't?"

"No, I did. But what if I didn't?"

He kissed my upper cheek. "Then I wouldn't like it either."

"Bull*shit.*"

"Well it's true, Kathy." He got up on one elbow and looked me long in the face, his mustache and eyes calling dark attention to themselves. "It's true."

I kissed him, opening my mouth, and he slid back on top of me. "Man, I'm in trouble, Les. I believe everything you say." He began to move and my mouth tasted sour and I wanted one of those tall Budweisers in the ice chest downstairs. I raised my legs up and held his back and I wanted him to let go inside me, deep inside, where everything I say has another side to it, like telling him to wear a condom when I know I don't want him to do anything like that at all. Not at all.

⋮⋮⋮⋮⋮⋮⋮⋮
⋮⋮
⋅⋅

Quite early sunday morning i carry to my son's room a tray of sugar and hot tea and I tell to him everything we face as a family. Esmail sits up in his bed with no shirt upon him, his eyes still heavy with sleep, his black hair uncombed. He drinks his tea and listens quite intently as I explain the young woman with whom he spoke on the grass Saturday afternoon. He looks away from my eyes.

"She said this is her house, Bawbaw-jahn. And it was taken away from her for no reason."

"No, as I have just said, there *was* a reason. She did not pay her taxes, Esmail. This is what happens when we are not responsible. Fardmeekonee? Do you understand?"

"Yes, Bawbaw."

I do not like lying to my son, but I am certain if he knows the woman's home was taken from her due only to bureaucratic mistake, he will not be able to keep all of this from Nadereh.

"We own the home now, Esmail. We purchased it legally, and that woman has no right to harass us. This is why I do not want you telling to your mother any of these things. You know how easily she can become sick with her worries."

"Moham-neest, Bawbaw-jahn. No problem."

I nod my head and drink from my tea, weighing whether or not I should tell to him more, that I had planned for us to stay here until cooler weather began but now I feel compelled to sell and leave while it is still clear no one has legal recourse against us. And I enjoy sitting here with Esmail, discussing serious matters. It has been the nature of my life's work to keep secrets, and to bear heavy responsibility for others. But oftentimes, I feel very tired and quite alone. And of course it is an important moment for Esmail, to have his father confide in him for the first time. My son sits straight in his bed, his brown shoulders pulled back while he holds his teacup and saucer and nods his head along with me.

"You know I must raise money for your university education."

"I can get another paper route."

"Man meedoonam, I know. And you must begin saving your money."

"Yes, Bawbaw."

"Tomorrow, people are coming to view this house for buying. If we are fortunate, we can make a large amount of money. Wish me bright eyes, son."

"Will we have to move?"

"Yes, but we will have enough pool to live well, perhaps to buy more property or start a business."

My son stares across the room at the blank screen of his computer, but I know he is not seeing this. I begin to regret telling him my affairs.

"Bawbaw-jahn?"

"Yes."

"We were rich in Iran, weren't we? Weren't we pooldar?" He regards me as if he has not seen me in a long while, his mouth open slightly. I stand to leave.

"Yes and no, son. Yes and no."

IT IS MY belief people feel more free to spend their money in good weather, so I am disappointed today, Monday, with its gray sky and its fog bank along the beach. From the widow's walk I can see no ocean, only a whiteness down beneath the rooftops of Corona. Also, my first appointment telephoned to cancel, stating they had seen a property over the weekend they could not turn down. I tried to talk the gentleman into at least seeing my bungalow, but he was not to be moved.

At noon Soraya arrives to take Nadi to lunch. My daughter is dressed tastefully in a skirt and blouse and jewelry, her black hair held back with a silver ornament. I am on the roof as she steps out of the car and waves and blows to me a kiss. This morning she told Nadi on the telephone she is enjoying decorating their new condominium in Mountain View, over one hour's drive south of us. And she is a good daughter to have driven so far to lunch with her mother at a fine restaurant in San Francisco. I did not tell Nadi of my appointments today, and I am grateful she will be gone from the house.

After they leave I descend the stairs to ask Esmail to do the same, to leave, but he has already disappeared, his skateboard gone as well. I suspect he is making friends with the local young people along the beach here. Now the bungalow is empty and silent and for a brief moment I feel quite lost standing in its rooms without my family. I inspect it once more for order and cleanliness, but I need not worry. Nadi takes care of every room as if we are expecting special guests each day.

L<small>ES WOKE ME BEFORE DAWN MONDAY MORNING WITH A CUP OF THAT</small> too-hot cowboy coffee from the woodstove. The Coleman lantern was turned low, not even hissing, and in the shadows I could see he was in his uniform, with his badge and gun, his hair combed and still wet from the river. He squatted on one knee at the corner of the mattress and said he'd heated me up a basin of water to clean up in, I could stay here or he could drop me off at the Eureka to get my things.

"Get my things?"

He glanced down at his hands. "If you want to."

"I do, Les." I nudged his back with my foot. "You've got a weird way of asking, though."

"I'm shy, Kathy." He smiled, then stopped. "Will you know how to get back here on your own?"

"Yep." I dressed in front of him, then peed in the dark woods and brushed my teeth on the porch, using a cup of warm water to rinse my mouth.

On the drive back to San Bruno, Les told me about the two lawyers he knew in town who would get me back into my house in no time. The sky was beginning to lighten, though it was gray and the beaches seemed to be one long fog bank. I sat there in the passenger's seat with my feet up on the dash feeling almost confident that everything would get worked out. At the motor lodge Les paid the bill and carried my suitcase to my car. We kissed goodbye and promised to meet back at the fish camp by seven o'clock tonight. He said to be careful driving that luxury car of mine up the pine trail, then he was gone.

I sat in my car a few minutes and smoked a cigarette, flicking my ashes out the window. I was starting to feel jittery, though I'd only had half a cup of Lester's coffee, and my fingers were shaking a little as I smoked my second cigarette though I'd meant to light just one. In Group, we'd coax all our snakes and gargoyles into the room and smoke our lungs sore and our eyes bloodshot while we got "clear" on everything else. And I knew to any of my counselors back East my life wouldn't look very manageable: I was drinking again, and smoking; I was sleeping with a man who'd just left his family, all while I was supposed to be getting back the house I'd somehow lost. I knew they would call the drinking a slip, the smoking a crutch, the love-making "sex as medication," and the house fiasco a disaster my lack of recovery had invited upon itself, and on me. In RR, it would be time to turn to self-control and self-worth reminders, use my powers of reason to tell myself how lovable I was, how I didn't need to do anything dangerous because I'd be endangering a good person, me. I knew what all the rationally recovered assholes would say, but it wasn't me loving me I was interested in. It was Lester loving me, he and I living on Bisgrove Street, both working during the day only to spend time together at night, snuggling in front of the TV, or else going to bed early to make love. And that's what it was beginning to feel like, *love*.

Later, as I cleaned my Monday residential, running the vacuum over carpets, mopping the floor, you'd think my mind would be on my house for most of the day, but it wasn't; it was Lester, his tall skinny gentleness, his smell—like sweet damp ground—the way he paid such attention to me. And I was thinking of kids again. I wanted to see pictures of his son and daughter. I wanted to know their ages, and their favorite snacks. I knew lots of men who'd started second families, had babies again when their first kids were almost on their own. But I was getting way ahead of us, wasn't I?

Around noon, I picked up my mail at the post office, then went to a shopping center sandwich shop to sift through it all while I ate. It was only ten days' worth but it took up all of my table, and I put it in two piles, one for the trash can on the way out, one to keep. The trash pile was mostly junk mail, the other was bills: car insurance, gas, my final phone and electric. The electric bill was the most recent and I opened it and read the cutoff date for the last billing period: just two

days ago. I tore into my turkey sandwich and drank down some Diet
Coke, and I shook my head at how fucked-up this was. It was the
same with the gas bill.

My first thought was to call Connie Walsh again, but I knew she'd
only tell me to call the utility companies and set them straight. I
didn't want to hear that. I pushed my sandwich away and lit a cigarette, looked out the window at the shopping center parking lot, at
all the cars under the hazy sky. I was reaching for the ashtray when
I saw the postcard in my bill pile, a glossy picture of the Hilltop
Steak House back in Saugus on Route 1. In front of the restaurant
was a huge fiberglass cactus maybe fifty feet high, and all around it on
a small fenced-in lawn were a dozen life-sized steers. I knew the card
was from my mother and I took another drag and drank from my
Coke before I started to read it:

Dear K,
    Your telephone is out of order. Have you two got an unlisted?
Your aunts won two round-trip tickets to San Francisco. I may go
with them Labor Day. Send me your new number.
                                                            Mother

I left the sandwich shop and stepped into a drugstore for a notebook. Back in my car, I wrote:

Hi Ma,
    I'm sorry I haven't called you. A bad earth tremor rolled
through here last week and a tree hit the phone lines down the
street. As soon as they're fixed I'll let you know. Also, that's good
news about your coming out here but Nick and I won't be in
town that weekend. He's taking me on a business trip. Sorry to
miss you.
                                                                 K

I wondered if I should put in anything extra about the tremor,
what it feels like to be in one, maybe, but then thought no, she
wouldn't expect that from me.

Then I wrote letters to the gas and electric companies explaining
my situation, telling them to bill a Mr. Barmeeny instead of me. I
drove back to the post office to mail them but when I dropped my
mother's letter into the box I felt as if I'd just heaved my last sand-
bag against rising water and there wasn't much time left.

It was barely one o'clock and I had six hours to kill before I met
Les back at the camp. I thought about going there early to make us
a nice dinner, surprise him, but then I pictured myself trying to build
a fire in the stove, not having an oven to use. And my specialty was
casserole dishes; lasagna, veal and eggplant Parmesan. I decided to go
to a movie instead, one or two weekday matinees at the mall Cineplex in Millbrae off the Camino Real. Last night, as we were drifting
to sleep, my cheek on his shoulder, I asked him his kids' names again.
"Bethany and Nate," he said, his voice full of gratitude. Then I asked
him where his house was and when he said it was in Millbrae, in a
housing development you had to drive by to get to the mall, I told
him I'd probably driven past his house a dozen times, maybe I'd even
seen his wife.

"Carol," he said.

"Yeah. Carol."

But now, instead of passing through San Bruno for the highway to
Millbrae, I drove into foggy downtown Corona, then right up the
long hill of Bisgrove Street. I wanted to pull over beside the woods
across from my house and just look at it a few minutes, maybe remind
myself of what was mine before I went off to numb my afternoon
away in a dark theater. And I guess I didn't really expect to see anyone there, but a station wagon was parked by the woods so I could
only park near the house and I didn't want to do that because there
were people standing in my yard looking at my home: a man and
woman and a young boy, maybe eight. He had his hands in his shorts
pockets, and he was kicking one foot into the grass. His father's hand
was on his shoulder and they were all looking at what Colonel
Barmeeny was pointing out to them, the new deck on my roof. The
bald Arab wore a tie and a short-sleeved dress shirt that looked very
white in the grayness. He glanced at me in my car, but then turned
away as if he hadn't seen anything. He was talking fast, officially,

though I couldn't hear his exact words through my open window. He looked back at me one more time before he led the young family up the steps to the roof for a view that must be foggy. I couldn't believe what I was seeing and a sick laugh rose up from my stomach: *the fucking bastard was trying to sell my house!* Then I just honked my horn, leaning on it with both hands. I looked straight ahead and I could feel the steering wheel vibrate. Two houses up, a woman stuck her head out her front door and stared. But I kept my weight on the wheel, letting that sound tear through the air until my wrists started to ache, and I let go and yelled through the window, "He can't sell you that house! He doesn't own it! He's trying to fucking *steal* it! He's trying to sell you a *stolen* house!"

The man was half-smiling like he didn't know if this was a joke or not. He looked from me to Barmeeny, then back at me again. His wife stepped closer to her son, and the colonel's face was still as stone. I pushed on the gas, sped up the hill, and turned around at the dead end. I drove back and honked the horn again. The colonel was standing near the railing talking to the man and woman, and now he nodded his head and pointed in my direction as if my noise proved some point he was trying to make. But I didn't care what he said; I kept going, my hand pressed to the horn all the way down the hill.

. . . .
. . . .
. . . . . .
. .

Nadereh returned from her afternoon with Soraya in high spirits. After their luncheon they had shopped, and Nadi was quite excited to show to me my new shirt and tie, the pants and sweatshirt she purchased for Esmail. She also pulled from her bags more tape cassettes of Persian music and she put one of them into the machine while she set about preparing our dinner. The music was most recent, and I did not like it. There were still the old instruments being used—the tar, kamancheh, and domback—but electric guitar as well, and the singer sounded to me like a whining child; I was surprised Nadi had chosen it. I watched her fill the rice pot with water from the sink, moving her head slightly in feeling with the music, and I pressed the machine's off button. Nadereh turned her head to me immediately. "Nakon, Massoud. What is wrong for you?"

"You must not spend so much money, Nadereh."

"It is not so much money," she said in Farsi, smiling. "There are school sales now. Even your clothes, Behrani." She walked to me, drying her hands upon her apron. She kissed my cheek, then pressed the music on once again and resumed her cooking. And I knew I could not tell her my worries. I knew I would prefer to have her this way, cheerful and innocent as a child.

BUT THERE WERE flames in my stomach, and now, after dinner, I sit upon my widow's walk at the new table under the umbrella looking down over the rooftops and streets of Corona to the gray fog that enshrouds the beach and the sea. It is two or more hours to nightfall. I drink hot tea, strong from brewing in the samovar since morning, and I can hear my wife in the house below washing dishes in the kitchen sink. The sky and ocean are so gray and white as to be inseparable. I sit and think. I must weigh my options regarding this Kathy Nicolo, but my hand trembles, my mind roaming elsewhere, to Jasmeen, my cousin, who was nineteen years old and very beautiful. Her voice was low for a woman, but her body was long and thin, her hair quite thick and black, and when she thought something was humorous she would laugh without reservation, letting her teeth and bright eyes be seen by anyone. But she had an affair with an American oil executive, who they say was rich and quite handsome. She committed this in a townhouse which one of her own neighbors cleaned three times per week. Soon, all the village women knew she had given her girl's flower away without marriage, without the blessing of God and the holy mosque, and to a married foreigner from the west. And it took a full month for the news to reach her father, my uncle, and her two brothers. My uncle was a trader in carpets, though

not highly successful, while his only brother, my father, was a respected lawyer who would one day become a judge. When my uncle
finally heard the gossip of the old khanooms, he did not believe it,
but Jasmeen was not capable of telling lies well and so he knew it was
the truth and he beat her. For two weeks he kept her locked in the
home. He began to drink vodka nightly, at first with the neighborhood men, but he could not bear their silence so he drank alone, usually at his shop in the back room where the carpets hung from the
walls or were stacked in long rolls in all four corners. My uncle rolled
his own cigarettes and I imagined him smoking his black Turkish to-
bacco and drinking in the stillness and quiet of his office, the walls
threatening to collapse upon him. He would return home very late,
often in the early morning, pull Jasmeen from her bed, and beat her
with his fists, crying, "Gendeh! Whore!" My aunt would sometimes
attempt to stop him, but he would beat her as well, calling her,
"Modar gendeh! Mother whore!"

On the first morning of the third week, his eldest son, Mahmood,
returned home from the bazaar after having overheard five market
women speak of the Behrani family, of the shame their kaseef daughter had brought upon their heads. It was a cold winter morning, and
my uncle had not yet left for his shop. He sat by the woodstove with
his tea and bread, though he took neither; he had once again not
slept through the night and was still mast, drunk. My aunt had left
the home early with Mahmood and she was at the bazaar, while my
cousin Kamfar, the youngest child, sat at the wooden table with his
morning's schoolwork, and it was his brother who rushed into Jasmeen's room and pulled her out. She was dressed in long white nightclothes, her hair loose and wild upon her shoulders, her small face
bruised and swelled from the beatings. He brought her before their
father and yelled he must do something. *The family is disgraced, Bawbaw! We are all disgraced, because of this stinking GENDEH!* Jasmeen
struggled with her brother, cursing him, but he would not release
her, and my uncle looked away from his son and daughter and stared
into the fire as if he could not hear or see or smell anything around
him. At last he stood. He left the room, and returned with his

German-made Luger pistol. Jasmeen was still attempting to free herself from Mahmoud's hands, but when she saw her father and his
gun she began to scream until it seemed she could not breathe. She
began to cry Kamfar's name, but when he stood, his father pointed
the gun and ordered him to stay seated. He took Jasmeen by the
hair, and with his eldest son's help, dragged her outdoors.

The ground was frozen but there was no snow. The house was
only a short walk to the village square, and one could see the long
bread and trinket tables of the bazaar, a cage of chickens, the
butcher's meat hanging from a timber. Already passersby stopped to
view the spectacle of the carpet dealer pointing a pistol at his dirty
kaseef daughter whose hands were held behind her by her bearded
older brother who stood to the side, his eyes on the eyes of their father. The girl was in white nightclothes, her feet bare, already beginning to turn blue, her black hair hanging before her face as she
cried so hard she was unable to speak. The men and women of the
bazaar began to look as well, and perhaps they saw the youngest son
run from the house just as his father pulled the trigger, the sound like
the cracking of ice, a wisp of smoke entering the air, and the young
beautiful Jasmeen, the gendeh, the whore, falling to the ground, curling herself up as if she were cold, moaning, then becoming quiet and
with great concentration sitting up and pressing her hands to the
hole in her chest. But in seconds the front of her gown was completely red and wet, and quite soon she lay still, her eyes open, steam
rising from her wound into the early-morning air of Tabriz.

I hated my uncle, believing he had acted rashly and with too
much passion. We are an educated family; we do not need to live as
the peasant class, resolving our troubles with spilled blood. My aunt
took Kamfar and moved to her family in the south, to Bandar Abbas,
on the Strait of Hormuz. But none of her brothers or uncles would
take revenge on Jasmeen's killer. A man has the right, even the obligation, to protect his family name. Many years later, when I was married and Esmail was not yet born, Kamfar told to me the details of the
story while we were mast with Russian vodka, and we both wept for
Jasmeen. Soraya was a girl of eight or nine years and in my drunk-

enness I could not allow myself to even *imagine* raising merely an unloaded pistol to her. And over the years I have dreamed of Jasmeen in white falling to the ground, Mahmood standing over her as she attempted in vain to keep life from leaving her, pressing her hands to the torn opening between her breasts.

The hurting of women I have not approved of, though, yes, I have struck my wife on occasion, but I regretted each incident deeply. Once at our home in Tehran, I slapped Nadi's face for raising her voice to me in the presence of a junior officer. Her eyes filled with sadness and humiliation and she ran crying from the room. Later that evening, when she would still to me not speak, I rolled up my shirtsleeve, lighted a Turkish cigar, and pressed the glowing ash into my flesh. I wanted to cry out but did not. I relighted the cigar and burned myself again. I did this five times, and I asked God for forgiveness with each burning of the flesh. The white scar on my forearm remains, and it is a reminder to me for controlling my passion, but today, when this woman Kathy Nicolo assaulted my buyers and me from her automobile, when I felt the sale of the bungalow begin to slip past me like the wind, I wanted to shoot her in the head; for with each of her false accusations, she was attempting to take from me not simply my future, but my family's food and water, our shelter, our clothes. I explained to the gentleman and lady that this was a crazy woman, she knows nothing of which she speaks; I am pleased to show you all the paperwork for the sale of this home; *I* am its proper owner. The man and woman regarded one another and then we spoke of other matters such as the proximity of the home to the beaches and San Francisco, the quiet nature of this street. The husband said they would telephone me with a decision, but I knew as I escorted them and the child to their family automobile, I had lost them.

Perhaps I should reconsider my decision to complete these dealings without a real estate agent. I have heard of many people who have put down payments upon homes after only viewing color photographs of the property in the Realtor's office. This would allow me to not worry about this kaseef woman spoiling things.

But no, I cannot allow a salesman to take a heavy percentage of what is rightfully mine. I will wait for calls on the property and if this woman troubles me again, she will simply wish she had not. That is all. There is no more to consider.

⁂

MY VISIT TO BISGROVE STREET LEFT ME FEELING WORSE, LIKE I'D JUST fanned a fire I was trying to put out. I skipped the matinee and went food shopping instead, then drove south to the fish camp to surprise Les with some kind of meal when he showed up at seven, hopefully with some good lawyer news. It was only two-thirty when I drove the Bonneville up the pine trail, but I couldn't go very far because Lester's Toyota station wagon was already parked there. In front of it was a red pickup truck and on the rear window was a faded LET GO AND LET GOD bumper sticker beneath a small trout-fishing decal.

I got out with my two bags of groceries and squeezed past the station wagon and truck, the pine branches messing up my hair. As I carried the groceries into the clearing, I saw Lester and a man on the front porch, though they hadn't seen me yet; Lester was sitting in a cane chair against the wall, still in his uniform, looking down at the floor, a beer can in one hand. The man was leaning against the railing with his back to me and the woods. He was wearing jeans and a dark blue short-sleeved shirt, his arms thick. I stepped on a twig and Les raised his head, but for a half second his face didn't change from what it was before; he looked at me like I was someone he didn't know who had just walked in on something private. But then his face softened up and he stood and met me at the steps, taking a bag and kissing me on the cheek.

"You're early," I said.

"You too." Les motioned to his big friend and introduced us. His name was Doug, and this was his camp. Doug smiled, nodded at me, and drank from a can of ginger ale, his wedding band catching my eye. His square fleshy face might've been good-looking if his head weren't practically shaved. I noticed how big his chest and biceps were. He reminded me of a lot of men back East, and I didn't like it. I followed Les inside with the groceries. He seemed skinnier than usual. I went over and hugged him. "You look pretty low. What's up?"

He held me for a long quiet minute, then let go. "Carol's real upset."

I heard Doug step off the porch and walk away from the cabin, and I didn't know what Lester was trying to say. I took the food from the bags, a sudden current in my chest.

Les looked out the screen door, at the trees on the other side, though he didn't seem to see them. "She was waiting in the car with the kids when I got to work this morning, and she began shouting and crying. Hitting me. The kids were still in their pajamas and they were crying too. It was bad."

I had that floating feeling again, my heart beating somewhere in the air in front of me. I started to fold an empty paper bag. Les stayed quiet and was putting a crease in a bag that was already creased. "Are you going back to her, Lester?"

"That's not an option, Kathy."

Why? I wanted to know. Because she would never take him back now anyway? Or because he was really committed to this new road he was on? This road with me? But there was an edge in his voice, like he could yell or cry or both if I pushed him, and I pictured his son and daughter in their pajamas crying in the car. I wanted to hold him, but I lit a cigarette instead, blew the smoke out the side of my mouth. "I'm sorry your kids had to be there. That must've been hard."

"It was." Les pushed open the screen door with his toe, his back to me. "I should go help Doug with his boat. He's trading it in for something bigger."

I inhaled deeply on my cigarette, then rested it on the very edge of the chopping block, balancing it there, a tremor in my fingers as I let all the heat out of my lungs. "Les?"

"Yeah?"

"This all would've happened anyway, wouldn't it? If you hadn't met me?"

He turned to me, like he was surprised I'd said that, his lips parted under his mustache. He let the screen door close behind him and came over and hugged me, told me of course it would, it was all going to happen sooner or later. He stepped back and looked at me with a hand on both my shoulders. "It's not you, Kathy. It's not you at all."

I felt better but also left out, like a little sister, and I stepped away from him to finish my cigarette. "I know this is shitty timing, but did you get a chance to call your lawyers about the house?"

He said no, he hadn't, but he was planning to do that before tonight. He came over and kissed me, tasting like sour beer, the way it gets old in the mouth. Then he said he'd drive up to Half Moon Bay right now and make the calls, be back in no time. I told him I was blocking them both in with my car and I handed him my keys as he stepped out into the gray light, ducking his head as he left the porch. I moved to the door and watched him walk to the river trail, his shoulders hunched slightly, his head low, like there was still something he had to duck.

I smoked a cigarette in the doorway while they carried the aluminum skiff through the clearing past our woodpile, then up the trail until I couldn't see them anymore. I could hear Doug's calm voice, and I wondered if they were talking about me. I wondered what Les had told him about us, and I pictured Doug and his wife having dinner with Lester and Carol Burdon. I felt like leaving, like getting in my car and driving for days and days. But Lester was taking my car anyway, and he was doing it to call lawyers for *me*. I sat at the table and looked around the cabin, at the bare pine walls, the black iron stove, the groceries on the wood chopping block, the steep staircase to the loft. I could hear the Purisima River through the trees. All this quiet was making me more nervous and I'd wished I'd brought my Walkman from the car. I went outside, squatted at the woodpile, and loaded myself up with a stoveful of split logs.

LES WAS GONE almost two hours, longer than it should've taken him to drive five miles to make a couple of phone calls. I'd bought two jars of marinara sauce, and I was planning to heat that up in the stove while I boiled some pasta and cooked hot Italian sausages in another pan. But I didn't want to start any of this till Les got back, because on a hot stove it would all get done fast. So after finally getting the fire going, I tossed a three-green salad on two paper plates, peeled eight cloves of garlic, diced them with a dull knife, made half-slices in the French bread, then scooped in spoonfuls of margarine, sprinkling in the garlic before I wrapped the loaf in foil. I sat on the porch and smoked a cigarette. Any minute I kept expecting Les to come out of the woods into the clearing, but I sat there for close to an hour listening to the river, an occasional bird, the crackling of the fire in the house behind me. Every twenty minutes or so I'd go back inside to add a split log to the flames to keep the temperature of the stovetop up. There were only two pots and one pan in the crate under the stairs, and the pots were small. I'd filled both with clear water from the river and each had a slow boil going in it. I was going to have to cook the vermicelli in both, then dump the water to heat the sauce, hoping that and the sausages from the pan would be hot enough to reheat the cooled pasta, though I wasn't too worried about anything cooling off in that cabin; it was hot as a sauna. My shirt was sticking to my skin and the sweat was beginning to burn my eyes. I poked the fire with a stick, shut the oven door, then walked down the short trail to the Purisima, where I pulled off my top and bra, stepped out of my shorts and panties, and waded out in the cold water and dived in.

It was a shock but I felt instantly cleansed to the bone, and I let myself surface, turning on my back and kicking until I was away from the treetops and there was nothing but the gray western sky above me. I closed my eyes and drifted a minute, but the water was cold and I didn't know how deep it was and for some reason I pictured the fish camp on fire, tall flames curling out the windows, black smoke snaking out the shingles of the roof. I swam back to the mossy bank and dried myself as well as I could with my underwear. I dressed without them and walked back to the camp, which wasn't burning, and there was Lester lugging my suitcase into the clearing from the cars.

In his other hand was a covered Styrofoam cup of coffee he tried to drink from as he went, his dark eyes on the ground in front of him. When he saw me he swallowed and lowered his cup. "Go for a swim?"

"You get lost?" I reached for my suitcase but he stepped away with it.

"Your foot."

"It's fine." I tried to take the suitcase again, but he wouldn't let go and he walked ahead of me while I stood there watching him make his unsteady way up onto the porch. He dropped my suitcase against the wall and sat down. I stayed where I was. "You go drinking?"

Lester looked at me with his eyes narrowed a little, like he didn't quite know how to take what I'd just said. But really, he seemed put out, as if I was interrupting an important train of thought. He flipped the plastic lid off his coffee cup and drank. I crossed my arms and stared at him, my wet underpants balled up in one hand. I was hurt he didn't bring me a cup. I felt refreshed after my swim, and coffee would've been nice right then, before I cooked. I knew I could go inside and make some, though. And I couldn't stand myself looking at him this way, my arms crossed, my head cocked. Why didn't I just start tapping one foot?

I sat on the top step of the porch, my back against the post. Lester had both elbows on his knees, holding the coffee cup between his hands, and he gave me a weak smile, then looked over the railing into the woods. His uniform shirt was wrinkled and sweat-stained in the back, and his pant cuffs were riding high on his calves, his black socks fallen to his black shoes, his shins skinny and hairy. A rush of air seemed to go through me.

"You don't have good news for me, do you?" I felt selfish asking this, and I wished I could take back the question. Lester studied me for a long minute, then shook his head.

"I don't have good news for anybody, Kathy."

"What do you mean?"

"I mean I'm just a Bad News Bear, Kathy." He raised his eyebrows at me like it was my cue to laugh.

"Did you get loaded before the calls? Or after?"

Les stared at his small woodpile. "After. But I didn't get loaded. I started to, but then Doug steered me away from it." He looked over at me. "You're so beautiful with your hair wet like that."

I was thinking of Doug and the twelve-step, Higher Power bumper sticker on his truck, of letting go and letting God. "They can't do anything to Bahroony, can they?"

Les shook his head and I felt my chest sort of disappear.

"I called three lawyers. Two of them said if he bought it legally he can do whatever he wants. They say your case is with the county, Kathy."

"But the county said they'd sell it *back* to him. And I don't *want* them to buy me another house. Can't we *make* him give it back?!" I jumped up and walked out into the clearing. *"That fucking prick's trying to sell my house, Les!* I saw him showing it to people this afternoon."

"Today?"

"To a *family*. That fucker just wants the cash. He probably does this all the time, makes money off people's problems! What did the third lawyer say then?"

"That was my lawyer."

"Well? Did he say something different?"

"I didn't call him about that, Kathy."

"Oh." My cheeks got warm and I felt like I'd just walked into a stranger's living room, plopped down on their couch, and started watching their TV. I'd been thinking Les came back from his phone calls all down mainly because of *my* bad news; now I was ashamed of myself and I didn't know what to say. I needed a cigarette. I went inside the hot cabin and lit one on an ember from the woodstove. I stuck another split log inside, then went back out on the porch and sat on the stoop smoking. Les stood and tossed the last of his coffee over the railing. He leaned against it with his hands, and we were both quiet. Far off in the woods a dog barked.

"I guess my wife never saw this coming. I feel pretty bad about that."

"You think you're making a mistake?" It was strange, but I felt calm. Les stood there all long-armed and still. He could answer any way he wanted.

"What do *you* think?"

"Do *I* think you're making a mistake?"

Les nodded.

"I can't answer that. Maybe if you have to ask me, you are."

"Then I'm not asking that."

"What are you asking me, then?"

He didn't answer right away, just looked at me. He finally said: "Can you put up with me through all of this?"

"That's what you're asking me?"

"Yes, I suppose I am."

"I think so. Depends on what 'this' is, though."

Lester flicked a paint chip off the railing. "Carol's on sort of a rampage. She called the lawyer before me and she's already petitioned for dissolution."

I made some kind of face.

"Divorce," he said. "We don't use that word in California. We *dissolve* marriages here; it's supposed to be a lot nicer for everyone, just slide into the hot tub and disappear."

"And you don't want that?"

"I want what's best." He peeled up another paint chip and glanced at me. "And I know that's what has to happen, but she also asked him some nasty questions about custody and property. She can't do anything against me without mediation, but just hearing it kind of put me over the edge."

I went over and hugged him. He felt to me like an old friend, though I didn't have any. It must feel like this though; they're warm against you and you love and respect them and are on their side no matter what. I asked him if he'd like a nice Italian dinner, and he said yes. We kissed and made our way inside, starting to undress, needing to do it, but it was so hot in there we ended up hurrying back down the trail to the Purisima, our arms around each other, and we took off our clothes on the mossy bank, then made love there, Lester pushing in and out of me so fast it hurt a little. His face was all bunched up with the effort of it, and I suddenly felt far away, closing my eyes just as he let out a short groan, pulled out of me, and came across my stomach in a warm wet line.

MAYBE IT WAS the hot cabin that got to us, to him. Maybe it was the quiet and the stillness. I think it was all three. The dinner came out better than I would've guessed and because it was too hot inside the camp, we ate out on the porch off plates in our laps. Halfway through supper the mosquitoes began to hit so we sprayed each other down with repellent, something I wished I'd waited to do because the rest of the meal didn't taste quite right.

We sat on the porch awhile, the two of us looking out at the small woodpile and trees like old people waiting for someone to visit. The sky was still gray, but darker, and I knew we were close to nightfall. Les was sitting straight in his chair. He'd changed into jeans and that tacky striped golf shirt, and he wore sneakers without socks. But he didn't look relaxed; he'd been sitting with his arms crossed over his chest, his feet flat on the floor, and sometimes he'd wave a mosquito away from his face, then cross his arms again. I thought of my mother and her two sisters and their plan to fly west, and I wished I'd written a better reason for them not to come. I knew if they thought Nick and I would be gone for the weekend they'd still fly out, and worse, they'd probably want to stay at the empty house. "*Shit.*"

"What?"

I told Les about my mother's postcard, and about the rest of my mail, the bills I was supposed to pay to keep the Arab family comfortable in my stolen house.

"You're right, you know." He sat back and looked at me. "This guy's received stolen property and now he's trying to pawn it off."

"It's not really stolen, though, right?"

"Technically." Lester's breath was starting to rise. "That's one thing I hate about law enforcement, Kathy."

"What?"

"Do you know how many times I see people violate the spirit of the law without actually breaking it? Like the DV law: no matter which spouse does the violence, we have to take them in. That means if a two-hundred-pound artichoke rancher in Pescadero slugs his wife and she hits him back, she gets charged, too."

"For defending herself?"

"That's right. We took in this one guy who did a number on his wife, really worked her over. She wouldn't take out a restraining order, and when he got out on bail he went back to the house and coaxed and taunted her until she started clawing his face. And he stood there and let her do it because he knew the law and he knew now it would be *her* turn to sit in a cell. And I can't *not* take her in. And this Arab son of a bitch—he knows what he's doing is wrong, but the law saves him anyway. The day we drove by, you see the kinds of *cars* parked in front of your house? You see the *clothes* those people had on? And you're out in the cold."

"I'm out in the heat." I was smiling. It felt so good hearing this kind of feeling about me and my problem coming out of Lester's mouth. I lit a cigarette. "I can't believe we can't just evict him. That's what's so fucked up."

Les gave me a long look, his dark eyes narrowed like he was thinking of something else. "You said this guy was a colonel?"

"That's what he said."

"From what country?"

"I don't know, but his wife hardly speaks any English at all."

"Maybe they haven't been here very long, Kathy. Maybe they don't know their way around." Lester went inside. I could hear him undressing.

"I'll call INS tomorrow, Kathy, see if they have anything we can use."

"Use?"

He didn't answer me. I could hear him pull the plastic off his dry cleaning. I was really enjoying this. "Use for what?"

"For the greater good."

I listened to him dress, then he stepped back outside, zipping up his deputy uniform pants, tucking in his shirt. He reached into his pocket for some uniform emblems and his gold star badge, pinning them on.

"What the hell are you doing, Lester?"

"Officers tend to listen to other officers, Kathy. It's worth a shot." Les began to finish buttoning his shirt, but I stepped up and took over, like I used to do for Nicky.

"What if he doesn't listen, Les?"

"Then we turn up the volume." He laughed at his own line, at the cowboy toughness of it, it seemed. I told him to stay still, and I straightened up his shirt collars and kissed his throat. I was about to say thank you but he was already stepping off the porch, so I put on my Reeboks, then went out and started the Bonneville while Les unlocked his car. I watched as he straightened to buckle his gun belt on. He looked perfect walking to the passenger's side of my car, the creases in his uniform sharp and clean, his badge positioned just under his heart. I noticed he hadn't pinned on his name tag. When he got in and shut the door, I leaned over and kissed him and said, "I love you for doing this, Lester. I really do."

A HEAVINESS OF HEART POSSESSES ME ON OUR NEW WIDOW'S WALK. ITS cause is remembering Jasmeen, but I begin to worry once more of the difficulties I already face in the selling of the home. Even if I were to sell the bungalow at the profit I have projected, I must still be prepared to move my family once again, and this time it will have to be a modest apartment in one of these modest villages along the coast. This will of course be the best way to avoid spending my pool while I search for suitable investment opportunities. But I recall my daughter's face, the fashion in which she regarded me at her homecoming dinner, the aggressive and rude way in which she all the night long repeatedly apologized for the family's present living situation by recalling our old life. How will she regard her mother, brother, and me living in a cottage in a place such as San Bruno perhaps? Or Daly City, with all those Filipino people? Will she be too ashamed to visit? To bring her husband and his family? These thoughts begin to anger me, for who does she think she is to judge her own father? To perhaps pity me? And yes, it was pity I saw in her face that evening as she viewed me in the candlelight at the sofreh, that, and a degree of shame as well. But also, she seemed to me confused at the change we are undergoing, and that is where I blame myself, for I have never let her know of our finances. Even when I worked two jobs for so long to uphold our charade, she never knew what sort of work and where, and of course I would leave the home well dressed and return as such. Perhaps I maintained this mask for my children out of pride and vanity. Perhaps I was being soosool.

But enough of all this self-examination. It is a habit I only began to assume after the fall of our society when I found more time on my hands and upon my shoulders than I would ever wish. I never wanted so much time. I must discpline myself to keep my attention on my present tasks and challenges, to drive into Corona before the department store closes to purchase one or two signs further advertising the sale of the home.

I BUY TWO signs, bright crimson letters over black, stating home for sale and for sale by owner. As the sky darkens, I secure the first with string to a utility post at the base of Bisgrove Street. In the sign's space reserved for the telephone number, I draw a blue ink arrow pointing up the hill. The second sign I did not think to purchase a stake for, therefore I tape it to the left of the door over the lighted house bell button. Inside our bungalow, Nadi has for me drained a glass of hot tea from the samovar and placed it upon the counter. The sofreh is gone from the floor, and I see my wife has changed into her expensive French exercise suit which hangs upon her so loosely. Over this she wears a cotton apron, and she does not approve when I wash my hands in the sink near her clean and drying dishes.

"Nakon," she to me says and she slaps me playfully on the shoulder. I attempt to kiss her quickly upon the nose and she pushes me away but her eyes are smiling and I sit upon the counter and eat a grape. From down the corridor come the strange electronic sounds of Esmail's computer video game. Today, by his own decision, he acquired another newspaper delivery route. In my office, shortly before Nadi called us to the sofreh for dinner, my son told to me he would give me every penny he earns to go towards his education and his future. "And you can buy food with it too, Bawbaw-jahn. Whatever you wish." He stood straight before me, his knees skinned once again from skateboarding, his thick hair in need of a brush, and I wished to hold him as tightly and completely against me as I did when he was a small child. But now he was approaching me as a young man of responsibility and I did not wish to diminish this, or take this from him. I stood and shook his hand, which was smooth and warm and no longer smaller than my own.

I drink my hot tea. I watch my Nadi dry the rice pot with a towel, and I feel much better than I did only a few short hours ago; this family has overcome challenges far more difficult than the selling of a small bungalow, and with the new signs in place and the advertisements still in the papers, I feel confident we will meet our true buyer very soon. Nadi turns to me with the dry pot in her hands and she begins to remind me tomorrow is her sister's birthday. She has sent her a gift, but she would like to telephone her early in the morning, before the day becomes too late in Iran. She lowers her eyes at me like a young girl and says to me in Farsi, "I promise we will not talk long."

I am filled with that old love for my wife, a love of nearly thirty years, and I cannot possibly allow a "no" to escape my lips. The house bell sounds. Nadi appears startled, and I go directly to the door expecting a buyer, a lady or gentleman who has seen my signs and is stopping to inquire. But standing on the step beneath the exterior electric light is a tall policeman with a thick mustache, and I think immediately of Soraya, is she all right?

The policeman points to the right of the doorway. "Did you post this sign, sir?"

"Yes." I feel relief instantly. "Is there a difficulty, Officer?"

"And that's your sign at the bottom of the hill?"

"Yes."

The policeman looks over my shoulder into the home, his hands resting on his belt in a very relaxed manner.

"Please, come in, Officer." I step away and allow him inside. I look behind me and see Nadi has left the kitchen, disappearing into her room, I am certain. I say to the policeman I am new to the area, is a permit required to post signs?

"Not on the house, but the utility pole is city property."

"I see. Very well, I will put the sign elsewhere."

The policeman regards the painting of the battle of martyrdom on the wall, stepping closer to view the framed photograph of myself and General Pourat with Shahanshah Pahlavi. I move to the door. "I will remove the sign immediately, sir. Thank you for informing me."

But the policeman does not acknowledge my movement. He turns to me and I believe he is smiling beneath his mustache, which I see now is trimmed in a slightly disorderly manner. He says, "You're a long way from home, aren't you?"

"This is my home, sir. I am an American citizen." I smile, but a stillness has entered my chest. The policeman walks over the carpet and inspects our family portrait on the table beside the sofa.

"Were you a general, sir?"

"I was a colonel." I leave the door and join this man, but I stand at the kitchen's counter so he cannot easily look down the corridor to our bedrooms. Now there is a heat in my stomach. I can no longer hear my son's computer video game. The bungalow has become very quiet. "Tell me, Officer. What more can I do for you this evening?"

He pulls from his belt a small leather notepad. "You can give me your full name."

"Are you penalizing me?"

"No sir, I just need your name for my report."

I spell for him my name, and then he inquires the names of anyone else living on the premises.

"I do not understand. Why is it necessary for to have the names of my family?" I regard the policeman's badge, a gold star, and beneath it, a smaller badge of two pistol barrels crossed together, then another pin, the gold letters FTO. "And what is *your* name, Officer?"

The man regards me, his jaw muscles tightening a brief moment. "Deputy Sheriff Joe Gonzalez. Let me ask *you* a question, Colonel: are you selling this house on your own?"

"Pardon me?"

"No Realtor or agency? 'For Sale by Owner,' right?"

"That is correct."

"Have you got a title or escrow company to handle it?"

"No, I do not." The home is too quiet. Nadi is certainly listening at her door, and I am confused. Why is this deputy asking these questions? I move away from the counter and walk back into the living-room area, hoping he will follow. "I do not wish to offend, Officer, but if you will excuse me I have work I must do this evening."

"Civil Code 1101, for starters."

"Yes, you have informed me of this. I suggest you come with me to witness my removal of the sign." I open the door, holding it for him.

"I'm talking about the disclosure law, Colonel. You're not aware of this law?" The officer stands and walks to the opposite wall, where he once again views the framed photograph of Pourat and me and Shah Muhammad Reza Pahlavi. The policeman keeps his back to me, a deep insult in my country. I still hold the screened door open, but my arm is beginning to tire and I must take a short breath. "No, Officer, but perhaps you will tell me."

"It means you have to *disclose*, Colonel. You, the owner, have the obligation to tell any prospective buyers anything about the property they have a right to know."

"I do not understand."

"You sure about that?" The policeman turns from the wall, regarding me with a smile.

I release the door and it closes quietly on its compressed arm. "Are you interrogating me, Mr. Gonzalez?"

"I don't know, Colonel. You tell me. I understand your friend the Shah used to make a real habit of it."

"I do not know who you think you are speaking to, sir, but I have had quite enough. You have done your job; now you may leave." I open the door once again, standing to its side.

The policeman walks to me. He is taller than I. He smells of garlic and charred wood.

"You're used to giving orders, aren't you, Colonel? Let me get right to the point here. San Mateo has offered to give you your money back so this house can be returned to its lawful owner. The county doesn't want litigation on its hands. In fact, Colonel, no one wants any trouble here at all. Except you. You don't seem to want to do the right thing, which is to sell this house back at the price you paid so it can be returned to the real owner. The *real* owner, Mr. Behrani. As far as I'm concerned, you're sitting on stolen property, and in my book, that just won't wash." The policeman walks out onto the step, but I can do no more than look at him.

"You have a family. I'd be thinking more about them if I were you. I have more than one contact at Immigration. People get deported every single day. There are a lot of things I can do, Colonel. I suggest you call the movers so I won't have to. Thank you for your time. I know we won't have to see each other again."

I watch the policeman walk across my lighted front grass and into the darkness of the street. There is no police automobile. No car of any kind. Soon, I can no longer see him, but I hear his footsteps as he moves down the hill.

I release the door and turn to see my wife and son, looking at me as if we had all just heard a very loud noise nearby.

"CHEEH SHODEH, MASSOUD?" Naderah says. "What is wrong?"

My son regards me a brief moment, then opens the refrigerator and begins pouring for himself a glass of Coca-Cola.

"Give to me answer, Behrani. What did that man say of deporting?"

"He said nothing, Nadi." I am suddenly so tired I cannot speak my words clearly. I close the door and lock it.

"Do not lie to me, Behrani. I heard him. Who was this man?"

"Do not call me Behrani. I do not like it." I sit down upon the sofa, but I can only look at the silver tea table before me. I do not understand the correctness of what has just occurred. How is it possible for the county tax office to send a policeman to threaten me? How is this possible in America? I have done nothing beneath the law.

"Beh man beh goo, Behrani! *Tell to me, what have you done?*" My wife stands in front of me, her eyes small with fear. I rise immediately.

"It is none of your business what I have done or not done, Nadereh! Have you no faith in me? No respect? I told to you the man said nothing, only that I must remove my sign from city property, that is all."

My wife tells me I am lying. She begins to tremble, raising her voice, demanding to know what is before us, her fears once again beginning to devour her. I must leave the bungalow, remove the sign, and contemplate what I am forced to do next, but Nadereh is screaming in front of my son that I am a kaseef liar, and a coward, and I seem to watch from far away as my hand slaps her across the face and I hold her thin shoulders and shake her, her head jerking backwards and forwards, and I am making some sort of noise from between my teeth. Then Esmail's arms are around my chest and he pulls me backward onto the tea table. There is a moment of stillness before its legs break and I am sitting on my son on the floor against the sofa, my wife screaming and crying on the carpet before us. I attempt to help Esmail to his feet, but he stands quickly with no help from me. He looks at his father only a brief moment before disappearing down the corridor to his room. Nadereh remains on the floor upon her knees, screaming, moaning of her dead mother's broken table, how I have ruined everthing in her life, *everything*. The black cosmetics have loosened under her eyes, and as I leave the bungalow she pushes me in the legs, but I ignore her, feeling curiously as if I am watching this moment instead of being a part of it, that it belongs not to my family, but another. Outside in the darkness, I smell the ocean. There are many stars above, but three and four homes down the street I am still able to hear my wife's crying. She curses me in our mother language, and I am grateful it is a tongue no one in this village understands.

AT THE HILL's bottom, in the dim yellow light of the streetlamps above, I see that my sign has already been torn from the utility post, a quarter of it still hanging from the tape. On the long climb back up the hill I am breathing with some difficulty, but I am not fatigued in the limbs, my mind is once again clear, and I no longer feel like a helpless witness to the unfortunate events of the evening. Why did this officer not have a police car in his possession? Why would he tear the sign himself? In such an emotional fashion? Why did he not have the name tag on his blouse that I have seen pinned to all other American law officers in uniform? And why did he hesitate in giving me his name, Gonzalez?

When I reach the bungalow I feel in my breast a very strong doubt that this is a genuine policeman at all. I know that America has its officials who operate over the law, but even corrupt county tax men fearful of a lawsuit would not send a uniformed officer such as that; they would send men who could not be traced back to them or their office. Dark men in suits. Savakis.

I cross the short grasses of my lawn and enter my home with a new resolve; tomorrow I will visit the same lawyer who advised me before. I will also visit the county tax office, as well as the San Mateo County Sheriff's Department to report to them of their "Officer Gonzalez" making threats. Or perhaps he was not making threats for any bureaucrats, but for this kaseef woman, Kathy Nicolo; perhaps he is her brother, or friend, or more.

I am surprised to see Nadereh has left the silver tea table broken upon the floor, a bowl of pistachios and wrapped chocolates scattered about. From her closed room comes the melancholy music of Daryoosh, that kunee singer with the pretty voice I have come to despise. But frekresh neestam, it makes no difference; I can no longer protect my wife from troubling news the way one would a child. If she is afraid and miserable and unable to adjust to our new lives as I have, if she cannot respect me or stand by me another day, then so be it. Een zendeh-geeheh, this is life. Our life.

I clean up the nuts and sweets, then inspect the broken legs of the table. They are made of cypress wood from Turkey, and two are split and broken. Tomorrow I will glue them. I lean the tabletop neatly against the sofa, the last remaining legs jutting out like a final salute. The door to my son's room is open and he is lying upon his bed, still dressed in shorts and tank T-shirt, his legs crossed together, his hands resting upon his stomach. He regards me as I enter, then fixes his eyes once again on the wall. I take the chair from his desk and sit. In Farsi I say that I am sorry for the fighting between his mother and me. "I was wrong to strike her, Esmail-joon. When you are one day married, please do not do as I did this evening."

My son says nothing. Nor does he turn his head to me. I reach out and squeeze his upper arm. He stiffens slightly, but I ignore it and tell to him how strong he is becoming. Soon he will be stronger than me in every way. My son blows air from his mouth, crossing his arms over his chest. He turns his head completely away from me now.

"Do not be disrespectful, son. Look at me when I speak."

Esmail sits up quickly. "Why did you lie to me, Bawbaw? You told me that woman didn't pay her taxes so they took her house."

"Yes, that is why they took from her this house."

"But I heard through the window everything that cop said. Why did he say she was the real owner?"

"Because they are all fools, that is why. The county tax officials made a mistake and took from the wrong person her house. Now she wants them to buy it from us so she may return here."

"Then we should return it, shouldn't we? Why don't you give it back to her? We can live someplace else."

I do not wish to discuss further these details with my son, but he regards me so intently, his dark eyes upon mine, I feel the time has come to give him something more of the burden I carry. "Pesaram, my son, I am sorry I withheld from you the truth, but that woman's house *was* taken because they thought she did not pay her taxes."

"But you knew they made a mistake?"

"Not when I purchased the house. But now I am quite willing to sell this home back to them so they may return it to her."

"Then why did that cop say he would send us back to Iran? Can he really do that, Bawbaw?"

"No. We are American citizens, they can do nothing to us."

"But—I don't understand."

"The tax bureaucrats will only pay to me what I paid to them. You see, they will not allow us to earn the profit we deserve, Esmail. I am therefore forced to sell it to someone else. We have no choice."

Esmail is quiet a moment. He looks beyond me at the wall. "But what about that lady?"

"I have told her myself she should sue the county officials for enough money to buy ten homes. With a good lawyer, Esmail, she could be very pooldar over this."

"But that day in the yard she told me her father gave it to her before he died."

I stand. "Her fight is with the men who took from her this place, Esmail-jahn, not us. We have done nothing wrong here. Remember what I've told you of so many Americans: they are not disciplined and have not the courage to take responsibility for their actions. If these people paid to us the fair price we are asking, we could leave and she could return. It is that simple. But they are like little children, son. They want things only their way. Do you understand?"

Esmail looks upon the floor, nodding his head. "I feel bad for that lady, Bawbaw."

"You have a good heart, Esmail, but do not forget this woman is refusing this new opportunity before her." I replace the chair beneath the desk. "I am pleased you have taken this newspaper job." I lean forward and take my son's face in both hands, kissing his forehead and nose. I smell traces of dried Coca-Cola upon his lips. "Soon all of this will be behind us. Wash your face before sleeping. Shahbakreh."

HOURS LATER SLEEP has still not come to me. I lie upon a blanket on the floor of my office in the darkness, but I am unable to rest. Earlier I knocked upon Nadereh's door but she did not answer, though I am certain she heard me over her music. But this is not what keeps me restless. It is that man's final words to me, his threats of contacting Immigration. Of course he can do nothing to the Behranis—we are all citizens now—but there is Soraya's new family; her husband has applied for his green card, while his mother and sister are still waiting to be granted asylum. But I did not tell him of the existence of my daughter, so perhaps he will miss this altogether.

These thoughts increase the speed of my heartbeat. The muscles in my back and neck become tight. I think of this Gonzalez telling me there are many things he can do. Late in the night an automobile passes by and I rise and walk to the dark living-room area in my underclothes. My bare leg knocks against the extended leg of the table, and I curse it on my way to the door. Its lock is secure. I turn on the exterior lamp, seeing nothing but a few flying insects, the small lawn beyond. I leave on the light and make my bed upon the sofa.

I WAS SMOKING BEHIND THE WHEEL OF MY BONNEVILLE WHEN LESTER marched back down Bisgrove under the streetlights, ripped the House for Sale sign off the pole, then got in. I drove off, holding my question about what happened until we were on our way. When I did ask, Les glanced over at me, his hands on his legs, looking almost like he knew I would ask and sort of hoped I wouldn't.

"This guy's obviously not right off the boat."

"What do you mean?" I flicked my cigarette out the window, my heart beating somewhere in my throat. We were riding out of town for the shortcut to San Bruno on the Junipero Serra Freeway. Earlier we'd decided to go to my storage shed and get some things to make life at the fish camp easier—a box of candles I hadn't opened since Christmas, glasses, plates, silverware, and the small hibachi barbecue Nick used to grill mushroomburgers on in the backyard. Fog was beginning to roll in from the beach and my headlights lit it up in front of us as I plowed through. "Well, tell me what *happened*, Les."

"He knew to ask my name, Kathy. I had to lie to him."

I didn't know how to read his voice. Whose fucking idea was this? Was he blaming me? I turned onto the lighted freeway where the fog was only a mist and I stepped on the gas. "So what did you say to that Arab prick?"

"He's not an Arab, he's Iranian. I think he's probably got money coming out of his ears, too. Or at least he used to. There's a picture of him on the wall with the Shah. The *Shah*. That guy had his own *mint*."

"What did you say to him, Lester?" My hand felt tight on the wheel. I wanted to scream. Les looked at me, then out the window.

"I swear to Christ, Lester, if you don't hurry up and tell me what happened back there I'm going to drive us right off the road."

"I gave him an ultimatum."

"What?"

"I told him I'd call Immigration on his family, and I hinted I could get nastier than that if he didn't clear out."

"You *said* that?" I let out a nervous laugh, accelerating to pass a muddy farm truck. "What did he *do?*"

"He asked me to leave, but I know I rattled him."

"Did you mention me?"

"Not by name."

"Shit, Les." I laughed again.

"You can tell he's used to giving orders all day long too. I think you were right—he probably buys up seized property just to make a killing. I did the right thing. He's scum."

"You think he'll call the department?"

"Not really. It's his word against mine. Besides, as far as he knows, I'm a Mexican named Gonzalez."

We both laughed hard, though what he said wasn't that funny. I was starting to feel like anything was possible again, and I think he probably did too. And that's what we seemed to have with each other, wasn't it? The feeling we could start out new again, clean, all our debts cleared.

At the storage shed in San Bruno, he held the flashlight while I went through my things for all we needed. We could hear a live band at the truck-stop bar next to the El Rancho Motel, a woman singing at the mike. I put the pillows and folded sheets in the backseat, and everything else in the trunk. My fingers were black from the hibachi and I went back inside the shed and wiped them off on some newspaper. I called out to Lester that I didn't want to go back to the camp yet. He said he didn't either but he couldn't go anywhere in his uniform. I took his flashlight and found one of Nick's blue button-down shirts. It was wrinkled and probably too big for Lester but he put it on anyway, the waist baggy when he tucked it in, the sleeves too short. He took off his gun belt and put it in the trunk, then stood there in just his police pants and those black shoes and that wrinkled shirt. I laughed. "You look like a laid-off security guard."

He laughed back, put me in a gentle headlock, and kissed my forehead.

We didn't drive far, just across the street to the truck-stop bar, which was crowded for a Monday night, mainly with truckers in work jeans, their T-shirts stretched tight at the gut. Some of them sat at small black cocktail tables with the wives or girlfriends they kept on the road, women who were dressed just like the men, some in matching T-shirts from rodeos or traveling carnivals. The floor, walls, and ceiling were painted black and the main light came from the theater lamps hanging over the band and the short plywood stage and small parquet dance floor. That end of the room was all red, orange, and green and the rest of us were in the shadows.

Les and I sat at one of the tables against the wall not far from the band, which was playing an up-tempo country song. He went up to the bar to get us something, and I lit a cigarette, a little preoccupied with what he'd bring me back to drink, and I watched a couple dancing out on the floor, a heavy man and woman, both in cowboy boots, jeans, and dark T-shirts, moving fast to the music.

Les came back to the table with a full pitcher of beer and two glasses. He poured me some until the foam started to flow over the top and I had to sit back and drink a third of it down. It was ice-cold and washed the cigarette taste from my mouth and throat. Les finished pouring for himself and he smiled at me, clinking his glass to mine, but the band was too loud for us to talk over so he turned sideways in his chair and we both watched the older couple dance. The band's lead singer was pretty, only twenty-five or -six years old. She had curly red hair—or at least it looked that color under the stage lights—and she wore tight jeans and her singing voice was really strong. The bass player was bald, closer to forty than thirty; I tried to picture Nick playing in a band like this, in a place like this, but I couldn't. One of the nights when I told him he should try and get a job with a local group, maybe play in the clubs, he just shook his head at me and asked if I'd already forgotten what the B in BEAST stood for. I told him no, I hadn't, but I felt ashamed of myself. Clubs were nothing *but* a Boozing opportunity. But now, as I finished my first mug of beer and Les filled my second, my head loose on my neck, I was sure fear of drinking had nothing to do with why Nick never took his bass guitar out to an audition; like most addicts, he had the worst fear of all, that his dreams would actually come true.

And I hadn't been in a barroom—warm and dark, loud and full of smoke—since I was a user working at the Tip Top with Jimmy Doran. But I felt okay because there wasn't a white snake in sight and that time seemed so long ago anyway, almost like somebody else had lived it, and now I had a mature man in my life, and not some addict trying to hang his own recovery on me. I looked at Lester's dark profile against the tangerine light in front of us, his deep eyes and small nose, the mustache under it. I drank most of my second beer and refilled my mug. The pitcher was getting light and I wanted Les to get us another one. He was such a serious man, and I knew he would get me back into my house and I wanted to make it worthwhile to him. I knew he was hurting over his kids. I wondered what it must be like to have children you have to live away from now because you no longer wanted their mother or father, and I got a nice picture in my head of his son and daughter visiting us at my house, sleeping in the guest room, or maybe even with us. I finished my beer, then poured myself some more, Lester too. He smiled at me and I held up the empty pitcher, but Les nodded at the dance floor that now held two more couples, and he stood up and took my hand and I was already feeling the alcohol, and I followed Lester Burdon out to the middle of the floor.

I WOKE UP to a patch of sunlight on my face. It came through the tree branches outside the loft window, and I turned over and kicked the sheet away. I was naked, sweating, and my mouth was so dry that when I tried to swallow, my tongue clicked a second to the roof of my mouth. I smelled coffee, which turned my stomach, and I could hear the crack of the woodfire going in the stove downstairs. I didn't hear Les moving around anywhere. I had to pee, but I wanted something very cold and sweet to drink, watermelon juice or mango. I remembered Lester driving the Bonneville after we left the bar long after midnight. I was sitting low in the passenger's seat, watching his face in the light of the speedometer as he drove, as he kept saying he was drunk but he wanted me, he wanted me so badly. Then we were parked off the Cabrillo Highway in the dark behind a beach shop, making love in the front seat. I must've been dry, because now I felt chafed, and I didn't remember getting from there to here. When I sat up, my head felt topheavy and my eyes hurt.

I pulled on my underwear, shorts, and Nick's button-down shirt Lester wore last night and I went barefoot downstairs. The tin pot of coffee was on the cool half of the stove, though it was still steaming, and I took a paper napkin and stepped out onto the porch. Lester wasn't anywhere, the sun bright on the trees and brush. I only walked as far as the woodpile before I squatted and peed, closing my eyes to all the daylight, smelling the split wood. I wanted four aspirin and a Coke, an air-conditioned movie. It was Tuesday, my day off from cleaning. Maybe Les would want to go with me, maybe even see two back to back.

I was brushing my teeth on the porch, using a cup of ice water from the cooler to rinse, when he walked up the trail from the river. He was bare-chested, his black hair wet and dripping, an empty coffee cup in one hand, his T-shirt in the other. He smiled and asked me if I slept well. I was rolling water and toothpaste foam around in my mouth, and I turned away from him to spit it over the porch railing. I wanted to be in a bathroom. I wanted a hot shower, a clean mirror, and a locked door. I didn't know how I looked when I turned back to him, but I hoped it was better than I felt. I wondered if he had a hangover like I did, but I didn't want to ask; I didn't want to draw any attention to my drinking. "I slept like a dead person. You?"

"I was too drunk to notice." He pulled on his shirt, then stepped up on the porch to hold and kiss me. He tasted like coffee, but smelled like the river, like mud and moss. "I had a great time last night," he said, but he looked kind of down when he said it, like it had happened a long time ago.

"Go for a swim?"

"Just my head."

I followed him into the house and he poured me some coffee, then refilled his cup and we sat down across from each other at the small table beneath the window, a sunbeam lying across the tabletop. Les looked outside, his face in shadow. I started to reach across the table to touch his hand but something made me stop. "You okay?"

He looked right at me. "Sometimes I feel guilty because I get paid to roam the countryside and think about things. You know how your mind can just drift off? And next thing I know I'm thinking about Carol, and how much I'd love to see her married to someone who loved her the way she loved him." He looked out the window. I wanted a cigarette, but was afraid if I got up for one he would stop talking.

"Once, outside El Granada, I drove up to a 7-Eleven right before they closed. Some boy had just pulled a Stop and Rob, but I didn't know it yet, and I was getting out of my cruiser just as he came out the front door, this real skinny Filipino kid, no older than sixteen or seventeen, holding a bunch of bills and a silver revolver pointed straight up at the sky from pushing the door open with that hand. And neither one of us moved, we just looked at each other.

"I wasn't calm, but I wasn't scared either. There was only my blood and my breath, and his too. I could feel it. Like we were the same body. Then I asked him if he wanted to talk, and he nodded his head, still holding that hogleg up in the air. I had both my hands on the top of the door where he could see them, but he seemed stuck where he was—he couldn't go back and he couldn't go forward. I could hear the cashier moving around inside the store, so I told the boy to bring his gun over if he wanted to, but he didn't have to give it to me, he didn't have to do anything he didn't want to do.

"And then he started to cry, Kathy. I don't remember leaving my patrol car but next thing I knew I was standing in front of him, and he was younger than I'd guessed—twelve or thirteen—and I was unloading his pistol and he was crying so hard I put my arm around him. His back felt so thin to me and I just held him, telling him he did the right thing. Everything would be all right. The store clerk came out yelling something, but I wasn't listening; my hands felt oily. My voice sounded strange to me. I kept saying comforting things to this boy, but it was as much for me as for him."

"Jesus, Les." I reached over to put my hand on his, but he stood and took his cup to the stove and poured himself the last of the coffee.

"And I kept thinking of my own son, of Nate, and I vowed for the hundredth time I would take such good care of him he'd never have to get that desperate. Get that turned around." Lester looked out the screen door, standing there tall and barefoot, his shirt hanging out of his jeans, his shoulders hunched slightly. There was something about him I'd never seen before, only felt, a goodness behind all the sadness in his eyes, maybe an acceptance for all we could never quite be, him included.

"I need to go home for a while today."

I nodded, but something dark and hollow opened up inside me.

"I need to explain things to Carol better. And Nate and Bethany. I should be home when they come back from school." He looked down at his hands and I was thinking how he'd just used the word "home" twice in a few seconds.

"It's okay, Lester. I'll go catch a movie or something and catch you when you get back."

"I don't deserve you."

"Yes you do." And I put on a smile, went over and kissed him, opening my mouth against his, but he cut it short and climbed up to the loft to get his shoes and all I wanted to know was this: was he telling himself he didn't deserve me so he could leave me? *Was he leaving me?* But the question was so ugly inside me I was afraid if I asked it out loud it would come to life between us with claws and fangs.

We were quiet as we walked through the woods to the cars. I was sweating, and I was sure I must smell bad. At his station wagon, Les turned to me, then both his hands were holding my face and he kissed me hard and dry, said he'd see me later, and he got into his car and I backed mine out so he could leave.

I sat on the porch in the morning shade and smoked my last cigarette. My mouth and throat felt like one long ash, and my fingers were shaking a little, though I didn't know if that was from last night's drinking, today's coffee and nicotine, or thinking now that Lester's pain about his kids was so bad he really wouldn't be coming back at all.

I drove the Bonneville to a mini-grocery gas station off the Cabrillo Highway and bought two Diet Cokes and three packs of cigarettes. It was still morning, but the sun was so bright off the white facade of the small building it hurt my brain just looking at it. I watched the sunlit cars and jeeps and vans go by, the people inside them young and cheerful-looking, and I pictured driving straight into them all. But no car was moving fast enough to do the job, to do more than just ruin the gift Frank had given me and Nick, my only asset now; no one was going fast enough to obliterate *me*. And that's what I wanted: obliteration. Decimation. Just an instant smear of me right out of all this rising and falling and nothing changing that feels like living.

My hangover had settled deep and black into me. I started to feel afraid of everything that moved: the traffic in front of me, the gas station attendant pumping gas into a jeep, a lone kite hovering so tiny above the ocean, my own hand as I raised another cigarette to my lips.

I put the car in gear and made my way onto the beach highway heading north. I turned on the radio, but a DJ was hawking a free trip to Cancún, his voice full of good cheer, and I switched him off, the air-conditioning too. I rolled down the window and let the beach wind blow into my face. I drove through Half Moon Bay for El Granada and thought of Lester's story of the Filipino boy, then I pictured him hugging his own two kids, his small son and daughter, and remorse moved through me so hot and thick my stomach felt queasy. I hadn't thought about any of this the way the kids would. I only pictured them at my house laughing and playing, eating meals I cooked for them, sleeping in Nick's old practice room. Now I imagined them crying themselves to sleep at night, and I stubbed out my cigarette and lit another. I drank from my Diet Coke, but it was just sweet empty chemicals down my throat, and I felt myself get shaky knowing that I'd been too weak to keep my situation in my own lap, and now I was letting myself have a huge part in destroying someone else's family. As I drove through Montara, heading north for Point San Pedro and Corona, I tried to do what they used to encourage in Group: ask yourself the questions in life that scare you the most. But I already knew the answer; I knew why I had gotten drunk last night, was smoking so much again, and why I was sleeping with Lester Burdon: losing my father's house had been the final shove in a long drift to the edge, and I thought about calling Connie Walsh again, just tell her to sue the county for as much as she could get. But that would take months, maybe years, and still my father's only heirloom to Frank and me would be gone and even though it was just a little place in a low-rent beach town, I refused to be the one in the family who had let it slip away.

I started driving faster and kept seeing my mother's face, a different look of hers this time, one she'd sometimes give me after Nick and I were married and rationally recovered, both working, when at a family gathering—a christening or a birthday, or Sunday dinner— I'd catch her watching me; I would just glance over and see her taking me in, her lips parted but slightly bunched, like she wasn't quite sure what to think. Had she been wrong about me? Was I actually going to turn out all right? And somehow her watching me, looking like she was holding her breath doing it, was also me watching myself. I was her and she was me, and I couldn't stand not tolerating my own company, not tolerating the very center of me.

The beach wind through the driver's window was warm and I could smell car exhaust and seaweed. I was sweating under my clothes, sweating out the beer and last night's nicotine. I wondered if Lester, in his drunkenness, had come inside me. I felt suddenly close to crying, and I didn't know if that meant I loved him or not. I didn't know. I needed badly to take a long shower.

As I drove into downtown Corona, slowly passing the one- or two-story shops, the glare of the sun off their windows making my eyes ache even with the sunglasses on, I thought about renting a motel room for the day just to recoup. But recoup for what? More waiting? More sliding over the dark edge? Instead I drove out to my Colma River residential, the divorced accountant's house, and let myself in. I showered in the downstairs bathroom, wishing my suitcase was still in the car. Maybe I should have taken all my things from the fish camp, put them back in storage, and just let Les off the hook completely.

I towel-dried my hair and walked naked down the hall into the daughter's room. Sunlight came through the sliding glass door to her small deck overlooking the river, and her bed was made. Propped against the pillows was a Cabbage Patch doll, a stuffed Garfield cat, and two teddy bears. I walked barefoot over the carpet, opened her top bureau drawer, and pulled out a pair of rolled yellow cotton panties. They were a little tight around my hips, but clean. I snapped on my bra, stepped into my loose khaki work shorts that still smelled like mosquito repellent and wood smoke, and used the blow dryer on her dresser to dry and feather my hair. Then I opened the rest of the drawers, pulled out an oversized turquoise T-shirt from Fisherman's Wharf, and put it on, telling myself I would return it clean and folded. In the mirror my face looked pale, my eyes tired. There was a purple cosmetics bag on the dresser, and I poked around inside until I found some eyeliner and blush. The blush was too pink for me, so I thumbed away as much as I could, but it still showed. It was a color cheerleaders wore, so bright and instantly cheerful their faces could sometimes look almost fluorescent. It was okay if I looked cheerful, but I didn't want to look cheap, not for the colonel's wife. Somewhere between the fish camp and here I'd decided that's who I had to talk to. If she really didn't know the situation, then I would tell her. Just drive up there, wait for her husband to leave, and talk. No threats. No men shoving their weight around. Just two women talking out our problem.

I went back to the bathroom, folded the damp towel neatly over the rack near the sink, then opened the medicine cabinet and shook four Anacins out of their bottle, tipping my head back and swallowing them dry one at a time. Outside, a car drove up nearby, the engine shutting off, and I held my breath and didn't move. The car door slammed, then I heard the door of the next house down open and shut and I let out my breath. I took one last look around the bathroom, put on my sunglasses, and left, thinking this is wrong; it's so wrong to invade someone else's home.

I IS A DAY OF BRIGHT SUN, TOO WARM FOR THE FULL SUIT AND SILK tie I wear as I drive past the large shopping malls and automobile dealerships, the restaurants and clothing boutiques of Redwood City. Since I left the lawyer's office in Corona, I have allowed myself the relief of air-conditioning, but I feel no other such relief. Over weak American coffee and for another one hundred and fifty dollars, the lawyer with the bow tie confirmed for me my suspicions of our visit from this Joe Gonzalez. He told to me it is highly unlikely any persons at the county tax office would send a police officer to threaten me. And when I informed him the man wore a gold star from the Sheriff's Department of San Mateo County, but no name badge, which I know to be required in this country, a look of concern passed over the short lawyer's face and he said to me that Corona was in the jurisdiction of that department. He telephoned them directly, but I was not surprised he discovered there was no such officer of that name. The lawyer passed to me the telephone, and a man who identified himself as a lieutenant asked if I would care to travel to Redwood City to discuss this further.

The Hall of Justice building is eight or nine floors tall, across the street from a courthouse whose roof is a very large dome of stained glass. It momentarily reminds me of a mosque in Qom, its mere sight bringing me a comfort and sense of confidence I have not otherwise been feeling. And it is a comfort being inside the building as well; the ceilings are high, the floor hard and polished, and I am directed by a court officer to the fifth floor where men in the same uniform as the so-called Mr. Gonzalez sit at desks, attending to computer keyboards or telephones. I am reminded of my old life again, my offices at Mehrabad, and I stand erect when I am greeted by the lieutenant with whom I spoke from the lawyer's office. He is dark-skinned and quite trim, with the very short hair of an American marine or army officer. He announces he is with the Internal Affairs Bureau, and he leads me to his office, where he requires a physical description and I of course mention the man's tall height and his mustache. The lieutenant asks of any particular pins or badges on the officer's blouse, and I inform him of the gold star, the badge of two pistol barrels crossed together, and when I tell to him of the gold letters FTO, he regards me quite carefully, then excuses himself from the room only to return very soon with a single sheet of black-and-white photographs of officers' faces.

"There are only eight field training officers in the whole department," the lieutenant says, though he does not smile at our good fortune. I immediately point to Mr. Gonzalez's face, which is in the second row of photos, and I take note of his name: Burdon, Lester V.

"Are you completely confident this is the officer, sir?"

"Yes. That is him. That is the man who threatened me."

The lieutenant writes something upon a pad of paper. He then asks me additional questions as to why this man, a stranger to me, would want me to leave the property, and so I explain our situation, saying as well that I do not know the reason this man is involved. Perhaps he is a friend of the previous owner? The lieutenant hands me an official complaint form, and I take nearly three-quarters of the hour to record in my neatest writing and my best English grammar what happened the evening before. The lieutenant thanks me, and as he escorts me to the elevator, he assures to me he will pursue the matter and please do not hesitate to call us should there be any more disturbance.

I drive northward upon the Bayshore Freeway. I make loose the tie at my neck and I am thinking and feeling many things. Among those law enforcement officers in that very orderly building, I felt in the manner one does when meeting a distant cousin and seeing one's own brother or sister in the face of that cousin; even if you have never before met this relative, there is the urge to embrace him simply because you share a measure of the same blood. That is how I instantly felt among all those uniformed men. And I begin to question my desire to find work only with aerospace companies. Perhaps, after selling the bungalow and while searching for the prudent investment opportunity, I might attempt finding a position with a local police department. Chera na? Why not? I am a naturalized citizen. And I would be quite content taking only an office position, answering the telephone, or perhaps watching over prisoners, taking their fingerprints or some such detail. I would be able to work amongst men of duty and discipline.

But meanwhile, I have of course several pressing concerns. In all my military years I witnessed many times what could happen to a soldier who reported the infraction of another soldier to an officer. He is no longer to be trusted; he is shunned and usually beaten by many. One man, a young air soldier named Mehran, was drowned in a toilet at Mehrabad, his killer never proven. And I have no illusions of how this man Burdon may take my reporting of him. As I drive the Buick Regal past the San Carlos airport, the sun bright upon the runways beyond the tall hurricane fence of the freeway, I consider simply selling the bungalow back to the county for what I paid, perhaps even taking a loss for the widow's walk. We would have nearly as much as we started with and all these troubles would be behind us. But then what must I do? Work upon the highway or at another convenience store or even in a police department while I watch the remains of our savings disappear? No, this I can no longer do. It is evident now that I have discovered a real estate opportunity that can only come about as the result of a bureaucratic mistake. It is unlikely, given the marketplace, that I will triple my money as surely as I can with this bungalow on Bisgrove Street. No, we must stay and sell. Sometimes in this life, only one or two real opportunities are put before us, and we must seize them, no matter the risk.

But now I must consider how I may protect myself and my family, and I grip tightly the steering wheel that I am forced to even think of these things. I have no weapons. There is only the Cossack dagger I purchased from an Azerbaijani at a summer bazaar on the Caspian Sea, and that I use as a paperweight. Perhaps I was not wise to report this Burdon. Should I have left matters as they were? Simply attempted to forget the man's threats and proceeded with selling the property? In Tehran, my driver Bahman carried a pistol and of course I had a private weapon of my own, though until the fall of our society I had no need for it, a gift given me by an American defense executive in Tel Aviv to celebrate the completion of a large sale of F-16s to the Imperial Air Force, a silver-plated .45-caliber pistol. In its handle grips was etched an American cowboy on a rearing horse, and the night we fled Tehran I kept that weapon fully loaded in the waistband of my trousers. Once we arrived in Bahrain I wanted no legal delays in our flight to Europe so I was forced to sell the pistol. But now I wished to feel its weight in my hand, the cowboy and horse against my skin. But then what, Genob Sarhang? Do I shoot this Lester V. Burdon if I am to see him again? Or do I simply point the weapon at him so that he is forced to reveal his own and we both shoot one another? No, man beehoosham, I am so very stupid; this line of thinking will bear no fruit, only destruction. And I am not my uncle from Tabriz.

Near to San Bruno I leave the highway and drive for the mall to purchase wood glue for Nadi's table. It is close to the noon hour and I have a thirst and a hunger as well, the sun hot upon my bald head as I walk through the massive parking area. I am reminded of last spring, our thirty-day fast of Ramadan, when I ate one small meal only before sunrise and then again only after nightfall. These days I was still working as a garbage soldier and when the fat radish Torez would stop the truck for lunch I would only rinse my mouth with water, then spit it out. Nothing more. The old Vietnamese Tran offered to me a portion of his rice but I quietly declined. Having been an officer for so many years, I was not accustomed to the effects of physical labor combined with Ramadan's hunger and for the first days, especially those that were warm, I would feel weak, my limbs heavy and sluggish, and if I moved too quickly, the grass and highway would spin a moment in my head. One afternoon, after watching me for ten days go without a midday meal, Torez asked me to his

truck where he offered me a large meat and cheese sandwich. I
thanked him, explaining our religion, that Ramadan comes every
year for us, the ninth month of our Muslim calendar. He nodded
quietly as if he respected this answer, but then he told to me: "Suit
yourself, Camello. But go tell Allah I have a crew to run, man." The
Panamanians and the pig Mendez said nothing to me in those days,
for I think they could see I had something they did not, a belief in
more than today's work and tonight's wine. Although in my country
I would not be considered a religous man, but simply one of the
many comforted by its ancient practices. After those first ten days,
the midday hunger and weakness disappeared, replaced by a lightness
in the body, a clarity in the head, a wide and open space in the chest.
As I worked stabbing bits of trash with my spear, shaking them into
my yellow plastic bag, I had visions of what this country might yet
offer my family: Soraya was still in the season of hastegar and I imagined her contentedly married with many children of her own. In my
mind, Esmail was a young handsome man in a finely tailored suit.
Perhaps he was a successful businessman, engineer, or doctor. Yes, a
surgeon of some sort, a savior of the sick. I saw Nadi and me living
in one of the white stucco mansions in San Francisco's Pacific
Heights. As in our previous life, we would have a driver. Our home
would be surrounded by high walls covered with vines and blooming
flowers. In my fast, all these things seemed more possible, especially
in America where—as in no other country—hard work, sacrifice,
and discipline can be rewarded one hundredfold. But then my imagination would become almost a fever in its lightness. To complete our
happiness, Pourat and his wife and children would be alive once
more, dining with us in our home, all of us; Soraya and her husband
and children, Esmail and his family, Nadi and I, all seated at a grand
sofreh upon a floor of the finest Isfahani carpets; we would drink
French champagne and eat the finest chelo kebab; we would laugh
at Pourat's jokes and riddles, his gentle teasing of the children. Nadi
and Pourat's wife would embrace each other in joy while Pourat and
I would retire to the balcony overlooking the city to smoke Cuban
cigars and speak of the old life we no longer needed.

Inside the air-conditioned mall, I sit at a white plastic table in front of the many food concessions and eat a Japanese lunch of fried beef and noodles, and I know in my heart that this is no holy vision of Pourat and me on a balcony in America; it is a lie, a dooroogh born of heat and hunger and thirst and a need for my old life that is sometimes so strong I feel I would do nearly anything to retrieve it. But I cannot, no more than Pourat can rise from the dead to extract the revolutionaries' bullets from his wife and children and then himself. And I am haunted once again with a picture of my dear friend's body hanging by its feet above the tarmac, the tails of his suit coat covering his head, blood dripping from the sleeves. I rise without finishing my meal. I walk through the corridors of the mall in search of a hardware store.

I WAS RELIEVED WHEN I DROVE UP AND DIDN'T SEE THE COLONEL'S white car in the driveway. I rang the doorbell, hoping she hadn't gone with him, wherever he went, and at the same time I was mad all over again that I was actually having to ring my own doorbell.

I could hear Middle Eastern music coming from inside the house, from behind a closed door, a man singing high to a backdrop of Arabian guitars. Sitars, I guess. I rang the bell three more times, then started knocking on the screen door. I put my hands and face to it and peered in. Their silver coffee table was on its side up against the couch, two of its legs broken off and lying next to it on the carpet. I thought of Les, his visit here last night. But the rest of the living room and kitchen looked clean and organized, the stools pushed in neatly beneath the counter. On top of it were three vases full of flowers, and part of the kitchen floor I could see had a gloss to it. "Hello? Excuse me, is anyone home?"

The music stopped and I heard one of the bedroom doors open

down the hall. Then I heard the colonel's wife's voice, her thick accent: "Please a moment wait. Excuse for me, please."

I could hear her hurry down to the bathroom, shutting the door behind her. I wanted a cigarette, but didn't want her to see me smoking, looking as needy and hungover as I felt. The aspirin had dulled my headache but left my stomach burning. I had to pee. I started to rehearse what I was going to say. I tried to remember the right way to pronounce her name, the way Les had said it, but all I could come up with is the way I remembered first hearing it from the carpenter on the roof: Barmeeny. And were they Arab? Or Iranian? And what was the difference? I decided I would try not to call her anything at all, just get to our problem. When she finally came to the door almost ten minutes later, my bladder was so full I wanted to press my knees together.

She opened the screen door smiling. She wore a different designer sweat suit this time, maroon with silver lettering in Italian stitched on the sleeve. Her short thick hair was flattened on one side of her head, like she'd been sleeping on it, and I could see she'd put some eyeliner and mascara on in a hurry. Her lined skin was pale, but her smile was warm and she apologized in that accent for "keeping me to waiting." She asked about my foot.

"Deed your friend to leave more tools?"

At first I thought she was referring to Les, but then I understood; she really didn't know what was going on at all. But the pressure between my legs was bad enough I didn't think I could start explaining everything without going to the toilet first. I told her my foot was fine and with a pathetic smile on my face asked if I could use her bathroom again. She said yes, yes, of course, holding the door open for me.

When I came back out she had set a plate of red grapes and feta cheese on the counter.

"I am apologize for this mess. I cannot offer you sofa for sitting."

"That's okay." I stood at the counter and reached for a grape, slipping it into my mouth.

"Would you to like tea?"

"No, thank you very much, Mrs. Barmeeny—I need to tell you something; I'm not a friend of the carpenter you hired. I've never even seen him before.

"My name is Kathy Nicolo." I put out my hand and the colonel's wife took it. Hers was smaller than mine, and so soft I could feel my cleaning calluses against her palm. I let go. "My father was Salvatore Nicolo. This was his house and when he died he left it to me and my brother."

She stood very still, one small hand resting on the countertop, and she shook her head once. "I do not understand." Her eyes were a little shiny and there were deep lines around her mouth.

I ate two more grapes, more for the juice than anything else, and looked into her drawn, still face. "See, the county evicted me from this house by mistake. Your husband bought it, but now the county has admitted they screwed up and they'll give it back to me, but your husband has to sell it back to them first and he won't.

"They want to give him his money back, but he wants four times what he paid, and I have no place to live. I can't afford a motel any-more. I can't. I have no place to live. Do you undestand?"

Slowly she looked away from me, pulled one of the stools out, and sat on it, her back straight, her legs crossed as ladylike as if she were wearing a dress. She rested her hands in her lap and looked right at me. "Will they make us return for our country?" Her voice sounded thicker than before, and higher, like there was phlegm in her throat.

"Who? The county?"

"A policeman came to here last evening. He told to my husband he will deport us." Her eyes began to shine, but she kept sitting straight and still. "Please, you do not for understand, they will kill us. Please, they will to *shoot* my *children*." She began to blink, then cov-ered her face with both hands and pressed her chin to her chest. At first she made no sound at all; there was just the up and down move-ment of her shoulders, but when she got her breath she let out a long moan, and I reached over and touched her knee, small as bird bones. There was a box of Kleenex on the lamp table beside their family picture and I took some, and patted her small thin back, telling her not to worry, no one was going to deport her. But she didn't seem to hear me or understand. She held her hands to her face and cried. I patted and looked around my old living room, at the family portrait, the broken silver coffee table on its side against the couch, the framed painting of the swordsmen on horseback, the black-and-white photograph of the colonel with the Shah of Iran.

She straightened up and thanked me, taking a tissue and wiping under her eyes. I sat across from her, feeling a little hopeful all of this might get worked out after all.

"No one wants to deport anybody, Mrs. Barmeeny. I was just hoping if I talked with you, you might be able to convince your husband to sell the house back to me—I mean the county."

"Please, you are very nice girl. Please—" She reached behind all the flowers on the counter and pulled out a blank writing pad and pencil. "Write for me everything. I want for to understand for discussing with my husband."

I thanked her and squeezed her hand, the one with the wet tissue in it, and I started to write everything I'd just said. At the top of the blank page was someone's Middle Eastern writing. The letters were beautiful, long curving lines and loops and ovals, some with two or three dots marked in or around them, others underlined with a long snakelike curve. It looked exotic to me, and somehow the sight of it gave me even more hope as I wrote in very plain English, in neat block print, my situation. And while I did, she told me how hard it had been for her husband since the family left Persia, that he was a very important man there. He worked his whole life to be in that position and then came the revolution of the people and all was lost. "But he is good man. He wants for his family only the best, this is all. But these things I did not know you have told to me. You are nice girl. We never want cause trouble for people."

It was hard to write and listen at the same time, but I didn't want to offend her in any way so I kept looking up every line or two to nod my head. She said she'd called her country today because it was her youngest sister's birthday, who she hadn't seen in over fourteen years when her sister was only nineteen and now she is a wife and mother with three children, nieces and nephews she has never met, only received pictures of in the mail. She got quiet then. I glanced up at her and saw she was staring at the broken table on the floor, her eyeliner a faint smear on her cheeks.

I finished writing, and handed her the pad of paper and pencil. "Thank you so much, Mrs. Barmeeny. Am I pronouncing your name correctly?"

"It is Behrani." She smiled, her dark eyes bottomless, like she'd seen everything in the world at least once. "Do you not have husband? Children?"

I could see she was sincere, the rest of her face still and expressionless, as if I was a small animal she didn't want to scare away with any sudden movement.

"I was married, but we never had kids." I glanced over at the family portrait of her and the colonel, the two children in front of them, their handsome young son, their daughter dressed in white, her hair black and shiny, her eyes like her mother's, her teeth clean and straight as she smiled into the camera. "Yours are beautiful, Mrs. Behrani."

"You could be twin of our Soraya. You look as her, you see?"

I couldn't believe she'd said that. I was probably fifteen years older than her daughter, and even at twenty or twenty-one I never had the kind of light this girl let off. And it wasn't just her physical features; there was an air about her, even in a photograph, of being something special and knowing it, one of the chosen, and at that age I was married to a welder from Charlestown, both of us snorting white snakes until I guess *we* felt chosen. But every morning the kick was gone and left us thick-tongued and stupid, not even wanting to touch each other. But Mrs. Behrani was smiling at me, and I could see she meant what she said. She asked if my family was Greek, or Armenian.

"Italian." I stood to see myself to the door. The day had turned gray, the sun gone, but Mrs. Behrani squinted her eyes and held her fingers to her forehead. She was telling me in her thick Middle Eastern accent how much she loved the Italian people: Marcello Mastroianni, Sophia *Loren*, but I was already starting to brood; I would never have what her daughter did, her clean and respectful past, her comfortable present, her promising future; I wanted to get into my

car and drive, but Mrs. Behrani was telling me how she once met
Sophia Loren at a party on vacation to Italy long ago, so I waited,
smiling and nodding my head..

SAN BRUNO WAS UNDER THE SUN, BUT THE STREETS OF CORONA ARE
in a fog from the beach, a cool mist whose presence has convinced
me to nap as soon as I return to the bungalow. I did not rest well last
evening upon the sofa, and I of course was up with the morning birds
to wake Esmail for his new newspaper route, so I felt sleep coming for
me even as I purchased necessary items at the hardware store; glue for
Nadi's table, three new property for sale signs on wooden stakes, and
a long iron wrecking bar. It is a useful tool to own and I believe because of this fact I was able to purchase it without thinking of it as a
weapon.

At the base of Bisgrove Street, I halt the auto in front of the utility post I attached my notice to last evening and I use the wrecking
bar to drive into the ground one of my new signs. I tell to myself I
must return to draw an arrow upon it, one that points up the hill towards the bungalow, but this I will do after resting. Simply the effort
of swinging the iron over my head has fatigued me further, and as I
drive up the hill I am hoping—for this moment—that my wife is still
in her room with her melancholy music and her self-pity, that Esmail
has taken the BART train to visit his skateboarding friends in Berkeley, that I may lie upon the carpet in my office to sleep until I am
rested. But Nadereh is not in her bedroom. She is outdoors, standing
upon the step speaking with a woman whose back is to the road.
The woman wears short pants and the bright blue T-shirt of a tourist,
but I recognize her red automobile parked beside the woodland and
I accelerate and swing my Buick loudly into the driveway. Both

women turn their eyes to me, their faces masks, as if I have caught them openly discussing a precious secret. I stop the car so abruptly it rocks once forwards and backwards but my feet are already upon the ground as I approach my wife and this gendeh, this whore. Nadi says loudly, *"Nakon,* Behrani, *don't."* But I have put both hands upon Kathy Nicolo, squeezing her arms, pushing her back across the lawn, her face heavy with cheap cosmetics, her lips parted to speak. She attempts to pull away, and my voice comes through my teeth: "Do you think you can frighten me? Do you think you can frighten me with that stupid *deputy?* Coming here and telling *lies?"* I shake her, the hair falling into her face. We are nearly in the street and Nadi screams behind me to leave the girl alone, *velashkon!* But I shake the woman again, squeezing her bare arms with all my strength, pushing her backward. "Who do you think I am? Tell me that. Am I stupid? Do you think I am *stupid?"*

The woman is crying quietly, as if she cannot get enough air to breathe, her brown hair across her face. I want to break her, I want to push her against her automobile. Nadi's screaming grows louder, and I hear her running into the street behind me, but I do not stop. I pull open the car door, and push the crying gendeh onto the driver's seat. She bumps the back of her head upon the roof, and just after she pulls inside her bare leg I slam shut the door and lean into the window, my face only one or two centimeters from hers. I am breathing with difficulty. "In my country, you would not be worthy to raise your eyes to me. You are nothing. *Nothing."*

Nadi begins screaming at my back, screaming in Farsi that I am a beast, leave her alone, *velashkon!* But my wife's yelling is no louder than the blood in my head. I order the whore to ignite her engine and never return. "And you tell to your friend his superior officers know everything. You tell to him that." I grasp the whore's chin and force her to view me directly. There is fear in the moisture of her eyes, and Nadi begins to hit my back with her small fists but they are no more than the flap of a bird's wings. "You tell to him that. This is our home. *Our* home."

The gendeh pulls her head away, engages the gearshift, and speeds her auto to the top of the hill. She maneuvers around, and I push

Nadi back as the woman passes closely by. She is looking directly ahead, both hands upon the steering wheel, a strand of her long hair sticking upon her face. My wife has become quiet. I hear only her breathing, and mine as well.

MY UPPER ARMS WERE BRUISED, THE BACK OF MY HEAD STUNG, AND I was so angry I started to cry, and I kept on in ragged spurts all the way through San Francisco and across the Golden Gate Bridge, through Sausalito and Marin City, past signs for Mill Valley, Corte Madera, and Larkspur. At Route 580, up in the hills, I could see the sandstone walls of San Quentin prison, just the beginning of a guard tower, and I cut east onto the Richmond–San Rafael Bridge. San Pablo Bay lay stretched out under me in the sun. There were dozens of white sails, and the glare hurt my eyes. I wiped the stolen eyeliner off my cheeks, avoided looking in the mirror, and the bridge seemed to go on for miles.

In El Cerrito I stopped at a 7-Eleven to buy a box of tissues. I wanted bottled water too but didn't see any with the soft drinks, and I didn't want to ask, so I bought an ice cream sandwich. I knew I looked bad, but the Asian woman behind the counter was nice enough not to keep her eyes on my face. On the way back to the Bonneville I passed a pay phone bolted into the side of the building and before I knew it I was calling my brother Frank collect at his car dealership in Revere. It was almost one here, four o'clock there. Frank's partner Rudy Capolupo answered, his voice always low and wheezy, like he was being forced to talk with someone stepping on his throat. He asked the operator to repeat my name twice, then he paused and accepted the charges.

"Sorry to call collect, Rudy."

"Don't worry about it, I'll take it out of Frank's wallet at lunch.

Hey, how's sunny California anyways? I might retire out there, you know. Marina Del Rey. You been down there yet?" Without waiting for my answer, he said: "Hold on, sweets, your brother will want to talk to you."

It took a while for Frank to come to the phone. My hands shook as I opened the ice cream sandwich and took a bite. But I could hardly taste it and when it got to my empty stomach it was too cold and almost hurt. A bright purple jacked-up Chevy Malibu pulled up to the 7-Eleven. Three Chicano boys were inside. The driver went into the store, but the other two, both in flannel shirts buttoned up to their necks, one in a tight hair net, gave me the look from head to toe. I wanted to ask them what they thought they were staring at. Did they want their teeth kicked down their throat? But then Frank's voice came on the line, and I turned my back to the boys and slouched over the phone.

"K? Is that you?" He sounded so much like himself, his voice deep and peppy, the Saugus accent stronger than ever, that I started crying even before I could talk. I dropped my ice cream, covered my mouth, and twisted the receiver away from my face.

"Kath?"

"Wait." I pulled out a tissue and blew my nose, then got a fresh one, wiped under my eyes, and took a deep, shaky breath. "It's me, Franky. I'm sorry."

He said it was okay, no problem, but his voice wasn't peppy anymore.

"What's wrong, K? Is everything all right? Nick all right?"

I ran my finger over a number scratched into the phone. I began to turn from side to side.

"Kath?"

"Nick's gone, Frank."

"What do you mean, 'gone'?"

"He left."

My brother was quiet a second. I pictured him standing in his office in a monogrammed dress shirt, Hugo Boss pants, Johnston & Murphy shoes, a bright pastel tie, his hand on his hip.

"When, K?" Now his voice sounded testy, and I heard everything in it: my whole life, his opinion of it, his opinion of my marriage, which he really thought was doomed from the beginning. And now I knew Nick hadn't gone back home either, or else Frank would've heard.

"A while ago."

"Did he take the Pontiac?"

"No he didn't take the *Pontiac*. Christ, is that all you *care* about, Frank? The fucking *car* you gave us?"

"Hey, calm down, it was just a question." My brother blew his breath out into the phone. I could picture him shaking his head and I wished I hadn't called.

He was quiet a few seconds, then said: "Is this why you haven't been calling Ma, K?"

His tone was gentle now, but why did he have to ask me this? "Yeah, that's why. Frank, listen. I just—" The tears came with no warning. I saw again the colonel's raging face as he pushed me across the yard, his breath bad, like meat left out in the sun, his eyes wide and brown, the whites yellowed as he spit his words at me and pushed me farther and farther away from my house, mine and Frank's. "Frank?"

"K?"

"Yeah?"

"You still, you know, dope-free?"

"Please don't talk to me like this, Frank."

"Like what?"

"Like I'm a fuckup."

"I didn't mean it that way. Lookit, just come home. The hell with Lazaro. Come back East, K."

"I can't."

"Why?"

"I have a business."

"Cleaning?"

"Yeah." I blew my nose. He was quiet again, just long enough for me to imagine him rolling his eyes to himself.

"You can do that anywhere, K. Listen, Ma and the aunts are flying out there Labor Day weekend. They want to stay at the house anyway, so why don't you let 'em help you pack? If you want, I'll even fly out with them and drive back with you. Jeannie won't mind. How's that sound? You and me driving coast-to-coast together? By the time we get back to Mass., you'll be ready to start out with a brand-new sheet." He was about to say more, but then I heard Rudy grunt from a few feet away that Frank was going to blow a sale if he didn't get back out on the floor. "Kath, I gotta go. Think about it. I'll call you later."

I wasn't even mad anymore; I didn't feel anything really, just dried up and hollow, like I'd run out of something important. "Frank?"

"Yeah?"

I was past telling him about the house, past asking for any real help from him, but I could ask him this: "You can't call me, I'm going on a trip. I planned it a long time ago and I'm having some friends watch the house while I'm gone. Could you tell Ma that? Apologize for me? Tell her if I'd known earlier, I—"

"Okay, Kath, anything to help. Look, I gotta go. Chin up, hon. Call me."

I held on to the receiver until the dial tone came and listened to it awhile before I hung up. That old dark feeling started to open up inside me, like I was in the basement of a house I couldn't escape. I knew my brother would tell Jeannie about me and Nick, that she would tell my mother and then everyone would know the truth, that Kathy Nicolo hasn't changed; two steps forward and four steps back, and I knew as soon as I heard my brother's voice I couldn't tell him about Dad's house anyway. Not Frank, always looking out for himself first, keeping his clothes clean and his hair parted straight, only at his best when your problems don't have anything to do with him at all, when he can sit back in his expensive clothes at the lunch he's buying you and give cool, practical advice, show how much he believes in you by giving you and your new husband a brand-new Bonneville to drive west.

As I walked around to my car door, the purple Malibu was backing away from the curb. One of the Chicano boys leaned his face out the window, looked at my crotch, and slowly licked his upper lip. I acted like I didn't see him, but when I got inside the Bonneville I locked the door, started the engine, and waited for them to drive on to San Pablo. Then I lit a cigarette and drove south. The day had gotten brighter, but cooler, and I could smell rusted freighter. On the Eastshore Freeway I passed the huge parking lot of the Golden Gate Fields Race Track, and there was the long span of Oakland Bay Bridge a few miles ahead, the hazy green of Yerba Buena Island at its halfway point, a gray ship there, a place Nick and I had pointed out to each other on maps when we first got here. I thought about driving south to Millbrae, just cruise around the housing complex near the mall till I found Lester's car parked in front of his family's house. But then what? Sit there and wait for his kids to come home from school? Watch Les and his wife step outside to greet them? I remembered what the colonel had said about Les, that his superior officers know everything. I wondered if I should try and contact him, warn him, but I didn't know how I could do that without somehow making things worse, having his wife answer the phone or the door if I ever found his house in the first place.

I had the slow-blood sick feeling you get with a hangover that plans to last all day, that, and hunger pains, my stomach all tight with everything. I drove to the Mission District, parked on a street lined with palm trees, and walked two blocks in the sunshine past adobe apartment buildings to the Café Amaro and Connie Walsh's office above. Gary stood behind his desk on the phone. He was wearing a black-and-white *Les Misérables* T-shirt tucked into his jeans, his belly hanging slightly over his braided belt. The conference-room door was open, and there was no one else in the waiting area. I had a feeling Connie Walsh wasn't in either. Her receptionist hung up and put his hands on his hips. "Well look who the kitty dragged in."

I didn't know if I wanted to kick a hole in the wall or curl up in a ball in my chair. I asked if Connie was here and he said no, she wasn't, she's at court. "But she's tried to get ahold of you at your motel. She needs to know if she should begin proceedings against the county for you. My God, what happened to your arms?"

I lifted my elbow and looked at my right upper arm, then my left. They were already darkening to a light shade of purple. I looked back up at Gary, at his warm green eyes, the real caring in his face.

"Look, I'm not at a motel, I can't *afford* a motel, and I don't want to sue the county, all right? I just want my fucking house back." I moved to his desk, took a pencil from a coffee mug, and started writing my PO box number on one of the pink memo pads next to his phone. "If Connie can come up with something new she can write to me. Otherwise, there's nothing else to talk about."

I walked back down the dark stairwell to the café, and I should've felt guilty about talking like that to my lawyer's secretary, but it had felt good to let go at someone, *anyone*. I stood in the café, not knowing if I wanted to eat something or not, but on the sound system was that meditative New Age music, this very steady rising and falling of computerized notes that had all the rhythm of the respirator beside my father's hospital bed just before he died.

In Millbrae, I took the exit off the Camino Real and bypassed the mall's parking lot, all those cars baking in the sun, and I cruised through the housing developments with names like Hunter's Arch, Palomino Meadows, and Eureka Fields as slowly as a cop or a child molester, hating California houses, so flat and one-story, stucco and wood, so many pink or peach. Most of them had a short driveway leading to a carport, a basketball hoop nailed just under its green fiberglass roof. Inside on the smooth-looking concrete were beach balls, and plastic bats, and dog-chewed Frisbees. As I continued driving slowly by, I tried to remember the ages of Lester's kids, but I couldn't. Some of the houses were shaded by eucalyptus trees, their thin gray bark peeling like a molting insect's. Other homes were completely exposed with small flower gardens on each side of their front doors. I passed one stucco house the color of a banana and saw a tanned blond woman in shorts and a tank top lying out in the sun in a lawn chair. Her legs glistened with baby oil and her nails were painted bright pink. There was a Toyota in the driveway, heat flashing through my stomach, but I could see it wasn't Lester's, and I kept driving, wondering more than ever now what his wife looked like, what they were saying to each other right now. Were they making love one last time, the way people sometimes did at the end? And *was* it the end? I wasn't so sure, and I was surprised at how resentful I felt. I wondered again if I should try and warn him he might be in trouble at work, but that's not why I'd be calling him, and I knew it.

I lit a cigarette and continued driving slowly down one quiet winding street to the next, looking out at all this family life from behind Nicky Lazaro's aviator sunglasses, my stomach as tight and hot as stretched rubber about to break.

I GUESS I'D planned to get through the rest of the afternoon with a double feature at the Cineplex, but once I got inside the terra-cotta-tiled mall, standing in line with other people who could afford to see a movie in the middle of a weekday—kids out of school for the summer, retired old ladies straining to read the marquee—I stepped away, shaking my head like a crazy woman, the kind you see in the city talking to the air, feeding invisible birds.

My stomach hurt. In front of the theater was a granite wishing fountain and a pool full of pocket change. On the other side was a Mexican restaurant from a chain you only see on the West Coast, and I went in and sat at a blue-tiled table at the window, heard myself order a guacamole salad and a drink, a strawberry margarita. I could've asked for a virgin, but I didn't.

My order came right away, but the sight of the avocado cream spooned over lettuce made me feel queasy and I pushed it away and drank from the margarita, which was cold and sweet. Over the restaurant's stereo speakers came a fast salsa beat behind six or seven guitars. I could already feel the tequila in the blood of my face. I ordered another, my sluggishness from last night's beer replaced by a liquid lightness, and I smoked a cigarette and sipped my cool strawberry heat. I watched people go by in the main corridor of the mall, but I wasn't really seeing them, just their movement, their endless stroll to buy things. A man caught my eye, thin and blond, holding his little girl's hand while a baby slept in a sling across his chest. They walked right by the window, the girl trailing her fingers across the glass, her young father smiling at something she was saying. But they didn't look in and I drew deep on my cigarette and put it out before all the smoke had even filled me with what I knew, that Lester would not leave his family, he would stay with his wife, stay in his own desperation to spare his kids any. This was suddenly so clear to me I wondered if I'd really known it all along; Les wasn't the kind to turn his back on what was expected of him just because he was unhappy. Every two or three years he might have a week-long fling with someone like me, a street woman he'd meet through his job, but that was as close as he'd get to chucking the whole thing. I knew this. He might not yet. But I did. He might come back tonight, but if he did, he'd be full of family pain and resolve. He'd take me out for a memorable dinner date, or maybe cook me something, then make love to me like a man taking in oxygen before he goes on a long underwater trip. He'd pack his car and in the morning be gone, only to find out at work that his time with me would cost him even more than he thought.

My waitress came, asked if my salad was all right, and I said, no, it wasn't: "It's too *green*." She was young, short and chunky with shoulder-length blond hair. And she looked like she was about to explain to me that guacamole has avocados in it which are green, but I cut her off and asked for another drink, thinking as she left with my salad that *she's* green, she's new to the world and it's going to eat her. It eats everyone. I thought I was going to cry. I refused to. With my third margarita, she brought the check, a sign, I knew, for me not to bother ordering another one. I didn't like getting the message like that. I sipped my drink, as iced and fruity as the first two, licking the rim, turning the glass till all the salt was gone, swallowing it, telling myself I wouldn't be at the fish camp when he did come. The music stopped. I could hear the tink of someone's silverware, the opening of the kitchen door. My face felt as soft as a clay doll's. I wanted one more drink, but I knew it was no use to try and get another, that mall restaurants have three-drink ceilings for their customers because they think drunk people shoplift more or don't shop enough or scare away real customers. Knowing this didn't take away what I felt as I left my child waitress a good tip and stepped out into the main mall, looking for another restaurant, feeling watched, monitored.

The place was loud with voices, the ring of cash registers, different kinds of music coming from each shop—like it's all a test to see how much you can take—teenage girls talking and giggling in twos and threes, their hair high, their nails flashing. I passed some in front of a CD shop and one of them glanced at me, then turned back to the huddle of her friends.

I stopped and stood still, my face warm. Other shoppers walked around me as I watched these girls, waited for any of them to look at me again, try and say something cute or even make a face. They were all copies of each other: they wore jeans three sizes too big, pastel Gap T-shirts tucked in loose or tight—to either show off their breasts or hide them—tacky leather pocketbooks over one shoulder, loose bracelets jangling on their wrists, their makeup too heavy. They all chewed gum, talking at once, oblivious to the thirty-six-year-old woman watching them, wanting, for a day anyway—no, for just this minute—to be them again, though I never had been in the first place. Not really. Not a girl with girlfriends. Now, twenty years later, I could be their mother. But I wasn't anyone's mother, or wife. I wasn't a real girlfriend to anybody, or a friend; I was barely a sister, and whenever I thought of myself as a daughter my body felt too small and filthy to live in.

At the far end of the mall I wandered into an upscale pizzeria, sat in the back, and ordered a glass of white wine because they sold only that and beer. The lunch rush was over and just a few tables were taken up. The ceilings were low and the walls were covered with fake antiques: mirrors set in leather ox yokes, green-glass kerosene lamps, yellowed newsprint photos of strongmen, and wood carvings of Indians. It was quiet back here, dim and cool, no music, just the sound of the busboy still clearing the table. I smoked my cigarette, drank from my wine, and pretended to study the menu. When the waiter came for my order I smiled up at him, careful not to smile too hard, and tried to say very clearly, concentrating on not mumbling my words, "I don't see anything I want. I'll have another chardonnay, please."

He took my order and menu without a word. I must've just sat there a little while because when he came back with my second glass of wine and a basket of sliced Italian bread I went to put out my last cigarette and saw it was a long ash on a filter between my fingers. I took a tight, ladylike sip of my new wine. I started to butter the bread

I knew I wouldn't eat. My head and face felt blended, one the other, this second evaporating into my skull and hair and today might as well be yesterday when I was a girl, nine or ten, and every Saturday my father would take me with him on his rounds to deliver linens to restaurants and butcher shops and nursing homes up and down old Route 1, me in the passenger seat of his brown van, him smoking a Garcia y Vega cigar, the radio tuned to a baseball game or to a station playing music from when he was younger, but to me he had always been old, a small quiet man with thick glasses and thin lips, his hands always busy, and mine too, the two of us pressing clean linens on the electric roller we had in the basement, me on a stool at the feed end of the rollers, Dad sitting at the catch end because he could fold faster and better than me and he'd taught me how to use the knee lever that would open the hot rollers so I could slide in the first tablecloth or apron or napkin, but after doing that he didn't want me to use the lever again, didn't want to have to slow down to set in each piece of linen, taught me instead to take the corners of the next piece and with my thumbs and forefingers hold it to the corners of the last piece being pulled slowly through so one rolled straight into the other and we worked "like Henry Ford," and I kept burning my fingertips as I fed one piece of linen in after the next, but he seemed so content sitting on the other end of the roller from me, quiet but maybe proud he had such a useful daughter, that I never told him about my fingers because they seemed beside the point to me, and they always felt better when he'd buy me a cold Coke at one of the restaurants after and I'd put my fingers into the ice.

My wine was almost gone. My head and body were pulsing, and I lit a cigarette, held the lighted match close to my face, studied its flame, the blue and green sulfur colors at the base as it spread down the cardboard shaft. I watched it reach my fingertips, bumping up against flesh that wouldn't burn, and I didn't feel much and dropped it smoking onto the table, saw myself dropping one in the dry shrubs around my father's house, the flames rising up to the windows. Ashes to ashes. Dust to dust. I saw my house burning to the ground, the flames eating everything inside, the Persian carpets and fancy furniture, the pictures of the bearded horsemen on the wall, the colonel and the Shah, even their family portrait, the fire so hot the glass would blacken and shatter and the beautiful daughter would curl up into a fine ash. But then I thought of Mrs. Bahroony, the weeping little Arab woman and her love of the Italian people, her ability to be at the same party as Sophia Loren; I didn't want to hurt *her*, just everything she owned. I would have to find a way to get her out of the house before I burned it, the son too. A diversion maybe. A fire in the front yard. The bands in my stomach vibrated with this thought and I felt tickled by it, ready to laugh.

Soon, I was walking through all that bright noise into Sears, down the clean wide aisles past brand-new power tools and fishing gear, lawn mowers and lounge chairs, air filters and finally gasoline cans. I seemed to watch them from a distance, like I'd just been dropped off somewhere to run an errand for someone and I forgot what it was. There was a stack of them, five-gallon and made of tin, painted bright red with yellow stripes. They were beautiful in a way, and I thought how nice it must be for other people's husbands to buy these, to fill them with gas for their lawn mowers on a Saturday morning. I thought of Lester's house at Eureka Fields, the one I never found. Did he cut it himself? Was that part of his family life? Next to the gas cans were shelves of charcoal lighter and bags of charcoal. Should I buy some for the hibachi in the trunk? But after tonight, if even then, I knew the fish camp would be a memory, and so then what would I do? Spend months parking my car in rest areas, barbecuing my supper, looking for a safe place to sleep till Connie had settled the lawsuit with the county? Months? I picked up a gas can. It was light in my hand, only a reminder of what heavy could be.

The kid behind the counter asked if I needed a funnel.

"Nope," I said, no longer caring if I sounded loaded or not. "Just a book of matches."

And he smiled, this skinny-necked nineteen-year-old, like he knew firsthand the sort of problems solutions like this required, and out in the parking lot I carried my new gas can and saw the weather had changed to one of those West Coast fogs moving in from the beach, the sky gray, the air cooler, smelling like wet metal, though the cars were dry and the trunk lid of my Bonneville was still hot from sitting in the sun. I felt it against my palm as I steadied myself to unlock it, my gas can at my feet like a loyal dog, my face feeling strange, stuck in a smile that came from deep inside me. I was having a hard time sliding the key in. Cars were coming and going throughout the parking lot. I could hear the squeak of shopping-cart wheels over asphalt, somebody's child crying far away. The trunk lock clicked, I stooped for the can, and there in my trunk next to Nick's hibachi was Lester's coiled black leather belt, the fine checks in the grip of his gun, the worn black of its holster, and it was like being eleven again, walking into my brother's room for a pencil or pen, pulling open drawers and finding a color magazine of women sucking off men, when all the tiny currents open in you and they feel like evil and opportunity all at once, temptation and salvation, the cause and the cure, touch it, pick it up, take it away with you.

And so I did.

In one fluid motion I put the gas can in and pulled the coiled leather snake out, kept it tucked under my arm as I unlocked my door, rested it on the seat beside me, what Lester left behind before we went into the truck-stop bar for our last dance, his sheriffness, his sword, like a gift he'd willed me, a piece of him to carry and remember him by. I thought of us making love on the banks of the Purisima, him pulling out of me and coming all over my stomach, hedging his bets. I thought how a man's dried come smells like dead shrimp, how I'd never even shot a gun before, just held one, a small one my first husband owned for about a month when the white snake wriggled through us and in the fluorescent light of the bathroom he had me hold it loaded, point it at my reflection in the mirror.

I drove north on the Camino Real, the King's Highway. I reached over and rested my hand on the gun, felt its steel indifference. I kept my fingers on it as I drove the two miles to San Bruno, passing ugly housing developments on each side of the freeway, their hot top lanes broken up by an occasional grove of eucalyptus trees that looked olive in the gray light of the beach fog. I pushed in the Tom Petty cassette and turned him up almost all the way, turned into a mini-mall, placing the gun and holster on the floor, locking the Bonneville and walking into a package store next to a hair salon. I bought three Bacardi nips and two Diet Cokes, a pack of spearmint gum. Back in the car, I didn't remember who had sold me these things—a man? A woman? I parked in the far corner of the lot near a row of manzanita brush, dumped half of one soda out the window, poured in two of the nips, sipped pure Caribbean heat, smoking, listening to Tom Petty on the cassette player but keeping it low, not wanting to draw any attention to myself, feeling like a cop in a parked cruiser, looking out the window at cars, people going in and out of stores. I was waiting for something to happen.

Through the brush to my right was a self-serve gas station. I started the car, took a huge drink of my Diet Rum, but the bubbles were too much and I coughed and started to gag and had to lean out the window but nothing came. I smoked two cigarettes before I noticed the music had stopped. I flipped over the tape, turned up the volume, and drove around to one of the pump islands of the gas station. I freed my gas can from the trunk and pressed the pump button promising I would pay inside and I started to fill the can, my cassette player loud through my open windows—louder than I had thought it was. Lester's gun was still on the floor where anyone could see it, but there was no one around, just a woman in the pay booth reading something, her glasses pinching the end of her nose, her chin fat, Tom Petty singing, "Break down, it's all right," his voice as high and over the edge as everything I felt, what the rational would call an enemy voice, I knew, but to me the sound of him was good company, a warm drunk hand on my back, encouragement for what I had to do, the inevitability of it even. But the woman kept looking up from whatever she was reading, watching me with her head tilted back slightly so she could see me better through her glasses, so she could purse her lips at me like my own mother, already concluding just who I was and what I was up to before I even did. The pump clicked off, gasoline foaming up out of the can at my feet, the fumes so strong it was all I could smell or taste. I leaned into the car, Petty's singing a smear of sound, and I pulled a few bills from my pocketbook, but I didn't know if it was enough and I didn't stop to count, the music so loud the cigarette butts vibrated in the ashtray and all I could smell was gas and I didn't want to leave Lester's gun exposed in the car so

I unsnapped it from its holster and slid it out, black with a square barrel, lighter than I thought it would be.

I stuffed it into my pocketbook I hardly ever carried, hooked the
strap over my shoulder, and walked under the bay to the lady in the
glass booth. I could see my reflection in the window glass, my lips
parted like I was sleeping, my face as still as a nun's before she prays.
The lady's glasses were halfway down her nose, pinching the flesh,
and she had her fingers on the short microphone in front of her, saying something, but it was just nagging static to me, nothing I could
hear over my cassette player blasting from the Bonneville, Petty
pleading *Break down, it's all right, it's all right,* the pay drawer sliding
out and me dropping in my money, my left hand still in my pocketbook, resting on the hard checkered grip of Lester's gun. The woman
unfolded and counted the bills, three dollars. She shook her head,
the drawer pushed out empty, and she sat there looking at me, waiting, her head tilted slightly, her face in a squint, her eyes narrowed
like she couldn't bear me or the noise coming from my car another
second. She shook her head again, quickly. She put her lips to the
microphone, but then I stepped back, felt myself pulling out the gun,
saw myself pointing it at her through the glass, her hands jerking up
in front of her as she sucked her lips in as if she were holding her
breath, her pinched nostrils trying to flare, her eyes filling up behind
the glasses. I watched her, surprised, I suppose, at how suddenly
things had changed between the two of us. I wanted to tell her it's all
right; it's all right. Her lips were trembling and her fingers were
straightening into a church steeple. I lowered my arm, but her eyes
weren't on me, they were on the gun, so I stuffed it into my pocketbook and walked back to my car, a pickup truck pulling into the opposite bay as I got in behind the wheel, turned the music down and
drove slowly back onto the street, my entire body as thin and light
as the fog moving in around us, my trunk lid open, my full gas can
still at the pumps.

I KNEEL UPON NEWSPAPERS APPLYING GLUE TO THE BROKEN LEGS OF Nadereh's mother's table. It has been a very tiring afternoon; I have yet to nap, or take tea, and there persists an ache in my head between my eyes and ears, a sharp pulling in my neck. After the gendeh Kathy Nicolo drove away weeping, and my wife and I were back inside the bungalow, Nadi pushed into my hand a note written by this woman who is content to rob us of our future. Nadereh stood upon the carpet, her eyes shining with anger and distrust of me, and I saw there was no keeping the truth of all this from her any longer.

"Yes," I said in Farsi, placing the woman's note upon the counter. "These are our circumstances. What of it?"

Nadereh was quiet a moment, her eyes upon me but her face unchanged, her head leaning downwards to the side as if attempting to hear again what I had said. Then in Farsi she cursed me, calling me a thief, a dog, and a man with no father. She became ugly, zesht, her eyes turning small, the flesh between them deeply creased. But my own fury had been spent forcing this Nicolo woman from our home and I felt quite fatigued, empty of any emotion of any sort. Enough of these emotions.

I moved aside the broken table and sat upon the sofa, my hands heavy and loose in my lap, and I felt quite far away as I waited for Nadereh to finish insulting me and my judgment, my capabilities, my lack of forthrightness with her. All of these things I let pass over me like training jets with no ammunition, for I could see she was close to the tears of fear that have ruled her since the fall of our society. And yes, soon enough she was weeping, exposing to me her ignorant belief we would now be deported from this country for stealing the young woman's home.

"Did she say this, Nadi?" I asked of my wife as calmly as one would a child who has just fallen and struck her chin on a stone. But she did not answer me. She continued to curse me for ever being a genob sarhang, a high officer in a position of prominence that has secured all of our names upon the death list so we can never return home. From her I have heard all these things before, ever since our escape to Bahrain and Europe and now California, and I of course should have known, on this day when my wife telephoned her sister in Tehran, that she might show me continued disrespect all over again. But for perhaps the very first time, as I sat as heavy as sand upon the sofa while she continued to be as hysterical as a drunk gypsy, I wanted no more to do with this woman. I could not bear another moment. And I allowed myself to contemplate living the remainder of my days and nights without her. I would rent a small room on a quiet street, in a quiet city, and I would live as a holy man, owning only a single mattress, a simple samovar, and a few necessary items of cloth-ing. I would rise before the sun and pray to the east. I would fast not only for the month of Ramadan, but every week as well. I would free myself of all constraints. I would become as light as dust.

But I could not listen to Nadereh very much longer; she began to call me tagohtee, selfish, and this I could not bear to hear. I stood and inquired who she thought I was working so hard for. "Me? I do noth-ing for myself, heechee, nothing."

For a very long while we argued like city cab drivers, neither giv-ing way to the other, my wife insisting the young woman was very nice.

" 'Very nice'? She has sent an armed man to threaten us, Nadereh. Sang nan doz, do not throw these silly stones." Again and again I at-tempted to explain for her I knew nothing of all this at the time of the sale, and now it is the problem of someone else, not our own. "God has given to us this bungalow, Nadi. We will have no other op-portunity to make such money." I attempted to explain the young woman Nicolo had an even greater opportunity to enrich herself be-cause an entire county had acted against her. But to this Nadi would not listen. She has always been a superstitious woman, especially when dealing with people less fortunate than ourselves; in Tehran, at the bazaars and shops, she would bring extra money, handfuls of tomans, to give to any beggar that asked, the crippled and blind, those with burned faces and missing arms or hands, the victims of SAVAK. And if there was no beggar in the crowd, she would not leave her shopping until she had found one to give our money. And it is evident to me now this Kathy Nicolo has become a beggar for Nadi, one we must somehow appease, or be cursed.

And then my wife cursed *me*, barricading herself once more in her room.

. . . .
. . . .
. . . .
. .

I DROVE WEST FOR CORONA. AT THE WIDE DRY TURNOFF FOR A HOUS-ing complex, I stopped, slammed my trunk shut, and started driving again, thinking I only had so much time before the police came look-ing for my Bonneville, for the armed woman in it. My feet and legs and chest were a flock of drunk birds and I sipped my Diet Rum and smoked and drove, obeying all the traffic lights on Hillside Boule-vard, my window down, smelling the Pacific Ocean now, the air cool and wet, the sky gray, Tom Petty turned so low he was more like a small voice in my head which felt wide open in the back, birds fly-ing in and out of me.

In downtown Corona the fog was so thick I couldn't see the water or even the sand at the beach. The one-story shops and stores stood out in the gray, and as I passed the drugstore I saw a Corona police cruiser parked around the corner, a young cop sitting inside reading something, and I felt so thin and light I thought the birds would carry me away, Lester's gun on the seat beside me; I looked straight ahead and drove past the policeman, keeping my head still, check-ing the rearview mirror, but there was no one behind me and I drove through the blinking yellow light up the hill of Bisgrove Street. I wasn't sure what I was doing or what I would do next or even how the last few minutes of this day had come to happen, but as I crested the hill I could see the colonel's white Buick in my driveway, my lawn trimmed neatly, the widow's walk drawing attention to itself with the new garden furniture on it, the large white umbrella opened to the gray sky. Where else could I go but home?

I pulled the car into the driveway behind the colonel's, turned off the engine and radio, and just sat behind the wheel. My chin kept dropping to my chest, my hair in my face, my veins an alcoholic vapor ready to burn. Nothing but tequila, wine, and rum feeding me into a lava river, a huge molten mother rolling over me, ashes to ashes, dust to dust, and the small white house in front of me didn't even look like my home; it looked so white and square and orderly, the shrubs under the windows thick and green and well trimmed. I thought again of Lester, his crooked mustache and sad, brown eyes. I wanted to kiss him again, and hold him, but it felt like needing to see my father again too and Dad was dead and his little retirement house was gone and a whimper seemed to come up and out my mouth, and I felt sorry I'd scared that woman as much as I did. I felt the black gun on the seat beside me, a sleeping snake that woke up, now a silent prankster egging me on, and I reached over and lifted it, sniffing its small black hole, but all I could smell was the gas on my fingers. Then it was back in my lap. I could see it through the hair in front of my face.

I waited, but no one came out of the house. I waited some more, and I suppose I closed my eyes once, but that was a mistake, a night ship rolling in the surf. When I opened them again there was the sound of birds from the woods across the street, a gentle conversation.

Then, as if this was an idea I just wanted to try out to see how it fit, I pressed the end of the barrel to my breastbone, my eyes closed, the ship beginning to break up, my thumb against the trigger, everything coming to a fine dark point in my head.

I HAVE WRAPPED ONE TABLE LEG IN TAPE AND BEGIN WRAPPING THE other, its glue falling in droplets to the newspaper. My fingers are sticking, and the pain in my neck now rises up through the back of my head. I know I must lie down and rest, but I must first finish securing the table leg or it will set wrongly. From Nadi's locked room comes once again the music of Googoosh, this too-sweet sugar, the music of romantics ignorant of any history but their own. But at this moment, I find it more comforting than silence, better than the marching of my thoughts that do not end, those tired directives from myself to continue with the strategy I know is best for my family.

I think of my Soraya, so zeebah, of such beauty her name is no longer Behrani but Farahsat. I feel a pinch in my heart at the memory of her shame of us, of me, of the dinner we held for her and her quiet husband and his family. My head aches. It feels squeezed as if between two stones. My knees and back are stiff and tired. I feel so very poor, so old. But I will not be misunderstood by my own blood; I must telephone Soraya and arrange a time for us to meet, to eat lunch or dinner together, father and daughter only. Perhaps we will stroll along Fisherman's Wharf with the touring people in the city, her slender arm hooked inside my own, as I tell to her, as I tell to her *what?* What do I say to my daughter? Please do not look down upon me because I no longer have a powerful position in our society? I am not to blame our society no longer exists? It is not my fault we are in America now where only money is respected? Please daughter, make an attempt to forget how we once lived, put it behind you, and do not shame us by talking of it as if we are nothing at all now without recalling what we once were? We are your mother and father. Do not forget this.

I wash my hands at Nadi's kitchen sink, splash cold water upon my face, and I know I am a liar, for these words in my head are as hollow as a crippled man's wooden leg: I do not believe them myself; this small bungalow is not even the size of our outbuilding in which Bahman parked our automobile in the capital city. Perhaps Soraya was right to belittle it with her nervous recounting of who we *really* were, who her father was. But I must rest now; I am not yet beaten. Perhaps I must lower my price to secure a buyer more quickly. If I only double my investment with a sale, that will still be one hundred thousand dollars in our pockets. Surely, in this country, that kind of seed can yield a tree.

Outdoors the day is gray and there is fog hanging in the dark trees of the woodland across the street. The front lock remains engaged, and I am not certain Esmail has carried his key with him—he never carries anything in his pockets—but I cannot leave the door free for him; I will simply have to awaken to his knocking. I leave the long wrecking iron in the corner beside the door, and I am turning for my office when I see what my eyes do not believe they are seeing: behind my Buick Regal is the red automobile of the beggar Kathy Nicolo. I did not hear her arrive. She must have done so while I was washing at the kitchen sink. She sits inside her car, her eyes closed, her head resting on the neck support of her seat, her chin tilted upward, her throat long and white. Her black hair is tangled, and some of it rests upon her cheek, and I am feeling strangely because I did not hear her arrive and because at this moment she looks so very much like my long-dead cousin Jasmeen that for a moment I do not know where I am or what is the day, or how it is I came to be here. Is she sleeping? Is she this illogical?

But I feel little as I step outside into the cool gray air, only fatigue and confusion and a deep feeling in my heart that perhaps what I see before me is a dream. The woman Kathy Nicolo has not moved, her head still rests upon the seat and her eyes are shut, but as I draw closer she begins to weep silently, turning her face from side to side, her mouth open in words that do not come. Then she grimaces, her eyes squeezing closed and her shoulders curving forward. Her body becomes loose, her shoulders fall back, and she continues to cry, shaking her head and moving her mouth as if she were attempting to persuade someone yet unseen to do something quite urgent. She appears younger to me as she weeps, with not many more years than my Soraya, and I feel a tenderness as I move closer, a momentary regret at having treated her before so roughly, for having pushed her into her auto as if she were a man. However, I must tell her firmly that she must leave. Once more she makes a face, and the feeling I am in a dream increases for I see both of her hands upon a large automatic pistol, its barrel pushed to her heart, one of her thumbs pressing against its trigger which is evidently locked by its safety mechanism. Then I feel a witness to my own hand as it reaches inside the open window and twists the weapon from her grasp. She opens her eyes. They are reddened and she blinks them as if coming out of a deep sleep, but then she regards me and the pistol and she cries openly, her hair falling across her eyes and mouth. I press the release button, remove the fully loaded magazine from its grip, then pull back the sliding mechanism for any bullet in the chamber. There is none. My hands tremble as I deposit the ammunition clip into my pants pocket, as I push the pistol into the waistband of my trousers, and open the door to help this Kathy Nicolo from her automobile. The interior smells of benzine and she of liquor and cigarette smoke. She pushes my hands away and cries more loudly, but there is little strength in her and I lead her from the car, guiding her to the door, for she is drunk, mast, and once inside, standing unsteadily in the living-room area, my arm upon her elbow, she begins to speak through her crying, her hair hanging before her face. She speaks of not caring about this house any longer, simply not caring about anything. She talks loudly, the fashion in which the very drunk do, and I wish for Nadereh to come from the music behind her closed door and witness this, see this very nice intoxicated girl who was attempting to shoot herself in front of our home. My legs have become soft and I need Nadi's help, but I am fearful to leave this Kathy Nicolo even for a moment by herself. She cries more quietly now, swaying upon her feet like a marionette. I lead her slowly into my son's room, sit her upon his bed, and lay her down, stooping to lift her bare legs upon the mattress as well. To me she turns her face, wet with her crying, and she says, "I just—can't we just—" She weeps. But soon her chin lowers and she appears to relax deeper into my son's pillow.

"Nicky?"

"Nakhreh," I answer in Farsi. Then in English: "You must sleep now. You must rest." I place Esmail's chair in front of the bed and sit. The pistol is uncomfortably tight against me and I pull it free, hold it in my hands. I smell the lubricant on its surface and I think of Tehran. Where does a young woman acquire a weapon such as this? She appears to be sleeping and I consider for a moment removing her Reebok shoes, but I do not. I watch the young woman sleep, watch her mouth open slightly as she does. Beneath her brightly colored Fisherman's Wharf T-shirt her breasts barely rise and fall, and I regard the pistol in my hands, see Jasmeen falling to the ground, her long hair untamed, her hand pressed between her breasts, her white gown growing as red as saffron.

THE WOMAN KATHY Nicolo remained sleeping throughout the afternoon and into the early evening. I at first considered to tell Nadi directly, but my wife's door was still shut to me, Googoosh singing her away from her headaches and into a melancholy sleep. And no immediate good would come from her knowing our present situation. The panic of the weak never helps the strong. I poured for myself tea from the samovar in the kitchen and sat at the counter bar with the unloaded pistol and I once again began to weigh the alternative courses of action before me.

I could of course telephone to the police and pursue criminal charges against Kathy Nicolo, charges for trespassing on my family's property with a dangerous weapon. But upon opening the telephone book to the page listing the number of the Corona police, I found I was unable to make the necessary call for it was clear to me this woman was only intent on harming herself, and in my mind I saw repeatedly her crying face as she attempted—with great ignorance of side arms—to fire a large bullet into her breast. I put another cube of sugar into my mouth, took a drink from my hot Persian tea, and listened for a time to the muffled cassette music coming from Nadi's room. Yes, it was weakly romantic, but it put me in mind of my boyhood home in Rasht, of wrestling under the sun in the dusty road with my fat cousin Kamfar, his sister Jasmeen watching us from behind the wall of stones before my father's house, only the top half of her small face exposed, her large eyes smiling. I thought of Pourat's nephew Bijan, who would speak with impunity of severing the limbs of children while I drank vodka beside him, convincing myself that my refusal to dip into the mastvakhiar with him was a sufficient moral stand for a man of my station to make. But on those evenings, I would drink enough for three men and for days afterwards would carry out my daily duties in a joyless manner, treating junior officers in a lowly fashion, and giving orders whose sole design was to show my inferiors who was truly in charge.

Three times I walked silently down the corridor to make an inspection of this Kathy Nicolo. Each time I saw she had not moved her position, but continued sleeping as still as a small child, her face turned in my direction, her eyes closed, a portion of her hair lying across her lips which were partly opened. My son's room smelled of her now, of old liquor from the mouth, and for an instant I felt disgust rise in me. But then, perhaps like a bubble of air from deep water that dissipates once it reaches the surface, I felt no more disgust, only pity for this Kathy Nicolo, pity and a newfound pull in my heart to treat her well. In my country, there is an old belief that if a bird flies into your home it is an angel who has come to guide you and you must look at its presence as a blessing from God. Once, when Soraya was still a young girl and we were spending the summer at our bungalow on the Caspian Sea, she discovered at the base of a cypress tree a small young bird whose wings had been broken and she brought it to us. Nadereh made for its wing a wooden splint and they together nursed the bird with sugar water and bits of bread and by summer's end they took it from its cage to our porch overlooking the sea. Soraya parted her fingers and the bird flew up and away into the woodlands. For two days our daughter cried, though at the end she told to us she was very happy a broken angel had come to bless our home.

I return to the kitchen and drink more tea. The bungalow has grown quiet. No more Googoosh, only the silence of two sleeping women. The gray fog outdoors has not lifted, and I turn on the kitchen's overhead light. It shines upon the silver samovar on the opposite counter, upon the clean and dry plates in Nadi's dishrack. I feel strangely content, and I am put in mind of that afternoon with the Iraqi in his shop near the Highway Department depot when we played backgammon near the window, our silence a mutual acceptance to let the blood between our two countries flow under the bridge away from us. For days afterward, working as a garbage soldier on the highway with the old Vietnamese Tran and the Panamanians, I felt a lightness and goodness in me, and even Mendez, with the long scar upon his arm and the smell of old wine in his sweat, even he could not pull hatred from me as he called me old man in his mother tongue, as he dropped his empty water cup upon the ground for Tran to retrieve.

And this feeling is within me once more. Who can say how many more desperate and drunken moments would have passed before this Kathy Nicolo found the safety mechanism and then succeeded in shooting her heart very still? Yes, pride is weak vanity, but I do feel a sense of joy at having saved life. And yes, the woman is intoxicated but nonetheless I am encouraged by her words of not caring any longer for this house. Perhaps, after waking from her sleep, after eating a fine meal prepared by Nadi, Kathy Nicolo will be willing to put that in writing, will be sufficiently able to acknowledge who her real enemy has become, and she will begin acting accordingly.

But now I must rouse Nadereh to prepare an evening meal. I must enter her darkened room with its scent of facial cream and cotton bedding, and I must sit and tell to her of the sad drunken bird I found outside our door, of the beggar angel asleep in our son's room.

PART II

IT WAS DARK NOW, AND LESTER HAD BEEN SITTING ON THE FISH camp's porch for over two hours. The fog was thick in the trees, and it made the black woods around the cabin appear to be under a milky water. He could still smell the maple he'd cut, split, and stacked, and twice he heard a car go by on the asphalt along the Purisima and he waited for the engine to gear down, for the swing of the headlights through the trees, but they didn't come, and so he waited.

He was hungry, thirsty too, but he stayed in the cane chair near the screen door and didn't move. He kept seeing Bethany's face, the way she looked this afternoon standing at the kitchen table in her school dress. She had just come home, and already she was waiting to hear from him what was happening to them, to their family, standing there bravely waiting for the words to come out of his mouth. But then the phone rang and Carol answered it, her nose stopped up. In a tired tone she said it was for him and she left the receiver on the counter and went to Bethany, turned, and walked her gently from the room. Lester watched them go through the foyer and up the stairs before he moved to the phone. It was Lieutenant Alvarez, Internal Affairs. Lester knew him, but not well, because he was IA and because he was a short and humorless ex-marine who ran six miles every morning before work, whose on-duty appearance and professional record were as spotless as the tie he wore even during the summer months when the sheriff didn't require it. Other deputies felt automatically uncomfortable around him, but this was not what Lester felt as he picked up the phone, his daughter upstairs about to break;

he felt interrupted to an almost cruel degree, and he answered as if he didn't know who was on the other end. *"What?"*

The lieutenant identified himself in that calculated emotionless tone of his, pausing to give Lester a chance to get his protocol in order, but Lester stayed quiet and Alvarez had just a trace of heat in his voice as he asked Lester to dispatch himself immediately to Redwood City for a talk. Lester let out a long breath and could feel his heart beating in it. "Can it wait till I'm back on duty, sir?"

"No, Deputy. It cannot." The lieutenant said he would be in his office and hung up directly, but Lester had no plans to drive directly to the Hall of Justice to be interrogated by that prick about what could only be his after-hours visit to the Iranian colonel. And as he hung up he considered denying everything, just lying about it all. He wasn't up to facing any more truths right now, not after a day that began early this morning with him walking into the house hungover, his hair still wet from the Purisima riverbed, Kathy's smell still on his skin. Carol had been in the kitchen pouring water into the coffeemaker at the counter, and she had kept her back to him, said in a wary voice she wasn't expecting him. Lester apologized for not calling first and he sat at his chair at the table and watched his wife wash the kids' breakfast dishes. Her frosted hair was tied and pinned in a knot at the back of her head, and she wore khaki shorts and a white sleeveless top. Her upper arms looked fleshy, always had, though that had never bothered Lester and whenever she'd complain about them, he'd tell her she was fine just the way she was. And he meant it. She was.

When the coffee was done she poured herself some and sat down, leaving Lester to get up and pour his own. He stirred milk into his cup and asked if Nate was upstairs and she said no, she'd just dropped him off at her sister's in Hillsborough. "I have to go into the city today."

Lester knew what that meant. He sat back down, and in the next few hours watched his wife become four completely different people. For the first hour or so she was detached, speaking as coolly and rationally as the lawyer she was going to Frisco to see. She sat erect in her chair, and she spoke of their nine-year marriage as a contract they were both bound to because they had children now and it had to be honored. "What is a vow after all, Lester? What is a *vow?*" He told her he couldn't answer that, he didn't know what a vow was any-more. But by late morning all her rigid composure fell away and she began screaming that he was a weak, self-serving son of a bitch and so's the fucking whore you're sleeping with! And she threw her cof-fee mug at him, but it missed and hit the wall and didn't break. He picked it up, but didn't know quite where to begin, so he said very lit-tle as she paced back and forth, yelled until she finally crumpled, cry-ing into her hands, and that one Lester could no longer harden himself to and he went to her and held her and even cried with her, but he was feeling more relieved than anything else: the truth was out. Just hold on. Just ride out the storm. Then, inexplicably, the day was half gone. Where had it gone? It was already early afternoon, time for Bethany to come home from school, and when she came walking tentatively into the house, walking almost on her toes, Lester watched Carol become the mother she was, wiping the tears from her face, she put on a smile and squatted with her arms out-stretched to hold her daughter. Lester felt a distant but great admi-ration for her then, the same kind he had had for her ever since he first saw her in an ethics course in college, when she stood and openly called the professor a fool for insinuating a secular society was in-herently more tolerant, and therefore more democratic, than a reli-gious one, her eyes bright with conviction, her back straight, all ten fingertips resting on her desk so they wouldn't shake.

And after getting off the phone with Alvarez, Lester knew he had to at least fake that sort of courage, put on a father's capable face and with conviction walk upstairs to his daughter's room and say the right words, though it wouldn't be the whole truth, not just now anyway, not today.

His wife and daughter were upstairs in Bethany's room. She was on her bed on her back looking up at the ceiling, her face even more pale now. She was holding her stuffed Peter Rabbit to her stomach with both hands and Carol was sitting on the bed beside her smooth-ing her hair away from her face. He stepped inside the room, but when the floorboards creaked beneath the rug only Carol glanced up at him, her eyes narrowed, her lips a flat line. In the quiet, his daughter turned her face to him, her eyes as open and unblinking as when she was an infant staring up at him from her crib, completely dependent, yet completely trusting of his every move. And she trusted him now, he could see it in her face, though she was being so still and quiet it was as if she thought if she didn't say a word or move too suddenly everything would be all right again, everything would go back to the way it was. And Lester stood still too, conscious only of his heart beating, of the air entering and leaving his lungs, and his daughter's gaze kept him right there, though he wasn't quite sure just where that was anymore.

Carol's voice was calm: "Say something, Lester."

Then his voice came out of him, but it wasn't his really, more an approximation of his sound, of where he'd come from, and where he was, and where he wanted desperately to be next, though it wasn't down at the department where his voice told his wife and daughter he had to go for a meeting; it was at the fish camp with Kathy Nicolo, with that deep-eyed, sweet-tasting, tough and funny woman who was now lodged so deeply inside him it had become almost physically painful to continue enduring with Carol what he didn't share with her anymore, to sleep in the same bed with her, to eat at the same table, sit on the same couch and toilet. "I've been called in to work, Bethany hon. I can't talk now, but everything's okay, sweetie. You'll see. Everything's fine."

Bethany looked from him to her mother as if she were searching for some verification of what her father had just said. Carol smiled at her, bravely, Lester thought, then she shot him an icy glance and left the room. Lester kissed his daughter on her forehead, and he could smell the clean skin of her scalp. She looked like she wanted to say something, to maybe ask him something, but he had no words for her right now, not yet. "I've got to go to work now. Don't worry about anything, honey pie, everything's fine." And he said it in such a sure and solid voice he felt close to believing it himself.

Downstairs, Carol sat at the kitchen table, her arms resting in front of her. She was looking straight at the cabinets, and he wanted to say something comforting to her too, something that might fortify her for what lay ahead, but when he walked into the room she didn't look at him, just said, "Go, Les. Please. Just go."

LESTER KNEW HE should have gotten into his Toyota and driven the twelve dutiful miles south to Redwood City and his appointment with Lieutenant Alvarez, but instead he drove west on 92 along the dry bed of the Pilarcitos River past fogged-in fields of artichoke plant and occasional patches of manzanita he could barely see, for things were exceedingly clear to him, the kind of pristine clarity you can only get in the center of something big and reckless and on a path of its own. His heart beat at a high humming echo through his head and veins, and he kept seeing Kathy Nicolo, her lean no-nonsense body, the way she'd cock her head slightly whenever she looked at him, like she wanted to believe what he said but didn't, not completely, her eyes always giving her away anyway, those small brown eyes that almost glittered with this dark hopeful light. He had never seen eyes like that in a grown person before. They made her otherwise hard features soft—the dips in her cheeks, the lines around her mouth that seemed ingrained more from a grimace than a laugh. And he wanted to be inside her, to let go in the darkest center of her.

At Half Moon Bay he had to use his headlights in the fog and he cut south on the coast highway for the Purisima River and he couldn't get there fast enough. He was driving well over the speed limit, though he could only see three or four car lengths ahead, and twice he came fast on another car's taillights and he had to swerve, but still he only slowed once he got to the fish camp's dirt turnoff road, expecting to see Kathy's red Bonneville parked beneath the pine branches, but it wasn't, and so he hurried down the trail and into the cabin. Her suitcase was still up in the loft, propped open against the windows, and he climbed back down the ladder breathing hard, cursing himself for being so needy, for having so little faith.

For the first half hour sitting on the porch, he let himself imagine where she might be and what she might be doing. Maybe she'd gone to the storage shed in San Bruno to get more of her belongings, or she could be at a grocery store buying some fresh ice for the cooler, some charcoal for the hibachi in her trunk. That's where he'd left his gun belt too, and he shook his head at his increasing lack of judgment. She was breaking the law with that in her car, and he planned to take it from her trunk as soon as she pulled up.

In the last light, he sat there waiting, watching the fog grow thicker in the trees along the trail, and he tried not to but he kept seeing Bethany's face, the way she stared up at him from the bed, like she couldn't and wouldn't move until she heard from him what was happening and when and most of all, *why?* And he understood her stillness because he felt it too. All around him, all the daily and definite parameters of his life—Carol, the department, and even Bethany and Nate—they seemed suspended just out of his field of vision, his range of hearing, even his truest *feeling*. He thought of Carol's having missed her appointment in Frisco today, picking their son up at his aunt's in Hillsborough. He imagined how she would buckle their four-year-old into his seat while he asked if Daddy was home. Lester made himself picture this, but he allowed no more feeling to go with it than necessary. He knew Carol would say something comforting, like Daddy's at work, you'll see him tomorrow. And he felt sure what he'd told Bethany would hold her over till then too, that everything *would* be all right. She'd see. Later, he would add that divorced kids do fine. Half of all your friends go visit their moms and dads and their new boyfriends and girlfriends and everybody gets along. They even have fun. Maybe that's what he would try telling her tomorrow, Nate too, but in a different way, a less complicated way. But he was getting way ahead of himself. And Kathy, too. If only she'd drive up and walk into the fogged-in darkness of the clearing.

After the first hour of waiting, Lester began to worry that she might have been in a traffic accident, or was in a store when some kid walked in with a brand-new fifty-dollar handgun he was aching to use, or else she had gone to a movie theater that began to smoke and burn. But these were deputy sheriff demons and he knew it, the Whore Twenty-four, when you never really punch out, twenty-four hours a day you look at your world like you're out on perpetual patrol, the gold still pinned to your shirt; everybody even slightly out of line you give a double take, every loudmouth in a restaurant, every jackrabbit at a traffic light, every corner full of kids bopping at nothing to do—they all get your attention. You never say anything to them because you're off-duty and they're not usually breaking any rules anyway, but you're always poised for the outlaw: on a run of errands with your son in his car seat beside you, in your day dreams and night dreams too. And in Lester's dream he was always alone, stuck in his patrol car in a vacant lot in broad daylight, every perp he'd ever arrested standing around his car waiting for him to come out: the child abusers and wife beaters; the rapists and Stop-and-Robbers and drunk drivers; the B&E artists and teenage hookers; the car thieves and arsonists; and the only murderer he ever took in for a booking, a cleancut soft-spoken man in a white starched shirt and black tie who had flagged him down on the main drag of East Palo Alto on a hot, bright Saturday afternoon, his fingers and forearms covered with the dried blood of his wife, mother, and sister-in-law. He had quietly asked Lester to take him into custody, but in Lester's dream even he was out in the crowd, staring at him in his patrol car, waiting for him. Lester's doors would be locked, but the car engine would never turn over and when he picked up the radio he got nothing but silence. He'd reach for the pump shotgun in its rack beneath the dash, but it would always be stuck there, welded there, it seemed. He'd unholster his side arm, take the safety off, pull back on the barrel to slide one into the firing chamber, but then children would appear in the crowd, the kids of all the perpetrators, even the abused kids. They'd stand beside their mothers and fathers, their faces blanched and soft-looking, expressionless, and he'd put his gun down on the seat and just wait for help to come. But it never did. Some nights the crowd would push in close to the car, pressing their faces to the glass, the children too, and Lester would try and point his gun only at the adults, but the adult faces would become children's and the children would turn into their own hard-time parents, and Lester would just start shooting. The glass would pop and explode all around him. The faces would part and tear like thin cardboard, flapping open to the daylight behind them. He'd keep squeezing the trigger, feeling the kick in his hand, smelling the burnt powder in the air. Then the gun would jam and everyone—even those he'd shot— would look at him with great disappointment, not at what he'd done, but at what he couldn't finish, like it was a true shame this was the only fight he had in him.

Once in Daly City, Lester was working the six-to-six overnight and the bars had been closed a half hour when he got a call on a disturbance a block from the scene, an all-night self-serve gas station. He was in the lot of a coffee shop walking back to his car and he dropped his full cup into a trash barrel and got into his cruiser, accelerating with only his flashers on, no sirens. Two men were in the shadows just outside the light of the pumps. One of the men was small and lay curled up on the ground covering his ears and face with his arms while the other swore in Spanish and kept kicking him in the head, neck, and back. He pushed the man over with his boot, then began kicking him in the chest and stomach. The big one looked up only briefly at the blue flash of Lester's patrol car, but he didn't stop and Lester felt sure he was going to bolt any second, but even when Lester got out of the car and identified himself as a deputy sheriff, the big Latino kept kicking and Lester felt fear move through him like a cold wind. He called in for an immediate backup and for a second he thought about waiting for another cruiser to show, but the man on the ground had dropped his hands, his head jerking and rolling with each kick, his mouth and jaw flapping open.

"Step away! *Now!*" Lester unsnapped his holster, but the Latino didn't even look up, just kept kicking, and Lester repeated his command, this time in Spanish, and now the man stopped. He was breathing hard and in the light from the pumps Lester could see the shine of sweat on his cheeks and chin. His shoulders were wide and rounded beneath a black T-shirt, and there was the ornate crawl of prison tattoos on his thick arms. The Latino smiled, kicked the unconscious man once in the head, and Lester drew his pistol, flipped off its safety, but held it at his side and ordered the man in Spanish to lie facedown on the ground. But the Latino smiled again, cocking his head back slightly like he was on to Lester's charade, and he began to walk toward him. Lester raised his pistol and aimed it at the man's chest. "Get on your knees! *Now!*" Lester's own knees felt like spun glass, and his voice had a waver in it that he knew was betraying him. The Latino stopped and Lester felt his finger slide over the sheen of oil on the trigger, his heart pulsing in his nails. The backup car pulled into the lot behind him, its blue flashers spinning across the Latino's face like a strobe. But he didn't look or seem alarmed. He smiled hard at Lester, nodding his head at him and his pointed gun like it was a small problem he would take care of in due time.

The officer behind Lester ordered the man down and Lester jumped, his finger cramping away from the trigger as the big Latino became a shadow sprinting back over his victim and into the darkness around the corner of an auto parts store. Lester gave chase, but the long sidewalk was empty, its streetlamps broken except for one thirty yards ahead, casting a dim glow on the concrete beneath it, nothing but blackness on the other side. The quiet street was to his left, closed stores and supply outlets on his right, and he knew the man was probably in one of their doorways. He imagined him crouched down low, ready to pounce; Lester stopped and didn't walk any farther. He glanced once more at the lit section of sidewalk ahead of him, then the darkness beyond, and he backed away and returned to the young Daly City police officer who was calling in an ambulance for the unconscious man. Lester said he'd lost the perp, and the young cop, who was chewing gum, looked at Lester a long moment, then shook his head. "*Shit.*"

For the rest of his patrol, Lester tried to tell himself he hadn't let a dangerous man go because he was too scared to find him. He tried to take comfort in one of the major directives of the *Field Training Manual*: Don't get in over your head. Don't be afraid to wait for backup. But the truth was, Lester often felt he was in over his head, that one day someone would see just how unfit and weak he really was and then it would be all over, the true Lester would be revealed. And in Daly City, he knew if his backup had responded a half minute later, if that big Latino had kept coming, Lester would have shot him, and probably not in the shoulder or knee either, but where his gun was aimed, at the bully's heart. Because Lester had not only feared the big man with the dark mustache like his own, he had de-

spised him, despised him because he feared him and because he was
every Chicano Lester ever had to face in Chula Vista, his father gone
to Texas, his mother working, his little brother staying inside to take
refuge in hours and hours of television. He was Pablo Muñoz, Lester's
girlfriend's brother, who was over six feet and lifted weights and had
the flattened nose and cheeks of a Mexican Indian, his eyes dark
slits in an almost handsome face, pockmarked from acne. He had
dropped out of the high school and worked as a forklift operator at
the lumberyard across from Lester's house. Lester had first seen his sister at school in late spring with four or five Chicanas in hip-hugger
jeans and halter tops, their flat brown stomachs exposed. They all
smoked cigarettes and chewed gum except for Charita, who was short
and lean as a gymnast, her long black hair falling to her waist where
Lester could see two small dimples in the brown skin above her but-
tocks. By the end of the day he'd introduced himself and by the
weekend had shared two Tall Boy Schlitzes with her in the high
weeds outside the lumberyard fence and they had kissed and touched
and she tasted salty and sweet, like a spice he couldn't name. She
called him Lezter and one Saturday afternoon she sat on his porch
steps with him on Natoma Street, the sun high, all the adobe row
houses on both sides almost too bright to look at. She held his hand
in her lap and he could feel the warmth of her skin through the
denim. He wanted to take her upstairs to his room but his mother was
home so it would have to be the lot next to the lumberyard, the
weeds they could lie down in and be seen only by birds, and he had
stood to pull her in that direction when her face changed, her mouth
open in a sudden oval, her eyes on something across the street. It was
Pablo dropping down on the other side of the chain-link fence, his
forklift's engine running on the other side as he moved swiftly
through the litter, snatching off his work gloves, his eyes on Charita
as he crossed the street without looking. He wore a faded sleeveless
T-shirt, his brown skin sunburned, the muscles of his shoulders
rounded and defined. He pushed Lester down with one hand, grabbing Charita's hair with the other, jerking her onto the sidewalk.
Charita screamed, her face covered by her hair as she held on to her
brother's arm. And Lester jumped back up and didn't remember mov-

ing down the steps. He was on the sidewalk, close enough to Pablo to do what he hoped he was going to, to punch him or grab his arm or kick him in the knees—anything—but Pablo reached over with his muscled arm, put his free hand on Lester's face, and pushed him, Lester backpedaling eight or ten feet and falling on his side. Charita wasn't screaming anymore, but crying, saying something to Pablo. Lester stood but could no longer step forward; it was like trying to move quickly through waist-deep water, Pablo Muñoz and his thick arms and shoulders, his flat face sweaty and smeared with grime as he held his tiny whimpering sister by the hair and pointed a finger at Les. "I catch her with you again I will cut your white face off and toast it, *gavacho.*" He tightened his grip on Charita's hair and she let out another scream and Lester's stomach, arms, and legs were a storm of electric nerves; he wanted to run forward but Pablo's black eyes were on him, so Lester stayed where he was, everything backing up on him, his body suddenly concrete in damp ground.

Pablo pulled Charita off the sidewalk. She tripped on the curb, one of her sandals knocking loose, her brother letting go of her hair to grab her arm, and once they were halfway down Natoma, going around the corner for the main entrance to the lumberyard fence, Charita's small dark face looked once back at Lester for a long hot-faced moment, as if she wasn't quite sure what she'd see there when she looked.

Once again Lester had felt nauseated with shame. He went back inside the house, lay on his bed, and for hours imagined an entirely different scene, him taking Pablo's hand, crushing it in his own, then punching Muñoz so hard in the face he'd be unconscious for days and wake up in mortal fear of Lester Burdon. Or he imagined himself sidestepping Pablo's arm only to grab it, jerk it behind his back, and break it. And these pictures in his head were not new. He had them for every boy he ever had to fight at Chula Vista High. Maybe because he was tall and quiet and thin he called more attention to himself than the other anglos at school. But always it was the same— "Bur*done maricón!* Bur*done maricón!*"—and Lester would try to avoid the fight as long as possible. First he would deny to himself that that was where this name-calling was really going; he would try to smile off whatever insult was coming his way, and only when he felt the push of hands on his chest would he push back, hoping that would be enough, which it never was, and he would hold up fists he had no faith in only to be knocked to the ground, where he would stay curled up waiting for a teacher or someone to break it up or for the bully to lose interest and disappear. But they rarely did. Even when you arrested them, they showed up in your sleep, determined to unmask you, and show you to be the coward you really were.

Sometimes Lester would wake Carol and tell her his dream, but this was always a mistake, because it just gave her more ammunition in her nearly seasonal attempts to get him to quit the Sheriff's Department, a job she had never quite accepted or understood him training himself for in the first place. Not only is it too dangerous, she would tell him, but "my God, you are so above those cowboy simpletons you work for. Any lamebrain with a GED can go to the academy and do what you're doing!" She'd tell him he wasn't living up to his potential, he should go back to school and get his master's in education, and if there weren't any teaching jobs in California, then she was quite willing to relocate for any job he might get.

But Carol was wrong, Lester would sometimes remind her, because he was already a teacher, a field training officer for the San Mateo County Sheriff's Department, one of eight in the entire county, and of those eight, he was the youngest, with only six and a half years on patrol before they gave him the job. They were all assigned fresh recruits from the academy at Gavilan College, and for four weeks at a time—sometimes the six-to-six day shift, sometimes the overnight—he'd sit in the passenger side of his patrol car while his young trainee drove and he would deliberately and methodically begin to unload everything he knew about being a deputy sheriff. And what *did* he know? He knew if you were taking things personally you were more dangerous. He knew that he had once put a wife abuser away illegally, and that more and more he found himself coming down harder on some arrestees than others. Not the petty criminals—the car thieves and purse snatchers, shoplifters or even drunk drivers—it was the bullies, the wife and child beaters, the suspected rapists, anyone who used his weight to crush another. He kept his record clean but he took pleasure in the arrests, in jerking a wife batterer's arm far up behind his back while he lay facedown on the floor or sidewalk. He'd squeeze the cuffs on too tight, then pull him by the wrists to his feet. If he cried out, Lester would lean close to his ear and tell him to shut up. When he put him in the patrol car he wouldn't bother to guide his head and he'd let him bump it on the way in. Sometimes they were big men, usually drunk, and Lester would fear them and squeeze the cuffs so tight they cried out. But other times he'd see a wife or child bruised or bleeding, sometimes burned or unconscious, and Lester's stomach would fill with a galvanized, almost nauseating heat, a tremor in his hands and arms as he jerked the man to his feet, sometimes running him face first into a door casing on the way out, sometimes kneeling all his weight on the man's neck as he tightened the cuffs even more.

But after these arrests, Lester's rage and adrenaline would fade back and he'd feel spent and physically weak. Then the remorse would come, remorse that with each impassioned arrest he was doing his job less and less justice, and he'd vow not to get sucked in again, to instead perform his duties the way he was trained to. But these vows would fall away like cool ashes the next time he saw the bruised and broken evidence of one more man pushing his poison onto someone smaller and weaker and Lester's heart would take over again. And then after the booking, when he was back out on patrol, drinking a soda behind the wheel, trying to fill the desert in his mouth, fear would begin to pool at the base of his stomach like a cold underground spring, fear that he was beginning to lose control and it was only a matter of time before one of these perps saw through his uniform and badge and gun, saw that Officer Burdon was an impostor, that he was one of those men who has never been in a fight and come out ahead, that all his swagger was really nothing that couldn't be stepped on like a bug.

For a few months at a time, Lester was able to control his temper. He'd keep his eyes and ears off the wounded. He'd make the arrest and slip on the cuffs comfortably, escorting the man—and sometimes a woman—to his patrol car. He'd breathe deeply through his nose, ignore the onlookers, and open the back door. But sometimes the arrestee would struggle a bit getting in, or else yell something to a friend or family member standing nearby, or swear at Lester, and he would slam the door shut, pretending not to notice if his prisoner's shoulder or leg wasn't all the way in the car yet. Again, he was letting his emotion control the situation, even the Filipino boy out on the coast; he was young and scared and it would've been impossible for Lester not to feel fatherly toward him and do the right and patient thing. But what if the boy had been a grown man? Would Lester have drawn down on him? Shot him?

And at night, lying beside Carol, he'd dream of the parking lot and all of them waiting for him. One night his own wife and children were out there too, and even figures from his childhood, Pablo Muñoz, standing there holding Charita's severed head in his hands like it was something of Lester's he'd left behind.

By the third or fourth week of training, Lester would feel he knew the young man behind the wheel fairly well. They'd been spending nine to ten hours a day, five days a week, in a car together. Most of them were gym-hardened and in their early twenties, a slight shaving rash on the throat or upper cheek. And as he and his fully armed student drove through their assigned territory, either the wide green estates of Portola Valley or past the tenements and broken blacktop playgrounds of East Palo Alto, the bodegas, the barrooms with painted-over windows, the boarded-up drugstores, Lester passed on some basic tools and practices of the shift: the proper way to write clear traffic collision and crime reports, what to do when you discover a stolen vehicle, how you go about calling in a vehicle ID over the radio and get access to the computer through the dispatcher.

But a deputy's training wasn't all filled with material from the FTO Manual. Lester made a point of asking them questions about their home life, their childhood, why they were going into law enforcement in the first place. One boy, his face still full and soft-looking, said he hadn't made it through marine boot camp in San Diego, so he decided to try this instead. It was rare for Lester to hear such a naked admission from a trainee. Usually most of them spoke in slogans, the kind of language you see on military recruiting posters on bulletin boards in community colleges: I want to make a difference. I need to make a contribution. I don't know, I feel the need to *serve*. And that was all fine, but Lester noticed that eventually, as one hour became the next, one day another, spilling into weeks, more than one trainee would begin to open up a bit about his family, the muscles in his face seeming to stiffen as he mentioned his father or mother, the one who was either gone when he was still very young, or else stayed around the house much longer than was good for anyone. They spoke in vague terms like this, hunched slightly over the wheel, looking out the windshield into the sunlight at all the civilians in cars or on foot, and once again Lester would see himself, someone who wanted not only to clean up everybody else's act, but to make the world safe again by doing so, to make it right once and for all.

LESTER WENT INSIDE the cabin, lit the Coleman gas lantern, then took it out to the clearing and set it on the ground while he gathered an armful of logs for the iron stove. It was too dark now to see the fog in the trees and the clearing anymore, but the air was still heavy with it and he could smell the ocean, that and the almost earth-yielding scent of split hardwood. It wasn't cool enough to light a fire really, but he wanted it there anyway.

The gas lantern let off a breathing hiss and gave off a white light that gave Lester no comfort at all, and as he carried an armful of wood inside, he felt a well of self-loathing that comfort was what he craved; his young daughter was at home practically holding her breath, and what he really wanted was for Kathy Nicolo to walk into this one-room cabin lit up by the flames from the stove, a sleeping bag laid out on the floor in front of it, for the two of them to undress without a word, to make love without a word, then lie there, their sweat reflecting the firelight, and just feel what they would be now, the two of them. Kathy and Lester.

He lit the balled newspaper under the kindling, then got on his hands and knees and blew the flames higher, the newspaper perforated with heat, glowing orange. And he wanted that fireball to be inside him, incinerating those black tentacles. But it wasn't fear, was it? No, it was doubt. Black doubt. And it wasn't comfort he wanted from Kathy, it was reassurance, the silent kind that can show itself in the stillness after lovemaking, the kind that lives beyond speech. He didn't want to hear from Kathy that he was doing the right thing, because honestly, she could never know that. Only *he* could know that. And he also knew this knowledge would not be complete until he held her again, right now. It was why he didn't drive straight to Alvarez's office, and it was why he didn't take his daughter for a drive or walk and tell her the truth of what was happening. Everything and everyone was stuck in time. It seemed like a month since early this morning when he'd given Kathy a distracted kiss before she backed her car up for him to leave. Where *was* she?

He squatted in front of the stove and laid in two split logs, the ash rising up, some clinging lightly to his forearm. He stepped back and watched the wood begin to burn. The fire seemed to at first diminish but then grow, blue-and-green flames flicking like snake tongues up through gaps between both logs, rising up around the smooth bark, lighting up what it would soon devour. The room felt suddenly too small, and Lester went back outside and stood on the porch, his hands in his back pockets. He thought of Alvarez probably writing up a report on his having disobeyed a direct order. That wasn't good. Men got terminated for that. But they also had sloppy jackets, a code violation here, a write-up there. Despite Lester's excessive arrests, his jacket was clean, not a coffee ring on it. And every time the Civil Service exam was announced, he'd get a memo from Captain Baldini's office suggesting he take it, move to the top seven, then complete the Civil Service Board interview for promotion to sergeant. Career enhancement, the captain called it.

But now there was the colonel incident to contend with. Only a couple of hours ago Lester could have driven into Redwood City and denied it all. His word against some rich Iranian son of a bitch who most likely wasn't even a U.S. citizen. But now, because he hadn't shown up, Lester's integrity and judgment would be called into question and so too would his innocence. Assuming that's what Alvarez wanted to confront him about in the first place. But Lester felt reasonably certain it could be nothing else. It would have been

relatively easy for the colonel to go to Redwood City and file a complaint against a Deputy Sheriff Gonzalez only to find out he did not
exist. This would have definitely piqued the curiosity of a prick like
Alvarez. He'd probably served the colonel coffee and had him go
through the department's photo ID catalog. And Lester thought
again how he should have considered all this before he ever put on
his uniform and went to Kathy's house, once again his emotion over-
ruling his better judgment.

But he didn't want to get caught up in a vortex of "should haves."
Regret was Fear's big sister, the one he believed should never be let
in the door. Lester preferred to watch Regret from the safety of an interior window, watch her standing there on the stoop beneath the
light waiting patiently, always patiently, to be let in, her long hair
prematurely gray, stiff with cold. Sometimes Regret would turn to
him and smile at him through the window, beckoning him, her teeth
straight and clean and transparent as wet ice. For years now she had
been standing at Lester's door, waiting, and sometimes she wore a
wedding gown, a constant reminder that only two or three years into
his marriage with Carol, he realized it was her conviction he had pro-
posed to, her way of looking at the world with such an angry and
compassionate eye.

He had assumed, because of her defense of organized religion in
their ethics class, that she was some kind of born-again evangelist.
But then he'd see her between classes working a political leaflet table
on one of the library patios under the sun. Her blond hair was long
then, and she usually let it hang freely past her shoulders and down
her back. She'd wear shorts, and her legs were thick and tanned and
muscular. One afternoon she'd be volunteering at the Palestinians for
Self-Rule table, on another day it would be the South African Al-
liance to End Apartheid, and on another the Coalition Against Intervention and Oppression. She was working that one alone, sitting
in the shade of a conifer eating a falafel pita sandwich when Lester
walked over and introduced himself. She nodded and said she recognized him from class, which emboldened him because it was a class
of a hundred and fifty students. He asked her what kind of intervention and oppression her coalition addressed.

"Multinational corporate intervention," she said, chewing slowly. "Like what?"

She looked him up and down, from his cowboy boots to his black Waylon Jennings road tour T-shirt. Then she drank from her bottled mineral water and pushed a pamphlet toward him. He told her he was a sociology major and had too much to read as it was, could she just give him a sentence or two? Months later, she said she was used to getting baited by Young Republicans and frat boys who would just end up cutting her off, calling her anti-American and a slut, but there was something in the way he had asked that made her talk; it was the sincerity in his voice, the lanky, slope-shouldered way he stood in front of her, his deep brown eyes empty of any judgment. And so she began to talk, and talk, unloading three history courses worth of news: the United States Marines being sent into Nicarauga in the early thirties to kill hungry peasants for United Fruit, the CIA killing the elected leader of Iran in 1953 for oil fields for the Rocke-fellers, the U.S. government supporting the fourteen murderous fam-ilies who own all the land of El Salvador. She talked and talked, her cheeks flushed red, her voice getting raspy. Lester finally sat on the ground next to the table, listening, feeling he was in the presence of someone he hadn't seen in a long, long time, someone who was as easily outraged by the unfairness of things as he was. The campus streetlamps began to come on, she began to run out of gas, and he asked her across town to an outdoor hamburger and beer stand over-looking a pink flamingo miniature golf course. They drank two and a half pitchers of beer and ate very little and they talked of their plans after school; she was going to travel to all the battle zones of the world with a camera and notebook and capture the truth of American imperialism, and Lester said he had no idea what he wanted to do, but whatever it was he wanted it to be good, he wanted to do good. And this seemed to touch something in her. She stopped talking and looked at him, her eyes slightly glazed, her lips parted as if she couldn't quite take in what she had just heard. She looked to him the way he felt, sweetly, almost sadly drunk; and they went back to her dorm room, wedged a chair beneath the knob in case Carol's roommate came home, and made love on the floor with their shirts still on.

The following spring they were married a month before commencement and three months before Bethany was born. Lester got a job with a custodial company cleaning restaurants from midnight to dawn, spending the mornings sleeping and the afternoons caring for Bethany while Carol took a photography course at the community college. Some days he'd tuck the baby into her carrier and go too, staying in the vocational guidance office to peruse graduate school manuals while Bethany slept or cried and he'd hold her and walk around the small office humming his daughter a tune, glancing at the announcements and posters on the walls. One afternoon a new one caught his eye, a huge color photograph of a young cop, barely thirty, a handsome Latino, standing between a man and woman, one hand pressed gently against the man's chest, the fingers of the cop's other hand just barely touching the woman's wrist. Her red hair was tousled and her eyes were wet from crying. The man's hands hung at his sides in loose fists, and he was looking down at the ground listening to or enduring what the cop had to say. Beneath this photo was WORLD PEACE BEGINS AT HOME, the phone number of the local police department, and a hotline number for the victims of domestic abuse. And there was something about the young cop's face— the strong jut of his jaw that seemed to keep the man in line that Lester had seen always on other men, and standing there holding his baby daughter to his chest, it felt like the time had come to finally try and take on that look himself. Soon he was at the academy, then out on patrol as a trainee, and when he became a deputy sheriff they bought the small house in the Eureka Fields complex in Millbrae. Carol got work as a part-time stringer for two local newspapers, and she covered town meetings, dog shows, and land dispute hearings. She was paid twenty-five dollars a story, and even though they weren't the kind of muckraking exposés she was still interested in, she told Lester she was content to be working at a job that challenged her, yet also gave her the time and flexibility to be a mother and a wife.

And there was the trouble; once the university life was behind them, once Carol's intellectual fires and righteous indignation had died down, Lester began to feel something wasn't quite there between the two of them, something as essential as this: that despite her loving company, her dry wit and erudite conversation, her good south-of-the-border cooking, even the warm timbre of her voice, Lester was no longer drawn to touch her, to hold her, kiss her, taste her, or smell her. And when he did, it never felt quite right. It was as if he was gearing himself to make love with a close relative, someone from his own family. It saddened and nearly disgusted him that this was all that seemed to separate him from Carol. It made him feel shallow and immature, almost scatological. Over the years, out on the street or on patrol, Lester saw women he could imagine loving, and sometimes he would take their image home with him—the bounce of one's hair, the sway of another's hips beneath her skirt, or the dark eyes of another that held the promise of something more sensual than intellectual. And while his wife and two small children were downstairs or outside, sometimes he'd lock himself in the bathroom, turn on the faucets, and like a teenage boy masturbate into the sink. And Regret grew only more insistent. She didn't just wait on his stoop any longer, she began to rap her icy knuckles against the door.

Lester began to feel as inauthentic a man as was possible, living in a marriage he no longer felt, working as a law enforcer when he'd never been able to face any man down on his own, to serve or protect anyone without the San Mateo County Sheriff's Department behind him. He began to imagine leaving Carol, just packing up and renting an apartment on the other side of town. But then he would think immediately of Bethany and Nate, their small round faces looking up at him in mute disbelief just before they cried, and cried. Also, he would be responsible for supporting two households. There would be child support, maybe even alimony, and the mortgage payments too, none of which, combined, he would ever be able to handle with his salary.

But this was not the whole story of why he stayed, and he knew it. Sometimes, while out on overnight patrol, driving down the dark

empty streets or back roads at three or four in the morning, his dispatch radio turned low, sipping a cool coffee, he knew what it was,
and he would allow himself to acknowledge that bright Saturday
morning in his boyhood in June, the used white station wagon their
father had bought for his move to Brownsville, Texas, parked in front
of their house on Natoma Street. It was the trunk and two suitcases
on top. It was the way the late-morning sun made everything almost
too bright to look at, the white wagon and its whitewall tires, his father's white button-down shirt, the way his gut always pushed his belt
buckle out, which was bright too. It was Lester's twelve-year-old
brother's T-shirt as he helped their father tie the canvas to the shining chrome rack. It was the smell of coffee and biscuits coming from
the house, the way his mother had made everyone breakfast as
though this was a normal Saturday morning. It was the way she'd
served them plates of eggs, pouring the boys juice and milk, their father coffee, all the while asking her husband sincere-sounding questions about his new job with the border patrol in Brownsville, as if
he didn't already have a job in Chula Vista, as if he was moving to
Texas for them. But mostly it was the way she stayed in the house
when it was time for their father to leave, the way he patted her
shoulder once on his way out the door, like she'd just gotten some
bad news he had nothing to do with. Lester sat on the porch steps
and he could feel the whole quiet house at his back. And his father
just stood there on the bright sidewalk, his hands on his hips, a package of Tareyton's straining against his heart pocket, and he looked at
sixteen-year-old Lester sitting on the steps like he was waiting for his
firstborn son to do the polite thing and stand and see him off. His father glanced at the house behind Lester, then looked at him again,
nodding once, as if to say, "Okay, if that's the way you want to play
it." Then he shook his youngest son's hand. Lester's brother began to
cry, and their father turned as quickly away as if it was something private he wasn't supposed to see. It was hearing the wagon's engine
start up, watching the car pull away from the curb and move past the
adobe row houses in the open sunlight for the stop sign at the corner of Las Lomas. It was seeing just the side of his crying brother's
face as he watched the car grow smaller, his thin shoulders jerking up

and down, his hands hanging loose at his sides. It was looking back at the corner and seeing no car at all. It was how hot it got that day, the way you could smell the old paint in the trim boards, the dog shit in the adjoining yard, the dry concrete of the sidewalk, the lumber from the building supply warehouse across the street.

For almost a decade with Carol, all the heat and light of that one day was enough to keep the cool regret of his own marital decision at bay. But everything changed when he walked into that little house on the hill in Corona with a suit from the civil division, Kathy Nicolo Lazaro appearing in her terry-cloth bathrobe, her toenails painted pink, her hair wild, her small dark face all incredulous but brave about the news they delivered. Lester had felt a wanting rise in him so deep and immediate his throat flushed, but still he couldn't look away from this Mrs. Lazaro as he watched her take in the bad news about her house, as he stood there in his uniform and gun belt, his desire so fierce it could almost be a noise in the room. And that changed too, his feeling there was no room to move. With his hunger for Kathy came the new belief that maybe it wasn't too late. And this feeling only grew when on a hard wide bed at the Eureka Motor Lodge she actually took him inside her, took in his hunger with a hunger of her own that was dark and slick and more heated than any day in Chula Vista. Regret seemed to slide away from his stoop, and with her absence came a picture in his head of having a place of his own, a house where his children would have their own rooms. Maybe a house on a hill in Corona. Kathy had hinted at this scenario, the fact her house had three bedrooms. Then Lester would only have to deal with child support payments and maybe half the mortgage on the house in Millbrae that wouldn't be his anymore. He could manage that. Maybe it was time he did take Captain Baldini up on one of his memos and go for his sergeant's stripes and the raise in salary that went with it. And with a sudden heat in his face Lester thought again of shirking off Alvarez; that wasn't smart. Maybe he should drive down there now and slip a note under Alvarez's door, offer his apologies and explain that circumstances beyond his control had kept him from reporting in. And that would be accurate, wouldn't it?

But that would take too long, and Kathy might show up while he was gone.

Lester went back inside the cabin and in the light from the fire in the stove he wrote her a note on the back of a grocery bag:

It's almost eight. Don't go anywhere, Kathy Nicolo. I'm off to make a call to work.

I love you.
Les

He put the bag on the table. Then, to draw her attention to it, he placed the empty wine bottle on top. He swung the fire door shut on the stove, then went out to the clearing lit by the stark light of the hissing Coleman lantern, picked it up, and walked back up the trail to his car. He hoped Kathy's Bonneville would pull into the turnoff road right then. But the road was dark and quiet, the cracked asphalt covered by a fog bed that, when he drove through it, rose swirling over his hood and windshield like spirits. He felt momentarily that he was somewhere exotic and dangerous, and he thought of the Iranian colonel, the photograph of him at a party with one of the richest sons of bitches in the world, a man with his own secret police force. The night Lester paid him a visit, the colonel had seemed to be in his walking-around clothes, but Lester had noticed how finely tailored the pants had been, the shirt too. And when Behrani spoke, his words were clear and unhurried, like a man used to being listened to. It would be hard for Alvarez to resist a slick bastard like that, Les thought, and as he drove through the fog up the coast highway, keeping his eye out for Kathy's Bonneville in the opposite lane, he wondered just how far this thing could go. Would he be charged simply with conduct unbecoming an officer? Maybe receive a letter of reprimand? Or a day's suspension without pay? Or could it get hotter than that? Would his threat to Behrani be interpreted as the extortion it was? Leave this property or else? But you needed evidence or corroborating witnesses for that kind of charge, so he was probably in the clear on that count. Still, there would be the dark spot in his file, which might very well hurt his chances with the Civil Service Board.

On the coast road in Montara, Les pulled the car into the lot of a gas station convenience store and used an outside phone to call the department in Redwood City. He left a message on Alvarez's voice mail, apologizing for missing him and saying he would be in the lieutenant's office first thing tomorrow morning. He hung up, then called the number that until this moment he had associated with home. He wanted to talk to both his children, even if it meant waking them up. Nothing too lengthy or serious, just tell them he was working and that he loved them and would see them tomorrow sometime. But on the fourth ring, the machine picked it up. He hadn't expected that. He pictured Carol probably reading a story to one or both of them, and he felt wounded at this image of her, holding herself up for the children. Then he heard her cheerful voice tell him the Burdon Family couldn't come to the phone right now, please leave your name and number or call us back. Les waited for the beep, but the silence that followed felt like a black emptiness he could not imagine speaking through to his son and daughter. He hung up, then felt like a fool because Carol would surely know it was him. A car passed on the beach road behind him and he turned quickly to its sound, but it was a black El Camino with mud-splattered wheel wells and he stood there and watched its taillights get engulfed into the fog. He could hear the surf out on the beach. He looked up the highway but saw no more headlights piercing the mist.

Something was wrong.

But then everything was wrong; he shouldn't be standing at some outdoor pay phone hoping for Kathy to drive by. And they shouldn't have to rendezvous at a place like Doug's fish camp either. Not tonight, squatting in some poker shack as if they were both on the run. Lester stood in the electric light of the pay phone and watched the fog move along the sandy surface of the parking lot. His hunger had vanished, but now he felt scattered and shaky, not quite rooted in his own feet. Nothing was rooted. Everything was suspended in midair until Kathy's presence—and then what they would do next—made it all move again. He could go inside the store for a chili dog or cup of coffee, but he knew the owner from night patrols, a big gray-bearded man who liked to talk and would never take Lester's money but seemed instead to expect conversation as payment. And usually Lester didn't mind this. The man was intelligent and genuinely warm, and speaking with him felt rarely like a waste of time. But Lester didn't want to talk. You had to look into a person's face then, let him look back into yours, and he didn't feel capable of either.

He was beginning to feel something was truly wrong. No longer demons of the Whore 24. And no longer simply the image of his daughter's face peering up at him so still from her bed. The stillness he felt was the kind a deer goes into right after the hunter's boot breaks a fallen twig; it raises its head and sniffs the air, the unlucky ones taking the moment to turn their glistening dark eyes to the trouble they smell, to the bright orange vest, the oiled bore of a large-caliber exit out of this life.

Lester got into his Toyota and pulled into the fog of the coast highway, heading north for Point San Pedro and Corona. The fog was so thick his headlights were reflected off it and he had to drive slow, and careful.

. . . .
. . . .
. .

I'M NAKED AND MY BREASTS ARE FLATTENED AGAINST A BED OF smooth black stones in shallow water on the beach. It's low tide and the small waves push me forward when they break, then pull me back, and I can feel the stones under me but instead of being cool and wet now, they're hot and dry, and I want to stand and leave, but my body is too heavy and the beach in front of me is as gray as ash and sticking out of it, in dozens of places, is Lester's black gun, the handle grip or barrel. Hundreds of them. And toys too, half buried in gray sand: old Frisbees, plastic bats and rubber balls, and a red tricycle, its wheels mostly covered. My throat is a scorched pipe to my stomach.

The waves roll me and now they're hot too, and I begin to cry and the water pulls back, dumping me into the gray sand full of guns and toys. And the waves are taking so long to come back I think they must be pulling up into one huge wall of water. I can feel the still air at my back and I dig my hands into the sand and drop my face to it and wait for the final crush of water, my whole body stiff, but nothing comes. Nothing happens. I hear birds. Seagulls. I raise my head and see my husband and Lester walking together on the gray sand. Their shirts are unbuttoned, both of them tanned, even Nick, who has lost some weight. I call his name, but my throat is so dry no sound comes. Then they see me and they both start fucking me, taking turns. Then Lester pulls out and comes onto my hip and side. And he keeps coming. And it starts to cover me, weighing me down, and doesn't stop, and now it all begins to harden and I've become a stone, a smooth white stone among all the black stones. And the air smells like spiced tea.

SOMEONE TOUCHED MY wrist and I saw the colonel's wife bending close, looking at me. Her brown eyes were a little bloodshot, and she looked at my upper arms and touched the bruise. She shook her head and said something softly to herself in her language, then she pushed my hair back out of my face and smiled. "Please, you must for drink this."

There was a tray on the chair by the bed, a clear glass of hot tea, a saucer full of sugar cubes, and a plate of sliced kiwi fruit, green with tiny black seeds in it. She sat on the side of the mattress and reached for the tea, but my stomach curled in on itself and my mouth filled with spit and I had to scoot past her to the foot of the bed and in the bathroom I threw up. Nothing but liquid. Then I heaved air twice, my ribs and throat hurting, and I rested my forehead on my arms. I still felt a little drunk. I closed my eyes but there was tilting dark. I opened them, remembered talking to Franky, getting nothing from him. And I was at the mall drinking there. And there was a woman crying in front of me. A cash register. A boy with a skinny neck. I wiped my mouth with toilet paper, then used it to clean the splatter on the rim. I sat on the lid, which was covered in thick lamb's wool, the kind rich people put on the front seat of their cars, and I wanted to press the flush handle down but I felt too weak right then to turn around and do it. The sink and mirror in front of me were so clean they were almost too bright to look at. I lowered my head and looked at the thick gray carpet on the floor. I tried to remember what this floor looked like when it used to be mine. My throat was dry as sand but I felt too shaky to drink. I remembered driving up the hill seeing the house, everything a white swirl.

The colonel's wife knocked softly on the door and I must've answered because she walked in carrying a fresh towel and a rose-colored bathrobe. She rested them on the sink, pulled the shower curtain aside, and started the bath water running. She turned and looked down at me the way mothers do with young kids who are sick, and she smoothed my hair away from my face. It felt so good and bad that my eyes filled up and I had to look down.

"Please, have bath for to relax. I'm for us cooking. Perhaps you will wish to eat."

She closed the door behind her. I stood to lock it, but I stood too quickly and the room seemed to pull me down and back. Through the door, I could hear water running in the kitchen sink, the colonel's wife speaking over it in their language. Then I heard the lower voice of the colonel and I remembered him as a blur against the gray light, unloading Lester's gun, putting it in his pants. Did I dream that? I didn't know. A black sky opened up inside me. I felt so suddenly afraid, so far away from the solid feel of a real moment in my old life that I couldn't move. I had a feeling about my chest, and I touched my fingers to my sternum. I could feel a tenderness: *the barrel of Lester's gun,* and I started to cry and I remembered the fat woman crying, me pointing the gun at her through the glass. And through the bathroom door I could hear silverware being pulled from a drawer. I could smell cooking meat, tomatoes and onions, and I thought I might throw up again, but I was too weak to get on my knees so I leaned my hands on the sink but nothing came. I looked into my reflection, saw the tear trails over the accountant's daughter's blush still smeared so pink into my cheeks, my eyes flecked with red veins, swollen underneath, my hair sticking out; I was so dirty, so deserving of everything bad that had ever come my way or ever would again. I jerked open the mirrored cabinet door. On the clean glass shelves were white boxes of Band-Aids and cold cream, tubes of antibiotic lotion, a jar of French aspirin, two small maroon boxes with Arabic or Persian writing on it, an alphabet of snakes. And on the lowest shelf, a brown plastic prescription bottle to Mrs. N. Behrani: Halcion. It was three-quarters full and my heart was beating in my fingertips, in the palm of my hands, my bowels loosening. I pressed down on the cap, turned, and pulled it off, my hands trembling, a chill up my arms and back, my nipples erect against a shirt I'd stolen from a girl, somebody's daughter, one I would never have, a son either. Family waste. My road was a circle of shit, rising up to the west only to fall back to the east, to this, to taking off all my clothes in a stranger's house, in the house of my father who was always a stranger to me, stepping naked over the carpet, running water in the sink. No more running, the tablets going down my throat like little embryos of solution. No enemy voices in my head, just a surrender to my cupped hands under the sink faucet as I drank and swallowed, seeing the cleaning calluses on my palms and wondering who will take over my clients' cleaning? This is what I thought of as I stepped into the water that was so hot goose pimples came out on my skin; I was thinking: who will keep the houses and offices clean of filth? Who will be there to take on everyone else's grit and dust and bad news? I lowered myself slowly in, my spine softening in the heat, my hands clammy on the porcelain bath. With my bare foot, I pushed the faucet knob in and shut off the water. Through the bathroom door I could hear Mr. and Mrs. Behrani speaking in that tongue that sounded older than the earth. No longer malicious voices to me. No great malice to accuse anyone of. Water dripped from the faucet into the bath and for a while I listened to each individual drop as it hit, the plimp of them. Their plimp, plimp, plimp. I began to count them. When I reached thirty-six, I started over, each drop a year getting sucked by gravity into everyone else's years, and thirty-six may as well be a hundred. I closed my eyes to a darkness that no longer moved, and I kept counting but did it from 1957 this time, '58, '59, and I hoped the colonel's wife wouldn't blame herself too badly. I hoped she'd lay me down on her brass bed in my and Nick's old room on those nice carpets—'70, '71—she'd wrap me in lamb's wool, and try to make me up as beautiful as her daughter. And they'd stand around me in the candlelight and speak in their old tongues. Mothers and daughters. Blood and breasts—'90, '91, '92—and the milk is for everyone. Please drink.

Please.

Please?

IT IS CLEAR TO ME ONCE AGAIN THAT MY NADEREH IS MOST HAPPY when called upon to serve and nurse the weak. While this Kathy Nicolo bathes herself in the washroom, I sit on a stool at the counter and watch my wife carry the steaming dishes of rice and obgoosht to the sofreh laid out upon the carpet in the living-room area. She has surrounded it with our fattest pillows from Tabriz, and she scolds me in Farsi to please remove the newspapers, glue, and mending table from the area, her voice still charged with the sense of purpose that lifted her from the darkness of her bedroom when I told her of the desperate girl under our roof. When I revealed the pistol she slapped me hard upon the shoulder and rushed to put on her robe, telling me in Farsi, "This is your fault, Behrani. You have done this."

But since that moment, she has spooned no more blame onto my plate. She is deeply occupied in her tasks, setting the mastvakhiar and bread upon the sofreh, placing a damp towel over the rice pot to keep the steam imprisoned there, and she hums a love song by Googoosh, as if there were not a pistol and fully loaded magazine upon the countertop, as if the woman inside our washroom had not actually attempted to turn it on herself in our drive earlier today. Nonetheless, Nadi's elevated mood helps my own, for she becomes quite beautiful when she is filled with the feeling she is needed, and I am of course hoping her beauty will further soften this Kathy Nicolo, that, and a traditional Persian meal and our forgiveness of what she had come here to do—well then perhaps, after all this, she and her friend Lester V. Burdon may be more willing to leave us alone, to aim their anger instead at the county tax men who took from her this home.

In my office, I carefully lay Nadi's mother's table on its face upon the floor. Kathy Nicolo is silent within the bathroom and I feel indecent to have taken note of this. I return to the kitchen and living-room area and sit at the counter. Between the steaming dishes upon the floor Nadi has placed three lighted candles in a small candelabra upon the sofreh, and she has extinguished the lamp near the sofa and the bungalow smells wonderfully of meat and saffron rice and cooked tomatoes. I have a large hunger and hope Kathy Nicolo presents herself very soon. I pick up the weapon once again. It is well maintained and smells strongly of gun oil. I pull backward on its ejection mechanism and allow it to slide back into position and the sound it makes startles Nadi and she nearly drops the warmed plates in her hands.

"*Nakon*, Massoud." She tells to me to put the weapon out of sight of the poor girl, and I apologize to my wife for frightening her, but I do not yet put away the pistol for I am thinking of Friday afternoons during the months before Ramadan, when Pourat and I would use the firing range built by the Americans at Mehrabad. We would wear headphones and smoke French cigarettes and we would fire with one hand or two, attempting to shoot holes into the black silouhettes of paper men at the far end of the gallery. Pourat was not comfortable with his weapon, a 9mm pistol such as Kathy Nicolo's, and he would jerk the trigger and miss the entire target, and his bullet would disappear into the sandbags against the concrete wall. But General Pourat did not care. He laughed at himself, even in the presence of the soldiers posted at the door, and he would give to me the weapon and I would allow him the use of my .45-caliber with the cowboy and rearing horse in its grip and Pourat would shoot even less accurately with that. But I was younger, my eyes clear, and many times I held my breath and squeezed the trigger and made a substantial number of holes in the chests and stomachs of the paper men. Later, Pourat would boast of my shooting to other officers. One year, all the spring season, he called me Duke Behrani after the American actor John Wayne, but of course Pourat's laugh was always last, for in Farsi Duke sounds very much like our word for liar.

I lay the weapon and its loaded magazine on a folded paper towel and set it against the flower pots upon the counter. Outdoors, in the twilight fog, comes the familiar metallic rolling sound of my son's skateboard wheels upon the concrete sidewalk. I begin to prepare myself for speaking with him and when he enters the home wearing only shorts and basketball shoes and a loose black T-shirt, I scold him for both underdressing and for dressing too darkly as well. In the doorway he stands as tall as a man. His black hair is matted wet upon his forehead from the fog and his own sweat, and his eyes survey the sofreh, the four plates there instead of three. Nadi is near to the sink preparing the samovar for later and she calls out in Farsi for Esmail to take off his shoes and then come into the kitchen for washing. She regards me, her hands upon the samovar lid, and she motions with her head for me to commence explaining. Esmail removes his shoes, asks me if the automobile in the driveway does not belong to that woman, Bawbaw-jahn? Again I am faced with the moment of not knowing how much of our situation to share with my son. But then I tell to myself it is his situation as well; the woman Kathy Nicolo has slept in *his* bed. I ask my tall handsome son of fourteen years to the counter where I show him the unloaded weapon and tell him everything.

Esmail's face looks as it did when he was a small boy, before he had his own television, computer, and video games, when he was still interested in stories of people, of hearing me talk of soldiers and their triumphs or failures, hearing his mother or older sister speak with pity of crippled beggars in the marketplace. His eyes would grow larger, more round, and a bit moist with a curiosity so sharp it became nearly fear as well. He appears this way now, and his eyes linger on the weapon as I speak. Twice he turns and looks down the corridor to the closed bathroom door.

Nadereh approaches him, wiping the samovar lid with a dry cloth. In Farsi she says that the woman is not well. "You must be a gentle-man, joon-am. Very kind. Very polite. Very quiet." She asks him to quickly retrieve long pants, a shirt, and socks from his room and he may dress in her bedroom and wash at the kitchen sink. Our son's eyes have changed now. They shine with the joy of adventure, and soon he is dressed and clean and sitting upon the floor at the sofreh, the light from the candles in his eyes. I sit there as well, giving to him permission to eat bread, perhaps a toropcheh, a radish. The covered dishes are cooling, the candle sticks burning shorter, and soon the scent of the samovar's tea will fill the room, so I tell to my wife to please inform Kathy Nicolo of her waiting meal.

Nadi disappears into the hallway, knocks upon the bathroom door. "Please, hello? Your food is to be eating soon. Hello?"

My son and I smile at one another over Nadi's English. We eat bread and listen to her knock again. But there is only silence. Too much silence. And it is in this silence my heart quickens and I stand. I hear Nadi turn the knob and open the door and I am moving down the darkened corridor in my socks, a prowler against my own knowl-edge of what is to come: I should have taken more precautions with this woman. I curse myself, and I am not surprised when my wife screams and I enter the bathroom and see in the sink the empty pharmaceutical bottle, Kathy Nicolo lying nude in the clear water, her face as white and still as if she were in the deepest of sleeps. Nadi cries out in Farsi that we must hurry, we must make her lose her stomach! I avert my eyes from the woman's breasts only to see the darkness between her legs. My face becomes very warm, my limbs clumsy. Nadi pulls on her wet arms and Kathy Nicolo opens her eyes, but they are narrow and quite dark, as if she were blind or seeing us only in a dream. Nadereh appears startled, but she regains herself and without turning around orders me in Farsi to leave the room imme-diately.

I obey. Esmail is standing there as well and I know he has seen the naked woman but I say nothing of this.

"What *happened*, Bawbaw?"

I tell to him to return to the sofreh and eat his dinner. My son opens his mouth to speak once more but I shake my head and point my arm to the living-room area. He does nearly as I instruct, except he does not eat at the sofreh. He fills his bowl with rice and ob-goosht and sits at the counter bar where he has a view of the corridor and me and the bathroom's closed door. I stand there listening, but the sound of my own heart fills my ears. I turn the knob and open the door a fraction. My wife speaks softly, half in English, half in Farsi, and the woman Kathy Nicolo speaks as well but I cannot understand her words, for they are in the high bewildered tone of a child.

"Yes, good," Nadi says. "Een bosheh. Beeah. Very good."

There is the sloshing of water, the rustle of a towel, and Kathy Nicolo's voice telling to my wife she is very beautiful, but the words are thick and her statement sounds more to me as a question would. Nadereh thanks her and tells to Kathy Nicolo that she too is beautiful. Khelee zeebah. Then Nadi says, "Bee-ah injah. Come to here, please." And I hear only silence. Then Nadereh speaks again: "Yes, your mouth to open. Khelee khobe, very good." Her voice is near the door and I am certain the two women are upon their knees at the toilet. Kathy Nicolo asks a question but once again I cannot understand the words. They are merged one over the other. She begins to cough and retch and there is a contracted silence, then her vomit hitting the toilet water.

I return to the living-room area, but the smells of obgoosht and saffron rice no longer attract me. I sit beside my son at the counter, my heart a presence in my hands, and tell to him to finish eating. He fills his spoon with rice. "Bawbaw-jahn?"

"Yes?"

"She took Maman's pills, huh?"

"Yes."

Esmail eats his rice and drinks from his glass of cola. He is excited by all this and I can see he is attempting not to allow this to show upon his face. Perhaps I should telephone an ambulance, but what can they do my Nadi is not already doing? And with them may come policemen as well, more trouble, though we have done nothing wrong. I pull the weapon to me once more, rub my fingers across its black plastic grip.

"Becaw uh thouth?"

"Chew your food before you speak, son. I did not understand."

Esmail swallows, wiping his face with a napkin. "I said, is it because of the house, Bawbaw? Is that why she keeps trying to kill herself?"

There is a grain of rice on my son's chin. His eyes look directly into my own. I brush the rice from his face and tell to him the truth: "Man nehmeedoonam. I do not know."

Esmail looks down the corridor to the closed washroom door, then he regards the food upon his plate, the stewed tomatoes and meat, their juices soiling the white rice. "I feel sorry for her. We should have moved, Bawbaw-jahn."

I take a deep breath, but my patience is not tested. I am simply very tired, tired of all this turbulence in our life. I want peace. I want peace and silence and no more loud emotion. Esmail does not eat. It is as if he is waiting for my response.

"Beekhore," I tell to him. "Eat." And I leave the counter bar and return to the washroom door to see if Nadi has finished saving this young woman's life, has perhaps even caught it in her own two hands.

IN CORONA THE FOG WAS SO THICK THE STREETLAMPS ABOVE THE sidewalk appeared only as dim approximations of light, and as Lester drove slowly by the beach shops and boutiques on both sides of him, he could only just begin to make out the square glow of their windows. In the ten blanketed miles from Montara only two cars had passed him going in the opposite direction, and one had the heavy

axle rumble of a half-ton truck, the other the high-rpm whine of a
small foreign car. But no Bonneville. He kept picturing Kathy at the
storage shed in San Bruno, all of her possessions there. Maybe she'd
loaded more things into her car and then was too spooked by the fog
to drive. There was no phone at the camp for her to call. She might
be at Carl Jr.'s a mile down the road waiting for the air to clear, or she
might have gone inside the truck-stop bar. Lester's stomach grew hot
at this image of Kathy, sitting alone in that dark place full of inde-
pendent truckers coming off days on the road alone, men who wore
their loneliness on their shirtsleeves like a badge in need of a polish.
And despite himself, Lester began to imagine one of the younger
ones—maybe a lanky kid from San Diego or Phoenix—buying her a
drink, or more, asking her for a dance. And he felt almost queasy at
this, like a high school kid desperate over his first crush. He was
ashamed of feeling this way, and he knew then he wasn't completely
sure he trusted Kathy, did he? Under the right circumstances, would
she give herself to someone else as completely and quickly as she had
to him? But again, he felt ashamed of himself. Right now everything
was floating completely out of proportion. Nothing felt grounded or
real. There was no proportion at all.

He would drive to San Bruno and look for Kathy there. It was
practically their entire geographical frame of reference. If she wasn't
at the storage shed or the truck-stop bar or the El Rancho Motel,
then he would try Carl Jr.'s on the other side of the freeway. And if
that didn't pan out he'd drive south to Millbrae to the Cineplex,
where she could possibly be at the movies. Ahead of him in the fog,
Corona's main street ended at the base of the hills and the intersection for the turn to Hillside Boulevard and San Bruno. The blinking
yellow traffic light above was so obscured it looked to Lester more
like a silent pulse. Kathy would not be at her stolen house up in the
hills but the colonel would, and there was no crime in cruising slowly
by; he was off-duty and out of uniform.

Lester downshifted and drove straight through the intersection to
Bisgrove Street. The fog thinned slightly as he acclerated up the hill
past the partially lighted shapes of houses on his left, the dark woods
on his right. His blood seemed to be moving faster, his senses height-

ened. He rolled his window down and could smell the ocean, the faint scent of something else in the salt water, his fingers after being with Charita, both of them fourteen against the sun-dry fence behind the lumberyard, the way she let him put his hand down her jeans into her underpants, and Lester had only heard of the hole there, never even seen a picture, and he kept rubbing the coarse hair over her pubic bone, waiting for it to open up into what was supposed to be there. They were kissing and his erection was bent inside his pants and she kept arching her back till finally his fingers slipped lower and inside the warm, wet answer to his own question. And there, near the top of the hill, in the light from the floodlamp over the front door, was Kathy's red Bonneville parked behind the colonel's white Buick Regal as if it had always been there. The colonel's light cast out over the small yard and made the low mist covering the ground appear almost like snow.

Lester pulled the car over onto the soft shoulder against the trees. For a moment he didn't move, just sat there and looked at the house, his confusion so stark he didn't feel relieved so much as he did hurt that Kathy had left him out of this, whatever this was, as if it were a party of close friends to which he hadn't been invited. Through the front window came the light from the kitchen, and Lester saw what looked like a teenage boy sitting at the counter eating. Low on the floor in the front room were candle flames Lester could see just the tops of, but no Kathy, nor colonel, nor his wife.

Lester was out of the car and across the road before he was even aware of his own movement. He ran bent over toward the relative darkness of the driveway and Kathy's Bonneville. He cupped his hands to the glass of the passenger's window and looked inside, though he had no idea what he was searching for, maybe more proof this was really Kathy's car, and of course it was. In the shadowed light that lay across the front seat he could see her worn canvas pocketbook. It was open and her wallet was open too, a five-dollar bill pulled halfway out like she had taken others in a hurry. And there was something on the floor of the passenger seat, something dark: it was his gun belt, half unrolled, the holster facing up, empty. A low tremor turned on inside him, and Lester glanced back at the house, then opened the passenger door. He smelled gasoline, the interior light coming on, the ignition buzzer too, so he closed the door quietly, pushing against it until it clicked shut, and he crouched low against the car, his heart beating in the cheeks of his face, his legs suddenly too light to hold him. *Could she have gone in there with his gun?* He heard voices coming from around the corner of the house and at first he thought they were outside and he was preparing himself to bolt right to them or away. But they were a bit muffled, more the sounds you hear from an open window, and he stepped onto the grass off the driveway and followed the voices to a light coming from a shower stall window eight feet above the ground. Lester kept his back to the clapboards. He could hear the colonel's voice, his and a woman's, both of them speaking Persian in some kind of heated exchange, though Lester couldn't be sure it was heated because all Middle Eastern conversations sounded that way to him, like something very important was always at stake. But where was Kathy's voice? Where was *she*?

Then their talking stopped and Lester heard a soft moan. The colonel's wife began speaking shrilly again but Lester was already running to the rear door of the house. There were tall hedges around the backyard and he shouldered himself between them, the branches scratching his nose and cheek, and he stepped up onto the concrete slab and peered inside the kitchen. He could hear his heart beating in his breath. The boy stood at the end of the counter watching whatever was happening down the hall and Lester could see a small section of the sofa in the candlelit living room, but his eyes were drawn to the flowers on the counter behind the boy, three pots of marigolds, ferns, white and red roses, others he couldn't name, and there was his service pistol, lying flat on a napkin next to one of the green-foil-covered pots. On a *napkin*. Like it had just been *cleaned*. Lester's confusion was black airless space. He could hardly breathe and he had to *move*. He gripped the doorknob and gave it a slow turn, but it was locked. He could step back and put his fist through the glass but by the time he got his hand around the knob the colonel or the boy or who knows who else could have his own pistol trained on him. More movement came from inside the house, and Lester

could hear the colonel and his wife arguing. The boy was still looking down the corridor, his long arms at his side, his mouth opened
slightly. Then Lester heard a muffled thump come from down the hall
and he stepped back and kicked in three window panes, the broken
glass and splintered wood skittering across the clean linoleum floor
of Kathy's kitchen, the boy jumping back so far he lost his balance
and knocked over the short lamp near the couch. Lester got his hand
around the inside knob, his fingers fumbling with the lock mechanism as he kept his eyes on the boy, who seemed momentarily pinned
against the lamp table. The knob turned, the boy straightened and
disappeared down the hallway, and Lester was in the kitchen, moving quickly through the smells of cooked meat and brewed tea and
old flowers. He slipped on a glass shard and fell forward into the
Formica countertop, grabbing his pistol and still-loaded magazine,
pushing the clip into the handle, then pulling back once on the slide
and sending one into the firing chamber, thumbing the safety off.

The colonel's wife was screaming something in Persian, the boy
too, and Lester turned to see them both standing in the darkened
hallway over Kathy, who was on her back in a robe which was parted
to the sash at her waist, one of her breasts exposed. Her eyes were half
open, looking up at the ceiling with either great interest or none at
all. Then the colonel stepped from the light of a side room holding
an iron wrecking bar, but with one hand, like he was simply trans-
porting it someplace else, and his wife was screaming even louder,
crying now, and the boy stood perfectly still and so did the colonel
because Lester had him centered in the tip and notch of his gun-
sights. He was yelling at the colonel to *drop it, drop it!* Though he
meant for him to only put it down because if he dropped it it might
hit Kathy, but he couldn't yell anything else. His heart was beating
in the grip of his hands, in the squeeze of all his fingers except one,
and it was a pained effort to keep that one from pulsing against the
trigger, pulsing until there was no more screaming, no one standing
over Kathy half naked on the floor, even the woman, and the young
handsome boy.

AGAINST THE WALL I REST THE IRON WRECKING BAR AND I LONG FOR putting my body between Lester V. Burdon's raised weapon and my wife and son, but I cannot do this without stepping over the nearly conscious body of Kathy Nicolo, and this I am quite certain the tall yelling deputy sheriff will not allow. My blood is thick and cold within me and I feel my arms have become mere threads. Lester V. Burdon keeps his weapon aimed directly at my heart and he is yelling many things at once. Questions and orders. What did you do to her? Step back! Pick her up! Shut up! This last to Nadi who is screaming uncontrollably, and he points the gun and she falls silent, clutching our son who has become completely still and quiet, watching the man and the gun as if from a great distance.

I attempt to begin explaining things, but I can only open my hands and say, "Listen. Listen." And he aims the weapon back at me, the flowers behind him appearing like evil wings. But then Kathy Nicolo makes a sound and Lester V. Burdon stops his yelling and watches as the girl moves her head once from side to side, her heavy eyes focused on the air above her. "Les? Don't, don't."

"*Move!*" Mr. Burdon waves his weapon at us, and my wife and son and I retreat to the rear of the corridor as he kneels at the woman's side, his back against the wall, his weapon resting on the carpet in his hand. He pulls the robe securely over her chest, then he places his hand upon her forehead, speaks her name, asks if she is all right. In the light from the bathroom, the color of the young woman's face is not good, like green olives immersed too long in water. She turns her head to Lester V. Burdon, and her strangely small and dark eyes do not appear to see him. She smiles weakly. "You're here."

"Yes, I'm here. I'm here." He pushes away the hair from around her face. I feel the time has come to speak but I must choose my words carefully. It is clear he loves this Kathy Nicolo; I must not have any disrespect in my voice. She has closed her eyes, a tentative smile upon her lips, and Lester V. Burdon regards us immediately. "What did you do to her?"

I take in a breath to speak, but Esmail steps forward. "She took a whole bottle of my mother's sleeping pills. You want to see?" And without waiting for a response from the armed Mr. Burdon, Esmail retrieves the empty prescription bottle from the bathroom sink and then returns to his mother's side, holding the bottle out in front of him for Mr. Burdon's inspection.

"Bring it to me." Burdon raises the pistol but does not point it at us. His voice reveals some emotion: fear. And I too am filled with it as my son stops at Kathy Nicolo's bare feet and gives to Burdon the bottle. He must narrow his eyes to read the label in only the light from the kitchen, the candlelight from the living-room area, and in English I ask my son to return to us, but he stays at the feet of Kathy Nicolo, as if it is important he wait there.

Burdon lowers the container. "How many? *When?*"

My wife tells to me in Farsi the bottle was nearly full, perhaps thirty to forty tablets.

"English!"

"My wife is saying in the bottle there were thirty tablets, but Kathy Nicolo was in the bathroom a very short period, perhaps only a half hour's time, and my wife has made her lose her stomach. She has vomited the pills."

Burdon looks down at the young woman once more. He pulls from her chin and mouth a strand of hair, then rests his palm on her forehead. I feel the moment has come to continue. "She also attempted to shoot herself with that pistol."

He regards me very quickly, the skin above his eyes drawn in tight lines, and I am careful not to use his name. "I discovered her with it in her automobile. She was quite upset. She had been drinking a great deal."

Lester V. Burdon looks from me to Nadi, to Esmail, then at me once more, his lips open beneath his mustache, as if this piece of information must enter his mouth as well as his ears. But then he shakes his head and stands. "Bullshit. Bull*shit.*" And he orders us to carry Kathy Nicolo to a bed.

There are tears in Nadi's eyes, but she appears relieved to be allowed movement again. She quickly administers to Kathy Nicolo, closing the robe around her bare legs, securing the knot more tightly at her waist. In poor English she directs me to take the arms of Kathy Nicolo while she and Esmail see to the legs. My back is stiff but I squat low behind the woman's head and place my hands beneath her upper arms. She opens her eyes, but again, they are quite small and dark. We lift and begin to carry her into Nadereh's room, and Lester V. Burdon is so close behind me I am able to hear his breathing. He tells to us to be careful, very careful, and in his voice there is still the menace of his anger and disbelief, but also his fear for the well-being of the young woman. But what concerns me more than these is this man's probable knowledge of my visit to his superior officer. If he is capable of breaking into our home, of pointing a loaded weapon at us, what more can we expect of him?

My mouth is quite dry, and as we lay Kathy Nicolo upon Nadereh's bed, I attempt to look into the faces of my wife and son but their eyes are on the task before them, Nadereh gently lifting Kathy Nicolo's feet so Esmail can free the light blanket beneath. They cover her to her shoulders and Lester Burdon orders us to step away from the bed. We obey. He sits upon the mattress beside her and he touches her face, speaks her name and inquires if she is awake. The young woman opens her eyes and smiles once more at him, but her eyes are wet and she begins to weep and says nothing, simply weeps.

Only a few moments before, when Nadereh and I were attempting to walk the woman down the corridor, we argued in Farsi of phoning the hospital. I had reached the decision we should, but my wife of course panicked and began screaming we will be arrested for stealing this woman's home, Behrani, for harming her, for the pistol, for—then she lost her grasp of Kathy Nicolo's arms and shortly thereafter Lester V. Burdon was upon us.

Now we watch as he strokes his lover's hair. Her eyes close and she appears to sleep once more. Her cheeks have a yellow hue, her lips a washed-away saffron. I prepare myself to step forward and speak, to recommend to Mr. Burdon he telephone the hospital, but he has already risen and picked up the receiver. He looks in our direction, then he places upon the bed his weapon and depresses the necessary telephone buttons, their computerized beeps the only sound in the room. He requests the emergency room nurse on duty, pulling from his trousers pocket the empty prescription bottle. To the nurse, he does not identify himself but simply states the facts. He tells to her the brand name of the drug. He gives the approximate height and weight of Kathy Nicolo. He tells to her how long a time he believes passed before she vomited. And he nods yes, she is responsive but still quite drowsy. He listens to the nurse, looking from Kathy Nicolo's sleeping face, to us, to the empty pharmaceutical bottle in his hand. He thanks the nurse and completes the telephone call without ever having identified himself, and I no longer possess hope we will be going to the hospital, to the bright lights and many faces of a public place.

Burdon once more retrieves his weapon, but as he views Kathy Nicolo he allows it to hang by his side like a forgotten artifact. Nadereh pushes her elbow into my ribs, but she says nothing and I do not turn to her although I am certain she is seeing this moment as a time for appeasement and reconciliation, and I should speak. But my better judgment is against this; in the lamp's light near the bed Burdon appears lost, gom shode. There are shadows in the cheeks of his face, and his eyes are narrowed in what I believe to be not only concern for Kathy Nicolo, but deep and painful surprise and confusion as well. No, in this moment he is weak. And it is the weak who are truly dangerous.

Esmail shifts his weight to his other foot and I touch his arm and squeeze. An automobile passes by the bungalow and down the hill. Burdon suddenly straightens and with his unarmed hand waves us from the room. "Leave, please. She needs rest. Go."

LESTER WATCHED THE YOUNG BOY LEAVE THE ROOM LAST. HE WAS AL-
most as tall as Lester and his hair was thick and black. Lester wanted
to look down at Kathy one more time before he left the room but
he'd just made the mistake of letting the colonel step into the hallway where he'd left his iron pry bar, so Lester hurried into the corridor only to see the colonel and his wife and son moving quietly
single-file toward the counter bar separating the living room from the
kitchen. The candles still burned on the living-room floor and for the
first time Lester saw the food there, the pot of white rice, the dish of
what looked like beef stew, the bread and yogurt and radishes. Three
clean unused plates. His belly felt as dry and empty as an old wine-
skin hanging on a line in the sun. The gun was suddenly heavy, almost obscene in his hand, as if he were exposing himself.

The small family stopped at the short counter bar between the
two rooms, turned and faced him, waiting for his next order, it
seemed. The boy wore only socks on his feet and he was standing on
the linoleum of the kitchen not far from a shard of glass. Lester
needed to sit and just think a minute. He found he could hardly look
into any of their faces. He waved his gun in the direction of their
food on the floor and told them to eat. "Just, sit down and eat."

The colonel looked like he was going to say something, but then
he kept quiet, turned, and led his family to their dinner. The son took
his plate from the counter and he gave Lester's gun a long look before he sat down. Lester pushed the safety on and just stood there a
minute, maybe more, half in the dark hallway, half in the light of the
kitchen, his head about as unclear as it could get without getting
drunk. His face was a windowpane and the inside was covered with
buzzing flies. And nothing was clear. Nothing. Kathy would pull
through. He had known that before he'd even called the emergency

room; if she could still recognize him and speak after taking all those pills, then not enough had been absorbed into her blood before she threw up. And he had no doubts about the throwing up because the entire hallway still smelled like it, so ripe it was sour. And when he'd just kissed her in the bedroom he had smelled the booze too, the gutrot scent it carries after being broken down in the stomach. Her cheek had been soft and dry and he'd wanted to lie beside her and hold her, as if holding her could begin to fill in the details for him, how this morning at the fish camp had led them to her stolen house in Corona tonight, to her doing what the Iranians say she'd done, to him standing there in her hallway while this family of exiles ate quietly on the floor in front of him, his loaded service pistol in his hand, a weighty reminder that *this* is where the ground met his feet, this is where Kathy was, so this is where he would be too. And there was no real reason to not believe these people. Lester had known this when Kathy turned her small, slightly puffy face to him, smiled a still-drugged smile and said, "You're here." Then in the bedroom she had cried looking right at him, her sweet, jaded face full of shame, and Lester had no more doubts the Iranians' story was true. This knowledge was a dark ball of sap in the pit of his stomach. He watched the Behranis eat slowly and quietly, using the back of their forks to push rice and stew onto their spoons, dipping radishes into yogurt, taking turns glancing in his direction but not quite all the way at him. He was tired and his eyes stung a bit. The kitchen smelled like spiced tea. The linoleum floor was covered with the broken wood and shattered glass of the back door that was now wide open. Against the wall beside it was a broom, and Lester held his service pistol to the light, pulled the hammer back to quarter lock, then reached around and pushed the weapon into the rear waistband of his jeans. He glanced down at the Behrani family, all three of them looking up at him from their candlelit meal on the floor, and he walked over the linoleum, took up the broom, and began sweeping, the 9mm a steel hand against his lower back.

．．．．．．．．．．．．．．．
　．．．．．．．
　　．．

IT IS IN THE MOMENTS LESTER V. BURDON IS SWEEPING FROM THE
kitchen floor the broken window glass that Nadi leans to me closer,
her eyes open wide with urgency, and whispers in Farsi, "Boro, invite
him to eat." Which, after having witnessed him put his pistol on
double safety, I was intending to do.

I stand so that I am able to view him upon the other side of the
counter, standing in the light of the kitchen as he empties the glass
and wood debris into our plastic garbage container. Upon his hand
is a gold wedding ring I did not before notice.

"Mr. Burdon," I say, and my face grows hot for I did not intend to
use his name, but it is too late; it comes from me as naturally as my
own air. He looks directly into my face and he slowly taps the pan of
dust upon the rim of the trash bin. He appears to be close to making
some sort of decision. I invite him with us to eat. But he tells to me
to sit and he does not join my family but moves to the counter bar
and looks down upon us, the handle of his weapon revealed at his
back. He looks beyond me to the framed photograph on the wall of
myself, General Pourat, and Shahanshah Pahlavi. He seems to be
studying it, his eyes smaller, his lips beneath his mustache squeezed
tightly. I do not care for his expression. It is one of judgment and who
is he to judge me? But I do not show my feelings. The smell of the
samovar's tea has filled the bungalow and normally, at this point in
the evening, Esmail would return to his bedroom and video games,
and Nadi would rise to clear the soiled dishes, to fill our cups with
tea. But she does not move. Nor does Esmail. I can feel my son
watching me. I take a breath and sit as straight as I am able. "Sir, my
wife would like to serve to us tea." But this is all I say. I will not request his permission for her to rise, and I regret having said to him
sir, but I could not use his name again only to risk reminding him I

went to the trouble to discover it. His eyes leave the wall and he regards first me, then Nadereh. He nods his head, and Nadi gathers our
plates and rises. Lester V. Burdon glances at my son, then again he
rests his eyes on me. They are dark and set deeply into his face. His
hair and mustache are dark as well and it occurs to me he looks very
much like Nadereh's younger brother Ali.

"What happened?"

I hesitate, for I do not know if he is inquiring of my reporting of
him, or if he is referring simply to Kathy Nicolo.

"When did she come here?"

"Late in the afternoon. My son was with friends. My wife was
resting. I do not know how long her automobile was in the drive before I saw it."

He inquires what she was doing, asking this quickly, as if testing
my story for the soft ground of a lie.

"She was weeping." I lower my eyes to the loaded pistol in his
waistband. "And she was aiming that at her heart. She was attempting to pull the trigger, but its safety mechanism was engaged, you see.
I took it from her and helped her into the home."

Burdon's eyes have softened, and he looks directly into my own
but I do not believe he is viewing me, but something else, a memory
perhaps, a memory of him and Kathy Nicolo, or perhaps simply a vision of what I have just reported to him.

"That's what happened," Esmail says. "My father wouldn't lie. He
never lies."

Burdon regards Esmail. It appears he wishes to tell to my son
something, but he does not speak. Nadereh places a cup of hot tea
before Mr. Burdon, then serves us as well. I put a sugar cube into my
mouth and drink. I then remove the sugar so that Mr. Burdon will
not think me rude when I must speak again. I see the question he is
perhaps ashamed to ask.

I answer it for him. "She was quite drunk."

"How *drunk?*"

I can see he does not like my use of words. His eyes become hard
again and I tell to myself I must stay cautious and respectful. I am
thinking I have never seen a woman as mast as Kathy Nicolo, only

prostitutes, gendehs in South Tehran. "She could not walk without help, nor could she speak very well, sir." I look down at the sofreh, but only for the briefest of moments; I do not wish Lester V. Burdon to mistake my gesture of respect as one of shame for the young woman. Nadereh sits beside me. She drinks her tea quite slowly. But when Mr. Burdon speaks again it is in a tone less interrogating. He inquires when Kathy Nicolo took the Halcion pills and I tell to him after she slept in my son's room. "It was my wife who discovered her in the bath and she forced her to lose her stomach immediately."

Mr. Burdon looks at Nadi beside me. I cannot read his face, for it is full of light and shadow from the candle flames. Nadi lowers her head. I regard my son. His elbows rest upon his legs, his chin upon the knuckles of his hands. He appears as if is watching a game of chess or backgammon between two professional players. I feel some irritation at this, but ebnadereh, it makes no difference.

I drink more tea and I wait for Mr. Burdon to say something or perhaps do something, for surely, the next move is his.

THE ROOM FELT TOO SMALL, AND LESTER NEEDED TO MOVE, THOUGH he had no idea where he could move to—the couch? One of the stools? What he should really do was carry Kathy to his car and drive her home to rest and wake up beside him. But where was home? The fish camp? A motel room over in San Bruno? And she shouldn't be disturbed anyway. Disturbed. The word seemed to linger in his head like a shred of silk on barbed wire.

And she had no home because of this colonel, who kept glancing over at his son, then his wife beside him, then he would look at Lester, but only very briefly. He would drink his tea and look back down at the burning candles. Sometimes the colonel's eyes shifted to the gun protruding from Lester's waistband, and Lester didn't like him looking at it; it was as if he was keeping an eye on the only true thing he had to fear, and Lester wanted to feel the pistol back in his hand, to let the colonel know one went with the other. But did it? Lester wasn't so sure. Part of him wanted to apologize profusely for kicking his way into this house—breaking and entering, in fact—and he wanted to take his service pistol, walk out the front door, and just come by in the morning for Kathy. She would probably be clear enough to drive her car then, and she could follow him to wherever it was they were going. But this part of him was a small voice up against one larger: he couldn't imagine leaving Kathy here for the night without him, not when he felt so shut out from Kathy herself, from the series of decisions she'd apparently made today that didn't seem to take him into account at all. From taking his gun to taking the pills in the bathroom, what could have happened since this morning to put her over the line like that? And all he could think of was her and alcohol. Lester still felt the dulled edge of his own hang-over from last night and he couldn't imagine having another drink today. But she had gotten drunk, and he was beginning to think that had to be the missing piece of things. He'd seen it time after time in his work, people doing things deep under the influence they wouldn't have even given a thought to sober, all the traffic fatalities, the petty thievery and arson. And she hadn't made things any easier for him. Did she give him any thought at all when she took his gun from the trunk? Did she *care* how entangled he'd become in this thing with her? And once he and she left this place, what was to keep this slimy officer from dialing the department, or even the Corona police? The Iranian had new charges on him now: B&E, and Brandishing a Weapon. And there were still the departmental code violations, any of which the colonel could pursue.

Lester was thirsty and he wanted to drink from the tea the colonel's wife had served him, but to do so at this moment would feel like a conciliatory move, as if he were a dog exposing his throat to one stronger. He glanced again at the framed photograph on the wall of Behrani addressing the Shah of Iran, a man who years ago Carol had told Lester all about, a man who had hundreds, maybe thousands, gunned down in one afternoon for daring an unarmed

protest against him and his entourage. And Behrani was smiling at
some kind of party with him, and now the colonel's eyes were again
on the gun probably just visible in Lester's waistband behind him.

Lester stared at him. Behrani looked back down at his tea and
slowly, almost casually, he stirred it with only his thumb and forefinger. It was such a self-assured gesture, a man adapting easily to his
new circumstances, and it left Lester feeling outmatched in some
sort of game he hadn't known he was playing. He began to feel afraid,
and he wanted to kick the colonel in the teeth, this friend of dicta-
tors, this man who had refused to sell Kathy back her house.

Lester pulled the pistol from his waistband and set it loudly on the
counter. "Go do something. All of you."

The boy stood first, then the colonel and his wife. She avoided
looking in Lester's direction and she squatted and blew out the candles. Then she picked up from the couch the lamp the boy had
knocked over and she placed it back on the end table, turned it on,
and began clearing the remaining plates and glasses from the rug.
The colonel stood there while his wife worked around him. The boy
looked from his father to Lester's gun to Lester's face.

"Go to your room, joon-am," the colonel said, and the boy began
to move down the hall.

"Wait." Lester turned to him and asked him his name.

"Esmail."

"Do you have a phone in there, Esmail?"

"No."

Lester glanced at the colonel, who was standing straight now, his
chin up, his eyes on his child. In the kitchen Mrs. Behrani picked up
a dirty plate and held it. Lester took a breath, this logical, inevitable
next step gathering in his chest, and he ordered all three of them
back into the hallway and the boy's room.

There was no phone, just a bedside lamp near a framed photograph. Tacked to the wall was the color poster of a skateboarder in
midair, no sign of the ground anywhere, his arms spread wide, both
knees bent. On a desk at the foot of the bed was a computer termi-
nal, keyboard, and a modem, its Internet and E-mail cable plugged
into the phone jack under the desk. Lester nodded his head toward

the boy and told him to unplug the modem on both ends and give it to him. It took him only a few seconds and when the boy handed it over he glanced down at the pistol Lester was careful not to point at him.

"Esmail, I want you to stay in this room until I say otherwise, all right? If you have to go to the bathroom, I want you to ask me first."

The boy looked over at his father and mother, Mrs. Behrani holding first the fingers of one hand, then the fingers of the other, and Lester heard himself order them back to the front of the house. He put the computer modem and its cables on the lamp table beside the couch, and Mrs. Behrani seemed to distract herself with work, with clearing the dining rug and rolling it up, her husband stepping to the side to allow her room, and Lester could hear the sounds of a video game coming from down the hall, a series of manic, off-key computerized musical notes followed by the scattered static of a simulated explosion. The colonel turned to Lester, his arms still folded in front of his chest. In the light from the kitchen he looked old and thin, an exiled patriarch.

"We have done nothing to you. What do you intend here?"

Lester had no idea. None. He sat down on the couch. It was soft and deep, covered with an expensive fabric. Everything in this house seemed expensive: the new brass bed Kathy slept on; the wine-red Persian carpets; the mosaic-framed picture of Persian horsemen on the wall; the heavy silver samovar on the kitchen counter; the gold lamp and shade the boy had nearly broken when Lester kicked in the door; even the late-model Buick out in the driveway. Again, Lester felt he was up against something larger than himself. His mouth was dry and he rested his weapon flat on the arm of the couch, running his index finger over the tiny ridges of the safety tab, his eyes on the carpet. "Who did you talk to in Redwood City, Colonel?"

"A lieutenant."

"What was his name?"

"Alvarez. His name is Lieutenant Alvarez."

Lester flushed on hearing what he had already assumed, and he tried to swallow but couldn't. The sofa felt too soft, as if he were sinking more deeply into it.

"Certainly you would have done the same, Mr. Burdon."

The colonel's wife was running water in the sink so Lester wasn't sure if he'd heard a challenge in this man's voice or had only inferred it because he'd just used Lester's name, but something shifted forward inside him—it wasn't Kathy; she wasn't to blame for any of this; she hadn't done anything that couldn't be traced to this prick, this man who was looking down at his hand resting on his leg, at a gold ring there with a red stone in the center. A *ruby?* Lester could feel the muscles tightening around his eyes and mouth. He sat up. "When do you plan to give this house back, Colonel?"

Mrs. Behrani was still at the sink drying plates with a white cloth, her face turned slightly toward the counter where her husband sat, though he remained silent, sitting with his back straight, as if he was above having to respond to Lester's question at all.

Lester took a breath. "Do you really *need* this tiny place?"

"This is none of your business, sir."

Lester pushed himself from the couch and was at the counter before he could even get a full grip on his pistol. He told himself to keep the weapon at his side, no need to dig a deeper hole, but the colonel's face was so still, so impassive, the whites of his eyes yellowed with age and a world-weariness that seemed to reduce Lester instantly to no real threat at all, only a mere nuisance, like Kathy, like the dispute over this house; Lester had no choice but to push the square barrel up under the colonel's chin. His heart fluttered behind his ribs, and his organs seemed to float inside him. He pulled the hammer all the way back, but kept the final safety on, and he could smell radish on the colonel's breath. The Iranian's lips began to purse like he was getting ready to speak, but Lester pushed the pistol harder into the underside of his chin. "That woman sleeping back there is my business. Everything about her is my business. Do you *understand* me? Now I want you to start thinking how we're going to solve all this."

The colonel's wife was crying softly, and in his peripheral vision Lester could see her standing there in the kitchen holding the white dishcloth in both her hands as if she were praying with it. "Please, please, we have nothing. Nothing. My husband only is good. Our son must to go university. That is all. Please, we are good people." She kept crying, quietly, taking in long shuddering breaths of air. The colonel's eyes were wet, though Lester didn't know if this was from fear or the fact he wasn't blinking. Lester thumbed the hammer back to quarter-lock, edged the pistol from under the colonel's jaw, and sat down on the stool next to him, facing him. He rested his gun on the countertop and he seemed to be waiting for the colonel's wife to continue, but she only sniffled and pressed her finger discreetly to her nose. The notes of the boy's computer video game sped into a high-pitched victory tune that soon faded into electronic space, and Lester's back and head felt suddenly too exposed to possibility and he stood and moved to the end of the counter, but the hallway was empty and the iron crowbar was still leaning against the door casing where the colonel had left it. Lester's arms and legs were heavy and there was a slight tremor in the forearm of his gun hand. He wanted to see Kathy, to check on her, but now he couldn't leave these people alone to do it.

"Tell to him, Massoud," the wife said. "To him explain."

But the colonel didn't seem to be listening. He was looking straight at Lester, the cheeks of his face empty of color, his eyes narrowed slightly, his lips a straight line, and Lester knew he'd just crossed a border not only in himself, but in the colonel as well. Lester waved his pistol in their general direction, then stood to the side of the hallway's entrance, told them to go first. "We're going to see how the owner of this house is doing." But the words came out sounding hollow to him, like there was a lie in what he'd just said, and as the colonel and his wife moved past him into the hallway, the wife still sniffling, Lester followed with his pistol hanging heavily at his side and he had a sudden wish for the colonel to do something, to grab the crowbar and try to swing it at him, to run, anything, anything that might make this gun in his hand feel less like the burdensome overreaction it had become.

Moments have passed since Lester V. Burdon pressed to my flesh his loaded weapon, yet still I am feeling it against my skin and it is no effort to imagine the large-caliber bullet tearing through my head like a missile, and I want only to kill this man who has broken into our home to do this after we saved his gendeh's pitiful life.

But I can of course do nothing with this desire, and my body has become quite stiff, the muscles of my neck, back, and legs as tight as if bound with rusted chain. The man orders us to Nadereh's bedroom. I move slowly. Nadi is to my back, Burdon to hers. I enter the room first. The gendeh sleeps peacefully, her thick hair a nest around her small face. Burdon orders us to the far side of the bed and with his free hand he puts his fingers to the artery beneath the woman's jaw. After a moment, he places his palm over her forehead. And he no longer appears confused. He touches her cheek, then tells to us we will visit our son, and he follows us. Again, I enter first. Esmail sits upon the bed in which Kathy Nicolo slept. The video game's remote control panel is backwards upon his lap, and the window behind him is open widely, the screen as well, the outdoors light shining upon the mist over the grasses, and Esmail's eyes are quite large and I feel in my hands the pounds of my heart; in Farsi I whisper to him to close it immediately: "*Holah, holah.*" He jumps to the task, the remote control box falling to the floor. I cough quite loudly but we are too late; Lester V. Burdon pushes past Nadi and me and with one hand upon my son's shoulder he pulls him from the window. Esmail nearly falls backwards from the bed but Burdon stops him with the side of his body, the weapon in his hand at his leg. It is within one step of me. I can reach and grasp it, twist it from him, but I do nothing for I imagine the gun firing, my son or wife hurt or worse.

Burdon pulls Esmail from the bed, forcing him to stand beside us.

My arm extends instantly around my son's shoulders. And I hold Nadi's small, warm arm. She is trembling, or perhaps it is I who tremble. I am surprised to feel my body standing at full attention.

"What am I going to do with you people?" He asks this of all of us but he is regarding only our child. "What were you going to do, Ishmael?"

"*Esmail*," my son tells to him. I squeeze his shoulder and I am hoping he does not misunderstand this as encouragement to continue with any belligerence.

Lester V. Burdon inhales a deep breath, exhaling it without turning his head. "Did you leave this house, Esmail?"

Against my arm upon his back I feel the beating of my son's heart. He shakes his head no, he did not. The video game emits the electronic music of alien aircraft flying off to battle in space, its refrain repeating itself every few seconds. Burdon regards the entire room, then he looks once more at my son. "Were you planning to use a neighbor's phone, Esmail?"

Esmail does not answer. Our captor rests his unarmed hand against his hip. In his other hand the weapon hangs straight at his side, his shoulders seeming to droop as if under a great weight. Burdon's face is lowered, but his eyes are leveled at our son.

"I am losing my patience, Esmail."

I again squeeze my son's shoulder. "Give to him answer, joonam."

"Yeah, I was going to leave."

The refrain of the video game continues, repeating itself every five seconds; it is the music of the microchip, as automatic and insincere as lies.

"Did you leave?"

"No."

Esmail has answered too quickly. Lester V. Burdon's eyes become smaller, and he draws in his lower lip. He regards first me, then Nadi, the computer game repeating itself again and yet again.

"This isn't working out," says Lester V. Burdon. "It just isn't." He orders us into the bathroom that still smells of Kathy Nicolo's vomit. The carpet is moist from her bath. The tub is full of her water. As my family stands close together between the sink and toilet and bath, Burdon looks behind and above us at the small window set high into the tile wall, his eyes passing quickly over Esmail and Nadi, then at the panjare once more before he nods his head to himself and touches the door's handle. "I don't want to see this move. Do you understand?"

"Yes," I to him say. "We understand."

Then Burdon stands more straight, as if has just slipped a heavy pack from his shoulders. He regards us once more, then he pulls shut the door behind him.

LESTER LOOKED AT THE DOOR A MOMENT LONGER, THEN TOOK THE chance and hurried to the front of the house. He stuck the pistol back into the rear waistband of his pants, switched off the exterior light, and stepped outside onto the front stoop. The nearest home was on the other side of the cars in the driveway, its screened porch light on, one in the family room too. Lester could see the corner of a TV set, the color flicker of its screen, then a man's wrist as he lowered a cigarette or cigar into an ashtray on the table beneath the window. No one stood on the porch, no one stood at any of the other windows looking in this direction. He glanced to his right, but the small stucco house there looked equally quiet and undisturbed, just a few lights on downstairs, no one peering through darkened or lit windows waiting for an emergency phone call to bear fruit.

He went back inside to Kathy's room. Her color wasn't any better; her cheeks still had a yellowish cast to them, but her pulse was steady and strong, and when he put his hand to her forehead it felt cool and dry and she raised her chin slightly and kept sleeping. He stood and slid open the closet door. He was looking for one of the colonel's neckties, but in this closet were only women's clothes, elegant-looking wool gowns covered in long sheets of dry-cleaning plastic, silk blouses and wool jackets; on the shelf above were oval hat boxes with French words embossed on their sides; and on the floor were twenty or thirty pairs of ladies' shoes, most of them stuffed with tissue paper. He could still hear the colonel's wife saying they have nothing, nothing, and it angered him further because he knew they had had at least enough to buy this place with cash at a county auction. From shelf hooks hung dress belts—silver, gold, black patent leather, one a brown alligator skin. Lester took that one, wrapped it around both fists, and pulled, but there was too much give in it and he put it back, glanced at Kathy again, her hair fanned out on the pillow, her lips parted slightly, and he went back into the hall and picked up the long iron pry bar.

He could hear the Behrani family whispering in Farsi inside the bathroom, and he walked into what looked like the colonel's office. There was a desk, chair, and typewriter. On newspapers on the floor was a silver coffee table on its side, two of its legs wrapped in masking tape. And hanging in the closet were twenty or thirty suits, some in fine leather garment bags. On the floor was a brass shoe rack six feet long and three levels high and it was full of dress shoes, loafers, white tennis and athletic shoes, three pairs of cashmere slippers, even a pair of worn work boots. The colonel's ties hung over the closet pole between a dark double-breasted and a military uniform, cobalt blue with garish gold epaulets, both breast pockets covered with brightly colored ribbons and tags.

Lester took two silk neckties, then went back into the hallway, stood at the closed bathroom door, and began tying both around the base of the doorknob. On the other side the foreign whispering stopped and Lester held the pry bar horizontally against the pine trim to the right and left of the door, wrapping both ties around it before securing them with two double slipknots. He pulled until the iron was snug against the door casings, then stepped back to survey what he'd just done. He took a deep breath and let it out, then went into the boy's room, shut down the computer, and moved to turn off the boy's bedside lamp. On the table beside it was a framed color photograph of the colonel in full uniform holding a toddler boy on his lap in a deep leather office chair, the green, white, and red stripes of the Iranian flag encased in glass on the wall behind them, the man and little boy smiling widely into the camera. Lester looked away quickly and switched off the light.

In the living room, he locked the front door and pulled down the shades. Then he looked through the kitchen cabinets for coffee, even instant, but there was none, so he took a clean cup from the dishrack and put it under the spigot of the silver samovar. It was strong black tea, steaming hot, and he carried it into the bedroom where Kathy slept, the room, he assumed, that had probably been hers in the first place.

He put the tea on the bedside table next to a new-looking cassette player. "Kathy?" He touched her shoulder and gave it a gentle squeeze. "Kath?" He had never called her that before, shortened her name like that, and it made him feel momentarily as if they had more of a history between them than they did. Her mouth had opened a bit, her face was turned to the side, and a thin line of saliva had run into the pillow, leaving a wet spot. Lester put his hand on her forehead and smoothed her hair back. It was thick and dry, and when his fingers touched the pillowcase she turned her head and let out a small sound, almost a whimper. Lester spoke her name again, but her mouth had gone slack and her eyes stayed closed. Her pulse was fine, though, and he sat on the bed and took off his shoes, the pistol barrel in his rear waistband pressing hard against his lower back. He could hear the muffled voices of the Iranians coming from the bathroom down the hall. The colonel seemed to be doing most of the talking, his Farsi sounding low and full of authority. A cool sweat came out on Lester's forehead and the back of his neck.

He stepped out into the dark of the hallway in his socks. Beneath the bathroom door was a thin crack of light, and the pry bar was fixed across the casings as if the room behind it had been condemned. Lester stood there a few minutes and listened. At first he thought Mrs. Behrani was crying again, because her voice seemed to waver, but then her words came spitting out, a barrage of throat-clearing vowels and consonants the colonel was talking calmly right through, his voice coming from someplace central inside him, as if he were right at home, leading his wife and son on an expedition through familar terrain.

Lester stepped back and kicked the door hard with the sole of his foot. The silence was instant. Something fell in the sink, maybe a vial from the medicine cabinet, he didn't know, though he did know this: this rich prick was not taking him seriously and that would have to change starting now. He pulled out his service pistol and drew back the steel slide, ejecting the live round onto the carpet before he let another slide loudly into place. He tapped the barrel lightly against the door, then paused, the silence on the other side like something he could reach out and squeeze between his fingers. His heart was beating fast and he pressed his nose to the door, smelling wood and paint. "Get some rest in there, Colonel, because tomorrow you're selling this place back to the county. Do you understand me?"

On the other side of the door, the colonel started to clear his throat but then stopped and said nothing.

"I asked you a question, Behrani." Lester imagined the little family crouched in various corners of the small room and his heart felt nudged by a dull stick; it would be better if the woman and teenager weren't a part of this but it was too late to back away, to let down his guard, expose his throat to any of these people, the boy and wife included. "Tell me, *Colonel*, what are you going to do first thing tomorrow?"

Again, there was no answer, not even the panicked whispers from Mrs. Behrani. Now Lester pictured himself talking to an empty room, the high shower window somehow dismantled and larger than he'd thought, the Iranian family running barefoot through the fog for help. And for a moment he felt almost nauseated at the thought of everything getting away from him, everything finally coming down on him.

Then the colonel spoke, his voice dry with fatigue. "I do not know. Perhaps you will tell to me what I must do tomorrow."

"Don't you patronize me." Lester pressed the side of his face to the door, the iron pry bar against his hip. "Tomorrow you are going to call the county tax office and accept their offer to give you your money back for this house. Then, while they're cutting you a nice big check, you and your family are going to pack up your things and leave. It's that simple. Understand?"

But was it that simple? What would happen after that? Did he just expect them to drive away and do nothing? For a brief moment Lester calculated how he might pull back from all this now, just let the family out of the bathroom, carry Kathy out to his or her car, and drive away. But they would have to leave a car behind, and Behrani would surely call the department. Then there would be new charges against Lester, far more serious: Brandishing a Weapon, Assault with a Deadly Weapon, and now that they're all locked up in the bathroom, False Imprisonment. Charges that could be corroborated by the son and wife, charges that would not only get him terminated but arrested and jailed as well, a cop among perpetrators, and Lester felt a hot flash of recognition and dread spread out inside him, and he kicked the door hard with his bare foot, an ache flaring through his sole and shin. *"Answer me, you son of a bitch."*

The colonel still did not speak, but his wife was whispering again. This time her voice was less harsh, more pleading, Lester thought. He closed his eyes, rubbed his forehead, and took a deep breath through his nose, his anger leaving him like something precious he wasn't sure he'd be able to get back again when he needed it. And now he felt queasy with exhaustion, the remorse beginning to move in on him like a cool fog. He told himself it wasn't smart to push the colonel for an answer right now; the ex-officer's pride and manhood were being tested enough as it was. The night had taken on a turn that, for better or worse, Lester had to commit himself to in order to get back on track; it was like riding a bicycle fast off smooth asphalt onto a sandy shoulder: if you panicked and put on the brakes or jerked the steering, then you went down. But keep up your speed and direction, he told himself, hold your nerve, and you'd make it back on the road unscathed.

"Sleep on it, Colonel." Lester put his service pistol on double safety, then squatted for the bullet on the floor. "You hear me? Sleep on it." He heard the boy's voice, high and full of questions, fear even. And that sound could have come from Lester's own body, which felt to him suddenly thin and inconsequential, his fingers shaking as he picked up the round. This was a familiar feeling, the fear that always followed his remorse, but this time there was no arrest or booking procedure to flush his prisoners neatly and safely away. What was he planning to do in the morning if the colonel still refused to cooperate? *Force* him to do it? And what was his strategy if Behrani agreed to sell the house back to the county? Just hope he and his family would then disappear? He didn't know. Right now all he could do was hope the colonel would agree to sell the house back. That would at least start to feel like progress, and he would just have to come up with something later to carry them both safely to the next step.

Esmail stopped asking questions and Lester walked back down the hall. He imagined Nate asleep now in his bed on his stomach, his face turned to the side, his bottom up in the air. And Bethany had probably gone to their room, the way she did sometimes after a dream that scared her, that left her feeling torn from the world she understood to be hers. She was probably snuggled up to Carol right now, his daughter's small body only beginning to fill the empty space that was his.

IT IS THREE HOURS SINCE BURDON MADE HIS THREATS THROUGH THE door. The washroom is now dark, but a soft light enters from the panjare above, for Burdon has not extinguished the exterior lamps over the automobiles in the drive. Esmail has grown more quiet than ever. He lies upon a bed of towels in the heavy bath, his feet resting upon the tiles above the faucet. I sit against the wall, my left arm on the porcelain edge so my face is only centimeters from my son's, but his is turned and I do not know if he sleeps or not. On the floor his mother lies curled upon two towels. The air is cool and smells slightly of the sea and of Kathy Nicolo's sickness. Nadereh appears cold and

I would like to cover her, but all the towels have gone beneath her and our son.

Before Burdon came to our door and affixed some sort of lock, Nadereh was telling to me in her panicked whispering to give back the woman's bungalow, what is the matter for you? We find another. But after Burdon's last threat, Esmail, who was already quite shaken, looked from his mother to me, then at his mother, then to me once again, his eyes no longer shining with adventure, but dulled by the suck of bowels that is true fear. I reached for him but he twisted his shoulder away. His eyes grew wet, and in Farsi that has not developed as well as his English he asked his father, "What are you going to do, Bawbaw?"

For a miserable moment I had nothing to tell to my son, no words formed themselves at my lips. I simply stood there mere centimeters away, my son's mouth partly open, his eyes blinking the water from them as he waited for what might happen next. It was Nadi who acted decisively: "Do not be afraid, Esmail," she said as she moved past him and began to drain the water from the bath. "Your father is a colonel, a genob sarhang. That man in our home is not even sergeant. Your father will easily take care of this business." She told to him to wash his face and clean his teeth, she would prepare him a bed in the bath. Esmail paused a moment, his eyes still upon me.

"Yes, joon-am. Clean yourself and rest. I have seen one hundred men like this; they are desperate for something so they use their pistol at the last moment but they are always bluffing. Do you understand? He does not intend to do anything he says."

"But Bawbaw—"

"Shh, shh, you clean and use the toilet—your mother will not look—and you rest. I will handle this man."

Esmail began to wash his hands and face at the sink and Nadi brushed past me to wipe dry the bath, her eyes upon me only a moment, narrow and shining, and I of course thought this was rage, rage at me for leading us all into this locked washroom. But her hands were trembling and she lowered herself to her knees and began wiping the bath in abrupt jerking movements, and I thought of the small bird Soraya discovered at the base of a tree, attempting to flap its broken wing but gaining no distance from where it began. Nadi prepared the bed for our son, directed him to it, and she said nothing more to either of us. She extinguished the light and lay upon the floor, turning her back to me with no apology. I knew her fear of Mr. Burdon, of what he may do, was so great she could not speak without betraying it to our young son, so I forgave her her rudeness. But I did not forgive her her fear.

She had less of it as Bahman drove us through the burning streets of the capital city before dawn, down darkened alleyways past the trash of American and French hotels, away from the main boulevards where students and bohemians, farmers and cargars burned effigies of Shahanshah and Empress Pahlavi, an offense that only months earlier would have brought torture and execution upon their entire family. In the rear of the limousine, Nadi held our infant son while my daughter of ten years sat upon my lap, her face pressed to my chest as she wept. I held her with one hand only, for in the other was the .45-caliber pistol given me by the American officer. Bahman drove us directly onto the tarmac at Mehrabad, past the lighted windows of the guard booth. The soldiers were obedient, waving us through immediately, but their faces appeared quite still, as if they were beginning to understand they may be the brunt of a cruel hoax. The jet engines were already roaring in the darkness, and I was afraid for my children's ears, especially my infant son's, as we hurried with them up the portable stairs to the aircraft. My copilot's wife and children were wrapped in blankets amongst their trunks and boxes and luggage. Nadi left the baby with the khonoum, Soraya with the other children, and my wife followed me back into the night, into the cry of the engine and the smell of jet fuel, to the tarmac, where Bahman handed to us our belongings from the limousine, only three trunks and four pieces of luggage. That is all we took with us of our lives. But Nadi did not complain. With both hands she carried a heavy suitcase and climbed the stairs to the plane while Bahman and I followed with a trunk, its leather handle cutting into my palm. Even then she was dressed stylishly, in a khaki safari suit, the jacket's many pockets full of anything she could carry from our home: earrings and necklaces, diaper pins, small kitchen utensils, a handful of French coins her father had given her as a girl. She helped me with the remaining two trunks, and once inside the aircraft, as I lifted the canvas flap to enter the cockpit, she squeezed my hand then pressed to my face her palm and fingers, her gavehee eyes full of gratitude.

But what if she had known then, at that moment, the revolutionary government would not collapse but grow more strong? That our names and those of all our friends and acquaintances would be placed upon a death list? That we would never return to our country, to our families, to the houses of our birth? Would she have been grateful still? Even for that one moment? For only in this bungalow did Nadi's old happiness begin to emerge once again. She was free of the pooldar acting of the Berkeley Hills; we were upon our own small hill with a widow's walk to view the sea, our daughter was newly married, and Esmail left the home early each morning to ride his skateboard joyously down the long hill of the street. I was no longer a garbage soldier with the rough hands of a cargar, my head and face burned by the sun. And she no longer had to lie at the dinner parties of the Berkeley pooldar, to lie with all her teeth and tell to the wives of surgeons and lawyers and engineers, "My sarhang has been playing tennis all day in the sun, golf as well." Because I had become an investor in real estate, a man who might once again provide an escape for his family, is this why Nadi invited me twice to share her bed?

But at this moment, in the dark, her back is turned. If I rest my fingertips upon her shoulder, she will pull away, for I know she is awake. "Please," to our captor she said. "My husband is only good." Perhaps Burdon understood this as a positive comment on my character, a wife attempting to expose only her husband's best side, the side she perhaps loves most. But this is not what Nadereh was saying at all: Please sir, my husband has only his good intentions remaining. He is nothing any longer. Nothing. And so I am nothing. Please sir, have pity upon us for we are nothing now. Heechee. Nothing.

Nadi is the lamb who wishes to sleep only with the lion. And now the weak lamb cannot sleep, for not only does she fear this tall thin policeman, but she fears she has lied to her own son as well, that his father is not capable to handle this man in his house.

"Bawbaw?" my son whispers, his voice thick with congestion from the nose.

"Yes, joon-am."

"I want to move back to Berkeley."

The muscles in my neck feel quite rigid. I close my eyes and inhale deeply, letting the air escape slowly, but no relaxation comes. Esmail turns over in the bath. "That was a good place, Bawbaw."

"Why do you say this? What was good about it?"

"We had an elevator and a pool. Maman-jahn liked to sit by the window and see San Francisco. It was good, Bawbaw. Nobody wanted to take it away from us. All our friends are there."

"I have no friends there. Those people were not my friends."

"But you had parties with them all the time."

"That was for your sister, joon-am. That was to help your sister complete her hastegar, to find a good husband. Now she has found one and we will not go back there."

"But where will we go, Bawbaw?"

"We are going nowhere." I stop speaking and in the darkness I regard the pale white of the locked door. I speak only in Farsi. "We stay in this bungalow until we are able to sell it, then we will have enough money to go many places, joon-am, to do many things."

"But that *cop*, Bawbaw. He told us to *leave*."

"I do not care what he told to us. He is no position to threaten anyone, Esmail. And I am quite finished with being forced from my home by thugs." This is a word in Farsi Esmail does not know, and he asks me to explain it.

"Thugs: these are people who hurt others merely to get things they want. Criminals, Esmail. Bad people."

My son is quiet for many moments, and I am grateful for the silence, the peace. Tomorrow I will pretend to do as Lester V. Burdon instructs, and when my family and I are safely away, I will report Mr. Burdon to his superior officers. I will press charges and he will lose everything, and we will sell the bungalow at a profit, then go where he cannot find us.

"Bawbaw?"

"Yes?"

Esmail sits up in the bath. His dark hand appears on the porcelain beside my arm, but he does not speak.

"What is it, Esmail?"

"Aren't we being thugs? Hurting that woman for her house?"

My face grows immediately warm. "*No*. We have done *nothing* wrong. *Nothing.*"

"*Nakon*, Behrani." My wife's face turns upward from the floor, a pale shape in the darkness. "Your son speaks only truth. You should have never kept this girl's home. *You* have done this to us—"

"Khafesho! Shut up!" I stand but have no place to move. I look down at the floor and into the bath, at the shadows that are my wife and son. "Do you think I do all this for me? *I* could live in the *street*. I do this for you, Esmail, because I am your father and you will take what I give you. Do you think that woman out there is blameless? This gendeh who comes here drunk to die? Do you think she did *nothing* to help her lose her own home? It is *I* who have done nothing. I simply purchased a property that can give my son a future. Is it I who has locked us in this toilet? Is it I who forced us from our old life, Nadi? *Tell to me.* What is it I have done except provide for my family? I think of nothing else. Ever. *Ever*, Nadereh. Only this. Only you. So close your mouths, both of you. You will show me respect or—"

"*What*, Behrani?" My wife stands quickly and I hear her fast breath, smell in it the old tea and obgoosht. "Will you call SAVAK? Tell to them we are not respectful? Do not throw these stones at us; they are lies. You want this home for you. *You.* You could never live in the street because there no one would respect you, Behrani, and you need everyone to respect you, even strangers must respect you. Here your uniform means nothing and this is killing you—"

"*Do not talk to me of this when it is you who made us spend all our money to impress people we do not know—*"

"For Soraya, yes. For *her*."

"But you—"

"But I nothing. I want only my children to be happy, Behrani. I do not care of anything else."

"Maman, Bawbaw, *please* don't fight, *please* don't make noise." Esmail is standing in the bath, his tall body only darkness against the tile wall beneath the panjare. His voice is high with fear and I feel my rafigh, Pourat, forced to watch his own son stand against such a wall; my anger leaves me as quickly as water from a broken urn.

"Yes, joon-am, you are right. We must keep our heads. Lie down and rest."

"I can't, Bawbaw. What are you going to *do?*"

"Shh, Farsi only," I whisper. "Lie down." I sit upon the bath's edge while my son carefully rests his feet once again on the wall of faucets and knobs. Behind me, Nadereh seats herself upon the closed toilet and exhales loudly. She rests her face in her hands and I am certain she has brought on one of her headaches, but for the moment I do not care.

"Bawbaw?"

"Joon-am."

"Were you a Savaki?"

"Of course not. You know I was not. Please do not even think this."

"But you knew them, right?"

"Yes, I knew some of those men."

"Did you meet them at Shahanshah's palace?"

"No, my son." I again see Pourat's nephew Bijan as we sat around the vodka and mastvakhiar, the reflection of firelight in his drunk eyes, eyes as dark and indifferent as a dog's.

"You know Soraya's new brother-in-law, Bawbaw?"

"Yes?"

"He said it was SAVAK's fault we got kicked out of our country, because they killed too many people. Is that true?"

"I do not know, Esmail. Rest. Tomorrow we must have our energy, our concentration."

"What are we going to do?"

I breathe deeply, allowing my answer to come with my breath. "We pretend that man is in charge of the situation, that is what we do. We let him think this, and when he is not looking, we defeat him."

"How?"

"Courage. He is attempting to frighten us away, but we will not be frightened, will we, joon-am?"

"I'm not scared." Esmail folds his arms in front of him.

"Good, good. But pesaram, my son, tomorrow I want you to appear frightened. I want you to do whatever that man tells to you."

"Why?"

I do not tell my son my primary reason, that I fear my child may attempt something youthful and heroic that may provoke Burdon to rash action. "Because if he thinks he has frightened us, he may feel secure to leave us alone."

"You mean he thinks we'll be too scared to try anything even when he's gone?"

"Yes, that's right."

"No problem, Bawbaw-jahn."

I kiss my son on his head. His hair smells of the sea. "Good night, my son." I sit once more upon the floor beside the bath. Esmail is quiet a few moments. Nadereh lies silently down upon her towels.

"Bawbaw?"

"Shh-shh. Sleep. Rest."

"Soraya's brother-in-law said the Shah ordered SAVAK to kill families, the kids too, just because the father read certain books."

"Soraya's brother-in-law is stupid. He knows nothing. Now please, sleep."

"But he also said—"

"*Saket bosh, sleep.*"

"Okay, Bawbaw. Good night."

Outdoors the night is still and I do not know if the fog has disappeared or not, but I suspect it has not. No sounds of any kind come through the panjare, not the call of a bird, not the working of an insect, not the fall of a dead pine twig in the woodland across the street. Not even the bark of a dog down the hill in the village, or the passing of a lone automobile, and so I of course imagine the entire land covered in a thick fog blanket, one that hides and protects and disguises, one that allows lies to live on untested. How can I tell to my son I have heard dozens of these stories as well? How can I tell to him that I drank vodka with a Savaki at the Pourats' home? How can

I tell to Esmail that I am sorry for yelling at him without my voice betraying this heat in my face, this feeling in my blood that if it was only me in this locked toilet and not my wife and son, then I would finally be receiving what I deserved, that the time had come for Colonel Massoud Amir Behrani to stand at the wall, to stand at full attention and face his accusers.

LESTER PULLED INTO THE PARKING COMPOUND BEHIND THE HALL OF Justice just as Lieutenant Alvarez was locking his jeep, his short hair combed back wet from his postrun shower, his briefcase hanging against his ironed pant leg. Lester parked out of sight in the motor pool between two K-9 cruisers and waited for Alvarez to go inside. It was only a quarter to eight, fifteen minutes before Internal Affairs opened, and Lester wanted to give the lieutenant time to hear his voice mail, to get Lester's message from last night. He checked himself in the rearview mirror; his own hair was wet from the Purisima spring at the fish camp, and he'd nicked his chin shaving without a mirror. He'd pushed a folded bit of toilet paper against it to catch the blood, and now it was a dry red speck on his face. His eyes were small and bloodshot from no sleep, there was a light scratch on his nose from the backyard hedge he'd shouldered his way through last night, and the slacks he'd pulled from his suitcase needed ironing, though the blue short-sleeved polo shirt he wore looked all right. Anyway, it didn't matter. This slightly disheveled look might even help his story, which was the truth: My wife and I are having serious problems, Lieutenant. I just couldn't get away, sir. Though Lester still didn't know what he was going to say about the colonel.

Just before dawn this morning, while Kathy and his prisoners slept, he sat at her kitchen counter and wrote:

Dearest Kathy,

I know this all looks very dramatic and wrong but the way it all came together seems inevitable now. *I think they're finally going to clear out.* Please do not let them out until I get back. (And don't let them know I'm not in the house.) I have to go into Redwood City. Be back by nine. You should drink plenty of water and juice.

See you then,

Les

—If you need to relieve yourself, I recommend the backyard!

Lester had folded the paper once. On the back was Persian handwriting, and he crossed it out and wrote Kathy's name in capital letters. He wondered if he'd written too little about what she'd tried to do to herself last night, if his directions on what she should drink would look like he was afraid to go any deeper than that, when the truth was he wanted to know more now than he ever had; he wanted to go so deeply inside her he would hardly even be him anymore. After his last talk with the colonel through the bathroom door, Lester had spent the rest of the night in a chair by Kathy's bed. Her hair was fanned out on the pillow, and in the lamplight her color was better. There was more pink in her cheeks, her lips didn't seem as dark, and all he wanted to do was kiss them, to taste again her tongue and teeth, to be inside her completely, all of him.

But first, there was having to slip himself free of his entanglement with this Iranian colonel and his family, coming up with something credible this morning for Alvarez, though the last thing Lester felt comfortable doing was leaving this house. What if Kathy woke and stumbled to the bathroom without reading the note and then let them all out? Or what if she kept them all locked up but the colonel realized Lester and his gun were no longer in the house? Would he encourage the family to start screaming for help? But what was the alternative? Lester had disobeyed a direct order from an LT in Internal Affairs, then left a message on his machine saying he'd be in his office first thing this morning to explain everything. If Lester didn't show again, then he would absolutely lose all credibility and any chance to talk away his incident with the colonel. What's more, Alvarez, who got paid to have a nose for worse-case scenarios, could want to speak with the colonel again, could call him or even send out a patrol car.

Lester left Kathy's note on the bedside table near his empty teacup, then thought better of it and slid half of it into the door casing at what he hoped was her eye level. He thought about kissing her cheek or forehead, but he didn't want to wake her; so much had happened since they last spoke, it would take too long for them to get things into some kind of even understanding before he could leave. He walked back down the carpeted hall, pressed his ear to the bathroom door, and heard one of them snoring, a light nasal snore that left him feeling he might pull off leaving after all.

He stuck his pistol down the front of his pants, covered it with his shirt, and left the house for the darkness outside. He urinated in the woods across the street. A fog hovered among the black trees, and the sky already was beginning to lighten. He put his car in neutral, left his door open, and pushed until the Toyota was off the soft shoulder and the hill started to take it and he hopped in and coasted silently down toward the sea.

Now the sun was bright off the chain-link fence around the motor pool, and Lester glanced at his watch. Five more minutes and he'd go in. And he was going to have to tell the truth. If he lied he would force Alvarez to call or even visit the Iranian for a follow-up interview. He imagined the Behrani family awake now, having to urinate in each other's presence, the mother too, a woman from a culture that demanded women cover themselves from face to foot. He pictured the colonel knocking on the door, prepared to do what he must. If Kathy was still asleep and no one answered, would he assume Lester was too and then tell his family they would all have to wait a bit longer? Or would he hear the silence and think the house was empty and begin making noise?

There had to be a better way to proceed, but right now Lester didn't know what it was, only that there was quite a bit he hadn't done as well as he could. He thought about Bethany and Nate, how sometime today he was going to have to get them alone for a talk. Maybe early tonight he'd take them out for hamburgers and choco-late shakes at a fast-food shack on the beach somewhere. He imag-ined Kathy with them too but then he let that one go; his daughter and son wouldn't be ready for that for a while, and the truth was he wasn't quite ready for it either. With any luck, Kathy would be mov-ing back into her place at dusk anyway, and he thought of Bethany one sundown when she was four and they were all at the beach. Carol was nursing Nate, and Bethany sat next to him in the sand, her *Star Wars* towel around her shoulders. She turned to him and asked where the new suns come from.

"The new suns? What do you mean, sweetie?"

"The new one that comes out every morning, Daddy."

"Honey, there's just one sun."

"No, 'cause look, Daddy, the ocean's putting that one out. *See?* It's getting all wet. They all do, Daddy. Didn't you know that?"

He'd laughed and pulled her onto his lap, hugged her to him, and kissed her wet sandy hair until his lips started to feel numb.

A truck horn sounded in the traffic out on Broadway, and Lester got out of the Toyota and locked it. His pistol was under the passen-ger seat and he wished he'd taken his holster from Kathy's Bonneville at dawn. He thought about how she might feel when she woke. Would the pills and his gun become something from a faraway drunk-enness she wouldn't even need to think about anymore?

He walked across the sunlit lot for the shaded doors at the back of the Hall of Justice, and he had to squint in the light, his head aching slightly at the eyebrows, his legs two long sandbags under-neath him. His mouth was dry and he planned on getting a cold Coke from the machines around the corner from the elevators. He took a deep breath and told himself just to speak the truth about Monday night—not a word about last night—but admit everything about Monday. His jacket was positively trouble-free; Alvarez might even let it all go with an oral reprimand.

"Hey, *Les.*"

It came from behind him, but Lester stepped into the shade of the building before he turned around. It was Doug, hopping out of his patrol car, leaving the engine running. His uniform was stretched tight at the shoulders and across the chest, and his forearms looked, as always, impossibly thick. He was chewing gum, something he always did on patrol, never any other time. He'd gotten a haircut, his brown hair shorter than Alvarez's, and Lester could see his scalp glisten in the sunlight just before Doug stepped up into the shade, saying, "I thought you were off."

"Left a book in my locker. Why aren't you out on patrol?"

Doug shook his head, said he had to clean up two arrest reports from yesterday. He looked straight into Lester's face and began to chew his gum with his mouth closed, as if chewing gum was a slightly indecent thing to be doing, under the circumstances.

"Barbara went over to see Carol last night. She stayed pretty late."

"Yeah?" Lester thought he knew where this was going, and he didn't like it. He also wanted to hurry inside, get his appointment over with, and get back on the freeway heading north.

"Carol wanted us both to come over, but, tell you the truth, Les, I didn't feel like hearing you get shitcanned all night. You look like crap, by the way. Sleep at the camp last night?"

"We're there for now." Lester looked away and over the chain-link fence to the old courthouse on the other side of the street. Its huge stained-glass dome looked cool and composed under the sun.

"*We* still, huh?"

"That's right, Doug."

"Listen, I know we've already done this little dance, but are you real clear on what you're doing?"

Real clear. Doug used that kind of language all the time, a vestige of all the inner healing weekend workshops he took with Barbara. Doug put his hand on Lester's shoulder, a warm calloused paw. " 'Cause you know you're throwing it all away, right, man? All those years between you two, you're trashing them. You *do* know that."

Lester took in Doug's face, his friend's forehead all ridged with concern, his eyes blue and bright and earnest as he'd ever seen them. But naive too. It's what Lester had always liked and disliked about him. "I don't look at it that way." Lester turned to open one of the doors, letting Doug's hand fall away. He could feel the echo of his heart in his veins, and he was thirstier than ever. "I appreciate you looking out for me, Doug, but tell you what: you go patrol your territory and I'll patrol mine, okay, man?"

Lester turned and walked into the air-conditioned Hall of Justice. Three lawyers in dark suits stood at the elevators with their briefcases and paperwork. He glanced at his watch and decided to skip the Coke. Maybe Alvarez would offer him coffee, or water. He stood and waited, his hands crossed in front of him, his eyes on the polished brass elevator doors. He could see his reflection there, taller than the lawyers, but divided by the center line where the doors met. Then the tone sounded, the doors began to part, and as Lester moved forward he watched his own image spread out from the middle then disappear.

THERE WAS JUST WHAT WAS IN FRONT OF ME, THINGS I KNEW BUT didn't: an empty chair facing the side of my bed; an open door with a brass-plated knob, the knob of all the doors of all the rooms I'd ever lived in; lamplight across the blanket that covered me completely, even my arms—it looked like wool, as brown and purple as eggplant, and I was too warm under it, but I didn't move.

My throat was dry and sore, and my face and head felt flat, part of the pillow underneath. I was sweating. I could taste the salt in my throat, and I was waiting for my mother to walk through the doorway to get me up for the busride to school. But this is where I lay and sometimes watched Nick walk in from the bathroom. He'd come back naked or wrapped in a towel, his love handles hidden beneath the terry cloth, then he'd dress quietly in front of the closet so he wouldn't wake me, stepping into his underwear, tucking his bobbing penis under the waistband, pulling on his suit pants and leaving them unbuttoned and unzipped until he found the right shirt. I'd sit up and light a cigarette, smoke it and watch him put on the costume he couldn't wait to shed each night when he came home to eat too much, then smoke too much while he played bass in his practice room till I made him come watch TV with me, or make love.

Now I heard muffled voices coming from behind a wall, an ancient language, the colonel's and then his wife's, and I sat up in their brass bed in a robe I didn't remember putting on. I held it closed at my throat though I was sweating and I felt suddenly queasy. The window shade was pulled, but a crack of white sunlight showed on one side of the heavy curtains I never hung. I remembered kiwi fruit sliced in half on a tray of tea, the colonel's wife on her knees beside me, holding my forehead.

I swung the blanket and sheet away and sat up for my clothes. But there was just the empty chair. I closed my eyes and took a deep breath, smelled tea. My mouth was so dry and it tasted terrible and I didn't want to step out of this room. I heard the front screen door open and shut, and I got up to close the bedroom door, but Lester walked in from the hallway and looked at me like he wasn't sure it was really me. Then he hugged me, pulling me to him, his neck wet with sweat. I put my arms around him and felt the gun handle sticking out the back of his pants, remembered my cupped hands under the faucet in the fluorescent light. Lester was hugging me hard, turning from side to side. I couldn't breathe. I pushed myself away from him and stood there looking at him. His eyes were small and bloodshot, and there was a scratch on his nose, a small cut on his chin, his mustache crooked as ever. He stood so still, his long arms hanging there, that gun hidden behind him; he was every boy I had ever fallen for—lean and dark and over the edge—and I started to cry, covering my mouth and putting my hand out so he wouldn't step any closer. I sat down on the bed and let it come.

Lester sat on the edge of the chair in front of me and rested both hands on my knees. They were big, his fingers so long I felt like a little girl, and I didn't know if this was a good feeling or not. Then he got up and left the room, came back with tissues. I wiped my eyes and blew my nose. I couldn't look at him and I didn't want him looking at me. My bare feet looked blurred against the carpet, my toenails chipped.

"Tell me what happened, Kathy." His voice was thin, exhausted. I could still hear the murmur of the Behranis in another room. "Do they know you just walked into their house?"

"*Their* house?" He looked behind him at the door, then down at the carpet. There was a piece of paper there and he picked it up, unfolded it, and handed it to me. I read it, my face turning hot, my stomach cold and hollow.

"They're in the *bathroom?*"

He nodded.

I thought of the colonel's wife bringing me tea and fruit, her lined, beautiful face giving me all her attention. "*Shit.*"

"Yep." He took the note from me, folded it tightly, and stuffed it into his front jeans pocket. "I waited for you at the camp, but when you didn't show up, I went looking for you and ended up here. I looked through the window and saw my gun on the counter and you weren't anywhere so I guess I just feared the worst." He kept his eyes on me a second, then looked away. He told me how he heard me moan, how he kicked in the back door and grabbed his gun, then saw me on the floor, and as he said all this, his voice steady, my head started to feel too heavy for my neck.

Now Les was using legal language about what he'd done: B&E, Brandishing a Weapon, False Imprisonment, all the real trouble he could be in. He sat in the chair with his elbows on the armrests, his shoulders hunched, his long fingers hanging there. I said: "I didn't think you'd come back."

"Why, Kathy? Why'd you think that?" He leaned forward and rested his hands on my knees.

"I don't know." I looked down at his arms, a long blue vein in the belly of his forearm. I told him about yesterday, when I started thinking for the first time how much he must love his kids and how they must love him, and how bad I felt squeezing myself into that picture. And so I made a sort of vow to myself to try and solve my problems without fucking up anyone else's life, drove here to talk to the colonel's wife woman to woman, but her husband came home and forced me into my car, and as I told Les this I felt angry again. I kept my eyes on the veins in Lester's arm the whole time I spoke. His foot was bouncing slightly, then it stopped.

"When did you drink, Kathy?"

I told him, but I couldn't remember what came first and what came later. I almost didn't tell him about the woman at the gas station, but then I did and he asked if she got a good look at me, at the plates of my car.

"I don't know."

We were both quiet. He got up and sat on the bed next to me, put his arm around my back. His body odor was strong and his breath was bad, like old coffee, and this made me feel a little better, the fact his smell wasn't pure and clean. Then I thought of my own teeth coated with dried stomach acid, and I kept my face down. There was a knocking on the inside of the bathroom door down the hall, the colonel's muffled voice calling Lester "sir," asking to be let out so his family could eat.

"This is crazy, Les."

"Crazy?" He was holding me against him, his voice hot in my ear. "What about trying to kill yourself, Kathy? What do we call that?" He let go of me and stood, the pistol handle sticking out his waistband. "Just tell me this: was it drinking too much on a really bad day? Or do you really want to die?"

The colonel knocked on the bathroom door again. I looked back down at the Persian carpet, at all those dark reds and purples. My throat began to close up. "I just—"

"Yeah?"

"I just want things to *change.*"

The colonel pounded on the door. It sounded like he was using his fist. "You must to allow us food immediately!"

Lester leaped over to the doorway. *"You'll eat when you call the goddamn county!"*

"Yes." The colonel's voice was low and dulled behind the closed door but I heard his next words clearly: "I will do as you say. We will sell."

Lester looked back at me and smiled so wide his mustache went up in a straight black line above his teeth. But I could hardly move. I just sat there not knowing what I'd just won. I put my hand over my lips, and he walked over and squatted on the floor at my feet. "How's that for a change?" He shook his head. "When I found out what you'd done, I felt stood up. Isn't that strange? What does that say about *me?*"

I didn't know what that said about him but I knew I felt closer to him when he said it. I reached over and took his hand, rubbing my finger over the ridge of his knuckles, down over his wedding band. "I don't think I would have done any of this sober, Les. If that helps you."

"It does."

The colonel knocked again, this time softly.

"I'm going to have to keep the heat on them until they go, Kathy. Maybe you should leave until then."

"I'm staying here."

"Promise?" Les was looking into my face, his dark eyes so warm and full of need I didn't know if I wanted to kiss him or move away.

He kissed me and one of his mustache whiskers went up my nose. I watched him leave the room, pulling out his pistol as he went. I looked around for my clothes, but they weren't anywhere. So I got up, stood in the doorway, and watched Lester set a crowbar against the wall, push open the door, and step back with his gun at his side. At his feet on the rug were two neckties, and he told the Behranis to go into the kitchen. As they came out I pulled the robe together at my throat. I felt like stepping back into the bedroom and closing the door, but I knew they'd already seen me. Lester walked backwards in front of them, stepping into the doorway beside me to let them by. The colonel went first, then his wife and son, the colonel looking straight ahead as he passed me, his chin high, like he was marching in a military parade. His shirt was wrinkled and there was a dab of shaving cream just beneath his jawbone. I was impressed by this, the fact he took the time to shave. And looking at him in that moment, Lester standing beside me with his gun at his side, I was glad things were turning out this way, that this hot-tempered shithead was almost Middle Eastern history for me. But then his wife glanced at me without turning her head, and I knew she was scared of Lester and was trying to see where I stood in all this. I looked down at the floor in time to see their teenage son's big brown feet.

Les nudged my shoulder and nodded for me to go use the bathroom if I needed to, then he followed the boy into the kitchen and I shut myself in my old bathroom, locked the door, and peed as quietly as I could. The room smelled like toothpaste and the colonel's shaving cream. My clothes were on the towel shelf across from me folded in a neat pile against the wall: my shorts, my client's daughter's turquoise T-shirt from Fisherman's Wharf, a corner of her panties and my bra under both. My Reeboks were set on the floor side by side. On the back of the sink was the empty prescription bottle. I didn't remember ever holding it in my own hand. But looking at it, I wasn't filled with the remorse and dread I'd felt before. Or even the dark rush I'd try again. I felt thankful, like the contents of that empty brown bottle had turned things around for me like nothing else could have. While I washed my face and hands with hot water and soap I pictured myself cleaning and returning the girl's T-shirt and underwear later this week. Today was Wednesday—yes, Wednesday—my Colma River morning, when I was supposed to clean her house anyway, but I'd have to call her father at his office and postpone a day or two because I was moving. *I was moving back into my house.*

I took a fresh towel and pat-dried my face, breathed in the clean smell of the thick terry cloth. I still wanted to disappear, but not completely. My mouth tasted horrible. I squeezed an inch of toothpaste onto my forefinger and used that, rinsing six or seven times. Then I drank from the faucet. On the towel shelf was the colonel's shaving kit but nothing of his wife's. No brush or comb, not even a compact. I bent over, letting my hair fall over my head. Then I snapped back up and ran my fingers over my scalp, straightening whatever I found, though I only dared to check myself in the mirror for a second.

I slipped out of Mrs. Behrani's robe and started to get dressed. I was a little dizzy from trying to fix my hair and I could hear the clink of silverware out in the kitchen, Lester's voice saying something about a phone book. He was talking louder and faster than he usually did, more jumpy. I knew he'd been up all night, that he was doing something now that could really go wrong if anyone found out about it, something he never would've done if not for me. But then I remembered his story about planting coke in the wife beater's bathroom, and I felt a little better as I pulled the T-shirt over my head and caught the faint scent of vomit and gun oil. Me and Lester.

I smelled toast. My stomach had never been so empty and flat. A hunger pain turned over behind my ribs. My body felt light, almost pure, but not my head. It was like I had cotton not in my ears, but in my thoughts. A cigarette and some tea, that's all I needed. I folded the towel and put it back on the shelf. I heard silverware tink once against a plate out in the kitchen. The colonel cleared his throat, then spoke into the telephone. There was a pulsing in my hand and fingers and I opened the door enough to hear him give his full name and my address to somebody on the other end. I stuck my head out the door and looked down the hall, saw their son sitting at the counter hunched over a bowl of cereal. I could see his mother's hands buttering a piece of toast as carefully as if it were something living. The colonel stood against the back wall near two or three pots of flowers holding the receiver with two hands. I didn't see Lester anywhere, but I pictured him standing in the living room with his gun, and as I left my bathroom, running my fingers back through my hair, I hoped he wasn't pointing it at anyone.

⁙⁙⁙⁙⁙⁙⁙⁙
⁙⁙⁙⁙
··

I HAVE FOLLOWED BURDON'S ORDERS AND COMPLETED THE TELEPHONE call and I sit upon a stool at the counter with my wife and son and drink black tea that is bitter for the samovar has been lighted all the evening long. Burdon and his gendeh sit upon the sofa at our backs, eating our bread, drinking our tea. Through the kitchen's window, beneath the steps of the new widow's walk, the sky is as clear and blue as when flying at high altitudes in air with no clouds. From the woodlands across the street come the morning songs of birds, and far away, perhaps down in the village, a dog barks. It would not serve Burdon's purpose to shoot us in the back as we sit, but I have the feeling my backside is not clothed, nor has even the protection of flesh over bone. Nadereh has eaten very little of the toast before her, and she drinks her tea without sugar in her mouth. This she does rarely and I assume it is to avoid the slurping sound it sometimes makes, the pull of air between the sugar and teeth. All the morning long she has been silent, the same quiet bird who clutched our infant son in the middle of the night as our bullet-proofed limousine drove through the alleys of the capital city. Once again she has surrendered the burden of action to me, and I am grateful and resentful as well.

My son has finished eating, and he sits and waits for what is to happen next. Again this morning, as we took our turn at the sink washing, I told him to do nothing but what Mr. Burdon instructs.

"Yes, Bawbaw," he said, his eyes upon mine, and in them was a dark, hopeful light that is now a heavy timber across my back for I have no real plan of any kind. I hear Burdon upon the sofa, whispering to Kathy Nicolo. As I spoke on the telephone with the same tax bureaucrat as before, Burdon sat upon our sofa's edge, his weapon placed on the cushion beside him, and the voice of the bureaucrat became nearly boyish, unable to conceal his relief at my news of selling back to the county this bungalow. For a brief moment, I felt a measure of his relief, a desire to simply follow his instructions, travel to Redwood City to sign the proper documents releasing a check in my name. Simply do as I am ordered and leave. But ordered by *whom?* This thin policeman sick and weak with love? And leave to what place? A hotel that will begin to eat our small nest of money even before we find a new home? One we would surely not be able to buy and sell at three times our investment? I drink my bitter tea, the whispering voices of our captors at my back. Many days, when I toiled as a garbage soldier under the hot sun or in the cool wet fog with the old Vietnamese, the fat and lazy Panamanians, the pig Mendez, the Chinese who smoked cigarettes as if it was air they had imported from their home country, as we fanned out along the roadside with our harpoons and bright yellow plastic bags, I sometimes believed I was being punished for the comfortable life I led as a high officer among beggars. But this belief came only on the worst of days, when my fatigue seemed to come from my own blood. Most days, however, I believed I was being tested by my God and that if I possessed a true desire to escape that life I must have patience and continue to endure until my opportunity revealed itself; this armed couple in our home is nothing more than a test within a test, something that comes when the prize is quite close at hand. Again, I must simply bow my head, and wait.

An automobile drives past the bungalow and someone rises from the sofa. There is the soft rustle of the drapery at the window, the footsteps over the carpet to the countertop and the telephone at my left. It is Burdon, the grip of his weapon protruding from the front of his trousers. He regards us all as he presses the receiver's buttons. He is perhaps twenty years my junior but my veins speed at the thought of grasping the gun from his pants. Have I grown too slow? If I must ask, it is already too late. I breathe quietly, turn away from Mr. Burdon, and look over Nadi at Esmail, who regards me, then Burdon's weapon, then me once again, his face still, his eyes bright.

On the telephone Lester V. Burdon identifies himself as a deputy and requests information on any dispatch of a weapon being brandished in San Bruno yesterday, a self-service benzine station off the King's Highway. He is silent for a long moment, and I do not know if he is watching us or his woman. He speaks again. "Was there a vehicle ID on that?"

Burdon thanks his colleague and hangs up the telephone. He does not move, and I regard him evenly. His eyes are small and moist with fatigue. It is clear he has not slept, but I do not know if this will be to my advantage or not.

"You and your son are coming with me. Get cleaned up. We have a lot to do."

LESTER ALLOWED THE COLONEL AND THE BOY TO GO INTO THEIR rooms one at a time for fresh clothes, then ordered them into the bathroom together to change. He stood in the dim hallway and waited, holding the pistol down at his leg, and even though it was on double safety he wished it wasn't part of the equation at all. But what was the equation? He wasn't sure. All he knew was they had a perp and vehicle description on Kathy but no plates, and his appointment with Alvarez had gone better than he had honestly expected. Lester had sat in a steel chair in front of the lieutenant's desk and told him most of the truth of Monday night, that he'd gone to the Corona address on behalf of a friend and simply suggested to Mr. Behrani that he do the right thing and move. He had never made any threats of any kind, was just trying to act as an intermediary in a dispute. "Unfortunately," he had told the lieutenant, "I made the mistake of leaving my uniform on. I know now that was highly inappropriate."

"He says you threatened to have his family deported."

Lester smiled and shook his head. "I'm not INS."

Maybe Alvarez had had an especially good run this morning, or maybe the sight of Lester's still-damp hair, nicked face, and wrinkled pants kept bringing the lieutenant back to Lester's phone message about family troubles. Alvarez sat back in the upholstered chair behind his desk, his elbows on the arms, the tips of all ten fingers touching.

"Are you and your wife getting counseling?"

"Yes." This was a lie Lester hadn't planned on, but it came out so naturally he had to wonder if he *was* getting help. The lieutenant looked at him for a long five seconds. Then he sat forward and picked a pen up off his blotter. "You're an FTO, Deputy. I shouldn't have to tell you squat about departmental code."

"Yes, sir."

The lieutenant tapped his pen once in his open palm, then he stood, and so did Lester.

"Consider this an oral reprimand to get back in line. And next time I ask you to my office I don't care if there's a death in the family, I want you in that chair. Understood?"

"Yes, sir."

"You have a bright future here, Deputy. I highly recommend you don't shit where you eat. Good day."

On the other side of the bathroom door the colonel was speaking low in Farsi to his teenage son. But the son was quiet and Lester wondered if he was scared. The colonel certainly didn't sound scared. Was he feeling resigned to this new situation? That he would just have to reverse the house sale and that was that? Lester didn't think so; he remembered the colonel's face after he'd pulled the gun barrel from under his chin, his narrowed eyes, his lips a straight line. Now Lester wiped sweat from his forehead, tried to breathe deeply through his nose, but the air wasn't coming fast enough. This *was* crazy; Behrani was too proud to take defeat so passively. Was he playing possum? Was he just biding his time until he and his family were free of Lester and his gun? And when would that be? After this little house was empty of their things and they got about four blocks down the road in their U-Haul to a pay phone to call Alvarez in Redwood City?

The colonel's wife was washing dishes quietly in a sink full of water. Lester could smell Kathy's cigarette smoke, and he thought he could get away with leaving Mrs. Behrani alone for a minute or two. He called Kathy's name and heard her get off the couch immediately. He didn't know how she would take what he was about to tell her, but he began by pulling the loaded magazine from the pistol and thumbing each 9mm round into the palm of his hand. She came up to his side, her hair a little wild, her face shadowed, and he kissed her quickly on the lips, tasting tea and nicotine, then took her hand and placed the bullets in it. One fell to the carpet and he stooped quickly and put it back in her palm. He whispered: "We have to bail out of this."

Kathy looked at him and shook her head, her eyes dark and moist, her lips parted like there was something she'd been prepared to say but now forgot what it was.

"This prick's not going to let this all slide, Kath. As soon as we send him packing he'll make his move."

"What do you mean? Let him keep the *house?*"

Lester could see her heart beating in her jugular vein. "No, you need to *sell* him this house. Take the money he gave the county and let him do whatever he wants with this little place."

"It was my *father's*, Les." A tear edged itself out her right eye, and Lester thumbed it away. He closed his eyes and breathed deeply through his nose. He was about to say he was sorry, he'd lost his temper and fucked up, but the bathroom door opened and the colonel and boy came out, the colonel in dress pants, white shirt, and silk tie, the boy in basketball shoes, bright green surfer shorts, and a tank top. Lester could smell the colonel's cologne, something sweet and European. He stepped with Kathy into the doorway of the boy's bedroom and waved his gun at them to move into the kitchen. He felt Kathy standing squarely behind him out of sight, sniffling and sticking the bullets into her shorts pockets. When the two Behranis reached the kitchen counter, their backs to the hallway, Lester told them to stay right there. The boy was taller than the father, and he was looking in the direction of his mother at the sink. Lester leaned back against the door casing so he could still see them, but Kathy too. She was looking at him, her eyes welling up. "This is my fault. I didn't mean for you to get into this."

Lester thought how it was true they wouldn't be here now if she had only met him last night at the fish camp, if she had gone there—drunk or sober—instead of here with *his* gun, but he could feel the Behranis waiting and this wasn't the time; they would have to talk later. He whispered: "I know you didn't. Listen, take his money and he'll still have his real estate and then maybe I can convince him to keep things between us."

Kathy wiped her nose and shook her head. "It won't work. You haven't seen his temper."

Lester looked at the father and son. The boy had crossed his arms across his chest, and the colonel was resting one hand on the countertop as if he were close to losing *his* patience. A warm flash passed through Lester's face and neck, and his mouth went dry. She was right; even if Behrani agreed to this sudden change in plan, they couldn't be sure he wouldn't turn on them anywhere along the line out of vengeance, the house in his hands or not. He felt Kathy's fingers on his arm.

"We have to get away, don't we?"

Lester nodded. But what were they going to do? Just drive away from here and keep driving? And in what? His Toyota and Kathy's wanted car? Or would they have to leave Kathy's car behind? Airports would be put under surveillance. So would all the bus and train stations. They would have to disguise themselves, rent a car under false names, and make their way north or south to the border. Lester's mouth tasted like metal, his legs seemed to have disappeared, and he was adrift in cold black space. How and when would he be able to see Bethany and Nate again? To hold them? Kiss them? But what was the alternative? Criminal charges? *Prison?*

"We're going to need that money, Kathy."

She looked down the hallway, then closed her eyes and shook her head. "I didn't want you to fall into my shit, Les. I really didn't."

"Hey," he said, kissing her quickly on the cheeks and lips. "Your shit's my shit. Think of someplace sunny we can go."

THE KEYS WERE still in Kathy's Bonneville, and Lester had the colonel and boy sit in the front while he sat in back. The upholstery was already warm from the sun, and the inside of the car smelled faintly of gasoline and Kathy's cigarette smoke. At Lester's feet was an empty Bacardi rum nip. He told the colonel to start the car and drive it over the lawn and around to the rear of the house. Behrani paused before putting the car in gear. The son glanced at his father, then looked away, and Lester leaned forward and pressed the gun barrel to the back of the colonel's neck. The boy seemed to stiffen in the passenger's seat, and Lester felt bad about that, but not enough to pull the gun away. The colonel drove slowly around to the back of the house. There were beads of sweat on his bald head. One dripped into another and caused a rivulet to run into the old officer's thinning black-and-gray hair.

"Pull right up to the hedge and give me the keys." Lester turned to the son, who was looking straight ahead through the windshield as if they were on the open road. The boy's sideburns were soft, downy hairs. "Esmail—am I pronouncing your name correctly?"

The boy nodded once.

"Good. Now I want you to listen to me, Esmail. Last night you did something that got your family locked into the bathroom, and right now we're going for a ride to Redwood City and I want you along for company. Look at me, please." The boy did, and Lester pressed the barrel a bit deeper into the colonel's neck. "Men learn from their mistakes, Esmail. And you don't want consequences to get any worse, do you?"

Esmail shook his head, his eyes on the trigger finger of Lester's hand.

"Good boy." Lester got out of the car and stuck his weapon into the waistband of his pants, covering it with his shirt. The sky was a bright gray haze that made him squint, and he had the colonel walk first, then the boy. The inside of the colonel's Buick was as clean as a model right off the lot, and Lester sat in the back directly behind Esmail in the passenger seat and stretched his leg out on the gray fabric. When the colonel started the engine, Lester pressed the window button for some air, held his pistol in his lap, and told the colonel to drive down the hill and take Hillside Boulevard for El Camino Real south.

Lester's mouth was dry from the black Persian tea and no sleep, and he wanted a cold Coke, though he knew he didn't need the sugar or caffeine; it was as if he was in a downward rush off a mountain, a fine electric current running from his feet to his brain, and the feeling wouldn't stop until he landed on solid ground. But where would that be? Mexico? Driving south through Chula Vista and the neighborhoods of his youth to the same border post his father had worked? No, they would drive north to Vancouver or British Columbia, where he'd heard there were mountains along the coast. He and Kathy could get lost in them, find a cabin where they'd spend the morning and early afternoons in bed, getting up to shower together, then dress and go into one of those seaside towns in search of a long hot meal. Lester felt Bethany and Nate standing outside this picture, and he tried to swallow, but couldn't. And would it be that easy anyway? Did the United States have an extradition treaty with Canada? Would they have to lie low there too? Lester didn't know. He would have to find out.

At the bottom of the hill the colonel stopped at the intersection before the main drag through downtown Corona. Across the street was a black-and-white from the city parked against the curb, and Lester recognized the young cop behind the wheel. His name was Cutler. One night last spring Lester had given him cross-jurisdictional backup for a jeep full of drunk fraternity boys from San Francisco State. Now he glanced over at the colonel's Buick just as it took the left for Hillside, and Lester slowly turned his face away, kept his eyes on the colonel's profile as he drove them up into the hills past pure stands of ponderosa pine broken up by the trimmed lawns of homes with seaside views from their second-story decks. The sky was still gray and it made the grass appear a heightened green, not quite natural. The colonel was driving with both hands on the wheel, checking the rearview mirror every few seconds. Lester turned and saw three or four cars on the incline behind them and he leaned back and told the colonel in a calm and relaxed voice to speed up a bit. The colonel obeyed instantly. Was he still playing possum? Or was he truly deep under Lester's thumb? Deep enough he *would* stay quiet after this was all through? Lester felt a rise of hope in him. Maybe there was still a way to work this out. He took his service pistol and slid it beneath his leg.

"We need to talk, Colonel."

Behrani's eyes darted to the rearview, and Lester saw new fear in them, that and a hardness, one he would have to start softening right now.

"How much did you pay for the house?"

"Forty-five thousand dollars."

Lester looked down at his hands, his long thin fingers, the fingers of a woman; he knew an auction price would be low, but he hadn't expected it to be a *third* of what the house was worth. He took a half breath and let it out. Why give this dictatorial son of a bitch the best deal? What had he done to deserve it? Why not take his money *and* the house? But it wasn't what the colonel had done last night, Lester knew; it was what *he* had done. And Kathy. There was still time to plea-bargain; they weren't completely on the run yet.

"Ms. Nicolo's not a well woman."

The colonel's eyes moved to the rearview mirror again, and this time they looked softer, curious, not about Kathy probably, but the direction of the conversation, the shift in tone. This was good, Lester thought, two men talking.

"You saw that last night, didn't you, Colonel?"

The boy looked at his father, then straight ahead at the road.

"Yes."

"What she really needs is rest."

Behrani looked like he wanted to say something, but was content to wait for hours.

"She's had a change of heart about the house."

"What does this mean?" The colonel glanced back into the mirror.

"It means you can keep it."

Behrani's eyebrows went up, two thin snakes springing out of nowhere. "She does not wish the sale to be rescinded?"

"Yes and no. Only she wants to be included in the transaction this time. No county, just a private deal."

"I do not understand."

"Between the two of you. You take the county check and sign it over to her. When the county returns ownership to Kathy, she'll just let you keep it and she gets some rest."

They were entering a small business district, passing a clothing boutique, a golf supply outlet, and a video store and sandwich shop. Behrani's eyes were back on the road, his face expressionless. "She will produce the proper paperwork for this amount? It will be in writing the bungalow belongs to me?"

"Yes."

Up ahead was the turnoff for Skyline Boulevard and the Junipero Serra Freeway. Lester usually took El Camino Real, but the freeway would get them there faster.

"Are we agreed, Colonel?"

Behrani glanced into the rearview. "Once the county bureaucrats have written the property in my name, I will give to her the money."

Lester took a deep chest-wavering breath and let it out. That could take days. "Take the Skyline, please."

The colonel took the turn slowly. He had just agreed to sign over the check, but why the somber, doubtful tone in his voice? It was the circumstances under which all this was happening, Lester was sure of it. It was the colonel's pride. Lester thought that maybe he should apologize, just explain that he hadn't known what had happened to Kathy, that he'd overreacted and now would like to put it all behind them if he could. But then he would be offering the captive colonel his bare throat, and a new fear was beginning to move coolly through Lester's ribcage; the county tax office was fifty yards from the Hall of Justice building in Redwood City, so he would have to let the colonel go in alone and hope he was sold enough on this new proposition just to sign his papers and leave without an extra word to anyone. And what about the boy? If Lester let him go with his father, then Lester would be a lone target on a shelf if Behrani concluded he was better off calling in the wolves than keeping his end of the agreement. And what *was* in it for Behrani to stay in the deal? He already owned the house. All he would be getting in return is what he already had, that, and Kathy and Lester off his back, which he could also get if he called the department from the county tax office and a half-dozen deputies descended on Lester sitting in the colonel's Regal. No, Lester thought, this was no time for false hopes; the thing to work on was getting back to Corona with the county check, then taking a reading on things from there. And he was going to have to reconsider the tone of this whole exchange; the only thing Lester still had going for him was the fact he *had* lost his temper last night, that he was still armed, and for all practical purposes was moving the colonel and son against their will and they still did not know what he was capable of, which meant Lester was going to have to keep the boy in the car with him once they got to Redwood City, keep the boy as some kind of human collateral, a thought that sent a tinge through Lester's shoulder and neck. He rotated his head once but his muscles were too tight for anything to crack.

He looked out the window. Skyline Boulevard ran along the spine of hills that divided the ocean side of the penninsula from the bay, and when he first began to patrol this territory, Lester had been taken by the absolute contrasts in vegetation on either side. The land to the west, from the hills to the beaches of the Pacific, was locked in fog and rain and so was thick with forests of live oak, digger pine, madrone, and Douglas fir. And south of Half Moon Bay the farmland was planted right to the shore, wide-open artichoke fields that were such a sustained green, Lester found it almost too much to take in while driving. Lawns came in thick and coarse, but *green*. But in towns to the east, from San Bruno to Palo Alto, the grass looked parched and yellowed. Even the watered grounds of estates in Woodside didn't have quite the same chlorophyll-rich look as those to the west. Lester's own lawn in Millbrae was too dry and coarse to sit on without a chair. And it was yellow at the roots. Instead of tall evergreens, the bayside towns were filled with dry shrub of manzanita, piñon, and toyon, plant life that did well in eroded soil.

Soon they were on the freeway and the colonel was driving at a normal speed. An eighteen-wheeler began to pass on the left and Lester could see only the spinning chrome of its wheels through the window. He lowered the pistol between his knees and placed it on the floor at his feet. On their left was San Andreas lake, the start of the fish and game refuge, the water catching the bright gray of the sky. Lester closed his eyes to it a moment but then opened them just as quickly. He still had that hum inside him and it was not unfamiliar; his limbs felt light, as if vapor moved through them instead of blood, and everything he saw had a new clarity to it: the small dots of lint in the gray fabric of the Buick's headrests; the colonel's profile whenever he would glance to the left or right, the way Lester could distinguish easily between each eyelash; the boy's hair, as black as a Mexican's, his pink scalp barely visible between thick strands, just the hint of smooth brown pigment. It was adrenaline but more; it was adrenaline that had stopped coming in amateurish gushes and instead shifted into a slow feed, the whole body on a sort of molecular alert. Lester had known this feeling from the births of both his children; he'd known it with varying degrees in his work; and now it seemed to come with the territory of leaving one's wife, with stepping so far over the line to do it Lester felt sure he was about to come up with a pan full of gold or else get swept down the river altogether. And you couldn't really call it a bad feeling. It occurred to him now it was probably how felons wanted to feel all the time.

The sun had burned through the cloud bank and was warm on his skin through the glass. He was thirsty and wanted a bottle of cold spring water, but he couldn't send the colonel or boy into a store to get some, and he couldn't chance all three of them going in either. In the lane in front of them was a municipal van full of Chicano kids, ten or eleven years old. Most seemed to be moving about in their seats laughing and shouting at each other. But sitting sideways at the rear window was a teenage boy wearing a white helmet, his mouth open, his chin wet with saliva, and he kept rocking back and forth, looking directly at the Buick, at all three of them, it seemed. The colonel slowly changed lanes to pass, and the boy began to rock faster in his seat, his eyes following the Buick as it began to pull out of his sight, his mouth nothing but a dark wet hole in his face.

FOR A LONG TIME AFTER LESTER LEFT WITH THE COLONEL AND HIS son, I just stood in the bedroom and listened to Mrs. Behrani quietly cleaning up out in the kitchen. I didn't like being left alone with her. I didn't know what I was supposed to do and I wished I hadn't volunteered to stay. Lester had told me to think of someplace sunny we could go to, but all I could think of was my family, my brother Frank and my mother, their faces when they found out I not only sold Dad's house without telling them, but that all I got was an auction price for it before I fled town to spend it. And then they'd get the whole story: my drinking, the gun, the pills, Lester and the family he took hostage. My brother would roll his eyes at me one last time, then write my name permanently on the expensive side of his internal cost/benefit sheet. My mother would just curse me for good. I felt queasy, like an important organ inside me wasn't attached all the way. My front shorts pockets were heavy with Lester's bullets.

Yesterday I was convinced that by this time today he'd be back with his wife and kids, back to his life in Eureka Fields. But instead he ended up committing a string of crimes to sit and watch over me in my drugged sleep while he didn't sleep at all. When he made the colonel park my car out of sight in the backyard, I came into the bedroom and watched from the window as he leaned forward and pushed his unloaded gun into the colonel's neck. Lester got out first, stuffing the gun into his pants and covering it with his shirt. And when the colonel followed, the morning sun in his face, it felt good to see him afraid, see *him* bullied by someone.

Your shit is my shit. But I never wanted this problem solved bad enough to scare a woman as sweet as Mrs. Behrani. And what was I supposed to do? Go out there and watch her like a prison guard? But then how could I do anything *but* help Lester get us out of this trouble, which was really more mine than his?

It was quiet out in the kitchen and I pictured her running down the hill into town to find a cop, tell him everything. Maybe they'd catch Lester on the road, think he was armed when I knew he wasn't. I let out a long weak breath, and stepped fast into the hallway.

She was still at the kitchen sink. The breakfast dishes were stacked neatly, and she was just standing there, looking out the window, though there wasn't much to see but the wooden staircase up to the new roof deck that was hers now. I used to like looking out that window while I rinsed a plate or coffee cup, see my small side yard and the drop of the hill into town.

Mrs. Behrani slowly turned her head and looked at me over her shoulder. It seemed to take her a second or two. Her hair was still flattened a little on one side, and I pictured her sleeping in the bathroom, in the tub or on the floor. I guess I expected her to look ready to fight me somehow, but instead her lined face seemed pained, her eyes taking me in like she wanted to understand me before it was too late. It was almost my mother's look.

"Please, your friend—" Her voice was weak and she looked down and pressed her hand to the side of her head, then took a deep breath and looked back at me. "Will he to hurt my son?"

"No, he doesn't want any more trouble, Mrs. Behrani. He's just trying to finish all this, I guess." I thought about reaching into my pocket for the bullets.

She stood still, looking at me, her hand pressed to the side of her head. I was about to tell her I was selling them the house, but her eyes were almost black, like she was imagining something that really scared her, and I knew what it was.

"He has a son of his own, you know."

She nodded once and took a breath. Then she closed her eyes and pressed until her fingertips whitened.

"Are you all right?"

"Migraine. Please, I must—" She moved by me and I watched her walk down the dim hallway as slow and careful as an old lady, one hand in front of her, the other pressed to the left side of her head. She left the bathroom door half open and I could see her feet and lower legs as she knelt on the floor at the toilet. I felt so strange, like it was almost fate that I walk over and hold her forehead as she retched her small breakfast, then sniffled and let out a long moan.

"Are you all right?"

She raised her head, her face grayish white. "I must to medicine."

On the sink was the brown vial I'd emptied the night before and my face flushed as I opened her medicine cabinet thinking, please, please don't be that one. But there were only vials with that snake alphabet on them, and I wouldn't know which one she needed even if I could read them. I picked up the empty vial on the sink and turned around, but Mrs. Behrani was up and halfway out the door.

"I'm sorry, Mrs. Behrani, I'll drive downtown and buy you some right now. I'm really sorry." I saw myself getting pulled over in the car, arrested for yesterday's slip over the edge at the gas station, never getting back here to relieve Mrs. Behrani's agony. I would have to walk or run down the hill into town, or maybe their son had a bike. But could she be faking all this to get me out of the house so she could call the police? No, she looked too terrible; she was dragging her fingertips along the wall, then she was in her bedroom and so was I, watching her sit on the bed and pull open the nightstand drawer, take out a prescription bottle. I was so relieved I hadn't robbed her of what she needed right now, I felt almost cheerful. She dropped her chin as she tried to get the lid off but couldn't, and I took it from her hands and opened it.

There was half a cup of cold black tea near the lamp, Lester's I guessed, and Mrs. Behrani shook out two capsules, palmed them into her mouth, then drank the rest of the tea. She pressed her fingers to the side of her head, her eyes closed, her hand shaking slightly. "I must for rest."

"Okay." There was nothing else to say or do. I watched her lie back on the bed and draw her knees up. She rested her arm across her eyes.

"Please." Her voice was almost a whisper. "Close for me window light."

I did as she said. I went to the window, my red Bonneville parked under it in the sun, and I pulled the heavy curtains shut. I heard the click of her tape player, then that same music she'd been playing when I came here yesterday to talk. I could see her thin arm adjusting the volume, though her other arm was still across her eyes, and I knew this was something she'd done too many times, come to this darkness and lain down on this bed with this music that at first made me think of fairy tales I'd read as a girl, snakes with the heads of princesses, carpets that would fly over black deserts under cold stars, men with long curved swords dancing around a pit of flames. But then a woman's voice began to sing in their language, high and mournful about something she'd lost, and I suddenly felt I was standing where I had no business being at all, like I was watching a stranger die, or two people making love.

I left my old bedroom and my old house. I went out to my fugitive car, sat in the driver's seat, and smoked. My head didn't feel stuffed with wet rags anymore, but still, everything seemed too bright and downy: the sun's glare across my hood, the way the hedges around my back door seemed to hover slightly off the ground, the muffled and tinny sound of Mrs. Behrani's music coming from inside the house. But the cigarettes were helping, the nicotine sticking its legs down into my chest like a baby, and I sat there in my Bonneville, the seat cover too warm under the sun, and I smoked and waited, waited for Lester.

LESTER HAD THE COLONEL TURN LEFT ONTO SYCAMORE STREET. THE county tax office was on the corner, not a half minute's walk from the old domed courthouse and the Hall of Justice on the other side of Broadway, and Lester was relieved there were no parking spaces this close to the corner. He began to tap his fingers on his knee, his mouth and throat as dry as paper. The colonel drove slowly, scanning both sides of the street for an available spot. The street was lined with tall laurel trees, and Lester was grateful for the shade. As soon as they'd turned east off the freeway onto Woodside Road, the sky had gone from its coastal gray to a pale, metallic blue, the sun shining brightly everywhere. Now it made Lester's eyes ache.

Nearly three blocks from Broadway a yellow cargo van pulled away from the curb, and Behrani began to take its place. He backed the car carefully, turning to look over his shoulder and out the rear window. Lester knew he was sitting directly in the colonel's line of vision, but he didn't move; to do that would be courteous, and right now, just before he sent the colonel out on his own to do the right thing, Lester couldn't afford to appear courteous. Or thoughtful. Or soft in any way.

Behrani finished parking and turned off the engine. Lester picked his pistol up off the floor, then pulled from his front pocket some loose change and handed two quarters over the seat. "This'll give you thirty minutes on the meter. They're expecting you, so you shouldn't have to wait." Lester made a point of looking at the boy, whose eyes were dark and expectant, seeing only his father, and again, Lester wished the teenager wasn't part of any of this at all, but he was and this was the time to use him.

"Your son stays here with me. If you're not back by then, Esmail and I will be gone. Are we clear on this?"

The colonel turned in his seat. His eyes were slightly yellow at the whites, and there were beads of sweat on his forehead and chin. He looked at his son, both of them locking eyes for a moment, and Lester felt instantly dirty and wrong, like he had just violated something precious, but he couldn't backpedal now; there was too much on the table and he was already waist-deep in his own bluff.

Behrani looked back at him, and Lester could see the twitch of a small muscle up near the Iranian's temple. "But we have an agreement."

"That's right, so go get the check and come back to the car, Colonel."

"No. I will for you do nothing without my son. *Nothing.*"

Lester took in a long breath and let it out. He imagined the three of them strolling into the county tax office together, his service pistol barely covered by his shirt while he somehow stayed close enough to the colonel and kept the boy in check too. And it was midmorning and at least a half-dozen men from the department would be on the sidewalk making a run to the bakery on Stockton and Broadway, and what if one of them happened to be Lieutenant Alvarez, or anyone else in IA who might know about this Iranian and his complaint against Les Burdon? The colonel's olive face was as still as a mask, but his dark eyes were full of heat and iron and the miles he was prepared to go. Then came the click of heels on the sidewalk outside, a young woman walking past, a black-haired stenographer Lester had seen in the old courthouse many times sitting erect at her small desk silently tapping in every word anybody said out loud, a shiny black crow on a limb. Soon she was out of sight and Lester could feel the heartbeats behind his eyes. He had to stay disciplined and controlled. Rational and in charge. The colonel's eyes were still on him. The truth was, Lester knew he'd never leave his son like this either; his judgment seemed to be getting worse with each breath.

THEY BEGAN WALKING toward Broadway in the shade, Lester keeping three steps behind them. Both father and son walked at a normal stride, not too hurried, with their backs straight. But Lester's chest felt sunken with fatigue, his neck and shoulders were stiff, he was thirstier than he could ever remember being, and every time he stepped forward the butt of his gun rubbed against his lower back. To his left was the bright concrete yard of the old domed courthouse, and just beyond the laurel trees a hot dog vendor was setting up his cart. He worked under the shade of his blue-and-yellow umbrella, sticking Coke cans into a cooler full of ice. Lester wanted one badly but the courtyard was full of people. A small group of receptionists leaned against a low concrete wall drinking from their office coffee mugs and smoking. Lawyers and clients stood in twos and threes conferring over cigarettes. And uniformed officers entered or left the building with paperwork under their arms. One of them was Brian Gleason, a stocky blond-haired kid Lester had trained eighteen months ago. He'd seemed kind and conscientious, and when Lester promoted him he'd found himself thinking Gleason wouldn't last. His heart was too big, too geared for the positive, and he wouldn't know what to do with all those images he would get of fatal car accidents, beaten wives and abandoned children, random shootings, drunk mothers you sometimes had to manhandle into the back of your patrol car. But now Gleason was cutting across the yard right for the vendor's cart, and Lester turned away, thick heat unrolling behind his face.

"Move, Colonel. *Move.*"

The colonel and his son were walking fine but it felt good to say that, to shove some of the edge back onto them. But now they were walking too fast, running the risk of drawing attention to all three of them, and Lester had to almost swing his arms to keep up. "*Slow down.*"

Behrani stopped there on the sidewalk. His son took a few more steps before he realized he was alone, then he turned around. But the colonel kept his back to Lester and Lester wanted to kick his foot right into the colonel's slightly wrinkled and damp white shirt. Who was he to keep his back to him? To stand there like he was waiting for Lester to make up his mind? His grip on the colonel's imagination was beginning to slide off like a hand that's fallen asleep, and Lester regretted ever having ejected rounds from his semiautomatic.

"Deputy Sheriff Burdon? *Sir?*" Gleason was walking through the row of trees onto the sidewalk, an open Classic Coke in his hand, and Lester needed to say something to the colonel's back, something to hold him and his son just where they were, but it was too late. He turned, putting his back and covered piece to the street, the smile on his face feeling waxy and wrong. "Hey, Deputy."

Gleason was smiling too, his cheeks flushed. He offered Lester his hand, and Lester shook it. The young deputy's uniform was clean and freshly pressed, his gold star polished and new, and Lester wanted almost desperately to be in his own uniform, to be behind the wheel of his patrol car driving up the coast with a cold Coke, the wind in his face, the green artichoke fields to his right, the Pacific with all its blue-gray possibilities to his left. Gleason let go and his eyes took in the colonel, who had turned around. Lester saw the question in Gleason's boyish face but no words came to Lester, nothing that would make any sense.

"Court, Brian?"

"A DV. I was an actual witness; the husband was going at her when I showed up." Gleason glanced from the colonel to the boy, then back at Lester. "I know you're busy, sir; I just wanted to tell you I really appreciate everything you taught me." The young deputy smiled. "It's funny. I keep hearing your voice while I'm out on patrol, you know, letting me in on this or that, on code and following your gut. I don't know, I just wanted to tell you, I guess."

"I appreciate that, Brian."

"Well—" Gleason looked once more at the colonel. "I'll let you go. Thanks again." He raised his hand, then cut back through the trees for the sun-bright courtyard and his walk to the motor pool. Lester nodded for the Behranis to keep moving, and as the three moved closer to the midmorning bustle on Broadway, Lester kept his eyes on the colonel's balding head, hating each hair, hating the fold of dark skin just above his starched white collar, hating the way he held his shoulders back, but more than anything, Lester hated the way he himself felt right now, hot-faced and thick-tongued with shame, undeserving of any of that young deputy's respect at all.

The Behranis began to cross Sycamore for the corner of Broadway, the boy glancing behind him at Lester, Lester following, his dream coming to him as suddenly as a wind that blows up from the ground, the image of him sitting in his patrol car in an empty lot with a broken radio while every man, woman, and child he'd ever confronted pressed their faces to all his windows, waiting for him. He came up behind the colonel and his son and ordered them to cross the street, but they took their time doing it, especially the colonel, as if nothing serious were at stake here at all. People were walking by them, a young woman pushing a baby in a jogging stroller, two young men in shirts and ties with short stylish haircuts and tanned faces, each holding a bottle of mineral water, both laughing at something, and Lester was breathing deeply through his nose, trying to get his feet flat on the earth, feeling his dream fade back and away like a car horn at high speed.

At the sidewalk the colonel stopped and Lester pushed two fingers hard against Behrani's lower back and walked him and his son quickly into the small shaded entryway of the county tax office, nudging the colonel ahead of him into the corner of the brick wall, the glass doors to Lester's right, his back naked to the bright sidewalk and street. The boy stood almost to his side, as if it was now the two of them against the colonel. Lester's face was so close to the Iranian's he could smell his old tea breath, and he just had to put things back where they belonged, to impress upon Behrani the new truth, that Les Burdon would do whatever it took to see this through to its just end. The colonel kept his arms at his sides and at first his dark eyes were startled but now they were calm, waiting Lester out as if he was a child throwing a predictable fit, someone's unruly kid. Lester poked a finger into the colonel's sternum and backed him a half step to the wall. He was gritting his teeth so hard his head hurt and he knew he had to pull away now before anyone began to take an interest, but it was like willing his body to stop sneezing or to hold off an orgasm once it had broken free. He could hear the scuff of somebody's shoe soles on the sidewalk as he stopped to watch, and he knew he wasn't gaining any precious ground now, but losing some, and with this knowledge he felt almost nauseated with a sudden weakness in his legs, stomach, and arms. He stepped back, and he wanted to say something to at least keep things on an even keel before they went inside, but then his service pistol was jerked free of his belt and he turned to see Esmail pointing it at him, backing into the sunlight, his other hand raised like he was getting ready to flee, his bare shoulders looking smooth and brown under the sun. A woman let out a shriek, and a businessman backed away as if the boy was a fire spreading at his feet, and Lester had one hand on the colonel behind him, was conscious of this just as his wrist was squeezed, his arm yanked down and twisted up behind his back, a burn ripping through his shoulder girdle. The colonel fumbled for Lester's other hand but Lester jerked it away, his attention still on the boy. Behrani yelled something in Farsi to his son, then in English for help, for someone to call the police. Lester could feel a half-dozen or more people watching, but he didn't look at them, only felt them standing there twelve or fifteen feet away, a man's voice telling someone to get to a phone. But Lester was looking at the boy, at his eyes, which were darker than his father's, more like his mother's—deep ellipses, beautiful really—now moist with fear and confusion. The boy's hand and arm were trembling, his lips beginning to move as if he wanted to say something but couldn't. He glanced quickly at his father behind Lester, then back again. Lester could hear someone running down the sidewalk, maybe into a nearby shop. It would take two or three seconds to get out of this hold, but by then the boy might flee and run down this congested street. His eyes were still on the boy's, and he knew he should tell him the gun was empty, that he was calling dangerous attention to himself for no reason, but saying that would rob Lester of any leverage once he got the gun back, would make it impossible to get both Behranis back down the street and into the Buick and away. Lester tried to be the boy, tried to will his own body to become blood and breath, but the colonel pushed harder, forcing Lester to bend forward even more, half in the sunlight now, half in the dark of the entryway. The colonel was saying more in Farsi to his son, his voice calm, waiting the moment out, as if he was sure things had turned now in their favor. Then Lester heard running footsteps on the bright sidewalk, the familiar throaty leather bounce of more than one departmental gun belt, and then he was them, running from the bakery, pushing through carelessly unshielded bystanders to see a dark boy holding a piece on two men, and there was no more time: Lester stomped the colonel's instep, heard him grunt as Lester pushed backward, then swung his free elbow twice into Behrani's temple, Behrani falling, someone yelling, "Drop it! Drop it!" And Lester jerked around, saw Esmail turn to the yelling, his eyes wide, his mouth a dark oval, the gun unmoving in his hand, pointing now in the direction of the man Lester couldn't see. Lester shouted: "Hold it! Wait!" He began to step out of the entryway but his movement had sound, a blast that hit the boy high in the torso and jerked him sideways, his arms swinging loose, Lester's pistol clattering to the concrete as the second shot buckled the boy's legs and he dropped to the sidewalk, his legs bent and separated, one arm stretched out as if he were reaching for something.

Lester could not move or speak. His veins had turned cold and thick, his lungs empty of air.

"Nakhreh! Nakhreh! Nakhreh!" Behrani was screaming, crawling past Lester, blood already spreading out around the boy's shoulder and arm and down his bare leg. Then the two deputies came into view, both of them still pointing their weapons at Esmail and now the colonel, who was wailing, holding his son's face, then turning him onto his back and pressing with both hands on the wound in his upper chest. *"Hospital! Call to hospital!"*

Lester's gun lay at his feet and he felt it like a pointing finger. One of the deputies crossed in front of him, rested his foot on the gun, and began to pull on protective gloves. The other had holstered his service pistol and was already on his hand radio calling for an ambulance or fire squad, and they were both young, in their mid-twenties, the one near Lester tall and thin, the other short and fair-skinned, and Lester had trained neither of them. They were failing to take in the wider picture, and Lester knew he could slip out of the entryway and disappear into the crowd right now. But the colonel was moaning, pressing down so hard on his son's wound his shoulders were hunched, and he was rocking slightly too, acting as a pump instead of a plug, blood leaving the boy's hip wound in pulsing gushes. The deputy near Lester had finished pulling on his glove, but instead of starting first aid, he bent down to pick up the gun at his feet. The radio deputy had finished making his call, but now he was fumbling with his own protective gloves and for Lester everything began to move again, he was as light and diffuse as smoke, his heart in his face, brushing by the deputy: *"Goddamn you, the kid's bleeding to death."*

Lester knelt by the boy and pulled Esmail's shorts down past the entry hole, then yanked off his own shirt and thumbed some of the material into the wound. The colonel didn't turn around but stopped rocking and was just pressing down, sniffling now, saying the same Persian sentence over and over again to his son. The colonel's shoulder and back were so close to Lester he couldn't see the boy's face, and he didn't want to. He lowered his head and put all his weight into his hands, which were streaked and spotted red. The two deputies had finished protecting themselves and were now pushing back the crowd, making a hole for the paramedics. He could hear the sirens of the fire squad only five, maybe six blocks away. Esmail's shorts and underwear were pulled almost to his penis, and Lester was looking down at the boy's pubic hair, just a small patch of black. He closed his eyes and pressed so hard his hands began to ache.

It took seconds and years for the siren to cut through everything,

then fall quiet, and he heard the doors open, the stretcher wheels hitting the pavement. Someone touched his shoulder and he stood,
watched as a man and woman from the fire squad knelt by the boy.
The man pulled Lester's shirt away, then put it back and wrapped a
yellow tourniquet around Esmail's thigh while the woman slipped an
oxygen mask over his face, and the colonel was still pressing, crying,
and he wouldn't move. The woman had her hand on his and she was
saying something to him, but still the colonel didn't seem to hear her.
The tall deputy came up behind him, then bent down, and Behrani
sniffled and finally let go, his mouth open, his eyes fixed on his son.
The deputy took the colonel's arm and helped him up while the
paramedics slid the boy onto the stretcher, raised it, and rolled it
past all the people to the street.

The boy's feet were splayed out, the soles of his basketball shoes
dirty and worn almost smooth, bouncing slightly as the stretcher
was pushed into the paramedic van. The colonel tried to follow but
the tall deputy held his arms, and as the van pulled away, Behrani
strained forward, the siren coming on again, the radio deputy stepping up to Lester and saying something, asking something, his name,
what happened? He had his notepad and pen in hand, and his breath
was bad, his voice tremulous, his fingers too. Lester looked down at
him, the shooter, at the twitch in his lip as he waited, treating Lester
like a civilian, a victim or perpetrator, the kid didn't know which yet.
And neither did Lester.

More deputies were coming, making their way through the crowd
in their French-blue uniforms, and the first was Brian Gleason. His
eyes caught Lester's right away and he stopped and looked down at
the blood on the sidewalk. Behind him was movement, Behrani
struggling with the deputy, trying to pull his arms free, his eyes on
Lester: "It is *him!* *He* has done this! It is *him!*" The colonel was swinging his elbows back, kicking his feet, and Gleason and another
deputy moved in and pulled Behrani's arms back while the other
handcuffed him. The colonel was still straining forward, the veins
coming out in his forehead and temple, his eyes on Lester: "*I will kill
you! I will kill you!*"

All three deputies were holding Behrani, and Gleason turned and looked at Lester. The crowd had grown; kids tried to make their way through to stand on their skateboards and look over the shoulders of lawyers and secretaries, of women still in their aerobics class sweats, of shoppers and store owners and salesgirls, all looking at the colonel now, at the boy's blood on the sidewalk, at the five sheriff's deputies, and at the man the bald handcuffed foreigner was yelling about, at Lester Burdon, who felt he was in the presence of a moment already dreamed and now real, not an accident, nothing random, but ordered and logical, an inevitable expression of who he really was. His throat was dust, his hands soft and damp, his legs brittle. The deputy was speaking again, asking Lester another question over the colonel's screaming, but Lester wanted only water, the cold sweet water at the fish camp. "What?"

"Your *name*, sir. What is your *name?*"

A patrol car had pulled up, and Gleason and the other two deputies pushed the colonel into the backseat, Behrani screaming only in Farsi now, a deep, guttural slash of vowels and consonants that sounded to Lester like a thousand-year curse on them all, on him, on his children, on their children—he looked down at the sidewalk, so dark and red where it was wet, and he wanted to see Bethany and Nate, to hold them and kiss them.

Gleason shut the patrol-car door and Lester could still hear the colonel's muffled cries. He turned back to the young fair-skinned deputy, whose face was pale, the twitch still in his lip.

Gleason stepped up, his hands on his hips, and he nodded his head in the direction of the blood on the sidewalk. "What happened?"

People were still standing around. The two young businessmen with their water and coffee were looking right at Lester. So was Gleason, and Lester wanted to rise up out of this like a cloud, to drift over the valley and shore to the Pacific, to dissolve into its huge green expanse like rain.

I FELT RESTLESS. I WAS SWEATING IN THE CAR BUT THE SKY WAS GRAY, and I knew a fog was unrolling itself down in Corona. I could smell the ocean. It was the weather I was used to, the way a normal day looked, and this made me even more antsy; what I really wanted to do was drive my car down the coast highway for hours and not come back until Les got here with the check. But I knew I couldn't, not in my red Bonneville. We would probably have to leave it here for good anyway, wouldn't we? And how would we get time to cash that big county check? Tie up the Behranis again? And it was Wednesday. Banks closed early. If Les didn't get back soon, we would have to wait till tomorrow morning and then keep the family tied up overnight. I felt sick at the thought. And I kept thinking of Lester having to run away with me from his whole life, his kids. I was outside, but I could hardly breathe.

I went back into the house. I heard the low Persian music. The air smelled like tea and flowers. I walked over the carpet and down the hall and I could feel my father like he was standing there in the dim hallway in his beige Nicolo Linen uniform, a smoking Garcia y Vega between his fingers, his eyes big behind his glasses, looking at me like he always did, like I was a rare bird he was still getting used to see-ing in his own front yard.

When I stepped into the darkened bedroom, Mrs. Behrani was lying as still as I'd left her. Her hands were crossed over her stomach, and her sleeping face looked pale in the shadow of the room. I wanted to do something for her, though I didn't know what that could be. On the cassette player a young woman's voice was reciting what had to be poetry, and there was a backdrop of drums behind her, that, and men letting long open-throated sounds out of themselves. My eyes were used to the dark now and I could see the rise and fall of Mrs. Behrani's breathing, her hands on her stomach. I remembered the way she looked at the bruises on my arm like it hurt to see them. I remembered her face as she washed my bleeding foot, then laid it on that thick white towel, her eyes full of warmth. I thought about wetting a cloth with cool water, laying it on her forehead, but for all I knew that could make a migraine worse. So instead I went into the kitchen and came back with a glass of ice water, set it near the tape player on her bedside table. The glass tapped against the base of the lamp and she squeezed her eyes as tightly shut as if someone had yelled in her ear. I stood as still as I could. Her face began to soften again and I tiptoed out of the room and went into the kitchen.

The back door was shut, shards of broken glass still in the lower windowpanes. There was a trash container in the corner and I carried it to the door and started to pull the glass out. The big pieces were easy to get free, but for the smaller ones I had to use a butter knife I'd pulled from Mrs. Behrani's dish rack. I squatted on the floor and dug the broken bits from the frame. Sometimes the knife scraped against the glass and made me shiver. I felt dirty: my skin and hair, my teeth and eyes and tongue, my lungs and stomach and the blood in my veins, still laced with what I took last night. I thought about taking a long hot shower, but then I would have to step back into these stolen clothes and Lester had already been gone close to an hour and I didn't want to be in the shower when they came back.

But I had to do something. I pushed the trash container back into the corner and stood there. On the refrigerator was taped a color photograph of the Behranis' daughter and her husband, I guessed, holding hands in front of a luxury hotel, all canopy and marble columns and gold fixtures on glass doors. The sun was on them, and they were dressed in matching polo shirts and baggy shorts. The husband wore glasses and was small, a camera hanging from his wrist by its strap. The Behranis' daughter was petite and beautiful, her smile posed but toned-down somehow, like she didn't want to flaunt too much what she knew she had. And looking at her on my refrigerator, I felt old, worn-out, and cheap. I wanted Lester here, but not because I wanted him to hurry up and finish all this; I just needed to see

him look down at me with those sweet eyes and that slightly dumb-
founded smile under his crooked mustache, like I was the answer to
every painful question he'd ever asked himself and he still couldn't
believe I was his. I hoped he still felt that way. I hoped this past
night and day hadn't changed that.

. . . .
. . . .
. .

I WANT ONLY MY SON.

They have sat me upon a soft chair in a new office and they ask
the same questions they asked me moments ago, and I answer, but I
want only to go to my son. They have freed my wrists and a large detective offers to me a wet towel for my hands, but I refuse it. The men
regard one another for they fear my son's blood. I look down upon my
red fingers. The skin has tightened as the khoon has dried and I do
not want it to dry. I fear washing it from my hands.

I stand. "Please, I must—"

Lieutenant Alvarez enters the room. One of the detectives rises
from his seat. "Burdon corroborates the whole deal, Lieutenant."

The Lieutenant does not look at the detective, keeps his eyes on
me only. "Mr. Behrani, this is your recourse." He begins to speak to
me of pressing charges, but I see only the movement of his lips, the
fashion in which his shirt collar presses into the flesh of his neck.

"Please, hospital. Where is the hospital, please?"

The lieutenant points to the large window overlooking the parking compound of officers' automobiles, the shops along Broadway
Avenue in the sun, a large gray building among others. He tells to me
this is where I must go, and there is the offer of an escort, a deputy
to accompany me, but I cannot urge my legs for walking quickly
enough. Soon I am among the people upon the sidewalk and I begin
running. A woman steps away as I pass by and her face is frightened.
It is the blood, the khoon, on my hands and shirt, my bloody peer-

han. It is that I am running, but I see only the face of Esmail as he held the heavy weapon on the man who would rob us, my pesar's eyes so dark with the question of what he should do next, the fashion in which he regarded me, his father, and I told to him, "Keep the gun pointed at his heart, do not be afraid."

There is across the street a sign for EMERGENCY. Into the khiaboon I am running and an automobile screeches to a stop. Another driver sounds his horn, and then another and another and I turn and curse them in my language, disgracing their mothers and grandmothers and sisters as whores. My throat aches and in my eyes there is a sting-ing sweat. A Mercedes-Benz drives very close by me and I hear the shout of a man inside but I do not care. I spit upon these people. I spit upon this country and all of its guns and automobiles and homes.

But inside the hospital it is cool, clean, and quiet. A kind desk woman looks directly at my son's blood and directs me to the area for emergencies. The corridors are wide and gray, shining from the light tubes above. The air smells of cotton bandages and floor cleaner. And I feel I cannot breathe. I follow the large signs for EMERGENCY. There are now many people in the corridors, some are in chairs with wheels and a husband or wife pushes them. Others walk with flow-ers and small children. They see the blood upon my hands and peer-han and look immediately to my eyes. And there are many sounds and voices and footsteps but I hear only my breath and I see my son's face as I pressed down upon his wound, his eyes were open but he no longer seemed to see me and I told to him to hold on, to keep his feet upon the ground, to grip his toes to his skateboard for he is de-scending very fast down a long hill and he need only hold on. Do not let go, Esmail-joon. Do not let go.

I am breathing with difficulty, speaking with a tall nurse who has as many years as I. There are deep lines in her face, and she does not fear the blood on my hands as she leads me to a sink and tells me to wash and I do not hesitate. Soon we are in the elevator and as we move upwards towards my Esmail, she holds a clipboard and asks me for the name of my son, my name, our address. I tell to her 34 Bisgrove Street, Corona, California, this property that is still completely my own, Burdon in the custody of his own officers; he has lost and I have won—the nurse two times asks a question of insurance but I do not speak: I must see Esmail. I must see him very carefully, I must see him.

The doors open and I walk along the empty corridor following the tall nurse who does not press me any further but only leads me. There is a sign for Surgery, a small waiting area with magazines and cushioned chairs, a window overlooking the streets and buildings below. The nurse tells me to please sit and she disappears behind a heavy door. But I cannot sit. Nor can I stand still. I walk back and forth over the thin carpet, and I see the magazines, the colorful covers of famous men and women, the rich and beautiful, and I remember my hand in Shah Pahlavi's; his palms were smooth as the face of babies and on his smallest finger there was a ruby ring as large as a grape.

For our excess we lost everything.

I kneel beneath the window, turn to the east, and bow my head to the carpet which smells of dust, and I curse myself for ever weeping over my lost position, for the respect I had lost among strangers. I must make nazr to God as did my uncle Hadi when I was a boy and his wife, Shamsi, lay sick in bed and my uncle made nazr to God that if he would heal Shamsi, Hadi would give thousands of tomans to a poor Kurdish family in the lower hills, and to seal this nazr, Hadi drove each day to the largest mosque in Tabriz and fed seed to the pigeons there, and after only five days my aunt Shamsi was well.

I press my head to the hospital's carpet, my eyes tightly closed: man nazr meekonam, I am making nazr for—but I know no poor families to whom I can give. I think only of the old Vietnamese Tran. Perhaps it is to him I must give. I again begin the words of nazr, but when I pray Tran's name I feel I am lying, telling dooroogh, and I do not know why, but this frightens me for there is very little time and I must be only pure in the nazr for my son. There must be nothing dirty or hidden in this prayer and now, at the thought of dirty, of kaseef, I know it is Kathy Nicolo, this beggar whore to whom I must make nazr. It is *her*. But I cannot. How can I give to this woman whose actions have led to my son's injury? This woman who has brought the weapon to our bungalow that resulted in Esmail's shooting? This woman who we took into our home when she was as mast as a drunk in the street? To whom we gave our son's bed? Prepared for her a hot meal? Offered her our bath which she defiled in her weakness before we saved her life again? How can I make nazr to this woman whose boyfriend has kept us hostage? How can I give to her anything from my heart but the poison she has given us? And I will press criminal charges against this Lester V. Burdon. I will sue the entire Sheriff's Department for what he has done. And I will sue the two deputies who shot my son. I will take from them their jobs and their homes—but I must not allow these thoughts to dirty the water of my nazr. I am weeping, seeing again my son's eyes as I pressed upon his wound. They were Nadi's eyes, and Soraya's eyes, and my father's, but they did not see me, but something else, a thing I cannot see. *God,* I am making nazr to this woman, Kathy Nicolo, and I to You promise if You heal my son I will return her father's house. I will also give to her all the money I have. Please, my God, Khoda, I make nazr for my only son.

"Sir?"

I beg you.

"Sir?"

I will do whatever is Your will. I will purchase ten kilos of the finest seed and I will find an American mosque and feed them to all the birds.

"Mr. Behmini?"

I will go to other holy places as well. I will feed pigeons in front of the churches of Christians. I will feed them at the doors of Jewish temples. I will let the birds cover me and then I will return with more seed and feed them again.

"Sir?"

And again.

"Mr. Behmini?"

My nazr is in Your hands.

I rise slowly. Beside the nurse is a man. He is short and very dark. An Indian or Pakistani. But as he introduces himself and offers his hand he speaks with no accent of any kind, and his eyes are black and he is dressed in the green clothing of surgeons, a paper mask hanging beneath his throat, and he does not release my hand and I know why and I begin pulling my hand from his, but it is too late, he has already released the words and they hit me like debris from an explosion. There is no air. No light. No sound. Only the dark vacuum of God's closed door, of his no to my nazr, of his no to my son to whom they now lead me, my executioners, this man and this woman, to Esmail who lies upon a raised stretcher.

Esmail Kamfar Behrani.

A white sheet covers him to the shoulders. They are bare and smooth and brown from his days in the sun, and the sheet is clean except for a spot of khoon at his hip, and evil rose in the snow. The doctor speaks softly, delivering to me the specifics of God's answer, but I see now only my son's face. It is turned slightly towards the wall. His eyes are closed but his lips are parted, as when he sleeps with a stuffed nose. His jawbone is long and beautiful, and I touch the soft black hairs on his cheek near to his ears. His skin is cool and does not feel natural. At once it is too hard and too soft, and I know my son is no longer here beneath my hand. There is a loudness in the corridor, the vibration of it in my head and bowels. It is me, silenced by my son's head as I hold him to my chest, his hair inside my mouth, his nose and lips pressed to my throat, and I would joyfully lie naked in flames for one thousand years to put life back into this boy. There is a hand upon my shoulder. It belongs to one of my torturers, but it does not pull me or push me, simply rests upon me as if it knows what it is I have lost, *my son, who as a baby walked before he had one year, his small brown legs as bowed as a wrestler in the zur khaneh—at one and a half years, his first words to me over the telephone at Mehrabad: "Salome, Bawbaw-joon"—his bare feet in Paris, black with dirt from the street where he led French boys in play we did not know—his ease with computer games which were sometimes as complicated for me as the controls of a jet—his kindness and character, waking me with tea at the pooldar apartments, telling to me in the early dawn he is sorry for his bad behavior, he knows how hard it is I work, he made mistake—*

I cannot breathe. I cannot see. My sound curls inside of me, releasing in the scream of his name. I kiss his closed eyes. His cheeks. His soft lips. There is a hand upon my back, the woman's, patting me, but she does not know how I have failed this child; she does not know I encouraged him to stand still with the gun, to stay in the line of fire of his killers. The sound that comes from me is that of a beast, a weak and primitive animal not even worthy of sacrifice. My Esmail's face is wet from my own and he must be washed.

He must be wrapped in white for his journey to God's door.

And Nadi must do it.

His mother must do it.

But how can I tell to her? How is it possible to tell her our youngest child has left before us? How do I tell my Nadi I could not protect him? How do I explain I ordered him to point the weapon at Burdon until the police arrived? These American police who shot down our son?

I lay Esmail down, lower my head, and rush into the wall, feeling too little, only the jolting warmth and confusion of impact. The surgeon's hand is upon my arm but I struggle away from this man who has killed me. The nurse calls my name but I am again running.

In the elevator I cannot stand. I cannot sit. I push myself from one wall to the next. In my mouth there is blood and I now know my dear brother Pourat was spared this torment, when at this hour he was shot instantly. But I have not been given this courtesy. And I will not spare the man who did not spare my son.

Again I am running. The streets are full of American people who walk along the sidewalks or stop in the shops or step into the office buildings as if my son had not just perished on this very ground. In my path walk two men in suits, their backs to me, and I force my way through their lack of respect, pushing them to the side, hearing their curses, the weak cursing of gentlemen, their voices high with fear and surprise that anyone would dare upset their calm water. In my mind I am spitting upon them. In my mind I am already preparing how careful it is I must be when I enter this Hall of Justice building, how it is I must walk through the clean glass door over the hard and shining floor to the elevators with no sweat or tears upon my face, no intent in my eye, only the impassive face of a man with business above.

And soon I am no longer in my mind but in the Hall of Justice. Men in suits walk by and they study my face and see the blood on my peerhan. I board an elevator, pressing the button which closes the door. I am moving towards the floor of detectives and Internal Affairs officers and I am certain I will find Lester V. Burdon, the tall thin lover of whores, the killer of my son, I will find him, perhaps being questioned in a soft chair, his friends and colleagues his only inter-rogators.

The elevator doors are brass and in their reflection is a man with blood upon his head, the dripping of it on his forehead and eyebrow. The doors open and I am not upon the floor of detectives and lieu-tenants but only deputy sheriffs in their blue uniforms seated at desks conducting their business. One views me, and then another, and both regard the blood upon my face, my peerhan. They call to me: "Sir, step out of the elevator. Sir?" But my hands press the buttons quickly and the doors close, the elevator descending when I want for it to rise, rise to the detectives, to where they are holding their fallen colleague. But now the door opens at the lobby, clean and spacious but full of men and women in the formal dress of courtrooms. A se-curity officer walks across the shiny floor, his eyes upon my blood. I turn, but the elevators have closed their doors.

"*Sir?* Hold on there."

Once again I am running. Outdoors the sun is upon my head and face. The air smells of engine exhaust, of cooking meat from a ven-dor's cart, transportation and hot meals continuing as if this mo-ment were any other. My eyes burn. I breathe with difficulty and stop running. I look once behind me but there is no guard. Across the khiaboon, in front of the tax office, many officers and men in suits talk behind the yellow tape of the Sheriff's Department. Men and women stare, talking amongst themselves, watching as one of the men stoops to investigate Esmail's blood. Who are these people to witness this? To invade my heart like soldiers with dirt upon their boots? I step into the khiaboon, but no cars sound their horns and I move quietly to the other side, to the rear of the crowd, searching for the men who shot my son, and I regard one of them standing in the shadow of the tax building, speaking with two men dressed in badly tailored suits. He is a young deputy. Round white face. His hands are upon his hips and he looks down at his shoes. One of the detectives speaks and the young man looks only at his shoes. He shakes his head. His lips move as if he might talk. He continues to shake his head. At his side his hand trembles and I would like to see him dead upon the ground but I have no desire to harm him. Only Burdon, our captor and his beggar whore, who is with Nadi still, and I feel suddenly my wife is in danger.

The highway is bright. I drive very fast, the white lines of the road becoming one. My drawn breath seems to reach only my skin. My fingers shake. I wipe the khoon from my eye and feel beside me the empty seat where sat my son, my abdomen heaving with crying I do not hear. The day's work was only beginning and the air was cool, the third day of Ramadan, and when I ate breakfast with Nadi before dawn she told me it was soon, and at dusk my driver Bahman was smiling, and before I entered the auto he spoke the news, that I had a son, Captain Massoud Amir Behrani is father of a son.

I do not see clearly and this does not matter. I drive into the fog of the hills towards Corona. I wipe my eye and nose upon my sleeve. The air here smells of the ocean, of rotted weed in the sand, of sea salt and garbage. My hands steer the automobile up the hill past the bungalows on the left which are small but newly painted, their stoops and sidewalks swept clean, the grasses of their lawn cut very short. This is an ugly street, zesht, and now I see our widow's walk rising from our roof, a foolish thing. My foot and leg are only the wood of a dead tree, and the engine responds with sound, carrying me and all I have done and not done to the drive. At the window, there is the parting of the drapes before they fall still and I slip from my automobile like black oil. I move to the front door of my home and for a moment my limbs are heavy as iron but then I am only empty clothes, the front door opening with a force that surprises me for I do not remember touching it. There is the startled hand of Kathy Nicolo as she raises it to her mouth. Between us is a sea of carpet from the house of my mother but now I am across it and I believe there is sound coming from the beggar whore's mouth but I cannot be certain for my limbs are again iron and my hands are fixed to her neck and throat. I seem to watch her face from a place higher, this struggling statue of a man and woman, her flesh warm and soft, the tendons of her neck I begin to break each at a time. Her hair has fallen over half her face, her eyelids fluttering, her sound quite ugly, a wet ripping, her tongue pink. Her fingers grasp my wrists and her nails pierce what was once my flesh. There is blood, but not enough, and I lift her from the floor, her feet kicking and dragging beneath her. I shake her once, twice, again, and again, her head jerking backwards and forwards. There is no end to my strength or how long I shake her, then her hand slips from my wrists and the bungalow grows silent.

There is only my breathing, the crash of khoon between my ears. I lower Kathy Nicolo to my mother's carpet. Her hair falls away, and her face is the purple-red color of saffron, her mouth open, a furrow between her closed eyes as if she were in the midst of dreaming badly. My hands release her and I sit upon her for a moment and I am once again in my flesh. In my chest is my thrusting heart, my palms are wet against my legs, and now I wait for the sound of Esmail's skateboard in the drive, the kick of it into his hands as he steps upon the stoop and enters his home. He has been away all the day long, on a journey he had not expected, and now I have called him home. I stay seated upon the dead woman's chest and I wait for my son, but I hear nothing.

Nadi. Where is my Nadi?

I rise and find her upon her bed, in her darkened room. Her small face is at rest. Her forehead is free of wrinkles and I see upon the lamp table her headache medication. I sit in the chair Lester V. Burdon carried here. I remember clearly how he watched over his gendeh, how he regarded her as if she were a precious stone. And now she will be a stone shot through him, and I pray his love for her was even greater than I witnessed. In the shadowed darkness of this room, Nadi's face has lost thirty years of living; the migraine has passed and she is in the deep sleep that comes to those relieved of their pain. It is a small face, with the soft skin of a girl. Her lips are dark, her jaw no longer set tightly with judgment, her closed eyes incapable of becoming narrow with fear and regret. Is it possible that from this rest she will rise to hear of her lost son? Is it in this small and pitiful bungalow she will know the final end of what we once were? And once again, while Bahman and my wife and children wait in the Mercedes, its trunk full of luggage for a week or weekend at the Caspian Sea, I am inside our empty home for something I had forgotten, my briefcase or perhaps a favorite pair of shoes, a last-minute call to Mehrabad, all these things that must occur before we can take our safar together, our long happy journey, these last-moment details that can be trusted only to a father and husband, my hands over Nadi's nose and mouth and eyes, this discipline to stand firmly in the face of her struggling, her grasping and twisting and kicking. My eyes fill and she blurs beneath me but I tell to myself it is only a small suffering she must endure before she is free to join our son, before she is free to return to the flowers of Isfahan and the mosques of Qom and the fine hotels of the old Tehran, before she is free to give money to the beggars in the bazaar, before she is free to claim her destiny—my wife's arms fall to her sides, and she is silent. I remove my hands from her face. Her brow is arched, as if she were on the moment of receiving a long-awaited answer, and her mouth now is open and I kiss her lips. Her tongue is warm. I kiss her nose and cheeks and closed eyes. *Sleep, Nadereh. Rest for your safar. Rest.*

The bungalow is quiet as a desert. I pass my son's room. No breath enters me and I must discipline myself to continue moving forward, to walk into my office, remove my clothes, and slide open the door. Take down my uniform which in this country I have never worn. Pull it from its clear plastic covering from a dry-cleaning shop in Bahrain, the fabric heavier than I recalled, the smell of its cedarwood hanger. The trousers fit perfectly at my hips, and the shirt is of soft cotton but needs pressing. I stand with no mirror and tie the cravat into the full windsor knot I then always wore. Inside the jacket pocket are gold cufflinks and a tie fastener, an engraved lion of the Pahlavi dynasty. I fold my shirtsleeves back one time and secure each with a cufflink, my family name carved in each one. To Nadereh's room I walk. I take from the bureau drawer my formal socks, black silk with small dark green diamonds sewn deep inside the leg. Nadereh lies behind me upon the bed, but it is no longer her; it is only a dress or overcoat she has forgotten to pack for our safar.

In my office I unwrap my uniform shoes, black and shiny and free of dust. I tie them securely with a double knot, then rise and slip into my jacket, each shoulder heavy with red-and-gold epaulet, my breast pocket covered with the ribbons, emblems, and badges of my service.

I secure the middle buttons and I stand at full attention, Genob Sarhang Behrani, Honorable Colonel Massoud Amir Behrani.

I pull paper from its box upon my desk, and in the kitchen I stand at the bar counter and begin to write in my mother language:

> Soraya-joon,
>
> I have done all that I could. Do not be sorry for us. Your mother and I await you upon your return. We love you more than we have loved life.
>
> After your dear brother name your first son.
>
> Bawbaw

An automobile passes on its way down the hill and I must hurry for I recall the lieutenant's orders as I left for the hospital, his request for a patrol car to be sent here. For the shooting of a boy they are efficient; for the rescuing of a woman held hostage they are late.

I take the second paper and write in English that I, Colonel Massoud Amir Behrani, leave to my daughter this bungalow and all of its contents as well as my automobile and all monies remaining in our accounts. I print my full name upon the document, then sign it.

This should be sufficient, but now I am troubled by the words "all of its contents," for I cannot leave the body of this gendeh and killer to my daughter, who I am quite certain will sell this bungalow as soon as she is able. I take up the pen and write again in Farsi at the bottom of my letter:

> Soraya-joon, live here if you like, but if you sell it take no less than one hundred thousand dollars.

I place both papers upon the refrigerator door, securing them with a magnet beside the honeymoon photograph of my daughter and son-in-law. They stand in the sunlight. They appear quite happy. I kiss my finger and press it to Soraya's heart.

I am too warm in my uniform. I feel the sweat at my forehead and neck and beneath my peerhan. There is very little time remaining. I stoop upon my mother's carpet, position my hand beneath Kathy Nicolo's arms, then lift and drag her into the kitchen area across the floor and outdoors onto the rear grasses. She is quite heavy, her hair loose upon my arms. I drag her through the tall hedge trees to her automobile. The air has grown cooler, but my eyes burn with sweat, and I lay her upon the earth beside the bungalow and open the rear door of her auto. There is the tired smell of cigarettes, and the seat fabric is still warm from the sun that is no longer. I look down upon her. Her mouth is open, one hand twisted beneath her. I think of Jasmeen, my dear cousin. I lift the whore and pull her onto the seat and bend her knees to shut the door and I think of what I will tell to Jasmeen, that I loved her always, that Kamfar and I wept for her. And I will embrace Pourat. I will kiss both his eyes and tell to him how I have missed him.

There is very little time. Inside the bungalow, I pull from the cabinet beneath the sink the roll of tape we used for our moving boxes. In my office I retrieve the plastic covering of my uniform. Then I enter the darkness of my wife's room, my heart once again thrusting inside my chest. My face and neck release sweat, and my uniform is fitted too tightly at the upper back; it is all the work here I have done, it is all those days in the heat and dust and fog, a garbage soldier working with men who before would have bowed their heads if I passed by. I sit upon the bed. I pull sufficient tape free of its roll, the sound like the cracking of ice over a frozen lake, what I felt beneath my feet as a boy with my father in the north mountains. I hold with both hands the tape and lean to kiss Nadi once more. Her lips are still warm but I feel if I do not hurry she will have left me behind. I apply one end of the tape to my knee, and my fingers shake as they did when I first undressed my wife on the night of our wedding, our new home silent as it is now.

I take the plastic covering and place it over my head and face. But there is a small hole near my mouth and I must double the layer and now I see only a vague dimness as I take the tape and secure it firmly around my throat and neck. My breath draws in the plastic immediately and I expel it with my tongue. I lie down beside my Nadi. I reach for her hand but cannot at first find it and my heart leaps against my chest, then I find it, small and cool, soft with expensive creams, and I am for the moment calmed. I close my eyes and mouth and breathe deeply through the nose, but the plastic quickly fills it and I again open my mouth to complete the breath but the plastic is there as well and I force it away with my tongue, drawing in more air, all that I will need, I tell to myself, holding it in, my chest weakened by its fullness. I feel Nadi's shoulder pressed to mine and I regret not having played music on her new player. I have a sharp desire to hear it, the poetry of Dashtestani, the ney and domback, the beckoning music of home. I release my breath, its sound a wind in my ears, the plastic slipping from my nose and mouth but then returning with the insistence of the sea, covering all the sand prints left behind, filling all the holes and channels. I attempt to force the plastic out once more, just once more, but the ocean is rising with the moon, its pressure growing in my chest, my heart and lungs beginning to burst beneath the weight of an unseen hand, my body struggling as it sinks into the bed. The plastic becomes iron against my face, and my arms float weightlessly as I attempt to pull free the tape but my fingers do not function correctly, fluttering uselessly against my throat and chin. I no longer have legs, and there is a terrible sound in my ears, the deafening pitch of low-flying F-16s, my chest beginning to fracture, my abdomen heaving, heaving—something beginning to open and release, a warmth filling me, vodka and fire, the hot wind of a desert sky, the earth falling away beneath me.

LESTER'S CELL WAS A STAINLESS-STEEL SINK AND TOILET, A STEEL WRITing desk, and two iron bunks recessed into the wall. Above each mattress was a small rectangular window, its bulletproof glass fogged so that all Lester could see was daylight, and the floor was eight feet wide and twelve feet long, the ceiling thirty feet above him, three iron girders painted as white as everything else. Lester sat at the edge of the bottom bunk, both hands resting on his knees. His eyelids were heavy and burned slightly, and his mouth hung partly open with fatigue. He was too warm wearing both jail-issue shirts and he lay back on his bunk, staring at the myriad of holes in the steel bed-frame above him. At the Hall of Justice, he had sat without his shirt in a hardback chair and heard himself tell the truth about every-thing, his voice low and subdued as he kept seeing the boy spin, his arms hanging loose as rope as he let go of the gun and landed on his side, one arm stretched out, almost pointing, the way toddlers do to something they recognize but can't name.

Someone had handed him a glass of water and Lester drank it down all at once. In the small room were two deputies, two detec-tives, and Lieutenant Alvarez standing with his back to the bright window, his face in shadow. The detectives were asking Lester about the Behrani family, their imprisonment overnight, Lester pointing his service pistol at them, moving the son and father against their will to Redwood City. They asked him about Kathy. Was she at the Corona address right now, holding Mrs. Behrani against her will? And Lester's voice sounded almost normal. "No, she's waiting for us to get back, that's all." Lester looked down at his hands, imagined Mrs. Behrani hearing her son had been shot. He imagined hearing his own son had been shot, how he would immediately picture the worst, little Nate's smooth face contorted and pale as too much blood left his body too fast. "Is the boy all right?"

One of the detectives said he was in surgery, and Lester turned his wedding ring twice on his finger. He'd washed his hands but there was still dried blood in the tiny cracks of his palms. He thought of Kathy, her red Bonneville in the backyard when a patrol car got there. He looked up. "I'd like to call my wife."

Lieutenant Alvarez was writing something on a pad of paper, and he stepped forward as quickly as if someone had just insulted him. "You'll get your two calls at intake, Burdon."

Lester had felt an impulse to look away, but didn't. Alvarez shook his head like even this, this eye contact, was way out of line, and he told two deputies to arrest him and take him across the street to the new holding facility, a short walk usually, but now it was long, Lester as handcuffed and bare-chested as a wino, a deputy at each arm, his face down. Inside they uncuffed him and Lester gave them what they wanted, his wallet, car keys, and wedding ring. One of the arresting deputies told him to hold his arms out and he gave Lester a pat search, his hands heavy and careful. The intake officer had broad shoulders, short red hair, and a small white scar on his chin. He sat behind glass and put Lester's keys and ring in a manila envelope, counted the cash in his wallet, then had Lester sign a form in two places, Lester thinking of Kathy being there when a patrol car pulled up, everything going as completely wrong as it could. He heard himself ask to make a call, but again, his voice was subdued, muffled somehow. The intake officer looked right at Lester but didn't answer him, just dropped his personal possessions into a box Lester couldn't see.

The deputies disappeared and one from the holding facility took their place, a short Chicano with a neck as wide as his jaw. He escorted Lester to a part of the procedure he'd never had to stay around for, to a fluorescent-lit room with no windows, a Filipino woman there in a white lab coat. She was small and dark and pretty, her hair held back with a red-and-purple pelican barrette, and Lester wished he at least had his shirt on. She wore white protective gloves. She wiped alcohol on the inside of Lester's forearm, then pressed a round TB skin pop into it, pulling it away just as quickly. She told him to sit down and she leaned against a counter covered with jars of cotton swabs, held a clipboard, and asked the Chicano jailhouse deputy Lester's name.

"Lester Veector Burdone." The deputy's accent was East Palo Alto barrio. Now the pretty nurse was asking Lester questions of his medical history, his body since he was a boy, his sexual relations since he was a man. Had he ever tested positive for HIV? She looked at him then, directly in the face, and it left Lester feeling he had something to lie about when he didn't. He answered no and then he was in the photo and fingerprints room standing against a wall in front of the Edicon machine, the technician telling him to look straight ahead at the blinking green light, Lester feeling he was being x-rayed, that this computer graphic of his face, this jailhouse mugshot, was really him, the true Lester.

The Chicano deputy called him over to the Identex and began rolling Lester's fingertips one by one onto the computer pad. It felt strange to have each finger guided like that, like someone was helping him to dress or feed himself, and as the Chicano officer finished, then escorted Lester down a bright corridor, Lester felt something was about to begin that wouldn't end for a long time. He knew the schedule for bail; he knew there wouldn't be any for kidnapping. That meant he'd be here until a hearing. And that could take months. Sometimes over a year. He felt queasy, his mouth suddenly full of tacky saliva. He thought of Carol, saw her in the kitchen dicing onions at a counter. He imagined the kids, both of them drawing with crayons on the floor of Bethany's room, and again he saw the colonel's son drop heavily to the sidewalk, blood pulsing from two wounds, and he felt afraid.

The deputy led him around a corner and opened a door for him. It was a small room with a desk and telephone, its white cinderblock walls freshly painted.

"Two calls on the county, Burdone. Five minutes."

The door was reinforced glass, and the Chicano officer stood on the other side, his arms folded, glancing in at Lester every few seconds. Lester picked up the receiver but didn't know the colonel's number. He dialed information, hoping that wouldn't count as one of his two calls, then he was ringing the Behrani residence, a brandnew listing. His throat felt thick and dry. The phone began to ring and he remembered Kathy as he'd left her, standing in the hallway of her stolen house in shorts and a Fisherman's Wharf T-shirt, her hair slightly unkempt around her face he'd kissed before leaving. By tonight, he'd imagined the two of them driving north in a rented car, maybe giddy for having just gotten away by a hair. Now he just wanted to hear her voice, a bit husky and unsure of itself. He just wanted to hear her say his name. But the phone kept ringing and no one was picking it up. A patrol car might have gotten there already, but he didn't think so. Maybe Kathy and the colonel's wife weren't in the house, but outside. He pictured them sitting up on that new widow's walk, waiting.

The deputy tapped on the glass and pointed at his watch. Lester

let the phone ring four more times, then hung up. He hadn't expected Kathy not to answer and now he felt as cut off from things as
he could imagine. For a second, it was as if she had never existed and
wasn't real at all; what they had started together was an illusion, just
a lovely rug thrown over a hole in the floor and now the rug was gone
and Lester was falling into something that had been there all along
and she had only come into his life to lead him to it. Cold spread
through his bowels and his face grew hot. He glanced at the deputy's
dark profile, thought of Behrani screaming in Farsi inside the patrol
car, the veins coming out in his forehead and neck. Maybe he'd
called his wife from the hospital and Kathy had taken a chance with
the Bonneville and driven there. *That's just what she would do.* Lester
dialed information again and was going to ask for the hospital's main
number when the deputy walked in and pressed the hang-up button.

"*Two* calls."

"Two were information. I didn't know the numbers."

The deputy took the receiver, hung it up, and motioned for Lester
to step back into the corridor. Lester felt a tightening heat deep in his
middle and he wanted to hit the deputy in the mouth.

"Let's go, Burdone."

"It's Burdon. Deputy Sheriff Burdon."

The Chicano smiled, blinking his eyes as lazily as a lizard's. "You'll
want to keep that to yourself around here, FTO. Now *move.*"

Lester walked with the deputy back down the corridor, his breathing shallow, the cinder-block walls a glossed eggshell white, not a
blemish anywhere, no scuff marks or chipped holes from a leg iron,
no graffiti, no dried spit and blood. A brand-new facility. He began
to feel that edge again, all of his tissues clear and ready, his stomach
a low fire.

Then he was in a small room with four or five others. Arrestees.
All waiting for dressdown. The deputy told Lester to have a seat
among a single row of steel chairs welded into two walls, facing each
other. The Chicano handed Lester's paperwork to a desk deputy,
then left without a word. Across from Lester sat a long black kid, his
skin the color of flan, his short hair freshly cut, his initials or his
girlfriend's shaved into his head. He wore a tank top, oversized jeans,

and white Converse All-Stars untied. He kept picking at his nails, three gold rings on the fingers of his right hand, two on the left.

The others were young too, an Asian and a white kid who seemed to know each other, the white kid whispering to the Asian about a dead boy named Beef, the Asian leaning his head back against the wall, his eyes half closed in a waking nap, a small blue serpent etched beneath the corner of his left eye like a tear. Lester glanced at the man beside him. He was sitting sideways in his chair, his wide back hunched to the others, his hair dark and matted, and when he saw Lester he looked away quickly and Lester did too, a gush of heat letting go inside him. The man was Filipino, a small-deal bookmaker out of Daly City, and Lester couldn't remember how or when their paths had crossed. For a moment he kept his face down, but then he thought he might appear weak so he raised his chin up again and sat back straight in the chair, his heartbeats lost somewhere inside his tongue.

The door opened and a jailhouse deputy called in the bookie, a name Lester didn't know, and he smelled him as he passed by: piss and sweat and cigarette smoke in old denim. The door shut behind him and now the Asian kid was looking right at Lester, his eyes dark slits, his head still against the wall, his arms crossed in front of his chest. The white kid stopped talking and looked too, taking in Lester from his running shoes and bare chest to his face.

"You looking for something?" Lester said.

The white kid shrugged and glanced at his friend. The Asian stared at Lester a few seconds longer, then smiled and turned his head away slightly, closing his eyes and leaving the smile on his face. The other kid looked at Lester one more time, then at a spot on the wall just to his right, and Lester glanced at the desk deputy, a lean man in his fifties eating a peanut butter and jelly sandwich on white bread, reading the *San Francisco Chronicle*. The Asian looked asleep, his eyes closed, his legs stretched out in front of him, but his lips were still fixed in that smile he'd given Lester, and Lester didn't like seeing it now; it was as if the kid had looked and seen the trajectory of Lester's entire life and was now gratified it had all come down to this.

The door opened again and the white kid stood but the dressdown deputy called in Lester, pronouncing his name perfectly, and soon the clothes Lester had yanked from his suitcase this morning at the fish camp were gone and he was pulling on orange jailhouse skivvies, orange canvas pants, an orange T-shirt, and a canvas button-down shirt with COUNTY JAIL embossed in black letters on the back. For his feet he wore orange socks under orange rubber shower sandals, and they clicked softly against each heel as he walked with a new deputy down a brightly lit corridor to Central Holding. The deputy was short and smelled of Old Spice cologne. It was what Lester's father used to wear, and the deputy was chewing gum as they walked, reading through Lester's paperwork. "An *FTO?* What *happened,* man?" He lowered the jacket to his side and picked up his pace. He didn't look at Lester, just kept his eyes straight ahead waiting for an answer, without judgment, it seemed, like they were two old friends running together, talking out a problem. Lester's legs felt heavy and stiff and he began to breathe harder, the jailhouse sandals slapping his heels like a reproach.

They reached a wide steel door at the end of the hall and the deputy pulled from his pocket an ID card attached with a clear plastic cord to his belt. He inserted the card into a slit in the wall, then opened the door for Lester, and they stepped into a cavernous room with three tiers of closed door cells, the fluorescent-lit ceiling over a hundred feet above. In the center of the floor was a rounded desk with two officers on duty, and in the corner of the second tier was a one-way-mirrored control booth. The air smelled of fresh paint and new air-conditioning, and Lester could hear the buzz of half a dozen radios in the cells above. Each cell door had a small window in its center and in one on the second tier was a man's face, a strand of white hair hanging over his eyes. Lester followed the deputy to the desk where one officer was on the phone and the other was checking off names on a headcount sheet. The escort deputy dropped Lester's paperwork on the desk. "When's the last time you guys had an FTO in Protective?"

The deputy on the phone stopped talking, looked up at Lester, then glanced through his jacket. He shook his head once, pushed the papers over to his partner, then hung up the phone and gave Lester his full attention, squinting his eyes like he wanted to pose a question but wasn't quite sure how to start.

"I haven't gotten through to my lawyer or wife yet," Lester said. There was a dull metallic bang from one of the upper tiers.

"You didn't get your two calls?"

"No one answered."

"Last meal's at four. We'll get you to a phone after that."

"Home Sweet Home." The escort deputy knocked once on the desk, then smiled and left, the electronically locked door closing behind him with barely a sound.

Now LESTER LAY back on his bunk. He could hear the faint bass note of another prisoner's radio, but nothing else. It was lockdown and the walls were thick. All was quiet and white. He was hungry and he had no idea of the time, but he knew at four they'd bring him food and then he could make his call. It would have to be to Carol, of course. He'd explain to her what he could, that one thing had just led to another, that he hadn't quite been himself lately and now things were upside down and inside out. But none of that was true; he couldn't remember the last time he'd felt more alive, more like who he might really be than in the last few days—making love with Kathy on the ground at the Purisima, coming inside her beautiful mouth, even sticking his pistol up under the colonel's chin. But he would tell Carol none of this. He would ask her to call their lawyer, ask him to hold off on their dissolution papers long enough to suggest a criminal attorney. A *criminal* lawyer. He would ask to speak with Nate and Bethany and he'd tell his daughter he'd see her at visiting hours and explain everything, that he was in this place because he did something wrong and people were right to keep him here for now. He imagined her face, more his than Carol's, her dark eyes filling up right then, and he'd say, "No, no, it's all right. Everything's going to be all right."

Lester closed his eyes, felt sleep waiting for him there behind his eyelids and in his limbs, a heavy dark warmth, and he opened them again; he knew the shooting of the colonel's son would add a decade or more to any conviction. And even if he was found guilty of lesser charges, his life in law enforcement was over. He wanted to see Kathy. The patrol cars would be at her place in Corona now, more men in French blue moving in on her, escorting her from her house, most likely charging her with everything they were giving him. But she hadn't answered, so maybe she'd left already. Maybe she'd dropped Mrs. Behrani off at the hospital and just kept driving. But he hoped that wasn't true. He hoped at the very least she was waiting for him somewhere. He wanted to see her right now. He wanted to stretch out beside her and rest his cheek on her bare breast, smell her smooth olive skin, hear the beating of her melancholy heart. He wanted to push himself all the way inside her and tell her not to worry, don't worry about anything.

Lester closed his eyes again, but when he did he saw the colonel's son standing there in the sunlight pointing the gun at him, his brown eyes moist with fear, one hand raised like he was getting ready to break and run, something Lester was certain the boy would have done if he'd known the truth, that the pistol was empty and useless. But Lester had denied him the truth to save himself; he had let fear have its way and now he could only imagine that it had been otherwise, that the boy dropped the weapon and ran through the coffee crowd and away, his lean arms pumping, his thick black hair jerking slightly, people getting out of his way, Lester wrestling himself from the colonel just to watch, watch that one boy fly to someplace better than this. And he thought again of the men who'd shot Esmail, practically boys themselves, letting their fear rule them as well.

After what seemed a long while, Lester's body began to feel like part of the bunk. He was breathing deeply through his nose, and as sleep began to take him he mouthed a prayer for Esmail, for his full recovery, and he saw himself holding and kissing Bethany and Nate. Then he was in a boat on some river and Carol and Kathy were lying beside him and there were thunderheads in the sky but there was nothing to do about them, and so Lester closed his eyes, one arm beneath each woman. Something rumbled far off in the eastern sky. The air began to turn cool. He breathed in the smell of fish scales and perfume and damp wood. One of the women let out a whimper, as if in the middle of a bad dream, but Lester just settled deeper into the bottom of the boat and waited, waited for the river to take them where it was going to anyway, to the inevitable conclusion of all he had done and failed to do, the air cooler now, almost cold, the boat beginning to rock.

THE SKY WAS BLACK AND TURNED TO BLUE JUST BEFORE A RIBBON OF bright coral opened like a cut on the horizon. At the edge of the parking lot, on the other side of a tall wooden fence, were juniper trees planted in a yard. The grass was thick and short, and there was a sandbox and swing set and jungle gym all made from dark beautiful wood—redwood, or maybe cedar. The house was beige stucco with a sienna tile roof and a low wide deck only a step off the ground, no railing, and four white plastic chairs around an umbrella table. Beside them, a child's plastic wading pool covered with smiling spouting blue whales, and I watched from the other side of the fence, two stories up, each swallow a hook in the stitched belly of my throat.

At seven, a male nurse brought me orange juice, coffee, and a bowl of soupy Cream of Wheat. But I didn't touch it and not long after, the back door of the house opened and a tiny brown-haired boy came running off the deck to the sandbox and blurred. I wiped my eyes. He put his hands in the sand, then lifted them over his head and let it sift down onto his hair. His mother set a mug of coffee or tea on the umbrella table, her long red hair catching the sunlight. She wore shorts and a loose T-shirt, and when she stepped off the deck and squatted at the sandbox I could see her thigh muscles. She was laughing, frisking the sand out of her son's hair, then she turned and went back to her coffee, sat at the umbrella table and started to read. The little boy sat with his back to the fence and the hospital on the other side, his thick hair sticking out in curls behind his ears. I stared at the miniature blue-and-yellow-striped shirt he wore, at his small bare arms and hands, at how big his head looked on his shoulders. Each swallow was thumbs crushing my Adam's apple all over again, and so I swallowed more than I needed, pictured the toddler in the yard growing into a boy with blue jeans and a red bike, then a teenager with a skateboard or maybe a beat-up car, and I swallowed twice and finally saw him as a man, a tall young man with a wife and child of his own. He'd drive up to that house across the parking lot and visit his mother and father—but the image wouldn't stay and instead I kept seeing Mrs. Behrani's son as I last saw him, climbing out of my car into the sunshine, glancing at Lester the way I'd seen high school boys wait for instruction from their coaches.

The boy lifted a truck over his head, dropping it onto something metal I couldn't see. The mother glanced up at the sound, then went back to her newspaper, and the door behind me opened and the deputy sheriff stuck his head in, saw me sitting at the window in my hospital gown. He looked at me like he was trying to figure out what else I might be doing besides sitting, then he closed the door.

Yesterday, in another hospital, I woke to see Lester standing at the foot of the bed, my throat swollen and so dry it had cracked. His uniform was clean, his dark hair seemed too short, and he'd shaved his mustache, but I wanted him to come closer. I tried to speak but a nurse put her fingers on my wrist and told me to stay quiet. She was old and slender. I looked back at Lester, but it wasn't him. This man was younger. His black hair was almost shaved and his eyes were not brown, but blue. I tried to sit up but the nurse put her hand on my shoulder, then showed me the button, and I pushed it and the mattress raised me forward and the nurse left the room. The deputy walked around to the side of my bed. There was another man in the chair behind him, older, with sandy hair and a tanned lined face. He had a piece of paper in his hand and he stood, introduced himself and the younger deputy, then opened it and read what I was being charged with: Aggravated Kidnapping, False Imprisonment, Brandishing a Weapon.

The young deputy leaned forward. My nose felt stopped-up, but I could smell his aftershave. "We know you're not able to talk right now, Mrs. Lazaro. Would you like us to call your lawyer?"

I remembered the screech of tires in my driveway, the front door swinging open. I had expected to see Lester first, but when I saw the colonel, his bald head silhouetted against the sunlight in the yard, I knew he was alone and then I couldn't move and his hands were around my neck, shaking me, my hair in my face, and I couldn't breathe and a buzzing darkness was rising up inside my head.

I nodded at the deputy. He handed me a small notepad and pen and I wrote Connie Walsh's name and number, then: *What about Behrani? What's* he *being charged with?*

The young deputy read my note, then showed it to the older one, who looked right at me, his eyes green and full of something that made me look down at his arms, at the thick tufts of hair on them. "Mr. Behrani's deceased."

I was lying down and they were standing there but the room felt so suddenly still and quiet I started to feel too far away to see and hear what would come next. I took the pad from the young deputy: *What?* I wanted to ask about Lester. Why hadn't he come back? Then I thought if they were calling me a kidnapper they had to be calling him one first, but I couldn't be sure so I didn't write any more. They didn't answer me anyway. The older one seemed to be in charge. He stepped away from the bed and told me to get the facts from my lawyer. Then the younger one called Connie Walsh's office and explained where I was and what I was being charged with. I heard the crimes again, and except for Brandishing a Weapon, pulling Lester's pistol out of my bag at the gas station, I had a hard time matching up Kidnapping and False Imprisonment with me. The older deputy held the door open for the younger one, then they were gone.

There was another bed in my room, but it was empty with no sheets, just a white plastic mattress cover, a TV suspended in the corner of the ceiling, the dark screen watching me: *The colonel was dead.* On the serving table was a pitcher and a short stack of paper cups. I poured water into one and drank, each swallow a spiny sea urchin in my throat. My window shade was pulled and I could hear the sounds of traffic nearby. I scooted to the side of the bed. I was dressed in a hospital johnny with nothing underneath. I moved to the window but my legs felt shaky. I opened the shade. Ten feet down was a flat tar roof with big air-conditioning or heating units on it. And on the other side was more building and windows. In one of them was the colored flickering of a TV. I couldn't see the sky but the daylight was overcast. I wondered if it was morning or afternoon. My neck was stiff and I could hardly look down or to the right and left. I remembered seeing the colonel's yellowed teeth grinding together, the flare of his nostrils, feeling my feet lift off the ground. I got back into bed and lay down, but it suddenly felt like a dangerous place, as if the bed were a thousand feet off the ground and if I turned over too fast or even reached for water, it would tilt and fall to rocks below; if Behrani was dead, I was sure Lester must've killed him.

Less than an hour later the deputies came back, told me I'd been classified a flight risk and was being transferred to San Mateo County Hospital. The older one rode in the back of the ambulance with me. He sat across from my gurney chewing gum, looking around at all the medical equipment. Sometimes his eyes would look into mine. The sky was growing dark as they wheeled me here and at the elevator an older woman with too much blush on her cheeks held the doors for us and she smiled down at me and said, "You are going to be just fine, dear. You'll see." There was a smear of lipstick on her front teeth, which were perfect and false, but I wanted to believe her.

The older deputy stayed here in my room until the nurse left, then he stood close to the bed and looked down at me like he was waiting for me to finish answering a question he'd never asked. I swallowed and had to close my eyes a minute. When I opened them he was shaking his head like I'd disappointed him. "Les Burdon and I used to be partners before they divided us up into single units. He was sheriff material, but he's all through now, I hope you know that. They've got him in Protective Custody, but that won't last. They'll throw him to the hounds." He stepped back from the bed and moved to the door. "There'll be a man outside till you're okayed to leave, then you're going right to holding in Redwood City. Think about that."

He left and I looked up at the white rectangles of the ceiling, the fluorescent light. I closed my eyes and swallowed what felt like a dozen thumbtacks, and I wanted that sandy-haired married deputy to feel it too, feel the colonel's thumbs breaking through his Adam's apple like it was cardboard; I wanted this old friend of Lester's to be at the fish camp when Lester put on his uniform and had me drive him to talk to the colonel; I wanted this friend to be in the house waking up to the whole family locked in the bathroom; and I wanted the deputy to be standing in the bedroom his father left him as Lester held his gun to the colonel's neck in my car. None of these things I asked for. I didn't ask for any of them.

A nurse and doctor came into the room. The nurse was younger than me. She smiled and introduced the doctor, a short man with silver hair and thick glasses that made his eyes look tiny. He read the clipboard at the foot of the bed, then came closer and put two warm fingers against my throat. My eyes began to fill up and I must've made a sound because the nurse took my hand and held it while the doctor looked down my throat with a tiny flashlight, then patted my shoulder and said my soft tissue was healing well and it would be best not to speak a word for at least two full weeks. Then they were gone, their white coats disappearing behind the door, and I didn't feel mad anymore; maybe I didn't deserve the deputy's judgement of me for things I never did, but now I felt even more that I didn't deserve the warmth the nurse just showed me, holding my hand like I was a victim in all this. Because I knew that wasn't true. Neither picture of me was true.

My door opened and a round Chicana woman brought in my supper on a tray: a glass of water, a bowl of clear yellow broth, and a dish of vanilla pudding. She smiled at me and I could see a gold cap on one of her front teeth. She left the room and Connie Walsh stepped in. Her dark hair was shorter than when I last saw her, cut close to the sides of her head, which made her pretty face look older and a little harsh. On her feet were brand-new running shoes and I started to smile but my face felt funny, my lips thick and twisted, and I couldn't look right at her.

She didn't say anything, just stood there, and I felt her looking at

me. She put her hand on my shoulder, pushed my food tray closer to
me, and asked if I could sit up. I pressed the button, and once I was
up, glanced at her, at her dark eyes that took me in with nothing but
concern. I thought of Mrs. Behrani, how she looked at me like that
too, and I felt I was with an old friend, one I was going to let down,
if I hadn't already.

Connie Walsh handed me a spoon. "How much do you know?"

I shook my head and pointed to my throat. She apologized and
waved her hand in front of her face, opened the briefcase in her lap,
then handed me a yellow legal pad and a pen. I pushed my supper
tray to the side and wrote: *They said Mr. Behrani is dead. Where's
Lester?*

She read the note before I'd finished turning it to her and looked
at me a second, her lips slightly pursed. I wrote: *What happened?*

She took the pen and pad and began to write, then stopped and
shook her head at what she'd just done. I smiled and she started to
smile too.

"Is Mr. Burdon your boyfriend?"

I nodded and I wished I could hear my voice as I answered yes.

"He's in custody in Redwood City."

I looked at her and waited.

Her eyes went to my supper. "The boy was killed."

My whole face felt squeezed, the air pulling back in my throat.

"Evidently he'd gotten ahold of Mr. Burdon's pistol on a busy
street and was pointing it at him." Connie Walsh's voice was calm
and controlled but she was looking at me like she'd only begun. "He
was shot by police officers."

This boy who this morning was walking so tall and straight down
the hall, his black hair still mussed from sleep. I reached for the paper
and pen, my fingers hot and thick: *I thought Mr. Behrani was dead. The
colonel.*

Connie Walsh looked at me like she'd been waiting for the conversation to reach this point and now that it had, she wasn't quite
ready for it. She was leaning away from me slightly, her hands on her
knees. I nodded for her to talk but even before she started to I
couldn't look directly at her anymore; I focused on her hands, on her

knuckles, which were wider than her long thin fingers. Her nails were short, some with tiny scratches on them, and for a second I saw her on her knees after work digging in a garden, but then she was telling me everything, her hands coming together, her fingers intertwined, Mr. and Mrs. Behrani lying dead in my old bedroom, Connie Walsh's voice talking of detectives reconstructing the scene. "They want to talk to you, Kathy."

Now I looked at her, but it was like seeing someone through the wrong end of a telescope. She wasn't talking anymore. She seemed to be waiting for me to try and speak, or write something, but her face was too far away to read, just an oval of flesh that was now asking me to write her everything, to write what the colonel did to me and when, to write how involved I'd been in holding this family against their will. "Write me everything, Kathy. Write me the truth."

The word was a black bat flittering between us. I looked down at my own hands, at the cleaning calluses on my palms. I saw again Mrs. Behrani standing in her kitchen, pressing her hand to the side of her head. I thought of the pain she must've been in, and I hoped it wasn't the last thing she'd felt. Connie Walsh's voice was more relaxed now and she was getting up, telling me she was late for an appointment but would be back tomorrow to read the facts. That's how she referred to what I would write. She touched my hand a second, then was gone.

I drank a spoonful of broth. It seemed to bathe my throat on the way down, but I didn't drink any more. I imagined the Behranis laid out on a morticians's table: the colonel, his suffering wife, his loyal son. My stomach drew backwards inside me and I sat up fast, my mouth filling with saliva. Connie Walsh's notepad and pen fell to the floor and I left them there, moved to the chair by the window and sat. I breathed long and deep through my nose and mouth till I didn't feel like I was going to throw up. Outside the window the parking lot was dimly lit with only a few streetlamps, and at the far corner cars passed on the road, their headlights and red taillights visible. In the hallway outside my door was the soft squeak of nurses' shoe soles as they passed by, the metal wheel roll of a food cart or gurney, the talking and laughing of three women at the nurse's station, a woman's voice over an intercom calling a doctor to ICU, then more talking, an elevator door sliding open and closed, the flushing of a toilet in a room not far from mine, then someone humming, the flap of a wet mop hitting the floor, the humming a man's voice, the tune unrecognizable; and I was unrecognizable. I could see my reflection in the window, a small shadowed face, hair flattened in the back. I looked like a sick child. But I felt dirty. My throat was dry and it was harder to swallow than ever, but I didn't care. I closed my eyes and tried to concentrate on the facts for Connie Walsh but I kept thinking of Lester in Protective Custody, sitting alone in some cell separated from the rest of the prisoners because he's a cop, the kind they would never understand, a man who would avoid shooting an armed Filipino boy, the kind that had risked his job to try and get me back into my house.

The mopping and humming had moved farther down the hallway, and I could hear the deputy on duty clear his throat, turn the pages of a magazine or newspaper. I got up and turned off the light switch near the door. The nurse's button glowed white at the head of my bed, and I made my way back to the chair at the window, the vinyl upholstery sticking to the backs of my bare legs, and I remembered Mrs. Behrani bringing tea and kiwi fruit to her son's room for me, her brown eyes full of compassion as she looked down at my bruised arms, as if her husband doing that had been the only reason I showed up at her doorstep drunk with Lester's gun.

But it was everything: it was talking to my brother Frank and hearing that same old patronizing tone; it was the Mexican boy flicking his tongue out at me, his eyes on my crotch like it was something he'd already seen a hundred times before; it was wearing stolen clothes; it was the bright sun on the day after I had drunk too much with Lester the night before; it was my dry mouth, and the deep hungover fear I had that Lester had used me up already and was going back to his wife; it was driving through his neighborhood of one-story ranch houses in the heat looking for what I hoped I wouldn't find—it was all of these things and none of them; it was Lester pulling out of me at the fish camp, coming onto me in what I was sure was a sudden change of heart; it was me letting Lester finish what we'd both started, letting all this happen so I could put off facing my mother and brother with the news that somehow Dad's house had slipped through my fingers: I'd been willing for Lester to do anything so I could put off that moment of judgment.

I looked out over the empty parking lot, at the shadowed wooden fence and the black trees behind it, and for a while I tried to tell my-self it was the colonel who had brought all this down on us. It was him not doing the right thing with my father's house. It was his greed, and it was his pride. I remembered him on his new roof deck with his wife and daughter and friends, his expensive suit, a flute of champagne in his hand, potted flowers set in the corners of the rail-ing and on the floor, laughing at something one of the fat rich women had said, the way he looked at me as we drove by, his eyes narrowed, all the muscles of his face still with some kind of concentration that scared me.

The door behind me opened and the light from the hall spread across the room. I didn't turn around but in the window reflection I could see the deputy's silhouette, his short haircut and baggy short sleeves, his gun belt. He seemed to look from the chair to the bed, then at the chair again before he stepped back into the hallway, the heavy door closing by itself. My throat felt like cracked stone and with each swallow my eyes would tear, but I didn't let myself get up for water or broth.

I slept in my chair at the window. When I opened my eyes the darkness was fading and I watched the light come from the east, spreading over the stucco house and its yard, and I couldn't take my eyes off it. Now the little boy's mother drank her coffee and read her paper on the deck. She leaned forward as she read, her thick hair gathered over one shoulder. I wondered what her husband was like. Was he kind to her? Did he want a child when his wife got pregnant? Did they make love early in the morning before their son woke up? My throat hurt worse than ever. I went to the bathroom, and when I came out, the toilet still flushing, a new doctor and the deputy were standing at the foot of the bed waiting for me. The doctor was tall. He introduced himself, then had me sit on the bed and he looked down my throat with his penlight, put his fingers on my lymph glands, and told me not to talk for ten to fourteen more days. The deputy's eyes were full of a light that reminded me of my brother: fascinated by other people's trouble, happy *he* was in the clear. The doctor wrote something on the clipboard, then left, and the deputy handed me my old clothes: my shorts, the girl's Fisherman's Wharf T-shirt, her too-small yellow panties. He told me I was being transferred to Redwood City to be booked, then he left the room and I changed at the window, my eyes on the boy and his mother. The underpants were still tight at my hips and as I pulled on my shirt and shorts the boy stood, his hands open at his sides. He climbed out of the sand-box and walked over the grass. He stepped onto the deck in front of his mother, then held his hands out in front of him, his chin pulled in slightly, his belly sticking out. His mother smiled down at him. She wiped the sand off his hands and lifted him onto her lap, his small back against her breasts, his sneakers just barely reaching her knees. The door opened behind me but I didn't turn around and I could smell the deputy's spearmint gum as he said he was sorry but he had to follow procedure and he took my wrists and slipped the cool metal of his handcuffs onto them, clicking them closed, my pulse pushing against them. I couldn't see the boy's face anymore, and in the hours and days that followed I would think of him, the way an important dream comes back to you throughout the day, a day that begins at six-thirty, my door unlocking electronically, me stepping out onto the second tier and filing downstairs with black women and white women, Chicanas, all of us dressed in the orange khaki pants and tank tops and overshirts of the San Mateo County Jail, over fifty of us.

On the bottom tier we sit at steel tables and eat toast and cold cereal or scrambled eggs and sausage links. Two color TVs are fixed to the wall, tuned to morning news shows, the anchorwomen pretty and successful. In the middle of the room is a control desk with four woman deputies on duty, and on clear days the door to the rec yard is open, though it's not a yard at all but a flat rooftop with a Universal weight-lifting gym set in the middle of it, a piece of equipment no one uses. One morning a young black girl pulled herself to the top of the chinning bar, sat there, and smoked two cigarettes. At the edge of the yard is a high hurricane fence topped with razor wire, then it's four stories down to the streets of Redwood City. You can see the old domed courthouse and part of the Hall of Justice building where Lester used to work. But of course Lester is here with me now, somewhere under us in another wing with the men, the carjackers and rapists and murderers.

On the bottom tier after breakfast, most of the women stay at the tables and smoke and talk. There are pay phones on the wall which never go unused, women calling their kids and boyfriends or husbands collect, their eyes miles away as they talk and sometimes yell or cry into the phone. Some even laugh. But I don't. I don't smoke either. My throat can't tolerate it, the smoke going down like grit rubbed into a raw scrape.

There's a black woman named Jolene who smokes pack after pack of Marlboro Lights. Her voice is as deep as a man's. She's short with boyish hips and small breasts, and her knuckles are wide and hard-looking and she never stops talking and even the big women seem smaller around her. My first week, one afternoon before the midday lockdown for lunch cleanup, she tapped me on the shoulder and said loud enough for an audience, "Why *you* here, girl?"

I was sitting at a table with two Mexican girls who spent their lunch talking to each other in Spanish. Three or four black women were standing around and behind Jolene waiting for my answer. At first I didn't understand her question and couldn't talk anyway. I pointed to my throat and shook my head.

"You can't *talk?*"

I nodded.

"You deaf?"

I shook my head again. One of the women behind Jolene smiled and I could see her teeth were bad.

"So you's *mute.*"

The one with the bad teeth laughed. A few others smiled. One of the deputies from the control panel called over to everybody to head back to their cells for lockdown. I nodded at Jolene and she was smiling like I'd just shown her something she'd been wanting to know a long time.

"You mean God sit back with the remote and motherfuckin' *mute* your ass?"

Jolene's girls laughed and I smiled and that afternoon after supper, while we all sat at tables in front of the two TVs on two different channels, waiting for our turn to go to the commisary or laundry exchange, Jolene yelled across the room at me: "Hey, Remote! Mute them motherfuckin' TVs!"

She laughed louder than the women around her, and from then on if a woman needed me to pass her the salt or hand off to somebody a lighter or cigarette, she'd say in a loud voice, "Send me the salt, Remote." Or, "Remote, pass this down to Big April."

After the first two weeks, when I was alone in my cell I tried talking again, naming the objects in front of me, "Floor. Wall. Toilet. Sink," my throat aching no more than when you have an allergy, my voice maybe lower than it used to be, but I still kept quiet on the bottom tier and in the rec yard and I let them call me by my new name.

These first weeks Connie has come and seen me three times, once with two detectives who took me to a room and had me write how the colonel tried to strangle me before he went on to do the rest. Lawyers and visitors have to go to the mezzanine on the second tier, a room of enclosed booths with thick glass separating us from visitors. Until I could use my voice again, Connie would talk into the phone while I wrote my answers and questions and held them up to the glass. Now that my voice is back I hunch forward and talk softly into the receiver so none of the other inmates with visitors will notice.

Every time, Connie wants to hear the facts. I tell her what I've done, wishing I hadn't said anything because her planned defense of me is that I was defenseless, suicidal, and drugged when Lester was locking the Behranis into their bathroom, that I was sick and physically weak, my judgment impaired, the next day when he forced the colonel and his son to Redwood City. She wants to argue that I am not who they're charging me as being, though she admits she has a mountain to climb to prove all this because my best witnesses are no longer with us. That's her expression, "no longer with us," though that doesn't seem true to me.

Connie was able to get me some money for magazines at the commisary, but during the lockdown hours after our meals, I sit on my bunk and can't even look at them. Instead, I keep seeing Mrs. Behrani, her small lined face, her deep brown eyes, the way she looked at me, one woman to another, when she asked if Lester would hurt her son, who I feel hovering in the corners of my cell, a young and polite presence. And I see his father in a way I never saw him, his bald head turned towards me, his face with no expression, like nothing I did to him can touch him now, but his eyes are two dark stars of grief.

Sometimes I sit against the wall on the rec roof with the sun on my face. I can hear the TVs inside, the chatter of the other women, one of them coughing. I look past the chain-link fence at the edge of the roof, the razor wire too bright, and I ache to see Lester, to lie beside him in the hot loft of the fish camp, to kiss his crooked mustache and hold his narrow back. I remember his ex-partner at the hospital saying he'll be thrown to the hounds, and I can only hope he's wrong, that the guards will look out for one of their own, though I feel like I'm lying to myself thinking this. I don't let myself think of his kids, or his wife, and if I think of the house at all it's only that I should've died there and nobody else, of how much better it would've been if Mr. Behrani never saved me from Lester's gun, if Mrs. Behrani never saved me from her own pills.

Today Jolene walks over to me, a cigarette smoking between her lips, her eyes squinting like a man's. "Mezzanine bitch sent me to get you. You got visitors."

I'm so surprised to hear this I almost ask out loud who. But instead I keep my eyes on Jolene, waiting for her to say more.

"That's right, Remote, somebody wants to do sign language."

Only two days before, I saw Connie. She's still working on getting my hearing date moved up. I told her I didn't want her to make me look like I wasn't responsible for what Lester had done.

"But you weren't, Kathy. We're not fabricating any of that." Connie looked at me through the glass, the phone pressed to her ear. I could see small red marks on both sides of her nose from reading glasses or sunglasses. She looked tired, her lips parted, ready to argue against whatever I was about to say. The other visiting cubicles were empty, but I kept my voice to a whisper as I talked into the phone. "I'll deny it. I'll say I was sober and never took any pills."

Connie Walsh shook her head, her lips pressing tightly together. "Then what *is* our defense, Kathy?"

"I don't have one. A family is gone." My throat started to close up and I turned my face away. I put the receiver back on the hook, left the mezzanine, and went back out to the tier where I knew I wouldn't cry, where I was relieved I didn't have a voice.

Now I climb the concrete steps to the second tier, thinking it is either Connie or she's dropped me as her client and it'll be a new lawyer, one assigned by the state. A blond deputy opens the door for me. Whoever has come is sitting, and I'm not close enough to see who through the glass over the cubicles, one of them taken up by a Chicana girl, her husband or boyfriend on the other side holding the phone to a little girl's ear. Then, behind the glass a few cubicles down, my brother Frank stands up. He's wearing a banana-yellow polo shirt, his black hair is moussed back, and there's a thin gold chain around his neck, a gold watch band on his wrist. He's gained weight, the curve of his belly pushing his belt buckle a little. He's squinting into the glass, his hands on his hips, but he doesn't see me. Then he does and his lips part, his eyes get shiny, and I want to turn and walk back out onto the tier: I hadn't sent a letter; I hadn't made one phone call; I guess I was waiting for Labor Day to come and go, for my mother and aunts to drive by the empty house and know Frank had been right, that I was away on a trip and wouldn't be back for a long time.

Franky begins to blur. I wipe my eyes, step into the phone stall, and there's my mother sitting in the chair looking up at me like I'm a vision she's been both praying and dreading would come. She's wearing too much makeup, the blush too pink and high on her cheeks, her lipstick too red. She's wearing her costume pearls and a purple-and-blue flowered dress. And she's just had her hair done. From where I stand, my breath high in my throat, I can see a round spot of scalp through her thinning hair. There are old-lady tendons in her throat.

Frank picks up the receiver and starts to say something, but then stops and waits for me to raise mine. I stay standing and hold the receiver, light as balsa wood, to my ear.

"Why didn't you *call* us, Kath?"

I glance down at my mother. She's looking up at me through the glass, her eyes slightly bloodshot. I swallow and point to my throat and am about to say I couldn't call at the time but Frank interrupts me.

"You can't talk?"

I don't answer but feel myself slide back into the lie like a warm bath. My mother turns and asks him for the phone. "K? Are you all *right?* Your aunts and I drove by the house yesterday and there was that police tape over the doors and windows. Why can't you talk? Franky flew out this morning. It took us all day to find you. No one would tell us anything, K. Honey, are you all *right?*" My mother was squinting into the glass like I was a ghost that might fade away any second. And that's how I felt, dead to them, nothing but a voice from the other side; I started to feel strangely at ease, safely out of their reach in every way.

My mother's lower lip starts to quiver. Her eyes go from mine to my county-jail orange, then back to my face, and I want to stand and show her all of it, the whole costume, every piece of it right down to the orange underwear that's as big and loose as a man's. I lean close to the glass and speak into the phone, "I'm all right, Mother." I have never called her that, only Mom or Ma, but I like the sound of Mother, the dignity it seems to give her, the bereaved.

"K? What *happened?*" She starts to cry. Franky puts his hand on her shoulder and hands her his monogrammed handkerchief. I look up at his face through the glass, but he isn't looking at me; his eyes are on the countertop, and he seems about to go off into a stare, like he'd just as soon sit this moment out somewhere else, but also there's hurt in his face, and for a second I wonder about Jeannie and the kids, is everything all right at home? I must have asked this into the phone, and the question props my mother up instantly.

"Of course they're not all right, they're worried sick about you. What have you *done,* K? Why are you *here?*" My mother still looks like she's going to cry, but there's something hard in her face now. She dabs at her mascara, her lips pressed together, bracing herself for what I am going to tell her. She's waiting for the facts, but her last question is still a wire of words in my head that won't stop vibrating, that's been singing the same thing for years and years: *What have you done?* Why are you *here?*

My mother is talking into the phone again, asking me about Dad's house, about the police tape across the front door, about the widow's walk Frank had never given permission to build. "Can't you speak, K? Is there something wrong with your voice? Did Nick have anything to do with this?"

Franky is looking down at me through the glass. He shrugs as if he's not quite sure he was supposed to have mentioned that but did. I look back at my mother, her eyes waiting, always waiting. Her last question seems as ridiculous and naive as can be.

"Nick left me, Mom."

"But why?"

"I don't *know* why, Ma. Why don't you go find him and ask him?"

My mother's eyes turn hard now. Her question might've sounded different coming from somebody else, more gentle, like the man who left me must've been in the dark about my best qualities. But from her it was an interrogation: What did you do this time, Kathy? How could you have let him go?

But now she looks confused, her too-red lips parted, her forehead furrowed. She shakes her head once, the way the hard-of-hearing do. A second ago I'd felt like hitting her over the head with the truth of my story, telling her the charges against me, telling her about the Behranis, holding her face in everything. But she looks so vulnerable right now, so pathetic in her pearls and dress and makeup, trying to make a good impression on my jailers, I can't say more. I shake my head and point to my throat. "I had an operation. I shouldn't talk right now. Call this number."

I write Connie Walsh's telephone number on the memo pad they leave in each cubicle for us, my shoulder squeezing the phone to my ear, and I hold the pad to the glass. My mother is quiet on the other end, and this should be familiar to me, her silence as I keep the truth from her. Frank is punching the number into the computerized Rolodex on his watch, and I'm looking into my mother's eyes, as dark as they've always been, tiny pink capillaries broken in the whites, but now they don't look cold or hard, though not warm either. Under her eyes is a small packet of flesh her pancake foundation can't hide. She raises her chin, her red lips pressing together, and I am the hunter who has caught an old deer in his range only to lower my bow. And this wall of safety glass between us doesn't feel like a bad thing, more like something natural, inevitable. Her eyes stay on mine longer than I can ever remember. I can look at her for days. Then she blinks, stands quickly, and turns to go as if I've already left. I wave at Franky but he is hanging up the receiver and I don't wait for him to look up.

I walk past the cubicles and out onto the second tier. I can hear the TVs and the chatter and Jolene's hoarse laugh coming from below. I see her sitting at one of the tables playing cards, blackjack, it looks like, and she's the dealer. The table is full of her women, all black except for a new blond girl who is sitting quietly between Jolene and Big April, an obese woman whose chins sag to her cleavage. I stop on the stairs and watch Jolene take Big April's money, a small mound of pieces of notepad paper. The air is heavy with cigarette smoke, and the sunlight from the open rec door makes it look heavier than it is, bluish, a wide band of it hovering over everyone's heads. I think of Lester, his Toyota station wagon pulling away from the neon light of the El Rancho Motel, disappearing into the fog. There is a loosening warmth between my legs and I want to feel him inside me again, but feel sure now I never will.

Behind and above me the deputy tells me to move along, no loitering on the stairs, and Jolene looks up and laughs. "Get down here, Remote." And I smile at her and nod like she's just said something I never understood before, but now finally do.

I descend the stairs, my eyes on the wide flat cloud as I walk down under it, this blue ceiling of smoke we make. And I feel it above me as I move past the women at the phones, past other women at other tables, all of them smoking, blowing out thin angry streams into the air, and I stand at Jolene's shoulder. She stops dealing and looks up at me, her dark eyes waiting, though she's never heard me speak, and I nod at her pack of Marlboro Lights. At first she doesn't seem to understand what I want, but then I smile, and put two fingers to my lips.